THE S

JON CLEA...   ...ad
througho...   ...irty
novels including such famous best-sellers as *The
Sundowners* and *The High Commissioner*.

Born in 1917, Jon Cleary left school at fifteen to
become a commercial artist and film cartoonist –
even a laundryman and bushworker. Then his first
novel won second prize in Australia's biggest literary
contest and launched him on his successful writing
career.

Seven of his books have been filmed, and *Peter's
Pence* was awarded the American Edgar Allen Poe
prize as the best crime novel of 1974.

Jon Cleary lives in Sydney and travels the world
researching his novels with his wife Joy.

JON CLEARY

The
Sundowners

FONTANA/Collins

First published by Werner Laurie 1952
First issued in Fontana Paperbacks 1960
Ninth impression April 1986

© Jon Cleary 1952

Made and printed in Great Britain by
William Collins Sons & Co. Ltd, Glasgow

To Joy

Chapter One

1

THEY ARRIVED in Bulinga late on the Friday afternoon. Sitting side by side on the stiff hard seat of the wagonette, they drove down the long dusty road that wound into the valley. Trailing them, the kelpie trotted thin-eyed through the dust disturbed by the plodding hoofs of the tired grey gelding and the creaking wheels of the ancient wagonette. In the back of the cart, home-wrapped in hessian and covered by canvas, was everything the Carmodys owned.

They came to a halt at the top of the final dip that led down to the floor of the valley. A high sunburned wind had polished the April sky to a pale brilliance; in the clear sharp light the hills at the far end of the valley seemed to be cut from blue steel. Below them, almost a mile away, willows fell in a sad thin curve above the twisted dazzle of silver that was the river. The road, running on to town, dipped to the narrow wooden bridge over the river, then climbed the opposite bank to wind away through the tall blue gums and finally appear as a brown rope thrown over the rising shoulder of a hill. A mile or so beyond the river was Bulinga, small and sprawling, looking from this distance like a jumble of wool bales dropped from some passing wagon.

"There it is," Paddy said: he had just discovered the Promised Land, take it or leave it.

Ida was willing to leave it. "Just another town. That's all. Just another town, doesn't even get into the atlas."

Paddy looked at her. "What's wrong with that? Who the hell cares about a bloody atlas? Any place is just another town, if it comes to that." He looked back at Bulinga. "But they're all different, somehow. That's the good part about coming into 'em for the first time, like now. You're seeing something different."

"What's different about it?" Ida was tired and irritable and

5

heretical; her behind ached from to-day and all the years on the hard seat of the wagonette. "Never mind. Don't worry yourself, trying to dream up what makes it different from Port Macquarie or Cobbadah or any other place. Where are we going to camp?"

"There you go again, changing the subject just as I'm gunna win the argument. I can easy tell you what's different——"

"Hey, Dad?" Sean said.

"What?" Paddy said. "Now you ain't on her side, are you?"

The boy hadn't been listening to his parents. He was staring down into the valley, his blunt brown face smooth and quiet with the faraway look of the dreamer in the daytime. "Ain't that a beaut farm?"

"It's all right," Paddy said; he could take it or leave it. "A bit small."

"Nothing like the size of the Carmody property," Ida said. "Is it a million acres you own, Mr. Carmody? Or am I just thinking of your backyard?"

Paddy faced her, sitting up straight. "I could tell you——"

"And you will," Ida said.

"You can be sarcastic, but you don't see the world like I do. The whole bloody country's me backyard," he said, singing it; the tiredness drained out of his back and he owned the world. "Even Sir Sidney Kidman don't own as much as I do. Does he own these hills," scooping the valley into the crook of his arm, "or the black soil plains where we spent last spring, or the river running down to the sea from the top of the country, down Adaminaby way? Are the canefields his, or the hills the back of Cairns? Can he sail down the Murray, like we done, and say it belongs to him? Can he live anywhere in this whole wide land, anywhere at all I ask you, and say it belongs to him, like we can?"

"Yes," Ida said. "Only a millionaire wouldn't live in a tent."

"That's all you know about Sid," Paddy said. "He ain't one of your luxury-loving millionaires——"

"Oh, you know Sid?" Ida said. "Never met him, myself.

Of course I don't get the opportunities you get——" She
delicately picked dust off her faded dress and flicked it away;
she ran a fastidious hand round the brim of the battered
man's hat she wore. "Drive on, Henry Lawson, and let's get
the tent up before dark. In bed to-night, in our tent that Sid
doesn't own, you can get poetical again and tell me about life
among the rich."

Paddy looked at her, then smiled, light winking on a gold
tooth at the side of his mouth. "You're a card, ain't you, Ide?
Dunno what I'd do without you."

"Neither do I," said Ida. "What do you reckon, Sean?"

The boy smiled at both of them. "I dunno, Mum. I reckon
he needs both of us."

Paddy threw back his head and roared as the wagonette
moved on down the steepening road. That was the year the
world was booming; everybody had money except the poor,
and the poor still had hope. That year Bruce was buttoning
on his spats in Melbourne, Baldwin was chewing on his pipe
in Downing Street and Coolidge was saying next to nothing
in the White House. The world and the men meant nothing
to Paddy: he was as good as the next bloke, and anyone and
anything beyond the next bloke didn't matter a damn.

There were times when nothing could touch Paddy Carmody, when he was as impregnable and bright as the distant
sun, and now was a time. For six months he had been stuck
in the one place, working as a railway fettler on the line just
north of Port Macquarie: no condemned prisoner had been
more confined and miserable. Then from a swaggie he'd met
one day on the line he'd learned of this droving job that was
offering at Bulinga, and that had been the end of railway
fettling. He had looked up from the railway sleepers that
stretched for miles like the dead of the world laid side by
side, from the blue metal that was never meant for tramping
on, he had looked up from the cold unfriendly rails and seen
the sun and the beckoning hills on the edge of the world.
Next morning, after arguing all night, they had loaded the
wagonette and headed north, taking up where they had left off
six months before, and Paddy had once more begun to live.
He laughed now, and it had the ring of freedom in it.

He was a small man, but tough and wiry as a mountain brumby. He was forty, but the years didn't count: he had been the one age a long time and would never grow older. Looking at him, you knew the years could chip nothing away and you would never know him as Old Paddy Carmody: suddenly one day he would be dead and the memory of him would always be as you saw him now. Short, hard-muscled, with a face that was almost square, with smooth leather for skin and candid, friendly eyes, with a gold tooth that winked as if he had caught sunlight in his mouth, with black curly hair that could catch a woman's fingers before she was aware of it, with two restless feet that had left prints in the dust of more roads than he could remember, he was Paddy Carmody, take him or leave him.

" Pull up," Ida said.

" I thought you wanted to make camp before dark," Paddy said. " Can't you hold it till then?"

" It isn't that," Ida said. " I went just after dinner."

" What is it then?"

" That," said Ida, and pointed.

" Cripes, it's all right, ain't it?" Sean said.

From that road they could see the farmhouse. It sat, small and neat, brown-walled and bright red-roofed, in the soft shadows of the hill that rose behind it, steeply like a breaking wave. Behind it, newly painted, was a white cowshed and beside that, also newly painted in white, was a low square barn. A creek, a wound in the smooth expanse of two large paddocks, pointed its way towards the river, where it would add just a trickle to the low flow of water already there. At the bottom of one of the paddocks eucalypts stood like a crowd of women after church, grey-gowned and grey-bonneted. Cattle moved in the paddocks, Jerseys cream and fawn-coloured, sleek as deer but without the grace or fear. Round all the farm was a two-railed fence, strong and well cared for: the farmer was proud of what he had.

" It's nice," Ida said. " It's the sort of place you wish you owned."

Sean sat stiffly in the seat, turned half-round as if about to get out of the wagonette. He sat in a silence all his own,

his eyes full of the golden light and the wide bleached paddocks and the inarticulate excitement of a dream beheld,
while the slight breeze came towards them from the farm and
insinuated itself into the kurrajong trees that bordered the
road.

"A place like that." He spoke with the softness of one
who had never seen a city, who had never had to raise his
voice above anything but the wind and the rain: life still
had to flatten it with bitterness. He was young, but you knew
he would never be as impregnable as his father: intelligence
gleamed in his eye like a weakness. "A place like that of your
own."

"Yeah," Paddy said, for the moment unhappy again. "All
the bloody worry of wondering if your cows was gunna run
dry, and when they ain't dry, getting up in the middle of the
night to milk 'em dry. Painting your house and your sheds
and then watching the sun peel it off. Watching the sky for
the drought to break and then when it does, watching the river
for floods——"

"Cripes, you do have trouble, don't you?" Ida said.
"You've just been through more in ten minutes than most
farmers go through in ten years."

"You think so?" Paddy said. "You think the cockies have
an easy time of it?"

"Nobody has an easy time," Ida said: hardship stretched
behind her as a long rough road. "Not even your mate Sid,
I'll bet."

"Leave Sid outa this," Paddy said. "You don't call him a
cocky. He's more than that, still I bet he's got his worries,
too. But I'm talking about blokes like that one," nodding at
the farm, a black curl dancing on his forehead like a bell on a
door, "battling all his life for bugger-all."

Ida looked at the farm. "He's got something for his
battling. Isn't that more than what-you-called-it?"

"How do we know he owns it? How do we know he don't
lie awake at night, worrying about the mortgage? Do I do
that?"

"If you did," said Ida, "you'd be the first man who'd mort-
gaged a tent."

Sean suddenly laughed and Ida, looking at him and feeling again, as she often did, the deep love she had for her son, also began to laugh. They sat on the hard seat, their backs arched with tiredness and their behinds numb, and laughed until they were weak, and soon Paddy was laughing with them. Merriment bound them closer than blood, and the argument was gone like the dust the wagonette had raised coming down the road.

They moved on along the road, the horse walking with head down, the kelpie trotting with the springy gait of legs that were as durable as rubber. The wagonette creaked and lurched, like a drunken man at the close of a long wet Saturday, and the dust rose behind it as a thin brown mist.

Sean turned round in the seat and looked back towards the farmhouse, now coming into the slanting late-day sun as the shadow moved round the hill. He stared across the paddocks at the bright colours of the house and sheds, seeing the eucalypts breaking into silver flame as the sun touched them, hearing suddenly, like an echo of their own laughter, the liquid mirth of kookaburras breaking the quiet stillness of the dying day, and he knew he would remember.

"That's what home looks like." His mother was talking softly to herself: Sean looked at her and saw the laughter draining out of her face like blood. "When you have a home."

2

"Paddy?" Ida said.

"Yeah?" He was sitting on the end of the mattress, taking off his boots. "Got another hole in me sock."

"Paddy, do I sound like a nagger sometimes?"

"Often." Paddy had begun to cut his toenails with a bone-handled penknife. "Why?"

"Nothing." Ida lay on the mattress that, spread on a large square of canvas, was their bed. She was naked beneath the thin grey blankets: you realised the pointlessness of night-gowns when you had no money to buy one. Her long, dark-brown hair lay in a wild splash beneath her head, and her tanned face, scrubbed just before she had got into bed, showed the bloom that had been hidden beneath the day's dust. She had long ago stopped admiring herself, but now and again, passing Paddy's shaving mirror hanging on the tent-pole, she would stop for a moment, caught by a memory of sixteen years ago.

Camden had been the place then, the only place, and she hadn't even been forty miles away to Sydney. Twenty, beautiful, some men had told her, and with a figure that was just the style then, all bosom and behind. Camden was a small town, and she had had a good time and paid the penalty: gossip had trailed her like the wake of a ship. But she wouldn't have, couldn't have changed. She had gone to church on Sundays, said her prayers, respected the Lord's Name, but the Lord had built her as she was. People could talk, but what was the whisper behind the hand to the whisper in your ear in the grass down by the river, the clucking of old women to the panting of a strong young man? Gossip was only envy, and she hadn't cared.

Although they had talked about her, watched her walking down to the river with the devil and every young man in town, everyone had liked her. She had known that, and it had pleased her because she liked people and wanted people to like her. It was her liking people and her generous way of showing it that had often landed her down by the river. That she had never got into trouble was something the town had never been able to understand; sometimes she hadn't understood it herself, but had never worried about it: she had been sure the Lord looked after sinners as well as saints.

She stretched luxuriously under the blankets, stirred warmly by a memory that had only touch, no likeness or shape.

"What's the matter with you?" Paddy said, switching the penknife from his left to his right foot. "Grinning like the cat that's swallowed the canary."

"Wouldn't you like to know?" she said, but he was included in the smile and the memory.

The bells in the tower of the church on the hill chanting song on the still evening air; the tall gums stretching to the

star-freckled blue; the river whispering its way past them like
an echo of the gossip; and Paddy, young and full of fire and
blarney, only a week in the district and already in love with
her and she with him. A wanderer even then, working on
Bonney's farm only while the mood held him, then at the end
of three weeks they were married and were gone. Just like
that, while the town stood at its gates and said she had thrown
herself away.

"But they were wrong," she said.

"Eh?"

"Just talking to myself. Come on, for goodness' sake!
Mucking about like an old woman."

"I ain't any old woman. I can prove it."

"That? I've seen bigger ones on statues. And they never
have much."

Paddy went outside to wash. Ida, listening to him with an
indulgent smile on her face, heard the splash of water in the
tin basin, the slubbering sound as he threw water in his face,
then the muttered cursing as he sought blind-eyed for the
towel. In a moment she heard him move away. The kelpie
barked tentatively, then there was the clink of hobbles and the
blowing of the horse. Paddy came back into the tent.

"Did you have a look at Sean? Is he covered up?"

"Cripes, the way you fuss over that boy!" Paddy hung his
grey flannel shirt on the rope that ran from pole to pole; he
began to peel off his trousers. "He's nearly fourteen. He
ain't a baby."

"I don't fuss over him," Ida said. "But he's the only one
we've got."

Paddy looked down at her and smiled; he could remember
the almost shattered look that had crossed Ida's face when
the nurse had told her there would be no more children after
Sean. "Yeah, he's all right. Snug as a rabbit in a warren."
Naked, he was lean and hard-muscled as a man half his age.
He patted his flat stomach. "You're lucky, married to such a
magnificent figure of a man."

"Go on." Ida waved a contemptuous hand. "You're a
midget alongside some of the men I used to know. Don't

know what was the matter with me, marrying a little squirt like you."

"You couldn't resist me winning ways." Paddy blew out the lamp and slid under the blankets beside her. "Or me loving ways."

Ida laughed scornfully. "I had to teach you."

Paddy ran a hand over her body, then let it rest on the firm plumpness of her breast. "I'm glad you're built like you are, darl. Plenty of it. I was looking at some of them skinny flappers when we come through Kempsey——"

"Don't let me ever catch you looking at any flappers. Or anything in skirts. I'll kick you in the you-know-where."

"You wouldn't spoil your own fun." He squeezed her breast and grinned at her in the dark. "Yeah, I was looking at these young sheilas. Gawd, what does a man see in 'em? No tits or hips, a behind you could hold in one hand. A bloke might as well go to bed with a broomstick."

"If you have to make a choice, you pick the broomstick. I'm warning you, my boy."

"Do you really think I'd muck about with another woman, darl?"

"I don't know." She turned towards him, her hand resting on the muscled hardness of him. "When you're drunk and don't know what you're doing——"

"When I'm *that* drunk, I wanna go to sleep. I don't wanna get into bed for any other reason."

"I love you, Paddy." She pressed herself against him, holding him tightly while she kissed him as if to bind him to her for ever. "I couldn't stand to think of you with anyone else."

"You ain't gotta worry, darl." His hand was stroking the soft thickness of hair at the back of her head. "You're the only one. Always."

"Ah, Paddy darling." She pulled him fiercely to her, but abruptly he struggled away from her and sat up. "What's the matter? Paddy, what's wrong?"

"Forgot to take Mickey out."

Against the starlit triangle at the end of the tent she could see him with his fingers at his mouth, removing the gold tooth. She flopped back, relief and annoyance banging together inside her. " You and that damned piece of gold."

" Think what I'd look like without it." He reached up and dropped the tooth in the pocket of his shirt hanging on the line; she heard it rattle against his tobacco tin. " Spoil me handsome looks."

He got back into bed and she drew him to her again. " Paddy, where are we going after this droving job? Here we are in Bulinga now, another couple of months it'll be Cawndilla. Where next?"

" I dunno. We'll see what turns up. You got any ideas?"

" Yes," she said. " Only they aren't the sort you go for."

" What's the matter, darl? You ain't been yourself to-day."

" Oh, I don't know. I'm getting tired of always being on the move, I think. I meant what I said down at the Port, Paddy. Why can't we settle down now? I see other women with a home, picking flowers in their own garden——"

" Ah, why d'you bring it up, darl? We been going over this for years now, and where does it get us? You know me. I could never settle down in one spot. Look what the six months at Port Macquarie did to me. I bloody near died."

" You're a selfish bastard, aren't you?" She felt him move stiffly with surprise. " Oh, I'm not wild at you, or complaining. It's gone on too long now for me to care much, one way or the other. But I think of Sean. He's not all you, remember. He's part me, and maybe he thinks like I do. You saw him this afternoon, looking at that farm."

Paddy was silent, lying without movement, almost without breathing. Ida could almost hear his mind ticking over in the darkness; any deep thought with Paddy was a major effort, needing time and concentration and even sweat. He wasn't backward or dull; he just didn't believe in thinking too deeply, that was all. But in the dark closeness of their bed, their limbs entwined so they were one, the night shutting out any distractions, he couldn't answer her with the usual laugh and changing of subject. So he thought deeply, then having thought sighed loudly.

" Righto. I'll tell you what. He'll be fourteen in a month, old enough to leave school——"

"What school?" Ida said. "He's been going to school all this time and I didn't know it?"

"He went all the time we was down at the Port, didn't he?"

"Yeah, he got there just in time to break up for the six weeks' Christmas holidays."

"Well, he had from February till this month, didn't he? And what about the time we was at Warialda? He went there for nearly five months. And six weeks or whatever it was down at Leeton. And a coupla months up at Innisfail."

"All that schooling, and he's nearly fourteen," Ida said. "He must just about be ready for the university. We going to send him there for a couple of months?"

"You're funnier than Stiffy and Mo," Paddy said coldly. "He can read and write, can't he? What more does he want?"

"He wouldn't be able to do that if I hadn't taught him."

"Well, it don't matter who taught him, so long as he knows it. Now where the hell was I?"

"Sean was just about ready to leave school," Ida said. "I'll get him a new suit for the occasion."

"Look, if you wanna be funny, I'll shut up." Paddy was writhing with indignation: try to talk sensibly to a woman, and all you got was sarcasm. "Are you gunna shut up or am I?"

"Go on," said Ida. "You're boss."

"Well," said Paddy, and lay back, drunk with power: all a man had to do was assert himself, "I was gunna say, we'll wait till he leaves school and is ready to start work. If he wants to be a shearer or a drover——"

"What if he wants to be a chemist?" Ida said. "Or a tram-driver or a lawyer?"

"Stone the bloody crows!" Paddy was horrified: she couldn't be serious. "And live in the city? Sydney or Brisbane or one of them places?"

"Yeah," Ida said. "People live there. Lots of them."

"Mugs who dunno no better." Paddy annihilated the cities with a sweep of his hand. "We'll keep moving around for another twelve months, then we'll ask him what he wants to do. If he wants to settle down, then we'll settle. Though Christ knows it'll kill me. All right?"

"Just another twelve months." Ida moved closer to him. "Paddy, darling, I love you."

He ran his hand over her plumpness and squeezed her. "Easy," she said. "Don't bruise the fruit."

"You're a wonderful bit of flesh, Mum. I said it this afternoon: I dunno what I'd do without you."

"You'll never have to," she said, suddenly weakening. "Not even if we never settle down, if we keep moving till we walk right into our graves."

3

Sean, as always, had been up almost from daybreak. He had crawled out from his bed in the back of the wagonette, pulled on his shirt and shorts, shivering a little in the early morning coolness, delicately washed his hands and face in the numbing water in the basin outside the tent, and had gone looking for the horse.

The day was still pallid, the countryside not yet awake. The scrub, still moist with night, loaded the air with its perfumes: take a breath and the sap of the bush flowed into you. Scraps of mist clung to the tree-tops, like clouds lost in the darkness and already moving back where they belonged, and the lightening sky beyond was sharp and fragile as new ice. A leaf or two fell with the slowness of dying hope, and shadows cut patterns out of the fading darkness. The river murmured its secret song and a long way off a mopoke tinged the morning with sadness.

The kelpie had followed Sean, wetting on bushes as they passed through the scrub, saving a squirt for each bush as if blazing a trail. Sean, reminded of his bladder, stopped by a bush.

"Makes you feel good, don't it, Nigger?"

The dog squirted again, a sort of off-handed assent. He wasn't a pure kelpie, but the breed had predominated in his appearance, and what he lacked in breeding he made up for in skill. Paddy and Sean were convinced there wasn't a better sheep-dog in the whole continent, *couldn't* be a better dog. The only thing the Carmodys had against him was his almost insufferable aloofness: if he had been clever enough to learn to spit, he would almost certainly have spat on the human race.

" Well, don't be so stuck up," Sean said. " You don't pee any better than I do."

The dog looked at him, turned and sniffed at a bush, lifted a leg and squirted, then trotted on, its behind a small insult in itself. Sean picked up a stick and hurled it, but the dog didn't alter its step or look round as the stick whistled past its head.

" You bastard," Sean said, and felt proud of the dog.

Guided by the small music of hobbles, he soon found the horse and led him back to camp. He fed him oats, then led him down to the river to drink. The sandbars were high and white, loose and powdery on top where the water hadn't flowed over them for months, and the bank itself crumbled as Sean and the horse slid down to the water's edge. Sean had been hoping to do some fishing, catch maybe a perch for tea to-night, but one look at the river told him the fish had gone downstream, looking for deeper pools. The river was just a silver wash over white stones and only slightly darker sand.

That summer had been a long one, beginning in September, burning out spring, and continuing on until now. From mid-November until the end of February the temperature had rarely dropped below the nineties; for three weeks in February, day after day as if the world had fallen into the sun, it had topped the century. Sometimes clouds coming in from the sea would catch on the mountains and rain would fall here in the coast belt, but it hadn't happened often and west of the mountains it hadn't happened at all. There the sky had been clear and dry for eight months, and Sean had lain awake last night, wondering what the country would be like out around Cawndilla.

He had seen only one bad drought, and even though he had been only nine at the time he would always remember it. At a little town in western Queensland, five years without rain, and the vast plain on which it stood turning to a thin powder, creeping on the town like a slow brown sea, the waves trailing a faint dry spume in the wind that came out of the Centre like the final kiss of death. Dried-up people, and everyone drinking beer because it wasn't as precious as fresh water and tasted better than bore water. The cattle lying dead in the paddocks, washed by the creeping dust, and only the crows happy.

Then the change of colour low in the sky that none of the townsfolk had noticed because they had long ago given up looking for it. The clouds coming fast over the horizon, at first indistinguishable from the dust, then suddenly the black sky and the silver lances of the rain driving hard into the earth. And the panic and the fear: that was what he remembered most. The children under five, the ones who had never seen rain, running screaming into the houses, shutting their ears against the drumming on the roof, burying their faces against their mothers' skirts, waiting for the end of the world; and the mothers unable to give comfort, for their minds and their praying lips were giving thanks. And the men standing in the rain, their faces flung back and their mouths open, drunker than they could ever get on beer. He didn't want to see another drought like that one.

By the time he had brought the horse back to camp from the river, his father and mother were up. They had breakfast, bacon and damper and black tea, then Paddy slung the old worn saddle on the horse and climbed aboard. He was going through to the other side of town to see Ferguson, the man who was offering the droving job to Cawndilla.

"Say a Hail Mary that I'll get the job," he said. "I hope it ain't already took."

"It's all ready for you," Ida said: she did the cooking, the washing and the praying for the family. "I was talking to Our Lady last night."

"Good," Paddy said. "How was She?"

"All right. Wished to be remembered to you. She said, 'How's that heathen husband of yours?'"

"And I'll bet you didn't even put in a good word for me. Just let Her go on thinking that of me."

"Why should I worry about you?" Ida said. "You seem set on going to Hell."

"I been living there for about sixteen years," said Paddy. "In a manner of speaking."

"Hey, Dad," Sean said. "What you gunna do about extra horses if you get the job? We'll need at least one more nag."

"We'll worry about that when I get the job," Paddy said. "Maybe your mum'll have another word with Our Lady. See you later."

He swung the horse about and rode up through the scrub towards the road that led to town. In a few moments he came riding back.

"Hullo," Ida said. "Get the job?"

"Forgot Mickey. Don't wanna go looking for a job, not looking me best." He favoured them with a gap-toothed smile. "You remember where I put him?"

Sean shrugged. "You didn't have it in before breakfast, I noticed. So we didn't throw it out with the scraps on your plate."

"There's never any scraps on his plate," Ida said. "Not with that worms' nest he has for a stomach."

"Thanks," Paddy said. "I got helpful lotta bastards in me family." He dropped down, lightly and easily; as a rider he was part of every horse he rode. "Well, don't stand there!"

Sean began to idly rake the ground with his bare toes. "What we want is a magnet."

"What the hell you doing?" Paddy said.

"Looking for your tooth," Sean said.

Ida was washing clothes in the basin on the rough bench Paddy had put up last night. "I don't know why you don't look after the damned thing." She vigorously soaped a shirt. "Why don't you get a string on it and wear it like a monocle, hanging down the front of you? You could pop it into your mouth every time you wanted to smile——"

"Jesus Christ Almighty!" Paddy yelled. "Quit the bloody yap-yapping and help me——"

"I'll knock the rest of your teeth out!" Ida said, and whipped the shirt out of the dish. Paddy ducked, sprayed by soapsuds, and the shirt flew over his head and landed in the dirt. "I told you before! Don't use the Lord's Name like that. It's bad enough——"

"There's your tooth, Dad," Sean said. "It fell outa the shirt pocket."

Paddy bent down and picked up the gold tooth. He wiped it on a clean but faded blue handkerchief, then fitted it into his mouth. "Tastes soapy."

"It'll help wash your mouth out," Ida said. "Righto, give me back the shirt."

Paddy picked up the shirt and dropped it on the bench. He kissed Ida on the back of the neck, slapped her on the behind and remounted the horse. He flashed the golden smile at them, then turned and rode up towards the road.

Ida, her hands resting in the basin, looked after him. "Sometimes I wonder if he doesn't need more mothering than you." She began to scrub the clothes in the basin; in the last sixteen years she had washed out half the dust of eastern Australia. "What are you going to do to-day?"

"I dunno," Sean said; sometimes the days were as blank as the summer sky. "Might go for a walk into town."

"Take the gun and see can you get us a rabbit for tea."

"I'm getting a bit tired of rabbit."

"When you're as old as I am, you'll be more than *tired* of rabbit. But if it's a choice of rabbit or nothing, I'll have rabbit. It's more filling."

"That's about all you can say for it," said Sean. "That was one thing I liked about living at the Port. No rabbit, except once or twice."

Ida paused, a pair of bloomers, trimmed with lace of soap, in her brown strong hands. She had never been really beautiful, despite what men had told her, but her neat firm features, the kind, yet impertinent, quirk of her full-lipped mouth, and the almost continual shine of laughter in her grey eyes, made you remember her long after a beautiful woman might have been forgotten. Her body had put up with a lot in the last sixteen years, but it had been strong to begin with, and she had had no soft living to let it grow fat and flabby. Her dark brown hair had but one grey lock along her left temple; it gave no suggestion of age, but had she been a city woman would have been used as an adornment. At thirty-six, she was *young*-looking, after a life in which youth should have died early, and in a country where women age quickly, still on happy terms with the world, the flesh and God. Only occasionally did she feel that she and life were going in opposite directions.

"There were many other things about the Port," she said, and there was no laughter in her eyes now. "We had only a tent, this one," she gestured at the patched, dirty-grey tent that hung dejectedly from its poles, as if ashamed of its own appearance, "but at least it was stuck in the one place, night after night. It wasn't a house, but it was almost home." She went back to scrubbing the bloomers. "That was the best thing about the Port, not that we had something else to eat beside rabbit."

"Well, yeah." Sean felt embarrassed. He had enjoyed the six months at Port Macquarie, going to school, getting to know the other kids, going to bed at night and knowing that when you got up in the morning you would be seeing the same kids you had seen to-day and would continue the game that had been interrupted. But he felt he couldn't side with his mother against his father, and that, in a way, was what she was asking him to do. It wasn't that he loved his father more than his mother; sometimes, lying awake in the wagonette, thinking in the quietness of the night, in the only time for real thinking, he knew he took after his mother more than after his father, but that didn't say he had to take sides. He admired his dad and sometimes, unaccountably, he felt a little sorry for him. He had never tried to reason out why he felt sorry for his father, it was just something that struck him at odd moments and left him bewildered and sad, but it meant he could never go against his father. Not even now, when he felt his mother was right and she had spoken things that had been in the back of his mind only last night. "Yeah, it was all right."

"It was more than all right," Ida said emphatically. "Now buzz off and bring home that rabbit. Two, if you can get 'em."

Sean got out the .22, cleaned it and set off for town. The

mile walk took him almost an hour. The day was too good
to hurry through; it was better to take your time and enjoy
it. Cicadas, still lingering on the long tail of summer, made
the trees just great shapes of sound. A willy-willy spun the
dust into a brown dancing wraith, then whipped it away into
the sky as he approached it. The paddocks sloped gently
towards the hills, and the hills leaned back against the
immense blue sky.

He saw two rabbits crouched in the yellow grass and shot
at both of them and missed; they were gone as grey-brown
tremors in the haze. He wandered off the road and down
towards the river to see how the pools were, but they were no
deeper here than back near the camp. He threw a stone into a
pool, but the only movement he got was the swirl of the
eddies. He turned and went back up to the road and a little
farther on he saw the kids playing football in the paddock.

He leaned on the fence and watched the pick-up game of
Rugby League, six kids on each side and all twelve acting as
referees. He could hear the yelling and, when the play veered
close to him, the puffing and grunting and self-conscious
swearing. Players in full flight were suddenly flattened as if
their legs had been cut off at the knee; the ball was kicked
and tossed about as if the death penalty hung over any man
who held it longer than two seconds. Then a tow-headed boy
broke away, holding the ball to him with desperate affection,
his jaw almost out of joint with savage determination and his
thin legs moving under him so fast they were just a brown
blur. He smacked a member of the opposing team with a
hearty chop of his fist that had all the enthusiasm of an
underworked policeman breaking up an unexpected riot, then
he was away, running the full length of the field, with both
teams baying at his heels in a mixed chorus of encouragement
and chagrin. Sean stood by the fence, thrilled to the core,
feeling the ball in his own hands, running all the way with
the tow-headed flyer. He could play as well as that, he knew,
if they would only ask him.

The kids came trooping back down the field. The tow-
headed boy, still holding the ball, noticed him and came

towards him, walking a little jauntily, the excitement of his
run still flushing him.

"G'day," he said; the other kids were backed up behind
him: the game was evidently over. "You new around here?"

"Yeah," said Sean, and tried desperately to belong.

"Where you live?"

"Well, not exactly anywhere." He suddenly felt the inade-
quacy of the camp. "We're camped down by the river, about
a mile back." Then, as if defensively: "Me old man's a
drover."

"And you go around with him all the time?" said one of
the other boys.

"Me and me mum."

"Cripes, that's what I'd like," the boy said. "Being a drover,
going all over the place, never going to school." He looked at
Sean. "You don't go to school, do you?"

"Only sometimes," Sean said. "I won't be going to school
here."

"You're lucky," said the tow-headed boy. "Old Randy, our
teacher, is a regular bastard." He looked at the rifle. "What
you doing with that?"

"Why?" Sean said. "You wanna use it on Old Randy?"

The boys laughed. "That ud be an idea. They'd take a fair
while to get someone in his place. Things don't move too fast
around here."

"Never anything to do but go to school," said the tow-
headed one. "And muck around like we are now. Never
anything exciting."

"How long you been moving around with your old man?"
said the boy who wanted to be a drover.

"All me life. I was born on the track, down near Jindabyne." Sean stood a little taller: it was good to know they
envied all the wandering he had done: he had nothing else
for them to envy. "We been on the go ever since."

"Where's Jindabyne?" said a boy hidden behind a mask of
freckles.

"Down Kosciusko way," Sean said.

"Hey, what's the snow look like? Is it pretty high?"

"What's Mount Kosciusko like? Is it pretty high?"

" You ever been ski-ing?"

" How cold does it get down there?"

The Carmodys had been on the track again when Sean was only a fortnight old, and they had been back to Jindabyne only once since then. That had been two years ago, and they had stayed in the district only a month because Ida had complained so bitterly about the cold. Sean remembered the broad glittering sweep stretching away beyond the town, the snow gums reared like skeletons against the sky, the clear air that was diamond-bright and needle-sharp against your skin, and the way he had fallen flat on his back every time he had tried to ski. He felt he was no expert on life in the Alps country, and he dug deeply and quickly for the touch of blarney he had inherited from his father. But it wasn't needed; from farther along the road towards town there suddenly came a commotion that switched everyone's attention from the Alps back to Bulinga.

" Get away, you crap-coloured, thin-gutted mongrel!" The voice came out of a tall, white-maned man like a wind out of a mountain-pass; the cicadas died and birds flew startled out of the scrub. " Who owns the bloody yap-yapping animal? Call it off before I kick it to death!"

" Here, Nigger!" Sean shouted, and moved down the road towards the two old men sitting in the sulky. " Here, boy."

The kelpie gave a farewell, derisive bark and backed off from the ancient horse that stood, sedate and oblivious, between the shafts of the sulky. Sean, followed by the crowd of boys, moved up to stand by the footboard of the sulky.

" I'm sorry, mister. He don't often do that." The dog had walked to the side of the road and lain down, facing away from them; it had completely forgotten them and was now contemplating a cluster of trees farther down the road. Sean felt embarrassed by the kelpie's rudeness. " He just don't seem to like people."

" Perhaps he's not as dim-witted as I thought," said the white-haired man. " There was just no need for him to be so vociferous about it, that was all." He looked across at the bored back of the dog. " He's making his point now with much more emphasis and less effort. A bloody clever animal.'"

The crowd of boys stood silent, their faces reflecting the sun as they looked up at the tall old man. Sean, who had inherited his father's short legs, saw the man as a giant. Sitting in the sulky he dwarfed his companion, his long bony frame stiff and straight in the seat, his left leg bent almost double in front of him on the footboard and his right leg hanging down beside the wheel as if it had slipped overboard and he was unaware that it had gone. Although his hair was snow-white, worn in a long mane under a black seaman's cap, and the skin on his face and neck had begun to loosen, he didn't look *old* once you were close to him. His appearance only seemed to emphasise the age of the small, quiet-looking man beside him.

"Who are you, anyway, son?" said the tall man. "I've never seen your dirty little face around here before."

"It's not dirty," Sean said.

"Don't argue, son. All kids' faces are dirty. Boys and girls and hermaphrodites. All of them dirty-faced little bastards."

"Well, mine's not dirty," Sean said.

"Go easy," whispered the tow-headed boy in his ear. "That's old Venneker. He'll skin you alive with that whip of his."

Old Venneker was already reaching for the long stockwhip hung over the front of the sulky. Sean felt the kids back away, leaving him alone and exposed. He stared up at the tall white-haired man, then slowly he brought the rifle round until the barrel pointed up at the big bony target.

"Hit me with that whip," he said, and tried desperately to keep the shiver out of his voice, "and I'll shoot you."

Venneker stared down at him, the lash of the whip still held against the stock, his long angular face growing longer with amazement. He continued to stare for almost a minute, Sean blinking back at him with nervous truculence, while the mob of boys stood a few feet in the background waiting for their first sight of murder. Then Venneker, dragging his eyes away from Sean, turned to the man beside him.

"Holy bleeding Jesus!" The storm of his voice disturbed even the kelpie: it got up and moved off down the road in silent annoyance; the crowd of boys jumped as if he had swung the whip at them. "Did you see that, Mac?"

"No." Mac was looking at Sean without seeing him; under the sandy-grey brows his eyes were pale and sightless as marbles. "But I heard it. He seems like a game 'un, without being a cheeky young beggar."

"He is, dammit, he is." Venneker looked back at Sean and shook his head admiringly. "I don't know who your father is, if you have one, but you're a piece of real, true-blue British stock."

"Me father's Irish," said Sean.

"That explains the mule-headed stubbornness of you," said Venneker blandly. "What's your name?"

"Sean Carmody."

"That's Irish enough," said the blind man. "Don't notice any true-blue British influence there."

"Nobody asked your opinion," Venneker said, not taking his eyes off Sean. "Where do you live, Michael O'Kelly?"

"Me name's Sean Carmody. We're camped down by the river back there."

"His old man's a drover," volunteered the freckle-faced boy.

"Who asked you to open your mouth, you spotty-faced Arab? On your way, all of you!" He raised the whip, letting the lash fall loose, then looked down at Sean. "With your permission, of course."

Sean hesitated, then said, "You better not."

Venneker paused, holding the whip as if to crack it, then he dropped it back on his knee. "All right, you accidents of birth. Your bacon has been saved." Then, in a giant roar: "Now get to hell out of here!"

The boys went off in a pack, running down the road towards the town, looking back over their shoulders to see how Sean was faring, but never stopping running. The kelpie chased them for a few yards, then grew bored again and flopped down once more by the side of the road.

Sean lowered the rifle and stood looking down at it for a moment. Then he said: "I wouldn't of shot you."

"I know that," said Venneker complacently, and smiled

the stiffness crumbled from his long face. " But we all like to play the hero, don't we?"

" Don't take any notice of him, son," the blind man said. "His bark's worse than his bite. Can we give you a lift?"

Sean looked along the road towards the disappearing boys, now just a faint cloud of dust going into town. There was no point in following them; they envied him, but he didn't belong. He clambered into the sulky, finding a cramped place to sit amongst the men's feet.

" What about your dog?" Venneker said as he slapped the reins on the horse's rump.

" He'll come when he's ready," Sean said. " There's no use whistling him."

" I'd shoot any dog that treated me like that," said Venneker.

" You wouldn't if you saw him work sheep," Sean said.

He was sitting with his back to the board of the sulky, looking up at the men. Now and again he looked at the small blind man, but the giant Venneker fascinated him. Some day he would like to be as tall as that: cripes, you could lick the world with one hand, need never be scared of anyone.

" You find me worthy of admiration, my boy?" Venneker looked down at him from the top of the world. There was something Olympian about his looks, in his great height, the set of his long head on the broad shoulders and the sweep of his magnificent white mane that was only slightly spoiled by the jaunty angle of his battered seaman's cap. His face was long and strong, with thick white brows that hung heavily over deep-set, lively blue eyes and a broad arrogant nose that jutted challengingly from between his deep flat cheeks. His mouth was wide and sensual, a mouth that had known a god's pleasure, and the long scoop of his jaw was the final arrogant insult. " I have been accustomed to it all my life, but it still gives me a small pleasure to bring a little of the unusual into other people's lives."

The blind man uttered an appropriate derisive obscenity, then turned his face down to Sean. " Excuse me, son."

"That's all right," Sean said. "It's one of me dad's favourite words."

"What is your dad doing up this way?" said Venneker.

"He's after a droving job. A bloke named Ferguson wants a mob taken over to Cawndilla."

"Yeah, I heard Ferguson was moving his mob," the blind man said. "Will you go with him."

"Me and Mum," said Sean. "None of us go anywhere without the others."

"How touching," said Venneker. "Are you all linked with the one umbilical cord?"

"Pardon?" said Sean.

Venneker smiled again. "Nothing, son. Now and again my tongue gets away from me."

"It'll be a dry route to Cawndilla," the blind man said. "It's bad enough here."

The full heat of the day was already coming down into the valley; it was hard to believe that winter had already begun its long journey up from the south. The pastures of the valley were brown, shot with yellow; the grass was dry and thin and short, looking almost like stubble. A few last cocks of hay lay sprawled dispiritedly in the middle of a paddock, like swagmen exhausted by the long summer, and on the flats down by the river the corn patches were brown and brittle-looking. The earth showed through the grass, hard and pale, and already the cracks of erosion marked several of the paddocks. The far sky was bleached by haze and the air had none of the usual sharpness of this time of year.

They turned off the road and drove down through the scrub and trees to the camp. The kelpie, keeping a suitable distance between itself and the sulky, followed them. Ida, cooking damper in the ashes of the fire, looked up as they approached. She saw only the men at first and stood up quickly, her mind at work; there always had to be excuses for camping on other people's land. The free life, Paddy called it, but somehow he never seemed to be around when the excuses were needed.

Then she saw Sean. "Oh, it's you. What have you been up to now?"

"Nothing at all, madam," Venneker said, and took off his cap with a flourish; Ida saw plumes waving, a sword flashing and a cloak being swung back over a shoulder. "Except to put me in my place with his gun."

Ida looked at Sean, then at this tall white-haired man with the tremendous voice and the grand gestures, and again at her son, still sitting quietly in the cage of the men's legs on the footboard of the sulky. "You mean you shot him?" she said matter-of-factly.

The blind man collapsed with sudden laughter, the tears running out of his useless eyes. "Gawd, that ud been a good 'un, missus! A shot in the pants is what he needs."

Venneker unwound his legs and stood up beside the sulky. He didn't appear to get out of the sulky; he just stood up from it. Ida looked up at him, her throat stretched and her head tilted back.

"Don't ask me if it's cold up here," Venneker said. "That little piece of high wit is no longer funny in my immediate vicinity."

Ida looked at Sean, now standing beside her. "I wouldn't have blamed you if you had shot him. He's rude enough to warrant a shot in the pants, like the gentleman said."

"Gentleman! Get that, Rupe?" the blind man said, and lay back in the seat wheezing with exhaustion from his laughter. "That's me!"

"You a gentleman!" Venneker roared. "Holy bleeding Jesus——!"

"Hold your tongue!" Ida suddenly produced a volume of sound that almost equalled Venneker's blast. He stopped with his mouth open and looked down at her in surprise. "You keep the Lord's Name out of conversation around here, unless you use it respectfully!"

"A revival camp," Venneker said almost incredulously. "They're not drovers, they're bloody evangelists."

"We're nothing of the sort," Ida said. "We just have respect for the Lord, that's all." Then, feeling she must be honest: "Or I do, anyway."

"Amen," said the blind man.

Sean, embarrassed by the way things had gone, looked up at Venneker. " Well, thanks for driving me home, mister."

" That means we can push off," said Venneker, then looked at Ida. He smiled and she, too, was amazed at the change in him. " I am sorry, madam, for my profanity. A cup of tea would convince me I am forgiven."

Ida was nonplussed for a moment, then she blushed. " I'm sorry. But you don't encourage anyone to be hospitable. Would you like a cuppa?"

" Thank you for your kind invitation," said Venneker, bending in the middle like a tree falling. " It is a most unexpected pleasure, and we should be glad to accept. Shouldn't we, Mac?"

" Considering we asked ourselves, I reckon we would." Confidently and without help, the blind man got out of the sulky. He stood beside Venneker: they looked like a freak vaudeville team, ready to break into a comic song-and-dance routine. " My name's Bert McKechnie, missus. The rude bloke's Rupert Venneker. He's English, which accounts for his rudeness. He still thinks we're wild Colonials."

" I've met some nice Englishmen," said Ida, and racked her brains to remember if she had met any Englishmen at all. Paddy couldn't stand the Pommy bastards, and they had never been encouraged around the Carmody camps. He had conveniently ignored the fact that Ida herself was only two generations removed from England. " I'm sure they're just like the rest of us."

" Thank you, madam," said Venneker. " The King will be glad to hear of it when I next write him."

" Do you write to the King?" Sean said in an awed voice.

" Yes," said Venneker. " But I regret to say that only his secretary writes back."

" Well, maybe he's busy," Sean said. " You know how it is with kings."

Venneker put a hand on Sean's head. " You'll go a long way, Sean, my boy. If ever you wish to be a diplomat, let me know. I'll give you a letter to a friend of mine in the Foreign Office."

" Talks like this all the time," McKechnie looked vaguely in Ida's direction. " It's better than reading a book."

Ida looked at the blind man. " Yes, I suppose it is. Well, the billy's boiling. How do you like your tea?"

" We'll have it as strong as you can make it," Venneker said. " Drop two good handfuls into the billy."

Ida looked up at him, squinting a little as she faced into the sun. " We'll have it the way I make it, Mr. Venneker. *If* you don't mind."

" Never in all my days," said Venneker, " have I seen such a stubborn family."

" You wait till you meet me dad," said Sean.

4

The two men spent the rest of the day at the Carmody camp. Venneker went down along the river bank with Sean and they came back with two rabbits, both the result of Venneker's skill with the .22. Sean had never seen anyone so deadly in his aim : two shots, two rabbits, both right through the head. A little later Venneker had excused himself, driving off in the sulky, and when he came back he was carrying a big bunch of carrots and a cauliflower, the lot held in one huge hand like a bouquet. McKechnie sat the while and talked to Ida.

" We live on that farm back at the bottom of the hill." McKechnie was a quiet peaceful man, as if he had a calm acceptance of everything that had happened and might happen to him. Sadness was a pallor in his thin face, but he would never embarrass you with it. His voice was a soft drawl and, although he laughed easily, his laughter too was soft. " We live there with me daughter and her husband."

" It's a nice place," Ida said. " We were admiring it last night when we came down into the valley."

" Everybody says so," McKechnie said without pride. " I was born on it and I can remember when it was nothing more than a tin humpy and one big paddock. It ain't the biggest, but I like to think it's the best-looking farm in the district. Everyone reckons it is."

" I'm sure it is. If ever we settle down, it's the sort of place we'd like to own."

" Ted, that's me son-in-law, and Rupe look after it pretty well. Ted seems to take pride in it, but I dunno, I don't feel his heart's in it. He comes from Sydney, and I think he's still a city bloke inside. One of these days, when I'm gone, I think he'll go back there. He come up here right after the war, and now I think he's had enough. When he goes, me daughter'll go with him. That'll leave just me and Rupe, and I ain't that much help about the place."

" It would be a shame to let a place like that go to pieces," Ida said: her voice was urgent, as if the farm were already in ruin. "My boy fell in love with it yesterday."

" Maybe you'd come back and help us." In his blindness everyone was a friend.

" Maybe," said Ida, and stopped the dream at the very beginning. " Who's this Mr. Venneker?"

" Rupe? He's a remittance man. He comes from a pretty important family in England. Venneker ain't his real name, but one night when he was shickered he told me his old man was a lord. I believe him. You only gotta know him as long as I have, that's the three years he's been in the valley, and you'll know he's no ordinary bloke. He turned up outa the blue one day and, right off, we became cobbers. He's been everywhere and done everything, and I think, more than anything else, he'd like to go home now. But for some reason, like all these remittance men, he can't. Or won't."

" He can be a bit rude and high-and-mighty," Ida said.

McKechnie smiled. " He don't mean anything by it. He just likes to pull people's legs. He really is a kind-hearted bloke. He'd give you the top brick of the chimney if you needed it."

Ida looked at the tent. " Yes, that's just what we need." But her smile meant nothing to McKechnie, and she said, " You like him, don't you?"

McKechnie faced down towards the clasped hands hanging between his legs: it was as if he held in the cup of his hands the last drops of friendship. "When he leaves here, and I got the feeling he wants to move on, I'm gunna be really blind again."

Ida raised a hand to put it on his knee, then changed her mind. She sat with her hand upraised, the great sympathy within her welling up to suffuse her face and bring on a glistening blindness of its own, then suddenly she brought her hand down with a loud smack on her own knee. " I wonder where that damned husband of mine is? All day, just to ask for a job."

Down by the river Sean and Venneker were skinning the rabbits.

"Do you want the skins?" Venneker said. "They pay a bounty on them in this district."

" You can have 'em," said Sean : it was rare that he had the chance to be philanthropic. " I don't reckon I'll have time to go in and collect the money."

"When does your father propose to be on the track again?"

" Monday, I think. Dad don't like to waste too much time in a place. He's a bit fidgety like that."

" And how are you?" The knife in Venneker's big hand was a stab of light; the pelt was peeled off in one slick flourish. " Are you fidgety too?"

Sean flicked his knife into the sandbank on which they squatted. " I dunno. I don't think I'm as bad as Dad. Now and again I wouldn't mind staying in a place a bit longer."

" There are a good many places that were invented only for leaving," said Venneker : he spat into the sand, as if bitterness were a phlegm in his throat.

Sean looked up at him, went to say something, then saw the distant look in Venneker's eyes and changed his mind. He liked this big bloke, but sometimes it was pretty hard to catch what he was driving at. Sometimes he talked down to you, then other times he talked at you as if you were a grown-up. When he talked like that, then he got a bit hard to understand : you didn't know if he was pulling your leg or talking to himself.

" I suppose I'm a good deal like your father," Venneker

said; Sean thought: crikey, you're wrong there. "I've passed through and been glad to leave more places than I can remember."

"Is Bulinga like that?" Sean was beginning to catch on: now if he don't go spouting above my head, I'm set. "Is that a good place to leave?"

"It depends on your frame of mind. Mac thinks it is a good place to stay. He likes it here, but then, what would be the point of his going anywhere else? Everywhere looks the same to him. And when you're on the move, you get only the *look* of a place." He talked like a man who could draw a map of the world from experience: there was the echo of distant places in his voice. "Yes, I suppose Bulinga is all right. But I have been here three years now. My eyes are tired of it all."

Sean sat looking up the river, wondering if he had caught all that Old Man Venneker had been trying to tell him. Upstream, a willow trailed thin fingers in the slow shallow water. A bird came down out of the sky, hovering for a moment as a small dark quiver in the blue, then settling down to be lost in the tree. Across the other side of the river a long line of galahs were picking their way across a paddock; something frightened them and they rose from the ground and went away as a swift grey-pink cloud. Then far away, in the shadow between two hills, a homestead was caught for an instant in a shaft of sunlight: it smarted against Sean's eyes and he turned his head sharply away and looked at Venneker.

"I think I'd swap places with you," he said.

They came up from the river as Ida stood up and looked into the tent at the cheap alarm clock hanging by a string from the tent-pole.

"Four o'clock," she said. "You'd better go looking for your dad, Sean. He's probably fallen off Tibby and broken a leg."

"Aw gosh." Sean dumped the rabbits on the bench outside the tent: flies came out of the air like black drops of moisture, and he dropped a cloth over the carcasses. "I'm always having to go looking for him. Can't he ever find his own way home?"

"That's no way to talk about your father," Ida said. "Even if it's true."

"I'll go with you, Sean." Venneker seemed to have odd moments of bombast and consideration; he was big enough for two men and he acted that way. "We can go looking for him in the sulky."

Ida was dubious; at any time Paddy disliked being sought as a truant, but to be brought home by a Pommy could precipitate another minor Sinn Fein uprising. "Sean'll be all right, Mr. Venneker. There's no need for you to bother."

"It will be no bother at all, madam. Otherwise I shouldn't go." Venneker washed blood from his hands in the basin on the bench and, unasked, dried them on the clean towel Ida had only just hung on the guy rope of the tent. "Absolutely no bother at all, I assure you."

"Loves to poke his nose into other people's affairs," McKechnie said. "Don't be too long, Rupe. We wanna get home before dark."

Ida wondered for a moment what darkness could mean to a blind man, but she forgot it immediately as she pondered the advisability of letting Venneker help Sean in the search for Paddy. She had enjoyed the day with the two men and she did not want it spoiled at the end by Paddy's bigotry.

"I'll tell you the truth, Mr. Venneker," she said finally. "My husband's more Irish than Australian, even though he was born here. And he doesn't"—she dug for a word and came up with an understatement—"like Englishmen."

"How big is your husband, madam?" Venneker said.

Ida was puzzled. "I don't know. About as big as Mr. McKechnie here. A little bit solider."

"A pity," said McKechnie. "He oughta be at least six feet three."

"If he gets obstreperous, madam, I shall break him in two." Venneker ran a comb through his hair and replaced the seaman's cap at its elegant angle. "Come along, Sean. We'll collect this rebel."

Sean looked at his mother, who shrugged as if to say the matter was now out of her hands, then he climbed into the sulky where Venneker had already draped himself.

"You said he was going out to Ferguson's to look for the job," Venneker said as they drove up through the scrub. He was like a general or an admiral mapping a campaign. Sean could find no reason for the resemblance, unless by some vague association it was the seaman's cap perched jauntily on the magnificent white head, but he had the feeling of being close to a man who had been born three hundred years too late. Drake and Raleigh, all the men he had read about in the books he had borrowed from the School of Arts library at Port Macquarie, must have looked and acted like this. "So we shall go there first. From there it will be just a matter of retracing all likely ports of call until we find him. Then we shall deal with him as the situation warrants. Does the poor benighted bastard imbibe?"

"Pardon?"

"Does your father drink? Is he a booze artist? What sort of an education have you had?" The sulky had now pulled out of the scrub on to the road. Venneker swung the whip above the head of the ancient horse, the lash cracking like a rifle-shot close to the limp scruffy ears. "Get up, death's head! We have a way to go."

The horse paid no heed to Venneker's encouragement. It plodded down the road at its one slow speed, and the sulky crept towards town.

"He's a bit of a goer, ain't he?" Sean said. "What d'you call him? Poitrel?"

Venneker again vainly cracked the whip. "This animal can't fathom any horse that breaks into even a canter. If he saw Poitrel or any other thoroughbred racing just for the fun of it, he would probably turn his back and head for the Never-Never."

Then at last they were coming into Bulinga. They drove up through the main street, past the shacks on the outskirts, clinging like poor relations to the town; past the weatherboard houses, all different yet somehow all alike, past the occasional brick house, looking no more permanent than the weatherboards, past the inevitable Commercial Hotel, the post office and bank, the school, the church: the town closed in behind them and Sean looked about him: born on the track, he searched for a home town. Then they heard the sound of a man singing, and clapping and cheering in a hotel on the corner of a cross street.

"Wait a minute," Sean said, and Venneker brought the horse to a halt by merely refraining from telling it to keep moving. The kelpie flopped in the dust behind the sulky, turning half away as if wishing to be considered alone. "I think that's me old man."

"How do you know?" Venneker said.

Sean sat waiting for the singing to begin again; it would, if the singer was Paddy. Then, in a reedy tenor torn with sobs and too much drink, the song was repeated. "That's him. He always sings *Little Town in the Old County Down* when he's drunk."

Venneker sat stiffly in the sulky, then he shook his head in pain and bewilderment. "A maudlin drunk! I can imagine nothing worse."

"He must of got the job," Sean said. "Well, I better go and get him."

"Stay where you are," Venneker said. "Pubs and brothels and parliament are no place for children. I'll get the sot. You look after the horse."

"Does he need looking after?" The horse slouched in front of the sulky: the shafts held it up, saved it from falling headlong into the dust.

"No," said Venneker, getting out of the sulky and going into the hotel, "but he'd be hurt if we didn't."

He was gone less than a minute. He came out through the open door of the bar, carrying Paddy over his shoulder and followed by a small crowd of men. They brought their glasses with them: they shouted encouragement, they yelled to let the poor little bastard alone. Paddy, his lungs constricted in an iron grasp, still wheezed *Little Town in the Old County Down*.

On the balcony of the hotel two men were sitting in rocking-chairs, drinking their beer and enjoying the peaceful afternoon. Hearing the noise in the street below one of the men got up and walked to the balcony rail and looked down.

"See this, Joe?" He took a swig from his glass, wiped his

forefinger along his yellow-and-grey moustache, then sucked
his finger. " Rupe Venneker's having a blue with a little
bloke half his size."

" Yeah?" The grizzled man didn't get off his chair; he
didn't have his spectacles with him and he knew if he got up
and went to the rail, the street below would be just a blur to
him. " Who's winning?"

" Looks like Rupe's already won. The little bloke sounds
like he's singing, or yelling, or something. Maybe Rupe's
hurt him."

" Yeah." Joe peered at his glass: six or eight beers hadn't
helped his myopia. " Did you tell 'em to bring up more beer,
Mick?"

" It'll be up in a minute." Mick was leaning on the balcony rail, looking down on the scene below. " Pity you ain't
got your specs, Joe. You oughta see this. Bloody funny."

" Wish they'd hurry up with the beer," said Joe.

The kelpie, aroused by the noise, cast a bored look at the
crowd outside the pub door. Then it noticed Paddy, obviously
the loser in an assault on his person, and instantly joined in
the commotion, whirling and snapping at Venneker's ankles,
barking with shrill anger.

Venneker gave vent to a storm of curses, drowning out
the dog's barking, Paddy's singing and the shouts of the men;
the bottom fell out of the peaceful afternoon. " Call off your
mongrel, boy, or I'll trample him to death!"

He swung a massive boot: the kelpie twisted away and
came back in, his barking even shriller. Paddy waved a weak
hand in encouragement: he suddenly stopped singing and
buried his teeth in Venneker's back. The men roared and
Venneker brought his huge hand down in a loud smack
against Paddy's behind.

" You sawn-off, carnivorous bastard! Do that again and
I'll trample *you* to death!"

The hotel keeper, a bottle in his hand, appeared in the
doorway of the bar, yelling to break it down or the bloody
copper would be down here in no time. No one paid any
attention to him, and he took a swig at the profits and yelled
again, but his voice was a whisper against Venneker's roar

and he gave up. He turned and went back into the bar, locking the door behind him: he wasn't going to have any disturbances in his pub, no bloody fear.

Up on the balcony Joe said, " You reckon they forgot about our beer? Gawd, I'm dying of thirst."

" Pity you ain't got your specs," Mick said from the rail. " This is funnier'n a circus."

Across the street the door of the post office and bank had been slammed shut: the postmistress's plump, frightened face was spread across a glass panel. An old lady came out of the church farther down the street, heard the Lord's Name being taken in louder vain than she had ever heard it before, and hurried back into the church before the lightning struck.

" Looks like the whole town's coming down for a look." Mick had finished his glass, but continued to lean on the rail gazing down at the scene below. " Here comes old Mum O'Brien. Trust her not to miss nothing."

The street, which had been almost empty in the lazy hush of the late afternoon, had abruptly come alive. People were hurrying from all directions. A police whistle blew, and at the far end of the street a stout figure hove in view.

" Here comes the Flying Squad," Mick said. " What the hell's he blowing his whistle for? There ain't another copper for miles. You only blow a whistle for reinforcements, don't you?"

" I dunno," said Joe. " How about blowing a whistle for some more beer?"

Somewhere a car, hurriedly started as its owner rushed to get to the scene before the riot was quelled, backfired loudly. People stopped running and looked around.

" Who's shooting?" Joe said.

" I dunno," said Mick. " I thought it might of been The Law, but here he is just arriving. He ain't got his gun, unless it's gone off in his pocket."

" I hope he bleeds to death," Joe said. " I've never forgiven him for locking me up, that time I was drunk."

" Which time?" Mick said.

The crowd had multiplied so quickly it was impossible to imagine where all the people had come from; from external appearance it would have seemed that Bulinga had had only one-quarter of this population. Saturday was shopping day, but most of the out-of-towners had already left to return to their farms; the crowd now thronging the street was the regular population of Bulinga, the workers, the loafers, the shopkeepers, the women, the children, the healthy and the invalids. No one knew what was going on: but whatever it was it was too good to miss.

"We ain't had nothing like this since the MacDougall boys burned down the gaol," Mick said. "Pity you ain't got your specs, Joe."

In front of the hotel now there was a mass of people. On the edge of the crowd the whistle was still being blown: a hoarse voice was bellowing to let the police through, but no one made way. In the centre of the crowd, backed up against the sulky, still with Paddy held over his shoulder, was Venneker still besieged by the kelpie. Cursing in a running blue streak, hopping on one leg like a giant bird while he swung the other, he was tall enough to be seen by people watching even on the outskirts of the crowd.

"It's old Venneker! What's he doing?"

"He's drunk! Shickered to the eyeballs!"

"No, he's not! He's being attacked by a dog!"

"What sorta dog?"

"I dunno. A mad one, I suppose. No other sort ud go near him."

"A mad dog?"

"Yeah, a mad dog."

"Mad dog?"

"Mad dog!" someone yelled, and the cry spread, leaping above the heads of the crowd like a startled pigeon. People running to join the crowd stopped, hesitated, then began running back the way they had come.

"What's that about a mad dog?" Joe said.

"I dunno," said Mick. "There's a dog down here yelping its head off at Rupe, but I don't think it's mad."

"I was bitten by a mad dog once," Joe said. "I ever show you the mark? They didn't think I was gunna live. Gawd, I was crook." He ran his tongue round his lips. "You think

I better go down for that beer? Only thing is, without me specs I might fall arse-over-Charlie down the stairs."

"I'll get it in a minute," Mick said. "Hey, the Flying Squad's flying back the other way now. Going for the lick of his coit up the street. Wonder if he's going back for his gun?"

"I thought you said he shot himself with it?" Joe said.

Down in the street Paddy had begun to wheeze his song again, Venneker was cursing and dancing, and the dog was barking and spinning in the dust like a berserk bunyip.

Sean, until now speechless at the disturbance that had been caused and at the sudden mysterious disappearance of the biggest crowd he had seen in a long time, at last found his tongue. "Nigger! Shut up!"

The dog stopped in mid-bark, growled a final insult at Venneker, then turned and trotted off down the street, back the way they had come. Venneker flung a medieval curse after it: he would have the last word, even with a dog.

Then he looked at the men about him. "That's all, you bunch of topers. All I tried to do was a simple good deed, but for some reason or other it caused more excitement than the announcement of free beer. I didn't realise any change in my anti-social attitude towards this flea-bitten town could mean so much to its addle-pated inhabitants. But," looking round the deserted street, "the demonstration seems to have been short-lived, and you may now return to your drinking."

"You'll do me, Rupe," Mick called down approvingly from the balcony. "Come in every Saturday and wake the place up like that."

Venneker looked up. "I thought I could hear your raucous voice while I was taken up with that man-eating mongrel. What were you yelling about?"

"Nothing," said Mick. "I didn't even open me mouth. Did I, Joe?"

"I could do with a beer," Joe said. "You think they forgotten us?"

Down in the street one of the men said, "What about the little bloke, Rupe? What you gunna do with him?"

Venneker dropped Paddy into the sulky, propping him up

against the front board. Paddy was silent now, looking about him, winking owlishly at the men and grinning vacantly at no one in particular. He looked at Sean and his grin widened. He turned to the men: Disraeli couldn't have been prouder of the Empire: " 'At's me boy."

" I am taking him home to his missus," said Venneker. " A charming and hard-working woman who deserves better than this midget-sized, drunken bellower of maudlin songs."

" Fair go," said Sean. " That's me father."

" My apologies," said Venneker, climbing into the sulky. " And my sympathy."

Sean jumped down from the sulky and disappeared round the corner of the hotel. In a moment he came back riding the gelding.

" I'll ride him back to camp."

Venneker turned the sulky round and they went out of the town along the road to the camp. The men outside the hotel gave a cheer: Venneker raised his cap and Paddy raised a drunken hand : the performance was over. Then the sound of the whistle was heard again.

" Here he comes again," Mick said, looking up the street. " Got his gun with him this time."

The men had hammered on the door of the bar and, after assuring the hotel keeper the riot was over, had been admitted. The policeman, red-faced and out of breath, his big belly bouncing in front of him like a huge wine-skin, arrived on staggering legs before the deserted front of the hotel. He looked about, grunting and blowing, his pistol raised at the ready.

" You looking for something, Baldy?" Mick said.

The policeman spun round, then looked up. " Where's this mad dog? Has he bitten anyone? Where's he gone?"

" Mad dog?" Mick said. " You seen any mad dog, Joe?"

" I ain't seen a flaming thing," Joe said. " I ain't got me specs with me."

Mick looked over the rail. " No, it must of been a false alarm, Baldy. But if we see a mad dog, we'll let you know. Keep your gun loaded." Then he turned to Joe. " Take me arm, mate, and I'll lead you down to the bar. I might even buy you a drink. I feel like shouting the whole town, what I seen this avro. Pity you didn't have your specs with you, Joe."

On the outskirts of town the small procession of the sulky, Sean on the gelding, and the kelpie was almost lost in its own wake of dust. Faintly there came the sound of Paddy once more singing *Little Town in the Old County Down*.

5

Paddy had got the job. His being drunk had been no sign of the outcome of his trip to the Ferguson place: he could have been celebrating or drowning his disappointment: either reason was a good enough excuse for getting drunk. He had fallen asleep half-way home in the sulky and had slept like a pole-axed bullock right through the night. It was six o'clock when he woke, clear-eyed, chirpy and with no traces showing of yesterday's bout with the bottle. His drinking was always that way: he drank only beer and though it could paralyse him on the day, next morning he was like a new man.

This morning he was a new man. He slapped Ida on the lump under the blankets that was her rump and almost shouted, " Hey, come on, darl! I got the job. We move out to-morrow morning."

Sean, leading the horse back to camp from the scrub where it had wandered, came running to the door of the tent. " Hey, Dad, is that right? I hear you say you got the job?"

" We get on the track first thing to-morrow." He gave Ida another thump on the rump. " Come on, darl, show a leg! We got a lot to do."

Ida slowly rolled over. " *We*'ve got a lot to do. What did you do yesterday? What stopped you from coming home then and giving a hand to get things ready? No, you have to land in a pub——"

" I met some friends," Paddy said. " A bloke's gotta be sociable in a new town."

" —get your nose stuck in a beer glass," Ida wasn't aware

Paddy had opened his mouth, "and in ten minutes we're forgotten, left to do the work, while you swell your gut——"

Paddy looked at Sean. "Stir up the fire and put the billy on for a cuppa. She'll keep going till the billy boils." He looked back at Ida. "Keep going, darl. What were you saying?"

"To-day is Sunday and I wanted to go into town to Mass, but instead I've got to stay here and help you get things ready." Ida stopped, out of breath. She looked at the doorway of the tent to see that Sean had gone, then she looked back at Paddy. "You're a bastard," she muttered.

"I know, darl." Paddy leaned over her, his hand pushing the hair back from her forehead. "I'm everything you don't deserve. But you'll never be able to get rid of me."

She stared up at him, then her arm went up round his neck and pulled his face down to hers. "I wish the shops in town were open."

"Why?"

"I'd send Sean in there," she said. "Get him outa the way for a while."

"We could send him up to the farm for some milk for breakfast."

"The man said he'd bring some down," Ida said. "If we had our own house, we could lock the bedroom door."

"If we had our own house——" Paddy kissed her and sat up; it was time the conversation was changed. "What man's bringing down milk for breakfast?"

"The man who brought you home from the pub. He was here practically all day yesterday. Mr. Venneker."

"Oh, he was here all day, was he?" Paddy began to pull on his trousers. "Ain't he got anything better to do? What was he hanging around here for?"

"Not for what you think." Ida pulled her dress over her head. "He's old enough to be my father."

"Age don't stop 'em." Paddy was lacing up his boots. "The older they get, the more ideas they get."

"I'll have to watch you when you get to his age." Ida wriggled her bloomers up under her dress. "You'll be bowling them over without asking them."

"Oh, he asked you?" Paddy stood up.

"Yes." Ida slipped on her shoes and also stood up. "But I told him I was too busy, cleaning up the camp, chopping wood, greasing the wagonette, doing all the things my husband should've been doing."

"Just as well I wasn't doing 'em," said Paddy. "You'd of had time."

"So I told him to come back this morning," Ida said.

On cue there came a stentorian bellow from up the road and as Paddy and Ida came out of the tent there was the sound of a horse coming down through the scrub. Venneker came into view, astride a giant chestnut stallion well suited to his own size. He swung down and towered over Paddy. He gave a milk-can to Ida, sweeping off his cap in greeting, then he turned and put out a hand to Paddy.

"The sot," he boomed. "And I must say, you don't look any the worse for it. Though God knows, you looked bad enough yesterday. Like something dragged up after five days in a beer vat."

Paddy stepped back out of Venneker's shadow. "And who the hell are you?"

"This is Mr. Venneker," said Ida. "The gentleman I was telling you about."

"He brought you home from the pub yesterday," said Sean.

"I see the billy is boiling. Let us have some tea," Venneker said to Sean, then turned back to Paddy. "I met Ferguson in town last night. I believe you got the job."

"That's right," said Paddy belligerently. "Any objections?"

Venneker looked at Ida. "Yesterday you complained about *my* rudeness."

"You want a punch in that long ugly snout?" Paddy was ready to let fly.

"You couldn't reach it," said Venneker affably: he appeared in high good humour this morning. "And if you could, I'd break you in half immediately afterwards. Now both of you wash up and we shall have breakfast." From the pockets of the faded army tunic he wore he produced a dozen eggs; he brought them out one by one with the flamboyant gestures of a magician performing to an audience. He turned out his pockets, emptying them of the straw in which he had packed the eggs. "I feel like a hen-house."

"You look like——" Paddy began.

"Don't be obvious. Just wash the sleep off your face, while the boy and I prepare breakfast." He walked across to the fire. "I have a few words to say to you that will be to your advantage."

"You sound like a lawyer," Ida said.

"I have a law degree," said Venneker, picking up Ida's frying-pan and inspecting it critically. "Sometimes one drops into the idiom of one's training. Your husband sounds as if he were brought up in the vicinity of a travelling boxing-booth."

Paddy took a step towards him, ready to commit mayhem before he blew a blood vessel, but he was restrained by Ida's hand on his arm. He turned to her, but she was just looking at Venneker, shaking her head in dumb wonder. She had the feeling that when she finally got to Heaven she would feel exactly this way in the presence of God. Paddy simmered down and stamped back into the tent.

"So help me Christ, I'll kill the long-legged bastard," he said. "Nobody's talked to me like that since I run away from home."

Venneker cooked the dozen eggs. He gave Paddy and Ida three each, Sean two and kept four on his own plate. "My appetite equals my size. Usually I have six."

"I'd rather keep you for a day instead of a month," Ida said.

"That is what I wished to talk to you about," said Venneker. "You could use my services on this trip to Cawndilla."

"No, we couldn't," said Paddy, stuffing his mouth with egg.

"Don't argue," said Venneker, blocking his own mouth with one entire egg balanced on his fork. "You know damn' well you could. You have yourself, the boy, a dog and one horse. Not enough."

"What about me?" said Ida.

Venneker bowed without rising. "Madam, my apologies. Your husband is most fortunate in having you."

"Fair go," said Paddy, suddenly suspicious again.

"And you have a mob of six hundred sheep," Venneker went on.

"That's where I come in," said Ida. "Just ahead of the sheep."

Venneker was ignoring the interruptions; he talked on past a steady stream of eggs disappearing into his mouth. "That is why you could use my services."

"We don't need another man," said Paddy.

"Perhaps not," said Venneker, conceding a rare point. "But you need another horse. Who is going to pull the wagonette? The good woman here?"

"I wouldn't be surprised," said Ida.

"I know Ferguson thinks you have at least two horses," Venneker said to Paddy. "I didn't enlighten him. But just where are you going to get that extra horse? You can't afford to buy one. I know he didn't advance you any money. Getting any sort of advance out of Ferguson is like getting water from a rock."

"Moses did it," Sean said.

"Is he with this party?" said Venneker. "No, Carmody. You need me. I am an experienced drover and I have two good horses. We are at your service."

"No," said Paddy.

"Don't be a fool, man," said Venneker, without rancour. "Where are you going to get your extra horses?"

"I'll borrow 'em," said Paddy: he was dug in, fighting to the last ditch.

"What from—the Mont de Piété? Who around here would lend a stranger—a drunken, disturbance-creating stranger, if you don't mind my saying so—a horse? This trip will take anything up to eight or ten weeks. Do you think they would let you have a horse that long?"

"I could borrow one from Ferguson," said Paddy doggedly.

"If you tried it, you'd lose the contract. I happen to know two other drovers arrived in town yesterday looking for the job."

"You know too bloody much." Paddy wiped up the remains of his eggs with a piece of bread, then sat chewing on it. "Do you know how I'm gunna hire you? What'm I gunna use for money?"

"You don't need to hire me," Venneker said. "My services are gratis."

"What?" said Paddy.

"He means free," said Sean. "For nothing."

"Thank you, son. It's a long time since I have needed an interpreter. Not since I was in Africa before the war."

"Have you been to Africa?" Sean said.

"I was a district officer there for some time. Best they had." He turned once more to Paddy. "Well, what about it, Carmody?"

"I dunno," Paddy said. "Why the hell would you wanna come along with us, working without pay?"

"There are a good many reasons," Venneker said. "One of them is that I am a restless person. I feel I have already stayed too long in this somnolent hole. One can have too much of the one place."

Paddy looked at him with renewed interest, almost with chill camaraderie. "Yeah, that's right. But who's gunna keep you?"

"We could afford that," Ida said. "If he cut down his appetite."

"I shall keep myself, if it comes to that," said Venneker. "I have a small income."

Paddy had been contemplating his empty plate; now he looked up. "Where do you come from?"

"England, of course," said Venneker. "Does my voice sound like that flat adenoidal whine an Australian uses for speech?"

"A bloody Pommy remittance man!" Paddy leapt to his feet as if the kelpie had suddenly attacked him. "I knew there was something that wasn't fair dinkum about you! From the minute I clapped eyes on you, I could see there was something wrong. No, no, a thousand bloody times no! I wouldn't have you on the trip if you were the last man on earth!"

"If I were the last man on earth," said Venneker, "you wouldn't be here. If you *are* a man."

" He is," said Ida.

" And you, madam," said Venneker, bowing again, " should know."

Paddy had heard none of this. He was storming about the clearing in front of the tent, consigning all Englishmen to the other side of Hell, asking God why he should have been inflicted with this stuck-up, overgrown Pommy bastard, telling the world he would rather lose the job than have to depend on a ——, —— sod from the Old Sod.

At the point where Paddy's language became too strong, Ida suddenly stood up.

" Shut up! I've told you before about swearing like that in front of Sean. Now cut it out and sit down."

" I ain't having any Pommy——"

" Cut it out, I said! And try and use that wooden block you call a head for something besides growing hair on." She stood stretched to her full height: she was tall with anger, the last couple of days finally stretching her to breaking point. " The Lord knows, I haven't any wish to go to Cawndilla. Or anywhere else for that matter. I wouldn't care if we never moved from this spot, if we stayed here for the rest of our lives and took to living naturally, the way other people do. But we haven't any money to build ourselves a home and I'm damned if I'm going to live out my days in a tent! If we have to live in a tent, and right now we haven't any choice, then I'd rather we kept moving. That way we have an excuse for having no home. If we stay here, we'll have no excuse other than that we're too poor to afford one. We'll be known as the Poor Carmodys, the people who live in a tent, the people that other people feel sorry for. And I'm sick to bloody death of other people's sympathy! I had enough of it from the women down at the Port." She walked stiffly to the door of the tent. She was flushed and the flesh of her face seemed to have hardened, so that the bones showed through, making her look suddenly older. But she was dry-eyed and her voice was steady. " So we'll be moving on to Cawndilla tomorrow morning. And no matter what you say, Mr. Venneker will be going with us!"

Then she had turned and was gone quickly into the tent.

S.—C

There was silence in the clearing for a long moment. Sean had seen his father and mother arguing many times, but he had never seen anything like this; he was suddenly afraid, waiting for something dreadful to happen. He looked at his father, standing stock-still beside the wagonette, staring with pained, puzzled eyes at the doorway of the tent. There was no sound in the clearing but the crack of a snapping twig in the fire, the slubber of the two horses, and a faint murmur from the tent that could have been anything, Ida praying or cursing or just weeping.

At last Venneker stood up. "I'm sorry, Carmody. I didn't mean to precipitate *that*. Forget I ever suggested my coming with you."

"Eh?" Paddy looked dazedly at him.

"You'd better go in to her," said Venneker. "The longer you leave her to herself, the worse she'll think of you."

Paddy shoved his hands deep into his trousers pockets and began to wander round the clearing. He was thinking deeply again; the muscles round his mouth moved as if he were chewing on tough meat. He approached the kelpie, lying with its head on its paws ignoring him, and when it refused to budge moved it out of the way with a sharp kick. He stopped by the gelding and patted its muzzle, then moved on to stand looking critically at Venneker's giant stallion. Then he turned and looked at Sean, who stared back at him, a little dismayed by this unusual quietness in his father. Finally, Paddy looked at Venneker.

"Righto, you can come along," he said, but you knew that the decision had been Ida's. "We'll go out to Ferguson's this afternoon."

Then he turned and disappeared into the tent to make his peace with Ida.

Chapter Two

1

THEY MOVED out on the road for Cawndilla the next morning. On the Sunday afternoon Paddy and Venneker, cool and silent as two strangers, had ridden out to the Ferguson property and stayed overnight. In the morning, while Ida and Sean were breaking camp and loading the last of the gear aboard the wagonette, they heard someone yelling up on the road.

"Hey, Mrs. Carmody! Hey, Sean! Are you there?"

Sean went running up through the scrub to the road. It was Bert McKechnie, sitting in the sulky, holding the reins of the ramshackle horse and waiting for them to come and lead him down through the scrub to the camp.

Sean clambered up into the sulky. "Don't you take a risk, Mr. McKechnie? I mean, coming out like this on your own?"

"I've been doing it for forty-six years, son," McKechnie said. "I went blind at fourteen."

"How?" Sean was still young enough to be direct.

"A gun back-fired in my face." It had happened so long ago McKechnie had forgotten the drama of it: he could have been talking about a minor childhood ailment.

"That must of been pretty crook. Did it hurt?"

"I don't remember that part. When I found out I was gunna be blind for good, there were too many other things to remember. But you don't lock yourself in a room because you can't see. I tried to do everything I would of done otherwise. I got married——" McKechnie suddenly realised he might be talking over the boy's head. "Well, I do all right. I don't think old Nugget will ever take me anywhere I oughtn't to go. It's hard enough to get him to take me where I *wanna* go."

They drove down into the clearing, and Ida already had the billy on the fire. McKechnie got out of the sulky and with

51

uncanny confidence walked over and sat down on the log on which he and Ida had spent most of yesterday afternoon. He took off his hat and ran his hand through his thick, sandy grey hair. Quite suddenly, to Sean, he looked very old.

"So you're on your way," he said. "Your husband got the job."

"Yes," said Ida.

"And Rupe's going with you." It wasn't a question; it was a plain flat statement, but the very flatness of his voice made it poignant. "I wish to hell I could go with you."

"Why don't you?" Ida spoke out of kindness and sympathy; there were times when her logic and realistic approach were forgotten in the rush of feeling within her.

"It's nice of you to ask me," McKechnie said. "But you know it wouldn't work out. I been telling Sean I've always tried to do everything I would of done if I could see. But that ain't right. I can't do half the things I'd like to do. It wouldn't be any good, Mrs. Carmody. If something happened to you people, I'd never be able to find me way home again."

"Nothing's going to happen to us," Ida said. "And if it did, you could write your son-in-law to come and get you."

McKechnie smiled, a little bitterly, if there were any bitterness at all in him. "I don't like to bother people more than I have to."

Ida turned away from him, as if to hide her sudden flush of embarrassment. She dropped tea into the billy and watched it boil. Then she poured the black brew into three cups.

Sean took his and blew the steam off it. "You gunna miss Mr. Venneker, Mr. McKechnie?"

"Mind your business," Ida snapped. "What's it got to do with you?"

"It's all right, missus." McKechnie took the cup she handed him. "Yeah, I'm gunna miss him, Sean. But I can't moan. I'm just grateful I got to know him at all. We been pretty good cobbers these last three years."

"I don't think he's gunna be good cobbers with Dad," Sean said. "They rode off to Ferguson's place last night like they'd never been introduced."

"Don't miss much, does he?" McKechnie spoke in Ida's

direction; she was moving about, loading a few final things into the wagonette. "Got his eyes open."

"He should keep his eyes open and his trap shut," Ida said. "In my day kids spoke when they were spoken to."

Sean grinned at his mother, but said nothing: he knew when he could and could not joke with her. He stood up and began to walk about the clearing. There was nothing left lying about: a hole had been dug and the rubbish buried: Ida left each camping spot as clean as a house out of which she had just moved. Venneker's extra horse, a bony bay gelding, stood patiently between the shafts of the wagonette. The wagonette itself, with the addition of Venneker's two suitcases, his blankets and a rolled-up stretcher, rested heavily on its flattened springs; like a completely exhausted old woman. Sean paused at the back of the wagonette and looked at the torn and faded labels on the suitcases.

"Mr. Venneker's been to a lotta places, ain't he?"

"He used to tell me about 'em," said McKechnie. "He's been all over the world. In the last thirty years, he says, he's been everywhere but home."

"Poor man," Ida said.

"Yeah," said McKechnie, and lifted his cup to his lips so his words were just a mumble: "I wish to Christ I been somewhere else *but* home."

Sean took the head of the wagonette horse and led him up through the scrub to the road. He vaguely realised that this morning was becoming painful to all three of them. He led the horse to the side of the road, letting him munch on the dry brittle grass, and sat down with his back against a fence post. A lizard, grey and twig-like, lay in the dust by his bare foot; when he touched it with his big toe, it was gone so quickly its movement could have been nothing more than a twitch in his eye. He picked a grass stalk and began to munch on its dry thinness: it snapped off in his mouth like raw vermicelli.

It would be crook being blind. Nothing to see all day, any day. The sky, the river, the road going away to anywhere, a horse, a dog. All of it nothing but noise and smell and a name. And feel. But how could you feel the sky or things like that? What was the feel of the sky, did a river feel like it looked, could you put out a hand and touch a farm and know it was the one you wanted more than any other you had ever seen (if you had ever seen)?

Anyone passing along the road at that moment might not have noticed him sitting against the fence post, or if they had they would possibly have paid little attention to him. He had that look about him that so many bush youngsters have, an almost perfect assimilation of their background. It was not so much just a personification of the physical bush: hair the colour of rich dark loam, eyes reflecting the sky, movement swift and graceful as any animal; there was something in him that suggested the lean of trees before the wind, moving water torn delicately on a smooth rock and bleeding sunlight, cloud-shadows flowing over the land and leaving nothing but an ache in the heart. He was not aware of suggesting any of these things, but they were as implicit in him as the blood in his veins and the quicksilver thoughts in his mind.

It was because they were implicit in him that he could feel McKechnie's blindness almost as a pain within himself. The bush was McKechnie's life, he had been in this one place so long now that the feel and smell of it were part of him. But the bush was more than rough bark beneath the hand and eucalyptus on the morning breeze; Sean could not have voiced his thoughts, but vaguely he knew that the tragedy of McKechnie was an accumulative one, every day being added to the ones that had gone, the beauty of years stacked unseen in everlasting darkness.

He was thinking of himself now. If he'd been blind like Mr. McKechnie, he wouldn't have seen the farm yesterday afternoon. If he'd been blind, would he have wanted a place of their own? Wouldn't any place at all, even a tent by the river, be just as good as the next place when you couldn't see it? Even as he asked himself the questions, he knew he was only kidding himself: crikey, how could you imagine being blind, when your mind couldn't stop remembering?

Abruptly he got to his feet and walked quickly and deliberately down the road. He came to a bend and there he stopped. He climbed on the top rail of the fence and sat there looking down the long paddock towards the farmhouse. Sadness came down on him like something from the warm winter sun; a crow cawed, a harsh bitter cry, and the sound was an echo in his head. He stared at the farm: after a while it seemed less solid, melting into the landscape, and soon it was gone and there was nothing. He stared with the sightless eyes of the disappointed dreamer, more blind than McKechnie had ever been, and there on the fence, motionless and small, he looked both very old and very young, sad and hopeless.

Then he heard his mother calling him, her voice floating lazily on the still air. He came back to life, taking one last look at the farm, trying to remember it for ever, then he dropped quickly from the fence and ran back along the road, wings of dust sprouting from his heels with his speed. McKechnie was sitting in the sulky, drawn up behind the wagonette, and Ida was leaning against the sulky's wheel, her old felt hat pushed well back on her head.

"Here they come," she said, nodding down the road towards town. "Where've you been?"

"Just down there." Sean jerked his head vaguely: there was no direction really for where he had been the last ten minutes. He looked at McKechnie. "Mr. McKechnie, if ever you gunna sell your farm, could you let us know?"

McKechnie didn't ask where they might find the money to buy the farm; a dreamer in his blindness, he saw no reason for opening the eyes of others by being realistic. "How will I find you?"

Sean thought for a moment. "How would it be if I wrote you a letter now and again? Could you get someone to read it to you?"

"Yeah," said McKechnie. "It ud be a bit of all right to get a letter that wasn't a bill. Me creditors are the only people who write to me. Write to me every town you come to, and tell me where you're heading next. That way I'll be able to follow you." He turned away to spit over into the dust of the road. "Get Rupe to write me, too."

"We'll all write you," said Ida, in an impulsive burst of

enthusiasm; she almost reached up and took McKechnie in her arms. "Dammit, I'll see you get a letter every week!"

"We might even get Dad to write," said Sean, then had a saner moment: "Well, anyway, Mum and me'll write."

Then the first of the sheep were straggling past and soon the road was flooded with a grey moving mass. The kelpie went leaping past on the backs of the sheep, keeping a neat but precarious balance as he went from the rear to the front of the mob without touching the ground. The dust floated up to thicken the air; it hung as a slow-moving haze above the road. The shrill barking of the kelpie, his ennui gone in the excitement of working sheep again after so long, was echoed at the rear of the drifting mob by the happy and individual cursing of Paddy and Venneker.

Ida and Sean said good-bye to McKechnie and clambered into the wagonette; they both felt the farewell had reached breaking point. Paddy waved to him as he would to any stranger on the road and rode up beside the wagonette.

"Who's the old codger? A stuck-up bastard, ain't he? I said g'day to him and he didn't even look at me. Must be a mate of your Pommy cobber."

"If you mean is he a friend of Mr. Venneker, he is," said Ida tartly. "He's also blind."

"Oh," said Paddy. "Well, I didn't know."

"No," said Ida, "you never do. You're a bit blind yourself."

Paddy let that one go. "Who is he, anyway?"

"Mr. McKechnie," Sean said. "He owns the farm down the road here. We're gunna write to him. If ever he wants to sell the farm, he's gunna let us know."

"Is he gunna let us know where they're doling out money, so we can buy it?" said Paddy.

"Well, no," Sean said, and turned away to call to the kelpie, which took no notice of him.

Ida looked at Paddy. "That's what I mean by you being blind."

Paddy rode away to move on a couple of straggling sheep, then came back. "Still, I'm sorry I said the old bloke was stuck-up. I don't suppose you can blame him for being a mate of that big Pommy bastard. After all, he can't see him."

"Stop calling Mr. Venneker a Pommy," Ida said.

"Well, are we gunna call him *Mister* Venneker all the bloody way? Who the hell's he? A Member of Parliament or a parson or something?"

"He's a duke's son," Ida said. "His father's an earl or a lord."

"You just said his old man was a duke."

"Well, does it matter? His father wasn't a post-hole digger like yours was."

"Leave me old man outa this. But what's wrong with digging post-holes? His old man probably never dug a hole in his life. Too bloody soft."

"Whether his father dug holes or not, he's going to be Mister Venneker until he tells us otherwise."

"He's just a big Pommy bastard to me," said Paddy, and swung his horse over to ease the press of the mob against the fence running beside the road.

Sean looked at his mother. "Gunna be a nice trip."

Ida looked back along the road. Venneker was riding beside the sulky, leaning down from the giant chestnut talking to McKechnie. He suddenly straightened up, leaning back in the saddle, and a great gust of laughter came rushing down the road.

"Good Christ Almighty, Mac——!"

Ida turned back to Sean. "All you've got to do is shut your ears when the two of them start arguing. The Lord's Name is going to take the biggest hiding it's had since Calvary. I'm going to have my work cut out."

"You should of been a nun, Mum."

Ida stared ahead at the bobbing ears of the horse. "I wouldn't have had you and your father then. God knew what was best for me."

2

By sundown they had reached the top of the road that led out of the valley. In mid-afternoon Ida and Sean had gone ahead in the wagonette to find a camping spot for the night.

They had pitched the tent and while Sean went off to gather wood, Ida began to run out the long screen of calico that, strung across the angle of a fence at the bend of the road, would make a break for the sheep for the night. By the time she had finished that, Sean was back with the wood and starting a fire.

Ida stood with her hands on her hips and looked down through a gap in the trees into the valley. The sun had gone, but there was still a shine on the air, except in the folds of the hills where the dusk was already turning blue. Far down on the road a fragile ball of dust was lifted and carried across the paddocks, then smashed into nothingness against a wall of trees. The tops of the trees were combed by the same wind that had lifted the dust, then the wind had passed on or died, and the valley was still again but for the bleat of sheep somewhere out of sight down the road. Ida hoped the mob wouldn't be too long getting here.

There was an ache in her back from sitting all day on the stiff seat of the wagonette and she would have liked nothing better than half an hour on the mattress before starting to get tea. Once, when Paddy had been too ill with pleurisy to work, she had taken a job as cook on a station near where they had been camped. Paddy had protested against her taking the job: he hadn't a great number of principles, but one he did have was a rabid objection to a wife supporting her husband, and although there had been times when *he* could barely support her and Sean, he had strenuously over-ridden any suggestion that Ida should go out and work. On this occasion, however, he had been too ill to argue and Ida had taken the job for a month.

It had been more than a job: it had paid more than wages and three meals a day. Despite her worry over Paddy and the two-mile ride at five in the morning and at eight at night to and from the homestead, she had enjoyed it and now, four years later, still retained memories of it. Memories of small things that an ordinary visitor to the homestead would have missed because he would not have been looking for them: the big stove, just the right height so that your appetite wasn't ruined by the kink in your back; the variety of pots and pans and the well-stocked larder; the cool smoothness of clean table linen; the feeling, not just the look, of a house being about you: floor beneath you, door to open, window to raise. On her last day at the job she had almost wept; it was like leaving home again.

"And I remember Mrs. Osbiston always had a rest about this time of day."

"What you say?" Sean looked up from the fire, his face flushed from the rapidly growing flames.

Ida blinked and came back out of the past: a little pain remained. "Nothing. Just talking to myself."

Sean stood up and looked around; Ida looked at him and realised with gladness that he was too young yet for memories. "Ain't a bad camping spot we picked. Hope Dad likes it."

The road came up a gentle rise, labouring over the last part of the climb out of the valley, then swung sharply west. It flattened out, exhausted, and went on between a thickly timbered ridge and a long narrow paddock. The grass of the paddock was thin and bleached: it covered the ground like a worn, sleazy shawl and in several places the earth showed through like dried sores. At one end of the paddock there was the red impression of wheel tracks curving in from a gate, the ruts getting shallower and shallower until in the middle of the paddock it seemed that the cart must have climbed into the air and gone on to greener pastures. The trees on the ridge, evergreens, still retained their leaves, but there was a sound of dying in their crisp hard singing in the breeze coming along the lip of the valley. The undergrowth on the steep face of the ridge was dead and brittle: the bright spray of a tree fern, like an arrested catherine wheel; the small grey explosions of wire grass; the wild tangle of leafless bushes; and the shifting, whispering face beneath it all that was the dead dry leaves: you looked and saw death and turned away, glad that the road ran on.

"We got a good fence to hold the sheep in," Sean said. "And this ridge'll keep the wind off us."

But when Paddy arrived he wasn't at all pleased. "Why the hell didn't you go on to Cawndilla? I kept wondering when

we were gunna catch up with you. These are sheep we're
droving, not brumbies. Gawd, we must of come about ten
miles with 'em to-day."

Ida was in no mood for a long argument. "We had to get
them up the hill. I wasn't responsible for *that*. There just
wasn't anywhere down there we could have camped them.
You've just got S. O. L., that's all."

"What's that, Mum?" Sean said.

"It's something dirty that I never allow myself to say," Ida
said. "But your father's got it."

"Is it any wonder?" Paddy asked the skies, and turned his
horse to go back and attend to the sheep.

Venneker and the kelpie were herding the sheep through
the narrow opening that had been left in the calico-fenced
break. The mob, weary after the long trek, went into the
enclosure without trouble.

"Well, that's the first day behind us," Venneker said.

"Had enough already?" Paddy said.

Venneker curled a magnificent lip, then turned away and
swung down from his horse. He walked stiffly towards the
fire. "A hell of a time since I've spent so long in the saddle."

"Getting old, maybe," Ida said.

"Age has nothing to do with stiff limbs, madam." Venneker took a deep breath of the steam rising from the rabbit
stew Ida had removed from the fire. "Not guinea-hen, but it
smells as good."

"It had better," Ida said. "There's nothing else on the
menu."

"No pudding?" Paddy was unsaddling his horse. "I
wouldn't of minded a nice rice pudding. Or a pie. Or something."

"Thinks he's at the Hotel Australia," Ida said to Venneker.

Sean came back from spreading his and Venneker's bed
rolls across the opening into the sheep break; they would
sleep there and be as effective as any gate. "I'll unsaddle
your horse, Mr. Venneker."

"Thank you, son." Venneker sat down with his back
against a fence post and luxuriously stretched his long legs.
"I'll sleep well to-night."

Paddy, struggling with a tight cinch buckle, looked across at Sean. "Ask him if he'd like you to rub his back."

Sean looked back innocently. "The horse?"

Paddy let out a curse that gave a deeper tint to the already blue dusk. Ida, without looking up as she served stew from the pot on to the four tin plates, said, "Cut it out! And hurry up and wash. Tea's ready."

"And it looks fit for a king," said Venneker from his throne by the fence post.

"We don't have kings around here," Paddy said. "Every bloke's as good as the next one."

"You're entitled to your opinion," said Venneker, and took his plate from Ida. "That's one of the drawbacks of a democracy."

Paddy stood for a moment, his wrists wearing cuffs of soap lather and his face stiff with concentration, then he spun as if Venneker had bitten him. "Why, you bloody high-and-mighty——"

"Dry your hands and start your tea," Ida said calmly. "He was only pulling your leg. Weren't you, Mr. Venneker?"

Venneker, his mouth full of rabbit stew, didn't answer. Paddy went off the boil, took his plate from Ida and sat down. The rest of the meal was eaten in silence.

Because they would be on the road again at sunrise, they turned in early. Paddy was already in bed when Ida came into the tent. She closed the tent flap after her and began to undress.

"I don't like that bloke Venneker." Paddy was lying with his hands behind his head, staring thoughtfully at the ridge pole of the tent.

"You haven't given yourself a chance to like him." Ida was naked; she had brought a basin of hot water into the tent and was now sponging herself. The warm light of the lantern hanging from the ridge pole became warmer still as it played on her rich curved flesh; her hair was pinned up on the top of her head, exposing the long youthful column of her neck; with her dress, she had taken off the dust and tiredness of the day and become suddenly beautiful. There was an animal grace about her as she went through the simple movements of washing; in all her body: the firm deep breasts, the good curved hips, the well-shaped legs, surprisingly long since she wasn't tall, and the smooth firm arms, there was a suggestion of earth in its wild state, of life not weakened and refined and debased by too much civilisation. Paddy, watching her, feeling desire uncoiling within him, was aware of another feeling, something that eluded him for meaning but which somehow gave him a sense of looking at more than the naked figure of his wife.

"I'm a lucky coot," he said.

Ida was drying herself, her body posturing as she moved the thin worn towel about it. "I know you are. But you don't often appreciate it."

"Get into bed and I'll appreciate you."

"That's it. That's the only way you men can appreciate a woman. If we didn't have this and these, you'd have no time for us. We'd just be cattle to you, something to work for you and be turned out at night."

"I'd never turn you out, darl. Not at night."

He had been in love with her almost from the first moment of sighting her and there had been no one for him since that moment. There had been a good many before her, loving some of them, leaving all of them, but none since: she was the one permanent thing in his whole life. His life: a long succession of roads leading back to the weather-beaten humpy where his father had beaten hell out of his mother and home sweet home had been a bitter joke. He had run away from there when he was fourteen and he had been moving ever since, no longer running and never looking back: it was one reason he tried never to think too deeply: if you thought too much you remembered and that way lay bitterness. All he wanted was Ida and the boy, and to keep moving.

Ida blew out the lantern and sank on to the mattress beside him. He threw the blankets over her, then held the warmth of her to him. She was silent, a long way away from him, and he pinched her gently.

"What are you thinking about, darl?"

It was the first time in years she had confessed it. "Home," she said, and was hardly aware of the brusque way in which he turned away from her.

In their blankets across the opening of the break Venneker was telling Sean, "I haven't been home for over thirty years, Sean. Too long. I've forgotten how England looks in the spring, and when you can't remember that, you've been away much too long."

"I'd like to go to England some day," Sean said; it was just over the rim of the world, not far at all in the short distances of the night. "Where else you bēen, Mr. Venneker?"

"Everywhere you can name. India, China, America, Brazil, Scandinavia. Everywhere. I've seen the world and the world has seen me." Venneker gazed reflectively up at the night sky. "I don't know which is the more fortunate."

Sean lay staring up beyond the stars. "What are other countries like, Mr. Venneker?"

"Never anything like you expect them to be," said Venneker. "Landing in a new country, one always has to readjust oneself twice. First he has to adjust his way of living, then he has to adjust his illusions." He rolled his eyes towards Sean: an eyebrow was a query mark on his forehead. "You follow me?"

"No," said Sean.

"I can see you and I are going to have some stimulating conversations. Let me put it this way: what do you think America is like?"

Sean searched among his paucity of Americana: half a dozen films, some paper-backed stories of the West, gossip of gangsters and something called Prohibition, three or four pages in the geography book those times he'd been at school. "Oh, I dunno. Everybody with a lot of money, cowboys shooting people, gangsters shooting people, everybody drunk——"

"Out of the mouths of babes comes libel," said Venneker. "I can see you have very few illusions about the United States."

"Oh, I like it," Sean said. "I'd like to go there."

"My mistake," said Venneker. "Your ambition is obviously to be a rich, murderous, drunken gangster."

" Or a cowboy," Sean said.

" Son," Venneker said, " you and I are going to have a few small educational talks between now and the end of this trip. You are virgin material and provided your brain is pliable— which I doubt, since you must have part of your father in you—I think there are great opportunities for me to bring you up out of the darkness in which you now flounder. You are extremely fortunate that I crossed your path when I did. You are probably unaware of it, but your life begins to-night."

" I'd like to learn," Sean said. " Sometimes I feel I dunno nothing."

" Grammatically, you don't," said Venneker. " But grammar will be only a small part of your education. I have in mind to teach you something about life."

Sean thought for a while: life lay round a bend in the road, like a new and frightening land. He wasn't sure he wanted to learn about it in advance: he had seen how un-happy some grown-ups had been at the secret, terrible things they had learned. Without knowing the words for it, he suddenly felt safe in innocence.

Up on the hill a night bird uttered a few broken phrases, sharp and carrying on the still air. A few sheep stirred rest-lessly, and one or two bleated. The kelpie, lying a few yards from Sean, got up and took half a dozen investigatory steps, then lay down again. From up the road came the clink of hobbles as the horses wandered seeking better grass. A bush snapped like a whip-crack as the heat of the day left it, and a sheep jumped nervously. Others stirred, pressing against the calico holding them in. Sean wriggled out of his blankets and walked up and down the length of both sides of the break. The sheep quietened down and he returned to his blankets.

" Don't take much to disturb 'em," he said.

It would have taken Gabriel's trumpet to disturb Venneker. Lying on his back, his mouth a gaping black hole in the moonlight, he was snoring loudly and in steady rhythm, work-ing a saw against the bone of his skull.

3

At sunrise Paddy and Venneker moved out with the sheep. They left behind them one of the bigger lambs and, while Ida let down the tent and repacked the wagonette, Sean killed it. He handled the long knife like an expert; he cut the woolly throat with one swift slice and held the lamb so the blood ran into the dust of the road and not down over his coat. He skinned it with the same expertness, working quickly and confidently, then rubbed the carcass with salt, wrapped it in a length of calico and put it under the seat of the wagonette. He pegged the skin to the back of the wagonette, where it was immediately blackened with flies, then climbed up beside his mother.

" All set," he said. " No bloody rabbit for tea to-night."

" Any more of that language," Ida said, " and there'll be no lamb, either."

The road wound through thickly timbered hills. The trees seemed to have lost their colour, bleached by the sun that had blazed so long, so that sometimes at no great distance it was almost impossible to pick where timber and bald hill face merged into each other. Sometimes, turning round a steep hill, they would see a small rock escarpment, grey and splintered, showing through the trees and it would take a second hard look to distinguish it from the trees: everything had the same dry fossilised appearance. Dead creepers hung down like giant spiders' webs and on the floor of the forest brittle leaves lay like the discarded shells of a million cicadas. Heat hung in the pockets of the hills as if it had been there all summer: it was thick and stale, almost explosive: the cool nights of the last month hadn't touched it. The road, grey and powdery, wound through the hills like a creek bed: the mob of sheep flowed slowly through it, dust rising above it in a fine dry spray.

Paddy and Venneker rode slumped in their saddles, Paddy at the head of the mob and Venneker tailing it. The kelpie trotted like an automaton through the heat and dust, occasionally barking as if to remind the sheep it was still with them. The sheep themselves gave no trouble; they plodded slowly after the man who led them.

Paddy rode with the thoroughly relaxed, almost boneless posture of one who was accustomed to spending hours in the saddle. Sweat ran down his sides and down the insides of his legs, but he felt no discomfort. He was the colour of the countryside: dust was a dry skin on his face and forearms, but he was unaware of it. He had travelled so many roads, eaten and breathed dust, had it ingrained into him, that it no longer meant anything to him.

His eyes, beneath the broad crumpled brim of his ancient hat, were closed almost shut against the glare of the road, but he missed nothing. He saw the eagle moving slowly in the high sky, disappearing in the blaze of sun, then drifting out to be once more a dark cross against the raw blue of the sky. He saw the wallaby, grey against the grey of the trees, loping away up through the timber, its bounding leaps disturbing the fallen leaves in small whispering eruptions. A carpet snake, lying like a dead branch by the side of the road, suddenly moved silently and secretly away into the timber, and he saw that, too.

He saw the small homestead as soon as he came round the shoulder of the hill. Tucked in behind the shoulder, either in fear or in ambush, the house merged with the trees behind it. Built of slabs, adzed smooth and fitting close, it had an iron roof, an outside stone chimney and a wide veranda that flung a welcoming mat of shade along the front. It was really little more than a shack, two or three rooms at the most, but there was a neatness about it, an unspoken sense of pride, that made it an insult to call it a shack. There were two windows facing down towards the road, both hung with bright green curtains, and at the side of the house, close by the large galvanised-iron water-tank, there was a brave attempt at a garden: a few flowers raised faded heads in a wilted protest against the drought. Running down from the house, beside the road and stretching back perhaps fifty yards to the timber, was a long cleared paddock in which half a dozen thin listless cows grazed. Almost half the paddock had been ploughed and cultivated, but it was impossible to guess what had been sown there: the faded brown corduroy pattern of the earth had no cross-weave of growth. In a corner of the paddock, behind the house towards the timber, was an open shed backed only by one wall and divided by single rails into stalls. There was no movement about the house, but from up in the timber there came the beautifully sharp ringing sound of a well-swung axe.

Then the sound of the axe stopped. There was the slow creak of wood tearing apart, the rustle of disturbed tops like a woman swishing her gown in anger, then a battery of hard flat sounds that came with the rapidity of barking guns. With the eye of memory Paddy saw it all: the tree falling across the sky, merging with other trees in a quickly increasing roar, coming down through them in a smashing, unstoppable plunge, branches snapping off and flying away behind it like the startled birds, then the roar suddenly an enveloping thunder, the tree gathering pace to hit the earth with an immense thud, to bounce and finally lie still. And silence rushing in for a moment after the thunder had abruptly gone, then the leaves falling in a sparse rain and the trees swaying back and forth with whispering sighs of relief.

Paddy turned his horse and moved the sheep towards the fence on the opposite side of the road from the cleared paddock. The leaders milled, turning back in on the sheep behind them, and soon the mob had come to a halt. Paddy whistled, blowing dust from his lips and wetting them with his tongue, and the kelpie, waiting just long enough to assert its independence, came running down through the paddock. It scrambled over the lower rail of the fence and without a word from Paddy began a slow patrol from one side of the road to the other. Having established who was boss, it lay down in the middle of the road and gazed at the sheep with a keen but supercilious eye.

Paddy pushed his horse back through the mob to Venneker. "We'll have dinner here. The missus oughta be along pretty soon."

Venneker swung down from his horse. He removed his cap and wiped a forearm across his sweat-muddied forehead.

"I've never known such heat at this time of year. That sun could very easily give one sunstroke."

"It wouldn't if you wore a hat, instead of that bloody silly kid's thing you wear."

Venneker looked coldly at Paddy's battered headgear. "Is that a hat or a discarded saddle blanket? This cap I wear, Carmody my man——"

"I'm not your man," said Carmody.

"No, that's right. You're not. I'm really your man. I suppose you would prefer I called you boss?"

Paddy considered this for a moment. "Yeah, that ud be an idea."

"It would be an idea, but it would be an extremely farcical one. Balls to that idea, Carmody," said Venneker, and took off his cap and looked at it with affection. "As I was saying, this cap has a history. It has seen the world, adorned the head of the master of a China boat——"

"What happened to him?" Paddy had unslung his saddle and hung it on the fence."

"Nothing happened to him," said Venneker. "He's just not going to call you boss, that's all."

Paddy looked at him, went to say something, couldn't think of anything and satisfied himself with spitting into the dust. He turned to face the four people coming down out of the timber and across the paddock towards the road. "All right to spell the mob here?"

The man and the woman came from the same mould, related by toil and care and hardship as much as by marriage: lean and strong in face and body, even their hair bleached to the same lifeless yellow, they were more part of each other than they could ever be in bed. But the two girls, one about seventeen and the other fourteen, were fresh as spring fruit, ripe and shining through the dust and sweat that covered their faces and arms.

"Don't let 'em get into the paddock," the man said; his tone was friendly, but with drovers you had to think of yourself first: once they had moved on they never thought of you. "Me grass is thin enough now."

"Looks pretty crook," Paddy said. "You been having a bad trot?"

"Terrible." The woman was plain to the point of

nonentity: she smiled and Paddy felt no better for it. "No rain for eight months now. They've had a coupla showers down in the valley, but we ain't even had a spit up here."

"We been trying to chop a fire-break over at the creek-bed at the back," the man said; his hand carried a blade of light as the axe caught the sun. "We been praying all summer there'll be no fires."

"It's dry enough," Paddy said. "You couldn't hold one if it started."

The girls had said nothing; they stood leaning against the fence in attitudes of negligent grace. Venneker took off his cap to them and bowed. "Morning, young ladies. It shortens the day, takes the stiffness out of a man's limbs, makes him forget six hundred mangy brainless sheep, to witness such unexpected beauty in such an out-of-the-way spot." He looked at the mother and father. "May I compliment you on the miracle you have achieved out of the material you had to begin with?"

The man and the woman stared at Venneker, then at Paddy, who shrugged as if to say he disowned the sun-touched giant. The two girls straightened up, unsure of Venneker, unused to flattery, especially in such extravagant terms. Then the elder one smiled, pleasure coming through the mask of dust and sweat as a brightness of fine teeth and a sparkling warmth in the blue eyes. She pushed back her thick blonde hair with the back of her hand: she had seen Dorothy Gish do it at the pictures in Bulinga.

"You ain't an Australian," she said. "Australian men don't talk like you."

"We wouldn't wanna," said Paddy, and winked at the girl's father. "A bloke ud never be able to hold his head up."

The woman looked up at Venneker. "I ain't seen anything like you since I used to go to the pictures down in Sydney. Francis X. Bushman would of talked like you."

"Thank you, madam," said Venneker. "I have never seen the character you speak of, but he has obviously impressed you."

"He could put his shoes under my bed," said the elder girl.

"And I'm sure he wouldn't refuse the invitation," said Venneker.

"Wanna come up and have a cuppa?" the man said to Paddy. "By the way, our name's Bateman."

"Mine's Carmody," said Paddy.

There was a deep silence, in which the Bateman family waited curiously. At last Venneker said, "His warped little ego recognises no one but himself. My name is Venneker."

Then the wagonette came round the shoulder of the hill, creaking and lumbering down the road to come to a halt with a groan of tired springs. Ida looked down with instant friendliness and smiled at the Batemans. "Hullo. These two been trying to start an argument?"

"Only with each other," Mrs. Bateman said. "You with them?"

"The little one's my husband," Ida said. "The big 'un is a friend of the family."

Paddy snorted and spoke to Bateman, man to man. "The star boarder."

Mrs. Bateman looked up at Ida. "We was just asking 'em would they like a cuppa tea. How about you and the boy?"

"Well, it's just about time for our dinner," Ida said.

"What were you gunna have? I've got a stove, if you'd like to use it. I reckon you don't enjoy cooking over an open fire. I know I didn't when we first moved up here. The first thing I got Ern to get me was the stove."

Ida swung down from the wagonette. "Mrs. Bateman, it takes a woman to understand a woman."

Ida cooked two legs of the lamb, having the time of her life over Mrs. Bateman's stove, her face flushed more with pleasure than with the heat, her eyes shining more than her sweat-wet forehead and upper lip, and both families sat down to an excellent meal. There was lamb, baked potatoes, dried green peas, home-made bread and a jam roly-poly: Ida had simple recipes, but she cooked well.

Sean stayed down on the road to mind the sheep, and the younger girl, who had just smiled at him when he was introduced to the Batemans, brought his dinner down to him.

"My name's Marge." With her fawn hair and her sleek

movements, there was a suggestion of young animal in her; she looked at him with frank curious eyes, completely sure of herself.

Sean nodded and hid his tongue-tied embarrassment behind a hugely piled fork. He had had very little to do with girls, and this one, ripe as a yellow plum, the same age as himself but already older, scared him a little. She sat down beside him, leaning back against the bottom rail of the fence, and hunched a provocative shoulder. Her young breasts came out against the thin faded yellow dress she wore, and Sean almost choked on a piece of unchewed lamb.

"What's the matter?" Marge said.

"Nothing." His voice had to push its way up past the meat stuck in his chest. "You have your dinner?"

"No," Marge said, unworried.

"Hadn't you better go and get it?" Sean said, worried.

"Yeah, I will." She scrambled to her feet, and Sean felt a mixture of relief and disappointment. "I'll bring it down here and have it with you. Won't be a minute."

She was back in no time at all, running with her plate balanced expertly on the palm of her hand. She spun to a stop and sank down beside him again. "Oh, you're finished! Crikey, you must have golloped it down."

Sean had. The lamb had lost all taste in his mouth, become almost as unpalatable as rabbit, and he had wolfed it down while his stomach had been temporarily receptive. He could not have finished the meal while this girl sat beside him. The meat lay like a busted rib on top of his stomach, but at least he had got it down: he could digest it later. Meanwhile he would sit and look at this girl who was giving him so much encouragement.

"Your mum says you're going to Cawndilla." A full mouth didn't hinder her talking. "Wish I could go with you."

Sean saw this as a hint, but he was too practical to be gallant. "Your mum wouldn't let you come."

"No, I suppose you're right." She chewed reflectively on a mouthful of meat and potato. "Crikey, I get sick of this place!"

Sean looked across the paddock to the house. "You can get pretty sick of being on the road, too."

"Oh, I dunno whether I wanna be on the road all the time. I like our place, I suppose. I just wish it was somewhere else but here. Down in Bulinga, or some other town, anywhere but stuck up here in the bloody bush." She looked at him. "Do you swear?"

"Yeah."

"You don't mind girls swearing?"

"I couldn't stop 'em, could I? Anyhow, *bloody* ain't swearing."

"Oh, I know worse than that. I was just testing you out."

He grew a little frightened: vaguely, sin had always had a woman's form and here was the first influence "Yeah, well so do I. Get on with what you were saying."

"Where was I?"

"Up here in the bloody bush."

"Yeah, stuck up here we never see anyone. Nobody but people like you, just going past, always going somewhere but never stopping so we can *know* you. Crikey, you must know hundreds of people. You're lucky." The kelpie was standing two or three yards from her, looking at her with a curious, but superior stare. She put down her plate in front of her and motioned to him. "There, boy. What do you call him?"

"Nigger," Sean said, and was pleased to see the kelpie was hungry enough not to be offensive. "He must like you. Generally he's too stuck-up to take any notice of anyone."

"I get on well with animals," she said. "That's all there is around here."

"What about your sister?"

"Mary? All she thinks about is boys. Not that there are any around here. But sometimes she goes down to stay with a girl friend in Bulinga, then she comes home and tells me all about it and that does her till next time. She has a pretty good time, but I'm always scared she'll have a baby. When Mum lets me go down there, she says I can when I'm sixteen, I'm gunna be more careful. I'm reading all about it now in a book Mum dunno I got. *What Every Young Girl Should Know.* You read it?"

"What would I wanna know about what girls should know?"

"Well, you can never know too much. Not about that, anyway."

Sean had had the facts of life explained to him in blunt awkward terms by his father a year ago, but his knowledge was still theoretical and he had never thought of discussing it with other boys: he had never known any long enough to get down to such intimate confidences. As for discussing it with girls, he would rather have died. He did his best to die now, strangling himself with embarrassment, but Marge was unaware she was provoking suicide.

"I wish you were staying around a while," she said, and looked at him out of the corner of her eyes.

Sean dragged himself awkwardly to his feet. "Gotta look at the sheep."

He walked blindly into the mob, pushing through it as if he were trying to wade through surf and out to the deep drowning water. Then he had pushed right through to the clear road beyond and was still alive; there was nothing to do but go back to the girl. Gosh, but she was a hot 'un! He had known for some time that when he eventually got a girl he wanted a hot one, he knew she would save time, but he hadn't reckoned on a girl taking any interest in him for at least another three or four years. Now here was one doing a line with him right out in the open, in the middle of the day, and he didn't know what the hell the next step was. He walked back through the mob, still blinded by excitement and confusion.

He was saved from red-faced seduction by the arrival of Venneker. "Some roly-poly pudding for you two youngsters. How are you getting on together? Has he approached you for a kiss, young lady?"

"No," said the young lady matter-of-factly. "I think he's shy."

"Is that so, my boy?" Venneker said. "Are you scared of the fair sex?"

Sean felt safer with a third person present. "No. Bloke

just has to take his time, that's all. Anyhow, there ain't nothing in kissing."

Venneker's eyebrows rested high on his forehead like two startled caterpillars. "In most cases, it's a beginning. Have you a subtler, swifter approach or do you just bludgeon your women into submission?"

"Pardon?" said Sean.

"No matter," said Venneker, and looked at Marge. "And how do you like your men, young lady?"

"Anyhow," said Marge. "I ain't fussy."

"Well, then you'll never suffer for lack of a husband. But I would advise you to use some restraint in your choice. The boy's mother evidently had your outlook, and look at what she landed."

It was Marge's turn to look puzzled. "What you mean?"

But Venneker had turned away to speak to Sean. "Let's saddle the horses. We'll be on the move again soon."

Sean finished his pudding and handed the empty plate to Marge. He got suddenly daring. "I hope we come back this way some time. When you're sixteen."

"I might have a boy by then," Marge said: her future was mile-stoned by men.

"Well, we'll see." Sean looked across towards the house where his father and mother and the Batemans were just coming out on to the veranda. "We might be able to stay a bit longer next time. That is, if you're still here."

"We'll be here, all right. Dad ud never leave here. He reckons some day this is gunna be a big property. Have a proper house and everything. We won't leave here, you can bet on that."

Paddy and Ida and the Batemans came down to the road. Venneker was already on his horse, getting the sheep on the move. Sean brought up the grey gelding and Paddy climbed into the saddle. Ida hoisted herself up into the wagonette and settled herself on the hard seat.

"This gets hard on your goat," she said, trying to spread her haunches comfortably. "It was a real treat to sit in that easy chair of yours."

"You'll be a bit stiff by the end of this trip," Mrs. Bateman said: it pleased her to know Ida had enjoyed herself in their house: it wasn't much, but she was proud of it. "How long d'you reckon it'll take you?"

"About eight or nine weeks," Ida said.

"Do you ever feel like settling down?" Mrs. Bateman was leaning on the gate: home was clutched in her work-scarred hands.

Ida looked down at her. "Mrs. Bateman, you're a lucky woman."

"That answers my question," Mrs. Bateman said. "I hope you have the same luck some day."

Bateman looked over the mob; Venneker had said good-bye and was already moving the sheep down the road. "They're not carrying much weight now. They'll be pretty thin by the time you get there, why didn't Ferguson rail 'em or truck 'em?"

"It's cheaper this way," Paddy said. "He don't care much what condition they're in when they get there, so long as we get 'em there. He ain't selling 'em. He's just moving 'em from one property to his other one at Cawndilla."

"He ain't picking a good time for it," Bateman said.

"I didn't ask him about that," Paddy said. "He just seemed to want 'em moved from here. I reckon he's more interested in feeding his cows." He looked down at the yellow paddock, the grass thin and short on the baked earth. "You wouldn't think this was dairying country."

Bateman smiled, a little sourly: the drought had begun to erode his face. "A man wants his head read. But you keep hoping——" He was a hundred years behind the pioneers but he had their faith: it would have to rain some time Then someday. . . . "Maybe in ten or fifteen years we'll have a decent place here. A bigger house, plenty of paddocks some good Jerseys or Aberdeen-Angus giving plenty of milk Then we won't remember this."

Paddy looked down at him. "You reckon you ever forget a drought?"

"No," said Bateman. "You never do. Or the floods or the fires, either. But you stay on, anyway." He looked up

and smiled again, the sourness gone. "You gotta be soft in
the head to be a farmer."

The Carmodys said good-bye to the Batemans and moved
on. In the wagonette Ida was talking to Sean. "They were
nice people. I admire people like that. Coming up here,
starting out from scratch without a cracker, nothing but their
hands and a few odds and ends and a lot of hope, and building themselves a home." She looked ahead at Paddy, pushing
his horse through the mob to take the lead. "Your dad
could do it. He has the guts, if he'd only stop still long
enough."

"Maybe he'll get tired one day."

"Then all he'll be fit for will be burying," Ida said. "How
did you like your dinner?"

"All right." Sean was only now beginning to digest the
lamb; he belched loudly and ducked the back of his mother's
hand. "It was better than rabbit."

"What was Marge like? You ought to meet more kids
your own age, like her. What did you talk about? We could
see you from the window. She seemed to be doing all the
talking."

"Yeah, she was a bit of a wind-bag. She just talked about
how she didn't like being stuck up here away from everything."

"Some people are never satisfied," said Ida.

Sean was silent for a while. "Mum, how old has a girl
gotta be before she can have a baby?"

Ida jerked the reins and the horse flung up a startled head.
"What the devil were you up to with that Marge? Did you
go anywhere with her while my back was turned?"

"Cut it out, Mum." Sean felt the heat of the day as
suddenly cool beside his embarrassment: he should have kept
his trap shut. "I ain't old enough for that sorta thing, am I?"

"That girl evidently is. Did she bring up this subject?"

"Yeah, in a way."

Ida was angry at the girl, but the anger was suddenly dissipated in memory: she had had her own first boy at fifteen.
Maybe the girl was lonely or, worse still, had recognised
loneliness in Sean and had offered a woman's comfort. She

looked for excuses, while a mile behind her the girl had already returned to *What Every Young Girl Should Know.*

" You should always respect a girl," Ida said.

Sean said nothing, wondering how you could respect a girl when she did all the chasing. Maybe Mr. Venneker would give him the answer: maybe this was one of the things that came under the heading of life.

4

They saw the curl of smoke on the ridge at four o'clock in the afternoon. Paddy saw it first. He didn't move in the saddle, but his body stiffened without straightening. His eyes came wide open, oblivious of the glare of the road, and he felt the chill run through him. It could have been another tree, just a little taller than the rest along the top of the ridge, its top fading off into a haze, but he could tell the difference between a tree living and a tree burning: he felt the skin over a scar on his back begin to shrivel as it had done once before. He had been looking for this curl of smoke all the way, almost from the moment he had looked at the map Ferguson had given him and had seen the road led through this thick timber.

The smoke was a thin curl, then in a moment it was a brown-yellow cloud coming up over the ridge like a runaway storm. Paddy pointed and yelled, " Fire !"

Venneker pushed his horse through the mob and pulled in beside Paddy. "We should be all right. That ridge is a good two miles from us. The road swings the other way just below this bend, doesn't it?"

The ridge, the top of it already disappearing under the broadening cloud of smoke, was to the south and slightly behind them. It stood out against the foreground of climbing ridges that came towards the road like grey-green rolling combers. The ridges were dense with trees, and Paddy could guess that in the small valleys between, the scrub was virgin-thick and explosively dry.

" Two miles ain't anything." He was too worried to think

of Venneker as anyone but a man who might be badly
needed. "You ever seen a bush fire?"

"Not a real one," Venneker said. "Just grass fires in a
paddock."

Paddy took another look at the distant smoke, then turned
in his saddle and yelled, "Come on up ahead! Get a move
on!"

Sean jumped down from the wagonette and Ida drove the
horse after him through the mob. It took them almost five
minutes, with the sheep packed tightly in the road as it
narrowed to run down between two steep embankments, but
at last they joined the two men.

They kept moving as Paddy talked. "Ide, you stay in front
here and keep moving as fast as you can. You stay out of
the cart, Sean. Keep the sheep on the trot after you. Me and
the old bloke'll be at the back pushing 'em. But keep on the
run. We gotta get down near the flat stuff before that fire gets
over this way. Righto, take your finger out. Come on,
Choom," he said to Venneker, "we got work to do down the
back."

Without a word Venneker swung his horse and followed
Paddy back through the mob. They got the sheep on the run
immediately. Sean got behind two or three of the leaders,
shouting at them and hitting them on the rump, and they
broke into a trot. The kelpie, catching the urgency in the air,
began to wheel and run, sometimes scampering in a straight
line across the backs of the mob, and the sheep were soon a
jostling, bleating grey mass moving at a good rate down the
narrow winding road.

Everything was noise now: the bleat of the sheep, the
barking of the kelpie, the crack of whips, the shouting of Sean
and the yelling and cursing of Paddy and Venneker at the
tail of the mob. Ida had pushed the horse into a slow trot and
the wagonette had moved ahead, everything in it clattering
and bumping, but she was unaware of it as she kept glancing
nervously across towards the ridge now almost lost in the
thickening angry swirl of smoke: there, in her mind, she
could hear a roar and a crackling that drowned out all the
noise here on the road.

With the sheep on the run Venneker pulled up close to Paddy. "Look, Carmody, I don't know much about bush fire. What's the danger from this one?"

"A bloody lot if the wind blows it this way." Paddy sent out his whip in a wide curl, keeping the rear of the mob together. "There's different kinds of bush fires. There's grass fires, like you seen. They don't mean much at all, just burn off your fodder, maybe catch your stock if you don't move 'em fast enough. Then you can have slow scrub fires, ones where there ain't no wind and the fire don't get up above the bush. You can belt that out easy. And then there's a scrub fire that gets along at a pretty good lick. You get that when things are as dry as this."

"Yes?" said Venneker. "There's another one. That's the one you're scared of."

Paddy didn't deny the fear. He swung away, moving in behind some lagging sheep and getting them on their way again, then he came riding back. "That's the sort I think this 'un might be. A crown fire. I just hope to Christ it ain't. If it is, and it catches us, we can forget all about the sheep and start looking after ourselves."

"What does it do?" Venneker had dropped his mock-arrogant air; he still sat straight and tall in his saddle, but he wanted to know what lay ahead of them.

"They're the worst bastards a man can meet. It goes through the tops of the trees, and it goes as fast as a brumby can run. Faster, in fact. You can't outrun it." The scar on his back pained until he wanted to cry out: he looked towards the ridge and saw the first flame, like a small yellow slash of lightning, come and gone while he looked at it, but leaving the burn of it against his eyes. "The timber and scrub burns and while it's burning the flames jump ahead like red spurts of water jumping out a dam. Just like that"— he made a swift nervous flash of his hand—" every bit as fast. You don't stand a hope. After a while everything's burning. The trees, the scrub, the ground, even the bloody air. It's no joke, I can tell you. I've seen it twice and I just got out by the skin of me teeth. Afterwards I went back and helped bury the blokes it caught, the ones who'd been caught in the scrub and them who'd jumped into the creeks and been boiled to death." He spat into the road. "I can still taste the sight of 'em."

Venneker looked at Paddy and recognised real fear, the sort that doesn't bear any shame; it communicated itself to him and he swung his horse forward, his great voice booming out, his whip a loud exclamation point behind each roaring curse.

Sean was alternately leading the mob and dropping back into it to search for young lambs. He would pick them up, one under each arm, and sprint ahead to the wagonette. Already there were half a dozen in the back of the wagonette and Ida was having a busy time preventing them from falling out as they maintained a precarious balance on thin unsteady legs atop the piled-up gear.

The heat of the fire had already come ahead of it: it stretched over the ridges to touch them like some breathless wind. Ida raised her hand and blessed herself: Take care of us, Lord; and looked towards the smoke as she prayed: fear was stronger than faith.

The smoke was rolling off the ridge down into the narrow valley beside it. The valley was flooded with the swirling grey-brown cloud: it flowed over the next ridge, coming closer to the road. The air now was pungent with the smell of the burning eucalyptus; even the sheep smelt it and began to run a little faster, bleat a little more loudly. Paddy saw the entire top of the second ridge burst into flame; he turned and yelled to Venneker, "It's a crown fire, all right!"

"What do we do?" Venneker swung his whip behind the tail of the mob. "Can we keep ahead of it?"

"Christ knows." The road twisted between the ridges: it was impossible to see farther than the next bend, sometimes a hundred, sometimes only fifty yards ahead. Paddy abruptly kicked his horse, swung it wide round the mob and went at a gallop through the scrub that bordered the road, ducking under branches, swaying with the sharp swerving of the horse, riding as only a true bush-man can, then he came out on the road again ahead of the sheep and was gone out of sight round a bend. A minute or two later he came galloping back.

"Keep it up!" he shouted to Ida and Sean. "We ain't got far to go. The road runs outa these hills another half-mile or so—no timber, just grass. We'll make it if we're lucky." He pulled his horse in beside the wagonette, slowing up for a moment. "All right, darl?"

She smiled: fear and love turned up the corners of her mouth. "All right." The beads hung from her wrist like a bangle: "I'm trying to say a whole rosary."

Paddy winked: he never took religion seriously, not even now. "That's all we need," and galloped back to join Venneker: the Lord rode with them, in prayer at the front of the mob and in curses at the rear.

Sean was running tirelessly by the head of the sheep. He had collected all the lambs he could find: the back of the wagonette was a seething, frightened woolly mass: it looked like a cart on the way to the slaughter-house. Sweat sprang out on his face, turned to mud instantly as it mingled with the dust that coated him. The dust worried him, hung round him like a faint brown halation; he breathed deeply, trying to smell the fire, but even that smelt of dust. His bladder bounced full in his stomach: he wanted to urinate, but there wasn't time. Already the sky above them had begun to turn yellow; smoke drifted thinly like the first clouds of a storm. His legs felt fine: he knew he could have run for ever if it weren't for this dust. A lamb fell out of the wagonette and he sprinted ahead to pick it up, glad to get away from the mob and the dust.

The sheep were running as fast as they could go now. There was no need to drive them; in their panic, the danger was that the leaders might go down, bringing those behind down with them, and cause a pile-up. Paddy, Venneker and the kelpie kept circling at the rear, pulling in the stragglers, keeping them out of the timber and on the road. The horses were responding to the riders' hands and knees, but fright was in their eyes: it wouldn't be long before they, too, would take a lot of handling. Fifty yards ahead, three wallabies suddenly bounced across the road and were just as suddenly gone. Other smaller creatures came out of the scrub, running with desperate, pathetic urgency. In the yellow sky there were the swift dark shapes of birds all flying in the one direction.

Paddy rode high in the stirrups: he couldn't sit, he had to keep looking over towards the approaching fire. The road came round the side of a hill now; the ground sloped away and on the other side of the valley the ridge was already burning. They could hear the roar and crackle of the flames: trees crashed with the sound of an artillery barrage: the heat and fury and sound of battle were just across the valley from them.

Smoke rolled up the hill like a fog: the sky above had gone in a yellow haze and the world below disappeared: all they could see were the flames and the crashing trees on the next ridge. The men, the boy and the dog were herding the sheep towards the inner edge of the road. The sheep needed no leading or driving now; they just had to be prevented from rushing headlong over the lip of the road down the steep slope into the smoke-filled valley. Paddy and Venneker had stopped yelling: they rode with neckerchiefs covering their faces, their whips doing their talking. Sean had taken off his shirt and ran with it wrapped round the lower half of his face: it almost stifled him, but it was preferable to the smoke, which was even worse than the dust had been.

Ida sat among her bleating struggling cargo and urged the wagonette horse into a shambling gallop. The wagonette bounced and swayed round the curve of the road; it began to gather speed as the road dipped, almost pushing the horse ahead of it. Some of the lambs had fallen off, dropping with a squeal into the smoke, lost immediately in the rushing mob as it came down the hill. The hillside below the road had begun to burn. The heat came up, more stifling than the smoke and the dust: it dried and tightened the skin as if to split it apart. Ida put her hand up to her left cheek: it was hot and smooth and lifeless, like something glazed in an oven.

The smoke thickened: the whole valley below them was alight. Paddy saw the tops of the trees burning, giant yellow and red flowers at the top of tall stems, then he heard the roar and screamed a warning. The sheet of flame went across the road behind them: for a moment the world was violently red: the heat was flung at them, and men, horses, sheep and dog all shrieked with the one fear. The trees on the hill above them, but behind them, broke into flame. The whole hillside was burning now; but the road had curved sharply, gone round an outcrop of rock and dipped to run across a sudden wide expanse of grassland.

Ida kept the horse at the gallop. The wagonette came out through the thinning smoke on to the flat straight stretch of road that led directly away from the burning hills. She had no idea how the horse had managed to follow the road through the smoke; she clutched her beads and looked back to see the leaders of the mob coming out of the yellow pall. She slowed the horse, still looking back, praying desperately: she saw the sheep coming out of the smoke, still running madly, then she saw Sean and finally Paddy and Venneker: she put the beads to her lips and kissed them and turned and drove on along the road.

Paddy kept them moving until they had gone another two miles, until they were well out on the plain and the fire was just a storm of smoke climbing over the hills behind them. Then he galloped up ahead of the mob to the wagonette.

"Righto, darl. This'll do." He took off his hat and wiped his face with his neckerchief: he wiped away sweat and grime and fear. "Jesus, that was close! I thought we were a goner, on that last bit."

She didn't hear the profanity: she wanted to weep with relief: she had never loved him more than now. "I heard you yell. I couldn't see you——" She stretched out a hand, leaning out of the wagonette towards him; he rode close to her and put his hand in hers. "Darl, if you hadn't come out of that smoke, I'd have gone back in there. I'm not being brave. I wouldn't have wanted to be out here——" She looked around at the flat wide paddocks, at the clear air and the sky above them: it was suddenly lonely as she thought of what might have been: she looked back at Paddy: "Thank God we're safe."

Paddy looked at the beads still hanging from her wrist; he put out a hand and touched them, pressed them between his fingers, as if he were shaking hands with God, then he smiled at Ida and rode back towards where Venneker and Sean had finally brought the sheep to a halt and were calming them down.

Sean had taken the shirt from about his face and was carrying it in his hand. His wiry brown body above his shorts was streaked with the mud of sweat and dust; his eyes were red and still watering from the smoke. "You reckon we lost any, Dad?"

"I don't think so, bar the lambs. We'll rest 'em for a while, then take 'em on and find another camp. When we put 'em into the break to-night we'll count 'em." He looked across at Venneker as the latter rode up. "You all right?"

"Did you think I might not be?" said Venneker; his craggy face streaked with smoke and dust and sweat, he looked like an apparition from some medieval witchcraft festival. "It was almost the end of the section for us, but it was no worse than a landslide I was in in the Himalayas."

"Always blowing," Paddy said. "We should of just turned you around and let you blow the fire the other way."

"I make no claim to miracles," said Venneker; he raised his chin and looked with white eyes down past his great smoke-streaked nose. "But where any bastard Irishman can go, there is nothing that will hold back an Englishman."

But Paddy was no longer interested in the argument. He rode slowly back along the road. The sheep, exhausted by their panic and hard running, were lying in one close huddle: for the moment they were too exhausted even to eat. The lambs were wandering nervously on the fringe, bleating despairingly: their mothers were too fatigued to come out of the mob looking for them. Even the kelpie seemed worn out by the last three or four miles: he lay flat in the dust, his head on his paws, his sides heaving like an anæsthetist's air bladder; it was the only way of knowing he was still alive. Paddy dropped down from his saddle and put a hand on the kelpie's head. It opened its eyes but didn't move.

"Nice work, Nigger. Good dog." Paddy knelt with his hand on the dog, holding the horse's reins with his other h·nd. He looked along the road, saw Sean and Venneker and, farther on, Ida just getting down from the cart: he felt

suddenly safe and surrounded by love and loyalty: he even
felt warmly towards Venneker. He patted the dog again.
" Good dog. A bloke appreciates it."

He stood up and looked back towards the hills. The sky
there still came down into a swirling bank of smoke, but the
fire had swung north-west along a flank of the hills that
petered out on the horizon. The hills themselves were black
and smoking: they were their own pyre and wore their own
mourning. Paddy knew that only great good fortune had kept
himself and the others from being a part of the blackness.

He mounted again and rode along the road. Sean had found
some sticks and had started a fire; Ida had the billy on.
Venneker was wiping the dust out of his horse's nostrils with
a damp rag. Paddy swung down.

" Fix the horses," he said to Sean. " Give 'em some water
outa the bag. We can spare some after what they been
through." He took out his tobacco tin and began to roll a
cigarette. He lit it and instantly dropped it and stamped it
out with his foot, almost savagely: the smoke of it mingled
with the other smoke still in his lungs. Smoke crawled up
from the fire where the billy boiled; he turned away from it
and said, " I'm going back when I've had a cuppa."

" Back where?" Ida said; she dropped tea into the bubbling
water.

" Back to see how the Batemans got on," Paddy said.

Ida said nothing; she stood up and went to get the cups
from the wagonette. Venneker led his horse off the road on to
the short grass of the paddocks, hobbled it and came back to
where Paddy stood motionless and quiet.

He said, " What are you going to do if they've been burned
out? Let me go instead."

Paddy turned only his eyes and looked up at him. " Why
you?"

" I can see you still remember those other people you had
to bury. You said you can still taste the sight of them. You
hate the job, don't you? Let me go. At least, now I don't
know what to expect."

" It's better you dunno. I'll go," he said almost desperately:
it was as if he were pointing a gun at himself, forcing him-

/self to do something that had to be done. "It's something you oughtn't to see unless you gotta. When you ain't seen it, you can't remember it."

Venneker turned away without a word and picked the billy off the fire. He poured the tea into the cups Ida held; they each took one, and Sean came back for his.

"Dad," Sean said, "how d'you reckon the Batemans——?"

"I'm going back to see." Paddy sipped the tea; it washed the smoke and dust from his mouth.

"Can I come with you?" Sean said.

"No!" Paddy spat tea with the word. "Nobody's coming. I'm going on me own——"

Sean was startled by his father's vehemence. He looked blankly at his mother, then at Venneker, who winked and shook his head. He buried his face in his cup, wondering what it was all about.

Paddy gulped down the rest of his tea and put his cup on the tailboard of the wagonette. He climbed slowly and deliberately into the saddle of his horse. He looked down at them.

"I won't be too long. Give the sheep a bit more time, then move 'em on. Find a place to camp, and I'll catch you up."

"Paddy." Ida put her hand up to his knee. "If they're all right, tell them I'm glad. Really glad."

Paddy patted her hand then turned the horse and rode off at a steady gallop down along the road. The three stood looking after him.

"What's the matter with Dad?" Sean said. "He nearly bit me head off when I asked could I go with him."

Ida could feel the memory of the scar on Paddy's back under her fingers: one night he had told her of what he had seen in the fires and as they had come down the road through the smoke she had remembered it all with frightening clarity. "He just didn't want you to go with him, that was all." She turned away, afraid the look in her face might scare him. "The Batemans mightn't have got out of the fire."

"I thought of that." Sean had no idea what human death looked like. "I thought I could of helped him."

"Your father was right, going alone," Venneker said. "If he

thought it was something I should not have seen, then it would be infinitely worse for you. Your memory is just beginning."

Sean still couldn't picture the horror that might be lying up there in the hills. " I just hope they're all right. It would be crook to think——" He walked down the road towards the mob: he was suddenly shocked and saddened, as if the terrible possibility were already a fact.

A mile along the road Paddy was also thinking of what might be up there in the hills ahead of him. He rode at a gallop, but without urging the horse on: he couldn't bring himself to hurry to the scene. The road began to climb; soon he was on the outskirts of the charred land. He rode up and into the aftermath of the fire: it was like riding through a smoking graveyard. The hills about him were black, trees standing gauntly, some still burning, long thin pillars of fire that petered out in the sky as pale columns of smoke, and the valleys still held the heat of the fire. The air was burnt: it hung in the nose, tasted on the tongue with a thick harshness that made him cough. The forest floor had been flattened by the stampeding flames, the scrub reduced to brittle black traceries through which smoke-ghosts danced slowly and weirdly, and the road was the only mark of colour, faded though it was, in the dark desolation.

Paddy rode stiffly, hardly aware of the movement of the horse beneath him. He smelt burnt flesh and saw the wallaby, black and stiff, trapped in the thin coils of what had been a bush; he rode by without looking back. He saw other stiff and blackened things: a dingo, some scrub birds, a snake that looked like another charred branch; and he saw some rabbits come out of the smoking earth and disappear almost instantly again as they felt the heat of the blackened forest floor.

Nothing but the rabbits seemed to have survived the fire. All about him as he rode was the silence of death, broken only by the crashing of trees that, finally burned right through, also fell and died. Paddy stopped thinking; he dug his heels into the horse and urged it forward and went up the road at full gallop.

He slowed as he came to the last bend before the Batemans' place He came round the bend at a steady canter and saw the paddock stretching away, black and smoking, to the stone chimney standing like a stunned person above the small ruins of the house.

Paddy walked the horse down the road. In the paddock were the Batemans' cows, lying on their sides in a heap in an angle of the fence, their legs stuck out stiffly and their bodies black and bloated. One cow had tried to jump the fence: it hung across the top rail, like a piece of black sculpture: its eyes had bubbled out of the sockets and hung glistening in the sun. The old taste came back into Paddy's mouth like bile; he spat and rode on until he was level with the house.

There was no sign of the Batemans. Paddy swung down and tethered the horse to the fence; the posts were smouldering, but the rails, above the level of the flames from the grass, were untouched. He pushed open the narrow gate and walked up towards the house. The ground was warm and stubbly; it crunched beneath his boots like a thin crust of black snow. He spat and the earth sizzled: he looked back and there was no sign of the spittle. In the timber behind the house, where Bateman had been cutting the fire break, there was the continuous sound of branches snapping and trees crashing. He walked slowly, hoping the Batemans had died somewhere but in the house, somewhere where he might not find them.

The house was no more than a broken shell. A black jagged piece of wall still held a window-frame: the glass was gone and the window faced down the paddock: it stared emptily at the dark heap of bloated dead cows. There was no furniture in the ruins: there was nothing but the ashes of someone's living. Blackened pots stood on the stove, cracked cups and plates lay among the ashes of what may have been a table. From the top of the chimney there drifted a peaceful curl of smoke: it had been built for fire. The water tank had collapsed: the water had run out and doused the burning grass about it: there was a darker patch, like the shadow of a futile gesture. By the side of the house a few clothes, smoke-darkened, hung on a line that ran from a peg in the chimney to an iron pipe driven upright into the ground. Paddy

stared at the clothes: the man's shirt and trousers, the girls'
dresses, the underwear; then he turned away and saw the
black figures, like aborigines, coming down through the
timber towards him.

He didn't move. He stood while they came towards him
slowly, then he took off his hat and said, "Christ Almighty,
I'm glad," and it was a prayer.

The women were dumb with shock. They looked at him
with frightened eyes and tried to smile, but the effort was
too much: their faces just grimaced. Bateman carried the axe
in his hand; the end of the handle had been badly burned.

Bateman said, "You people get out all right?"

Paddy nodded. "Yeah. Sheep and all, by the skin of our
teeth. We're out on the flat now, three or four miles farther
on."

"It was close," Bateman said. "Jesus, I don't ever want it
closer."

Mrs. Bateman and the girls had begun to wander round
the ruin of their house. They seemed unmoved by their loss;
they were encased in an armour of shock. Then Mrs. Bateman stopped beneath the clothes-line. She reached up and
felt a soot-covered blue dress. She took her hand away, looking at the blackened palm, then the stiffness went out of her
body. She dropped her head and began to weep. The two
girls went to her, each holding her, and they stood like that
while the three of them wept quietly and without restraint.

"They should of busted out sooner," Bateman said. "They
held it in more than they should of. They should of begun
crying soon's the fire went over us, but they kept holding it
in."

Paddy stood awkwardly by while Bateman tried to comfort
his womenfolk. Somewhere back in the timber there was the
thin crying of an animal, something that hadn't died in the
fire but had been left with pain. Three crows flew overhead,
cawing harshly; they went into the timber and instantly were
lost against the black skeleton of the trees. A charred beam
suddenly slipped and fell in the ruins of the house; the
younger girl looked fearfully over her shoulder.

Bateman came back to Paddy: his comfort was useless to

the women now: it was better that they cried, and later he
might be able to help them. He looked down the paddock
towards the burnt cattle. "Poor bastards. We didn't have
time to get 'em out. Anyway, there was nowhere to take 'em,"
he added almost defensively: he had a true farmer's regard
for his stock. "We couldn't take 'em with us."

"Where did you go?" Paddy said.

Bateman gestured with the axe towards the timber. "Down
through there to the creek. We got underneath an overhang
on the bank. The fire jumped across the top of us, but it was
gone pretty quick."

Paddy looked about the paddock. "Why didn't you stay
here? Christ, this ud been safer than down there in the
timber. All this open space. You could of beat out the grass
fire. Beat out enough to save yourselves getting roasted."

Bateman gestured weakly; the axe carved a thin slice of
light in the air. "The women wanted to go there. I couldn't
tell 'em this was safer. They didn't wanna see the fire coming
for 'em, they said." He glanced sideways at the burnt-out
house. "I reckon they didn't wanna see us lose everything we
got."

"What are you gunna do?"

Bateman looked at him, surprised. "What you mean?"

"Well." Paddy made a vague gesture; he felt the inade-
quacy of any help he could offer. "Can I ride down into
Bulinga and get 'em to come and pick you up? You won't
be able to stay here. Where'll you go now? What'll you do?"

"We'll start all over again." There was no bravado about
his quiet words; what he said was as much a fact as the
blackened ruins behind him. "I still own the land."

The land: Paddy looked over the desolate scene, then back
at Bateman. "You're a game bastard. Good luck to you."

The women had stopped weeping; they came and stood
behind Bateman. Together, there seemed to be a strength
about them: they had survived the fire and what lay ahead
of them could never be worse: they were familiar with
struggle and toil.

"We'll be all right," Mrs. Bateman said; Paddy looked at
her blackened, tear-streaked face and wondered how he had

ever thought she was plain. " We ain't the first that's had this happen to 'em."

Bateman drove the axe into a charred veranda post; he stood with his hands on his hips and looked at what was ahead of him. " Well, at least I ain't gotta build the chimney again."

5

That night Ida prayed long and with deep feeling. She prayed and wept with relief and gladness and thankfulness, as much for the Batemans as for themselves: she was like a cripple at some miracle spa who had stood up as the dumb man began to speak.

Paddy lay beside her in the darkness of the tent, his arm under her head as she wept. He could feel the heat of her crying running through her body; her tears ran down into his armpit like sweat. He was aware of more emotion within himself than he could remember ever before; he felt the urge to weep with Ida, but his tear ducts had shrivelled when he was a boy. Suddenly again, out of nowhere, he hated his father, then forgot him instantly as the day slipped back into his mind.

He had left the Batemans and ridden to catch up with Ida, Sean and Venneker. They had pitched camp close to a dry creek bed; some of the sheep wandered dejectedly among the dry sun-bleached boulders as if scenting the water that had run there many months before. As Paddy had come along the road, the black hills fading into the yellow-pitted dusk behind him, he had seen the camp ahead of him and for a moment had felt like a prodigal. The tent, the wagonette, the bed-rolls across the entrance of the break: it all suddenly looked more permanent than a castle: he dug in his heels and galloped towards home.

Ida, Sean and Venneker had been standing close together waiting for him. They had seen him break into a gallop a quarter of a mile down the road and when he arrived they were smiling; no one rides that fast to bring bad news.

" All of 'em all right." he said as he swung down. " Their

place was burnt right out, but they got out without even being singed."

"Praise the Lord," Ida said. "He does answer prayers."

"What are they going to do?" Venneker said. "They can't stay on there if they've been burnt out."

Paddy looked up; he suddenly felt proud of Bateman and spoke for him. "I dunno what they're doing to-night. I'll go back and see. But Bateman ain't leaving the place. He's gunna start all over again."

Venneker looked at Paddy for a moment, then lifted his head and stared across the darkening paddocks to the flickering stars of fire where the black hills met the black sky. "I can't remember what he looked like. A man among men, to shame the rest of us, and I can't recall his face. I should go back and apologise."

Ida had cooked a whole side of lamb chops and boiled some rice. When they had eaten, she put the rest of the chops in a bowl, wrapped up a damper, clamped the lid on a billy of tea and handed the lot to Paddy.

"It isn't much, tell 'em. But maybe some day we'll come back this way again and we'll have a real blow-out in their new house. Tell 'em I'll be praying for them."

Venneker had ridden back with Paddy, but when they arrived at the Batemans' someone was already there. A thin taciturn man named Gilderthorp, he had driven up from his farm in the valley in a battered old Model T and was taking the Batemans back to his place for the night. The Batemans and he were standing in the road by the car when Paddy and Venneker rode up.

"Thank your wife for her trouble," Mrs. Bateman said, taking the food. "We'd better eat it now, so you can have the bowl and the billy. We've got nothing to put it in." She looked away: darkness hid the gutted house, but ruin was an acrid smell in the air: then she forced a smile and began to undo the cloth covering the bowl of chops. "Here, you'll have to hold 'em in your hands. We're having no fancy stuff to-night."

Then later they had all said good-bye. Bateman had leaned out from the front seat of the car and shaken Paddy's hand.

".Hooray, Paddy. If ever you come back this way don't forget to look us up." He took Venneker's outstretched hand. "You too, mate. We'll be here and we'll be expecting you."

"It will be a privilege, mate," said Venneker, and gripped Bateman's hand so tightly the latter almost cried out. Then as the car drove away he looked down at Paddy and said, "Carmody, for the first time in many many years, I am tasting the salt of humility."

"I got a taste in me own mouth," said Paddy. "Whatever it is, I don't feel any the worse for it."

Then they had ridden back to camp. The hills were still burning: small flames, enlarged in the darkness, glowed against the black ridges, branches cracked off, sharp as rifle shots, and trees crashed invisibly: it was like riding through a town that had been laid waste and in which skirmishing still went on. Smoke hid the stars; the moon was a pale yellow light climbing in the east. The heat and smoke had ridden with them like an escort; when they had got down on to the flat, away from the hills, they had broken into a swift gallop, feeling suddenly free.

Ida sniffed. She sat up, found a handkerchief and blew her nose. Then she lay back into the crook of Paddy's arm. "You're quiet, darl. What's the matter?"

"Nothing," he said. "I was just thinking."

"What about?"

"The Batemans. I know he only done what ninety-nine out of a hundred would of done, but I still can't get over it. All he had was the axe he held in his hand. Nothing else, and he's gunna start all over again." He was talking to himself as much as to her: "He makes me feel a shiftless sorta bastard."

"Don't say that, Paddy." Ida turned her head on his arm and looked at the dim profile of him as he stared at the ceiling of the tent. "You did all right this afternoon. You got us out alive and you got all the sheep out. You did your job. You didn't pack it up and run, like some might've done."

"I don't mean that. I did all that without really thinking about it. Sorta instinct or whatever you call it. No, I mean, there he is with bugger-all, everything he's sweated his guts out for, burnt out around him, and he don't let it beat him. I'll bet to-morrow he'll go to the bank and get another loan, buy another horse and some more stock, and the day after, move back in again."

Ida felt a faint stirring of hope; she didn't want to rush it, for fear she would spoil it. " I suppose that's how you feel when you own something. You want to hang on to it."

" If that had happened to our place—if we had a place and it got burnt out like that, would you go back, darl?" He was still staring at the ceiling; it wasn't a direct question, she wasn't even sure he wanted an answer.

"Would you?" She suddenly saw nothing remarkable in the Batemans' action : she knew she would have done the same.

" I dunno. How can a bloke know till the same thing happens to him? Maybe some time——" He turned and looked at her. " If ever we get a place, Ide, I hope for your sake we're never burnt out. I saw what it meant to Mrs. Bateman this afternoon."

Ida said nothing. She just lay still in his arm and began to pray again : maybe some time. . . .

They did only three miles the next day. They rested the sheep and horses in the morning and moved on in the afternoon. The country had begun to flatten out. They were on a high plateau and it was another three days before they were in hilly country again. Fire had been through these hills two or three months before, but the undergrowth had begun to grow again, short and colourless for want of water : the gaunt trees stood like damaged statues above the weeds of a neglected cemetery. They kept the sheep moving : a week went by, two weeks, every day with the same dry blazing sky.

" I'm gunna post a letter to Mr. McKechnie at the next town we come to," Sean said. " You wanna put something on the bottom of it?"

He and Venneker were riding at the tail of the mob. Paddy was up ahead with Ida in the wagonette. They were down out of the hills now and on the fringe of the plains. They had passed through several towns, but Sean had never had the letter finished in time to post : he had finally signed his name last night, formally and with flourishes, Yours Truly, Sean P. Carmody, and had put the eleven pages in an envelope. He took it out of his pocket now and handed it to Venneker.

Venneker looked at the bulky package. "What's this? Carmody's Odyssey?"

"Pardon?" said Sean.

"Son, what did you see in McKechnie that made you want to write to him?"

"Well." Sean had to think back: once he had begun writing the letter he had forgotten the reason for it: there had been no one to write to before, and he had enjoyed the letter to McKechnie. "I reckon it was because I felt sorry for him. He looked as if he was gunna be pretty lonely once you'd gone. That was what he said."

"A barb," said Venneker. "It has sunk home, you keeper of my conscience."

Puzzlement aged Sean's face. "Cripes, you beat about the bush, Mr. Venneker. I never know what the hell—heck you're talking about."

Venneker was lost in the letter. They rode in silence for a while, then he folded the pages and with some difficulty managed to put them back into the envelope.

"You have the gift of the gab, Sean my boy. You have the style of a mail-order catalogue and the vocabulary of a backward boundary rider, but somehow you manage to delineate a scene. Have you ever thought of becoming a writer?"

"Cripes, no. Why, d'you think I could be one?"

"No. I was just suspicious, that was all. People who write many-paged letters are usually frustrated authors. I had a brother who was like that. He finally became a sort of unpaid staff correspondent to *The Times*. He was practically a personal friend of the editor, he wrote him so often."

"What did he write about?"

"Anything at all." Venneker waved a hand that took in all creation. "He was probably the most versatile man in the whole of England as far as subject was concerned. The strange behaviour of blue-tits, what we should have done in the Boer War, the bowling of Tate. Now and again I come across a copy of *The Times* that has inexplicably found its way to this illiterate corner of the globe, and I notice he is still writing to the editor. He now probably begins his letters Dear Dick, or whatever the editor's given name is."

"Would the paper print it like that? Dear Dick?"

"The day *The Times* does that, we can prepare for Armageddon. Nobody is ever referred to by his given name in *The Times*. Nothing as matey as that. Even music-hall comedians are called Mister."

"Anyway, are you gunna write something to Mr. McKechnie?"

"Don't seal the envelope. I shall add a postscript. Added to your long-winded epistle, it will be as a footnote to *The Decline and Fall of the Roman Empire,* but at least it will tell Mac I am still alive."

"Don't tell him about the bush fire. I already done that."

"I have no doubt of that. I shouldn't imagine you have missed a solitary incident of our journey, including the number of bowel actions you have experienced. No, I shall content myself with a small philosophical comment, something designed to convince him he is better off than we are."

"You reckon he is, Mr. Venneker?"

Venneker looked down from his Olympian height. "At least, his illusions are less susceptible to shattering than ours."

"There you go again," Sean said. "What d'you mean by that?"

"That blindness, once you have accepted it, has its compensations," said Venneker. "But I qualify it, strictly between you and me. I wouldn't change places with him, no matter what the compensations."

"Me neither," Sean said. "You might as well be dead as blind."

Venneker looked at him. "Don't ever make a slip of the pen and let Mac know you think that. I'll tan the hide off you, with or without your father's permission."

They eased the mob along, watering it at the infrequent bores along the road, and the sun came and went and always the sky was dry and pitiless. The sheep were thin now: the dust-clotted wool hung shapelessly on their bony frames like winter coats on a crowd of old crones: they clustered together, as if leaning against each other for strength. In the middle of the day and at night the mob would sink to the ground in one slow rolling movement, as if the earth had subsided beneath it; the sheep would lie there, thin and with fretting sides, dust rimming their eyes and thick in their coats and nostrils, and you wondered how they could be got back on their feet.

The paddocks were flat and brown as they stretched away to the sky; here on the plains even the sky, too, seemed brown, but it could have been just a condition of the eyes. The few trees were thin mocking traceries in the glare, throwing only twisted lines of shade, like cracks in the earth, beneath their bare branches. The scrub was the colour of the earth, bushes looking like ant-hills, and in places the earth had split apart like a melon left too long on the vine.

They passed through districts where the station hands came out and rode with them, keeping the sheep on the road: there was no grass to spare for itinerant mobs. For a day they followed the railway line: a train went past and the passengers threw them newspapers: they brushed off the dust and read of the disastrous floods in Queensland. Sean's birthday came and went, meaning nothing but that he could leave school now and go to work, something he thought about as he got up at four o'clock in the morning and went looking for the horses.

Then the heat suddenly ceased and winter was riding with them, cold when the winds blew, freezing at night, and always dry. Frost was brittle on the ground in the mornings; until the sun came up the dust was white like a thin fall of snow. Then as the day wore on it turned brown again and climbed in spirals on the cold westerly winds.

"I didn't think it was gunna be as crook as this." Paddy was riding beside the wagonette; dust blew across his words as a gust of wind slapped its way past him. "We got about another week to go. I dunno if some of the mob will last that long."

Ida irritably wiped dust from her lips with her tongue. "It would've been nice down at the Port this time of year."

"Don't start that," Paddy said. "I got enough on me mind

S.—E

already. It ud be pretty good up around Cairns, too. Only
we ain't either place, so don't make it worse by grizzling."

They were in flat scrub-land now, had been for the last two
days. The wind hissed among the saltbush and mulga; dust
writhed in the lively air. They had stopped earlier in the day
to let the sheep graze on the saltbush; soon Paddy would be
riding ahead to choose the camp site for the night.

"Dad!" Sean had been sitting quietly in the back of the
wagonette, hunched down against the wind; abruptly he sat
up and pointed. "A dingo!"

Paddy turned and saw the wild dog trotting through the
scrub about fifty yards away. It came in towards the outskirts
of the mob, then abruptly wheeled and trotted away again as
the sheep bleated and pushed together nervously. The kelpie
was on the far side of the mob, yelping angrily at some
stragglers; against the wind it had caught no scent of the
dingo.

"I'll try and get him," Paddy said, wheeling his horse
away. "Otherwise the bastard'll be back to-night."

He rode across the front of the mob, trotting quietly, looking for another glimpse of the dingo in the wind-disturbed
scrub. Then he saw the yellow form slip out from behind a
bush; he dug in his heels and went after it at a gallop.

In the wagonette Sean had stood up, his back to the wind,
watching his father ride. Some day he would be able to ride
like that himself, but he would be content to be second best
until his father gave up the saddle.

"Look at Dad!" He put a hand on Ida's shoulder and
squeezed in his excitement; she was tired and irritable, but
she turned and smiled at the look on his face. "Cripes, ain't
he a beaut!"

Paddy was swinging the grey through the scrub at full
gallop; he rode crouching low, his body seemingly another
part of the horse. The dingo was streaking between the
bushes, running hard and constantly changing direction, but
Paddy was slowly gaining on it. It whirled round a fallen
tree and kept running; Paddy took the horse over the tree at
full gallop and came down only a few yards behind the dingo.
Still riding at full speed, swaying with the twisting and

turning of the horse as it kept on the heels of the now frantic dog, he bent down and ran his right stirrup iron to the end of the leather. He swung the iron, getting the length of the leather, then suddenly urged the horse forward. He leaned down out of the saddle just above the racing dog. For a moment he seemed to be falling, then his arm went up and the iron came down in a swift swinging blow. The dingo crumpled, skidding on its nose in the dust, rolling over and over like a yellow bundle Paddy had tossed away, then it was wrapped round a small stump, lying still with the front of its skull crushed in.

Paddy slowed the horse, trotted back and swung down. He looked about and found a heavy stick. He walked to the dingo, stood looking at it for a moment, then he brought the stick down and finished the job of killing.

He rode back to the wagonette and Ida said, " I always feel sorry you have to kill those dogs. They're such lovely looking things."

" A dead sheep's lovely looking, too," Paddy said. " You're too sentimental, that's your trouble. You're the sort that ud raise rabbits as pets."

" I don't hate rabbits as much as I do this wind and dust."

" It's the bloody rabbits that's caused the dust. Or more of it. I've met blokes who can remember when all around here was thick with grass. You got droughts and the wind, but you didn't get this flaming dust."

" It's getting worse," Sean said. " We're in for a dinky-di storm. Look at it !"

The sky had turned tawny : the dust had begun to whip up above the scrub, whirling away to hide the sun : the trees creaked against the force of the wind.

" We'll hold the mob here." Paddy turned his horse about and rode back through the thickening dust to Venneker. " We'll camp here. We won't do any good going on in this blow."

The sheep turned their backs to the wind and lay down as soon as they were halted. The dust was like an angry swirling fog now ; viciously it attacked every crevice it could find : eyes, nose and ears were clogged with it. When Ida spoke to

Sean she had to turn her back to the wind; her face cracked as she opened her mouth.

"We'll just have to wait. You hungry?"

"Too right." Sean turned his back: they sat facing the same way, talking to some invisible third person. "But not that bad I wanna eat dust."

Paddy and Venneker each had taken a post at either side of the mob. They had turned their horses' heads away from the wind, had dismounted and stood close to the horses on the lee side. The kelpie was somewhere in the scrub: he could look after himself. The sheep lay huddled together; sometimes a thin bleat would be whipped away on the wind. The dust seemed to be the only moving thing in the world; occasionally dead leaves whipped past, but they couldn't be seen, only felt as quick soft scratches against the face.

Sean sat hunched down in the wagonette, his face buried in his arms as they rested on his drawn-up knees. He was below the level of the wind, but he could feel the dust falling on him like a dry rain. A Cobar shower, they called this: the people of the outback had long ago become sardonic about their climate. Something banged hard against the side of the wagonette; he resisted the impulse to look up, but spoke into his crossed arms.

"You better come down here, Mum. You might cop something up there."

Ida slid off the seat into the back of the wagonette and crouched down beside him. They lay there while the dust thickened on them; soon they were encrusted with it, looking as if they would crumble apart when they eventually moved.

The storm lasted an hour. The wind died suddenly; the dust began to fall slowly out of the sky. The sun came through, red as a boil; it went down beyond the edge of the plains, and the dust fell out of the air as a purple and gold mist. The plain looked like a vast silent moonscape; the scrub, the one flat brown colour, had been dead a million years.

They made camp where they were. Paddy rode on a mile or two, found nothing but a dry creek bed, and came back. They had no water for washing: they did their best to brush the dust from themselves, but they were all left with the same flat brown complexion: they merged with the scrub and the earth about them. They ate, tasting little but dust, herded the sheep together where two lines of stunted bushes formed a rough angle in the scrub, put up the calico to complete the break, and bedded down for the night.

Sean lay in his blankets, hearing the cold of the night coming in through the scrub: trees creaked, thin branches snapped, bushes stirred as if trying to get circulation back into frozen limbs. Most of the dust had gone from the air now; the stars were cold glittering flowers blooming on the black branches of the mulga tree beneath which he lay.

He wouldn't be sorry to see the end of this droving job. He had had enough of the silly bloody sheep: they were a stupid lot, brainless as only sheep can be, and they held you back. Never more than six or eight miles a day—cripes, where could you get at that rate? It didn't matter that after the sheep were delivered in Cawndilla they would have nowhere to go: they would move on, he knew that, and if they had to keep moving it was better to do it at a rate that got you somewhere.

They would probably go north, up into Queensland to get away from the winter. His mum didn't like the cold and he wasn't keen on it himself; he shivered a little and drew the blankets tighter about him. If ever they got a place of their own, he hoped it wouldn't be down in the south: he had been born in one of the coldest districts in Australia, but that didn't say he had liked it. No, somewhere up in Queensland would be the lurk, up on the Atherton Tableland maybe. Just a small place, a hundred or so acres: they would raise some crops, have a couple of cows, be farmers instead of nobodies. He dropped off to sleep, one dream sliding into another. . . .

He stirred restlessly, feeling in his sleep wetness on his face, dropping gently and coldly. There was a swishing sound that was whirling in his head and he was lying in a cool stream that was carrying him along, but dust was rising from the stream and he couldn't breathe, then he was wide awake and it was raining, falling heavily and straight, and he put out his hand and the dust beside him was already turning to mud.

"Sean!" Venneker was standing above him, huge and excited: his voice boomed against the beat of the rain. "Feel it, boy! Feel it! Rain, beautiful bloody wet teeming rain!"

Sean crawled out of his blankets, now heavy with wetness, and stood up. He felt something brush against his legs: he put down his hand and ran it through the muddied coat of the kelpie. He saw his father come out of the tent, heard him yell, nothing intelligible but full of a wonderful jubilance, and saw the glow in the tent as his mother lit the lantern. He stood there, the rain cold and clean on his naked body, and shivered with something more than the chill of it. He curled his toes in the mud, feeling the dust below the upper crust also turning to mud, life seeping down into the dead earth. He raised his face and closed his eyes against the sharp sting of the rain. He opened his mouth and the rain ran in, sweet against the dryness there, and he let out a wild shout that seemed to lift his body off the ground in a paroxysm of joy.

Then he had pulled on his clothes and was running through the pelting darkness to help his father and Venneker quieten the scrambling, frightened sheep.

6

A week later they had delivered the sheep. They had come across country that had turned to a smooth sea of mud. The grass was still thin, but it had lost its brittleness; fresh green shoots were coming up and the paddocks were changing colour. It rained twice in the week, cold driving rain that made them miserable; but on fine days, with the clear immense sky above them, the sheep moving steadily, and breathing the clean sharp air instead of the dust that had been with them for so long, they were happy. They delivered the sheep to Ferguson's station manager, were paid, and headed on into the town of Cawndilla.

"I'd like to buy a new dress," Ida said. "If I don't get one soon, I'll be running around in my birthday suit."

Paddy was riding beside her on the seat of the wagonette.
"I wouldn't mind that. Give me something to think about."

"It would give Mr. Venneker and Sean something to think
about, too. You think they would turn the other way?"

"I know the old coot wouldn't. I've seen him looking at
you a coupla times, even with your clothes on."

"You imagine things. You've just got it in for him, that's
all. He's been a big help to us on this trip. Have you paid
him yet?"

"No. I dunno whether I oughta. He said he didn't want
any pay."

"He wouldn't knock it back if you offered it to him.
Nobody's that cracked."

"He is. He's just as likely to tell me what to do with it.
I ain't gunna offer it to him so he can insult me."

"Well, I'll try him. If he doesn't want it, you can give it
to me. I've got to buy a couple of dresses, and a new shirt for
Sean."

"What do I get outa this?"

Ida looked him up and down. "How about a new hat?"

Paddy clutched his ancient headgear as if she were about
to whip it from his head. "Not on your life. This 'un is
comfortable. I don't wanna have to go breaking in a new 'un."

"You've had that one ever since we were married. It's
about time you threw it away." But she knew she was asking
him to dispose of a treasured possession; she had become so
used to seeing him in it, he would be a stranger if he wore
anything else. "Well, anyway, the first thing we'll have will
be a good hot bath."

Then they were coming into Cawndilla. At the edge of
town they passed the railway station; a train was in, the
engine grunting impatiently. There were more people on the
platform than in the three carriages. The train, passing
through twice a week, was more of a diversion than a means
of conveyance; the townspeople came down to meet it like an
old friend. There was a mob of sheep in the yards beside the
station. The bleating of the sheep mingled with the chatter
of the people on the platform: nothing of importance was
being uttered in either place.

The town sprawled across the plain as if blown there by the wind. The streets were at right angles to each other, but the houses seemed to have been built with the specific idea of destroying the pattern. At the far end of town a river with steep eroded banks curled under an iron bridge and went away to disappear in the far sky; red gums stood along its banks like old men and looked down into its yellow waters. The main street was paved, the macadam stopping suddenly short at each end of town: you could see where the rates ran out. The side streets were just ruts of mud: barefooted children were sliding down the slope of one street on a sheet of galvanised iron with the front curved up: snow wasn't necessary for winter sports.

"This'll do." Paddy brought the wagonette to a halt in front of a hotel, the fourth they had passed in the main street (*How big is Cawndilla? Well, it's got four pubs*), and helped Ida down from the seat. "We'll scrub the dirt off in here."

Venneker and Sean had tied their horses to veranda posts. They joined Paddy and Ida outside the private door of the hotel. From the bar, just round the corner, there came the sound of an argument: it was just a pub argument, that might lead to a brawl or might peter out; nobody really cared. Somewhere in the private quarters of the hotel someone was playing a piano: the pal that they'd loved had stolen the gal that they loved: you could trust no one, not even out here on the plains. Ida listened, then nodded her head appreciatively.

"That's one of my favourite songs. I heard a girl sing it down at the Port. All men are the same. You can't trust 'em."

"What about the women?" Paddy said.

"We're led astray by you men," said Ida, and smiled. "Well, let's go and get the dirt off."

They went into the small hall, stood among the dry faded palms in their boxes of earth, and a small blonde woman in gold-rimmed glasses and a fawn sweater suddenly sprang at them out of a small cubby-hole.

"My God," Venneker said. "A pixie!"

"Hullo." Ida smiled at her as at an old friend: she didn't get enough of the company of women. "We'd like to have a bath if we could. We've just finished a droving trip. We got nine weeks' dirt to get rid of."

The woman smiled back at all of them, her eyes bright and her glasses reflecting light from the doorway behind them: her whole face seemed to shine with friendliness. "Why, certainly! Too right. I'm Mrs. Firth, the owner here. Where you come from?"

"From Bulinga, on the North Coast," Ida said.

"Well, you lucky people! All that travelling, all the things you seen. My word, you're lucky. I've always wanted to travel. I come up here from Newcastle for a week fifteen years ago, and I never been back since."

"Have they missed you?" Venneker said.

Mrs. Firth arched backwards to look up at him; her prominent bosom rolled upwards under her sweater. "That's a good 'un!" She shot out a fist and dug Venneker in the stomach; he tried to wither her with a look, but she was unwitherable. She laughed out loud, with her mouth wide open showing all her teeth. "You're so tall, it's pretty hard to hear you down here. Us shorties miss a lot, don't we?" She beamed around at the other shorties. "Well, who wants to go first. Or is it all in together, this cold weather?"

"The Devil protect us!" Venneker made an unsuccessful attempt at a whisper. "Whimsical, too!"

"I think I'll have a beer first," Paddy said. "Me inside could do with a wash, as well."

"Just make it a wash, then," Ida said. "Don't go flooding it."

Mrs. Firth let them look down her throat again as she let out another clap of laughter. "Gawd, you have to watch 'em, haven't you? That's what killed my Alec. But he died happy, so I reckon that's something to be thankful for. I come up here fifteen years ago, bumped into him soon's I got off the train, married him a week later and he died three years ago. He was never sober, but, crikey, he was happy. Well, I don't suppose you can get into the bath too soon. Nothing like a good hot soaking, is there? Weakens the men and strengthens the women. Oughta be the other way round. Well, we got two baths and there's plenty of hot water in the kitchen. I'll get the girl to cart it up for you." She was hospitality itself: you felt she was willing to scrub their backs once they got into the baths.

" You men go and have a drink. The lady and sonny here can have first go. You're lucky, you know." She had begun to lead Ida and Sean up to the floor above. " A fortnight ago, we couldn't of let you have a bath each. You would of all had to use the one lotta water. The last one in would of been just washing the dirt back into himself——" Another laugh came ricocheting round a bend in the staircase.

Venneker stared up the stairs. " No wonder her husband was never sober."

The piano had begun again: a heavy hand was belting the daylights out of *Dinah*. Through a door they could hear the argument in the bar frittering away to a few grumbles: the voices were tired, sounded as if they were in need of another drink.

" I'm going in for a beer," Paddy said, and pushed through the door into the bar. Venneker followed him.

There were half a dozen men in the bar, all leaning on the bar counter; none of them was drunk, but they seemed incapable of standing upright, as if once they had entered the bar the atmosphere had drained some of the strength from their bones. They turned loose heads and looked at the newcomers; looked twice, first on Paddy's level, then up at Venneker. Then they looked back at Paddy, as if it were easier to talk to him.

" G'day. Just got in?"

" Yeah." Paddy ordered a beer, then with an effort looked up at Venneker. " What'll you have?"

" Whisky and soda." Venneker's voice boomed in the bar; one or two of the men involuntarily straightened up for an instant, but the effort was too much and they immediately relaxed again.

" You couldn't have a beer like everyone else, could you?" Paddy suddenly remembered his manners and he looked along the bar: when he had money, the world was his friend. "What'll you blokes have?"

They all had beer, everyone but Venneker, who drank his whisky as if he were dying of thirst. He ordered and drank another while the beer drinkers were finishing their glasses, then he ordered a third whisky for himself and another round for everyone in the bar.

"Where you heading now?" A bald-headed man with a red nose and pink eyeballs raised his glass to their health; Paddy had told the story of their trip from Bulinga, and everyone was interested in what would happen to them next. It wasn't just politeness in payment for a free drink: they had all been on the track at one time or another: it was like a common blood strain between them. "It ain't a good time for travelling."

"I ain't thought about it." Paddy leant against the bar like the rest of the men; only Venneker, because the counter was too far below the level of his elbow, stood upright. "What's doing around here?"

"Nothing. Unless you wanna join a shearing crew."

"Nah." Paddy shook his head. "Too much like hard work."

"What about you, Lofty?" one of the men looked up at Venneker. "You ain't saying much."

"That's a change," Paddy said into his beer.

"I am giving the matter some thought." Venneker put his hand up to the rail that ran round the top of the bar; like everyone else, he was now leaning off balance. "Like Shorty here, I am not over-fond of hard work. But there is good money in shearing."

"Nah." Paddy shook his head again. "That's out, definitely."

"Well, what do you intend doing?" Venneker said.

"I dunno," Paddy said, then looked hopefully up at Venneker. "You think you might go back to Bulinga?"

Mrs. Firth came into the bar, her bosom bouncing with her stiff springy walk, her smile still a mile wide. "Well, come on, you two. Your baths are ready. The missus has gone over to Porter's to buy some things." She looked up at Venneker;

her bosom shook like a jelly in the gale of her laughter. "You'll probably have to wash yourself in shifts."

Venneker looked down as if he were about to spit. "Madam, my ablutions have never caused me any trouble in the past. Let us keep my personal habits out of a bar-room conversation."

Mrs. Firth looked at the swinging door through which Venneker disappeared, then her bosom began to heave even more convulsively. Tears smeared her glasses and she took them off. "Gawd, he's a one! Where'd you pick him up?"

"I didn't pick him up," Paddy said. "The wife did."

"I don't blame her." Mrs. Firth was wiping her eyes: without her glasses, Paddy noted, she wasn't a bad-looker. "I wouldn't mind having him around the place, either."

"You can have him," Paddy said, and thumped his glass down on the counter. "We're getting rid of him when we move outa here."

Across the street in one of the town's three general stores, Ida and Sean were moving up and down a rack of dresses. A salesgirl hovered behind them like a black moth.

"I don't like the way they're making them nowadays," Ida said. "A person's got to be built like a stick to get into them."

"That's the fashion now, missus." The girl ran a satisfied hand down the stick of her own body. "These are the very latest thing up from Sydney."

"Well, I must be out of fashion or deformed or something," Ida said, conscious of her curves and not ashamed of them. She took down a red and green print and held it against herself. "How's this look, Sean?"

"Pretty crook," Sean said without interest. "You'd scare the sheep in that."

"It's just the thing for you, missus." The girl's tone implied Sean hadn't spoken, didn't exist. "The colour is just right for you."

"Green and red? You mean I've got a jealous temper?" Then she saw the pained look on the girl's face and she smiled. "I'm only kidding, love. I think it's a nice frock, but I don't know if it's right for where we'll be going."

"Well, if you're going down to the city, it ud be just the

thing," the girl said. "It's got real style. Look how it's cut——"

Sean wandered away and began to explore the store. It was full of everything you could want; the air smelt of wonderful mystery. He had wandered through general stores all over the country, but they never failed to fascinate him: he explored them as other boys might explore caves. He moved around amongst the stock. Treasure hung from the ceiling, lined the walls, was stacked all over the floor: cross-cut saws, corsets, shirts, trace chains, stock saddles, boxes of cutlery, coir matting, bolts of cloth, china: out of these things you could make a home. He came out from between some rolls of linoleum and a stack of fly-doors and joined his mother at the front counter.

The salesgirl was folding a green dress. Ida said, "And I want a shirt for the boy. A plain blue one, in something that will last a long time."

"Make it a brown one," Sean said. "It goes better with the dust."

Ida shot out a hand, clipping him under the ear, and smiled at the girl. "A blue one, please."

With Ida feeling almost a little proud of the brown-paper parcels under her arm, they came out of the store into the main street. People were ambling back from the railway station; in the distance the train sent back a long farewell whistle. The houses sat wet-bottomed in the mud of their yards; smoke from their chimneys were thin blue vines on the wall of the sky.

A cold silver sunset stood at the end of the street; a man on a bicycle came riding out of it. He rode down the street, slowly and a little unsteadily, and dismounted outside the hotel opposite the store. He propped his bicycle against a post, bent and stretched his legs as if to make sure they could carry him now he was on his feet, and went into the hotel.

"Another shearer," Sean said. They crossed the street and stopped for a moment by the parked bicycle. "Cripes, he's loaded down, all right."

The bicycle looked more like a rack on which its owner had hung the odds and ends of a lifetime. A blanket-roll was tied to a carrier above the back wheel; on a carrier above the front wheel was a wicker basket that had seen better days and a good many of them. The handlebars were festooned with a billy, a tin pannikin, a hurricane lamp and a pair of boots. From the crossbar there hung a water-bag and a small canvas bundle: the owner must have had either bow legs or hard callouses on the inside of his knees: the water-bag and the bundle bulged on either side almost in line with the pedals. The seat was a narrow racing seat over which an old felt hat, padded with straw, had been tied. The tyres were stuffed with rope and were tied on with strips of rubber: punctures would never worry the owner. The bicycle leaned tiredly against the post like an old man: Ida suddenly thought of swagmen she had seen like this, men with all they owned on their backs, worn out and yet never looking as if they would lie down and die. She had a sudden frightening spasm of weakness: Paddy might have been like those swagmen, like this bicycle, if she hadn't married him.

"They must be raising the teams." She looked along the street, saw one or two decrepit motor-cars, streaked with the mud of the winter tracks, three or four motor-cycles, loaded down with their owners' gear, then she looked back at the bicycle, an idea forming in her mind. "I'd forgotten it was time for the season to be starting."

"How'd it be if we talked Dad into joining a team?" Sean said. "I could get a job as a tar boy. I dunno whether Mr. Venneker can shear, he can do everything else, but they might give him a job as a wool picker."

"I've been thinking the same thing. I just wonder where I could fit in, that's all. If the three of us could get a job, we could make quite a bit of money——" She looked at him and smiled. "We might even make enough to buy a piece of land, get your dad to settle down."

"Yeah." There was some mud on the side of Sean's foot; he looked at it carefully as he scraped it off on the step of the hotel. "Yeah, we might even do that. Trouble is, can we talk Dad into joining a team? He's as good a shearer as any of 'em, but he ain't keen on it. You know what he reckons:

you work like heck and don't get nowhere. The money don't mean nothing to him."

"It's a pity it doesn't," Ida said. "Well, anyway, we'll try him. He can only say no the first time. If he does, then I'll get to work on him."

Chapter Three

1

PADDY SAID no the first time, but next morning the four of them went looking for a man named Quinlan.

They had stayed the night at the hotel. It had been Ida's idea: with her mind made up that Paddy would take a shearing job and already counting the money that would be coming in, she had decided on the extravagance of a roof over their heads and beds with sheets. Paddy hadn't grumbled about being civilised for a night: the bath and the beer had warmed him and he hadn't felt much like going out into the cold evening to put up the tent in the mud in which the town floated. Venneker had hesitated only because he reckoned they could do better at one of the other hotels, but Ida had refused to budge and in the end Venneker had said he would stay, but would keep his bedroom door locked.

"I shouldn't be in the least surprised if that baying pixie were a sleep-walker," he said.

Paddy had off-handedly offered Venneker token wages for the time they had been on the track and had almost fallen over when they had been accepted just as off-handedly, without comment and without the money being counted. But when the four of them had sat down at a table in the hotel's dining-room, with Mrs. Firth beaming at them through a window in the rear of her cubby-hole, Venneker had announced that dinner was on him.

"Not on your life," Paddy said, tucking a napkin into the neck of his shirt. "I always pay me own way. You don't owe us nothing."

"Not you, perhaps," Venneker said. "But I owe your wife a great deal."

"Now go easy," said Paddy. "Don't get too familiar. You're a bit too free with words about another bloke's missus. Have a bit of respect for me boy." He had had one drink too many; he turned slightly sleepy eyes towards Sean and grinned with sentimental paternal pride. "She's his mother, ain't she, Sean?"

"Mr. Venneker knows that, Dad," Sean said.

"Well, I dunno." Paddy looked suspiciously again at Venneker. "I wouldn't trust him."

"Well, trust me and shut your face." Ida was in high good humour to-night: she looked about the dining-room, at the herded tables, only two of them occupied, at the faded green walls, the Landseer prints with the stag and the dogs lost behind a mist of dust, the limp palms, the limp waitress, the beaming face of Mrs. Firth: this was the life, all right. "No, Mr. Venneker. It's all right. We'll pay for ourselves."

"Madam, for nine solid weeks I have been enjoying your cooking. The fare was simple, but you never failed to make it appetising. I have had a good many meals on the track. They have never before been anything more than just a means of avoiding starvation. But you, my dear Mrs. Carmody——"

"Fair go," said Paddy, and hiccuped delicately behind his hand.

"—are a *cook*, one to be complimented. In fact, one to be repaid. And that is what I am doing. Repaying you." Venneker sat back, arranging his napkin on his lap. "This dinner is on me. There will be no further discussion on the matter."

So they all had two helpings each of roast beef and apple turnover, which Ida silently decided hadn't been cooked enough, and they had toasted the future in beer, with lemonade for Sean, and when they had got up from the table even Paddy, his eyes half shut now, had taken Venneker by the hand and thanked him for a bloody wonderful blow-out.

Mrs. Firth had sprung on them as they had come out of the dining-room. "Going to bed right away?"

"And how are we meant to take that?" Venneker said.

Mrs. Firth's bosom jumped again; she almost broke her

hand against Venneker's hip. "Crikey, you'll do me! Ain't
he a laugh, Mrs. Carmody? My Alec was just the same.
Always pulling me leg. Come on into me private lounge. I
got a piano. You like to have a sing-song now and again?
Course you do. Everyone does, gets the dust outa their lungs."
She looked up at Venneker, her face splitting apart with her
smile. "I bet you got a voice."

"Mine's not bad," Paddy said, grinning fatuously. "Can
you play *Little Town in the Old County Down*?"

Venneker clapped a hand to his eyes and tried to turn away,
but Mrs. Firth was already pushing him through the doorway
into her private lounge. Paddy, humming to himself, followed
them. Ida, who also liked the sound of her own brassy singing
voice, pushed Sean ahead of her into the room. This was
going to be a real good night.

And it was. Even Venneker, encouraged by two or three
stout whiskies, broke down at last. He and Ida sang a duet of
There's a Long Long Trail A-Winding: the walls of the room
bulged with the volume of their voices. Paddy sang only
Irish songs, but he had an endless repertoire. As the singing
went on, other people began to poke their heads in the door:
Mrs. Firth welcomed them all with open arms and a gusty
burst of beery laughter in their faces. The room was soon full:
the air became thick with cigarette smoke; and Sean sneaked
away upstairs to bed.

He felt lost at these times. They didn't happen often, but
when they did he felt suddenly alone. A couple of times at
Port Macquarie his mother and father had been caught up in
parties; every Sunday night they had gone down the line to
play cards at the home of one of the fettlers. Then all the
good feeling that bound them while they were on the track
had instantly been dissipated: he had become a stranger on
the fringe of an adult world. It had been the same to-night:
his mother and father hadn't forgotten him, had turned to
smile at him while they sang, but he had been on the other
side of the border: he had no passport into the country of
the adult. He had been sullen and resentful and he had crept
away to bed, as if to make them suffer by his absence.

But now here in the wide double bed, seeing the stars

glittering like splinters in the pane of the window, he knew he couldn't blame his mother and father. How often did they have a really good time? His mother liked people; so did his father, if it came to that. He knew his father would prefer a card party to any other sort of party, but his mother liked nothing better than a chance to yell her head off. On the track, around the camp, she was always breaking into song. But to-night, before he had finally stolen away, she had been singing louder and longer than he had heard her before: each time he had looked at her, she had had a glass of beer in her hand, and it was really the shock of that that had finally driven him upstairs. He knew his mother had occasionally had a glass of beer, but to-night he had been frightened she was going to get drunk. He didn't mind seeing his father drunk. Men were expected to get drunk; but not women, least of all his mother.

The noise of the party came up through the floor at him: his mother and Mr. Venneker led the singing. He buried his head in the pillow and pulled the blankets up round his ears: if he couldn't hear, he might be able to stop thinking. He shut his eyes and in the blackness saw his mother stumbling up the stairs; he shook his head, wanting to weep. The singing went on: the voices rose and fell, rose and fell: the room was floating on a sea of sound. He kicked savagely in bed, hating them all: his mother, his father, Mr. Venneker, Mrs. Firth; then suddenly he fell asleep into a dream that had no meaning, only sadness.

He woke with a start. His mother was leaning over him; he could smell the beer on her breath, and he was both revolted and frightened.

"You all right, Sean? We wondered where you'd got to." She wasn't wavering as she leaned over the bed: it was hard to tell if she was drunk. "Are you warm enough?"

"Yeah." He slid a hand across to the empty side of the bed. "Where's Mr. Venneker? Ain't he coming up?"

His mother hesitated for a moment. "You'd better go off to sleep again. He may be a while. He's—he's helping Mrs. Firth clean up downstairs."

"I thought he didn't like her?"

"He must've changed his mind. Now good night. Go back to sleep."

He watched her walk across the room to the door; she walked steadily enough, and suddenly he was ashamed for what he had been thinking. She closed the door, and in a moment he heard the door of the next room open. He heard the murmur of his father's voice, then the sound of two people coming upstairs.

"You're a well-padded piece of goods." That was Mr. Venneker. "I think I'll call you Davenport."

There was a smothered laugh. "Crikey, you're a good 'un. Well, don't knock the furniture around."

"You'll be disappointed if I don't."

Again the laugh, not so successfully smothered this time. He lay stiffly in bed, waiting for Venneker to come into the room, but the footsteps went past down the hall and soon he heard another door close. Then in the next room he heard the squeak of bedsprings, and he turned his face towards the window, staring out at the stars and the impenetrable blackness in which they hung: once more he was on the other side of the border, an alien in his innocence.

Then in the morning the four of them went looking for the man named Quinlan. A man at the party had told them Quinlan was a shearing contractor who was still looking for men to fill his team.

They found him in the stock inspector's office near the railway yards. He was a barrel-bodied man with a square hard-fleshed face and stiff black hair that shied away from a centre parting. He spoke slowly in a voice that seemed to begin as a digestive rumble in his stomach.

"Yeah, I'm looking for some more blokes. A couple more shearers and a cook is what I want most of all." He looked at Paddy. "When did you last shear and where?"

"Coupla seasons back." Paddy couldn't have been less interested in the job if it had paid no wages. "Down at Burrambang."

"We'll finish up there, at Pearson's shed. We're working down through Condoblin, then east."

"I worked at Pearson's," Paddy said.

"What's your rate?" Quinlan asked. "I'm looking for blokes who can finish a shed in quick time."

Paddy stood a little taller; for the moment he had lost his look of disinterest. "I can usually better two hundred sheep a day."

Quinlan looked up. Until now he hadn't been very interested in Paddy, aware of Paddy's disinterest in him, but a "gun" shearer, a crack man, was always welcome in a team. "You can do that regularly?"

"Yeah," said Paddy; pride was a flush under his tan. "Me best is two eighty-two. I done that up at Shelton's shed at Coolabah about six or eight years ago."

"Righto," Quinlan said. "I'll sign you up."

Paddy slumped; pride drained out of him and was replaced by disappointment. "Well look, I don't want the job unless you can fix up the rest of us. One in, all in."

Quinlan lay back in his seat to look up at Venneker. "What about you, Lofty? You look a bit big for a shearer. You'd never get down to the sheep."

"I'm not interested in being a shearer," Venneker said. "I do not intend putting a kink in my back for anyone."

"Well, that puts the kybosh on it." Paddy looked down at Quinlan, then at Ida standing by his side. "We're sticking together. If he don't wanna shear, I don't reckon we oughta make him. I never believe in making a bloke do something he don't wanna."

"Can he cook?" Quinlan said.

"I have no wish to be a cook," Venneker said. "Not a shearers' cook least of all. To be the butt of morons with no more appreciation of good food than a jackal——" He wiped the spade of a hand across his face, as if the idea revolted him. Then he looked down at Sean, and after a moment looked at Quinlan. "But I have had considerable experience as a wool picker. I would accept that position."

"Aah!" Paddy turned away in disgust; he stared out through the dirty windows of the office. Then he had an idea and turned back. "But what about the missus and the boy? I ain't gunna leave them, and you don't want a woman coming along in the team."

Quinlan chewed on the end of a pencil. "You know, if I wasn't hard up for a shearer I'd tell you to get outa here and stop wasting my time. I got an idea you don't want the job. Do you?"

"Yes, he does!" Ida stepped in front of Paddy; she held him back with the point of her elbow stuck like a gun in his stomach. "We all want jobs. Have you fixed up for tar boys yet?"

"No-o," Quinlan said. "But how old is your boy?"

"He's old enough to work." Paddy opened his mouth, but Ida jabbed him with her elbow: his mouth shut like a sprung trap. "Right. You've got a shearer, a picker and a boy. Now you want a cook. I can cook, better than any darn man. How will I do for the cook's job?"

"Ah no, no." Quinlan shook his head: it was out of the question. "The men wouldn't have it. They want a cook they can abuse if the tucker isn't up to scratch."

"The food'll be up to scratch," Ida said emphatically. "Better than most of 'em are used to. Look, you haven't got a cook at all. You haven't much choice, and neither have the men. Call 'em together and we'll see what they say."

Paddy got a word in at last; he stepped back to avoid the poking elbow. "Nah, forget it, Mr. Quinlan. We're just putting you to a lotta bother. Let it go. If we hear of any shearers looking for a job, we'll put 'em on to you." He was edging towards the door. "Yeah, we're just taking up your time——"

Ida didn't even look at him. "Get the men, Mr. Quinlan. Sean here will run and get 'em for you. Where are they?"

Sean was back in twenty minutes. In another ten minutes all the shearers of the team had arrived. Among them were several men who had been at the party last night. They nodded to Paddy and Ida and Venneker, then stood outside the stock inspector's office and listened to Quinlan. No one spoke until he had put the case: they smoked and stood with their hands in their pockets and spat lazily into the mud of the yard: they were a very casual jury.

"No, I'm not keen on a woman cook, I tell you." He was

a heavy-set man with dull yellow hair and pale unhappy eyes. "As far as I'm concerned, the vote's no."

The other men stood considering for a while. They might have been choosing a candidate for the next elections; the choice of a cook was every bit as serious. Then a round-faced man with red hair and a happy grin said, "Well, if she can cook like my missus, I'm for her."

Then Turk Tuthill, the man with the pink eyeballs whom Paddy had met in the bar yesterday, spoke up from the back of the group of men. He had been at the party last night and several times he had joined Ida in a duet. His singing voice had been a hoarse gravelly bellow, as if his throat had been worn ragged by strong drink, and his speaking voice now had the same rough passage. "I vote we take Mrs. Carmody. She must be able to cook. Paddy and Lofty and the boy don't look like they're half-starved. And if we don't take her, Gawd knows what we'll cop instead. All the good cooks have been signed up by the other teams. I vote we take her."

Two or three others agreed with him, but the majority were still debating the matter quietly with themselves. All but the yellow-haired man who stood at the front of the crowd and said, "No, I tell you. I reckon we should have a man."

A middle-aged man with shrewd eyes and a hard-bitten air about him spat into the mud. "We wanna make up our minds pretty quick. Christ, the way we're arsing about——"

"Fair go, Chilla," said the red-haired man. "Watch your language."

The man named Chilla looked at Ida. "Sorry, missus. That slipped out. No offence meant."

"You see? That's what I mean." The yellow-haired man was working hard to prevent Ida getting the job. "We'd never be able to relax, could never be ourselves with a woman around the place. A bloke would always have to be watching his language. She'd be shocked at some of the things she'd hear around the shed——"

"That's what you think," Ida said. "Look, men. I've cooked for a shed once before. Nobody complained, once they'd tried my cooking."

Quinlan had done nothing to influence the men in making

up their minds. The choice of a cook was always left to the men, was something of great importance in which they brooked no outside interference. Paddy sat disconsolately on a bench outside the office. He was torn between loyalty to Ida and loyalty to his code of never working just for money: he didn't know whether to bust the yellow-haired bloke for insulting Ida, or just sit quiet and let the bloke talk the others out of giving Ida the job. He was ashamed of himself for what was the stronger feeling in him. Venneker leaned against the wall of the office. Ida had been expecting him to break out at any moment, to take over the meeting and tell the men what their decision must be, but for some reason he had been extraordinarily quiet. Sean stood on the step behind Quinlan, moving nervously from one foot to the other; his face was pinched with anguished pleading, but on the other side of Quinlan's bulk, the men were almost unaware of him.

" I've got an idea." The red-haired man grinned about him like a court jester. " I'm the brains in this mob. I'm full of ideas."

" What's this one?" The men were unimpressed with his genius. " Cut out the bull and let's hear it, Bluey."

" Why don't we let her cook a trial meal for us?" Bluey spread his hands as if the meal were already laid out before them. " We'll all throw in a few bob, and let's see what she can turn out."

" I'm not interested in that," the yellow-haired man said. " I'm not throwing in any money to see if she can cook or not. I'm not interested in her cooking. All I say is, there isn't a place for a woman around a shed, I tell you."

Turk Tuthill took off his hat and ran a thick hand over his bald head. " Well, my money's waiting for the hat to go round. Matter of fact, I'll supply the hat. Dib in three bob each." He begun to move round among the men. " Come on, get your hands outa your pockets. Spare a few bob for the Destitute Shearers' Society." He halted in front of the yellow-haired man. " Righto, Ocker. In the hat with your three bob." They stared at each other for almost a minute, then Ocker took three shillings from his pocket and dropped them into the hat. "That's the stuff, Ocker. If her cooking kills you, we'll give you back your three bob. We don't want money under false pretences."

Tuthill came up to Ida standing beside Quinlan and held out his hat. "There you are, missus. Thirty bob. You reckon you can turn on a meal on that? Nothing too fancy. Just what you reckon you'd give us any normal day."

Ida took off her own hat and poured the money into it. She looked at the men. "Where do you want it and what time?"

2

Quinlan signed Ida to the cook's job that night. Ocker Shand, the yellow-haired man, still thought a woman shouldn't be around a shearing shed, but he was the solitary dissident vote after the men had eaten Ida's steak and kidney pie, home-made bread and bread-and-butter custard. She had gone down to see Mrs. Firth, borrowed the use of the hotel kitchen, and at six o'clock she and Sean had served the men at a long table that had been set up at one end of the hotel's dining-room. The men had eaten a little self-consciously; all but Bluey Brown, the red-haired man, who ate with great relish and frequent comparisons of the meal to his wife's cooking, and Ocker Shand, who ate two helpings of everything and complained between every mouthful of what a woman would do to the shed's morale. At the end of the meal Ida had been elected and Mrs. Firth had suggested another party to celebrate.

Next morning Quinlan signed up his last shearer and several shed-hands and in the afternoon the team moved out for the first shed. Venneker and Sean had left in the morning, driving the wagonette and leading the two spare horses; it was twenty miles down the south road to Halstead's shed and they would be there about the same time as the rest of the team.

When Sean came out of the hotel with his mother, Venneker and Mrs. Firth were standing beside the wagonette.

"Just telling him he's gotta come back this way again some time," Mrs. Firth said to Ida. "Had the time of me life these last coupla nights."

"You mean at the party?" Ida said.

Mrs. Firth caught her look, then slapped herself penitently on the bosom; she quivered with remorse. "There I go again, big mouth and all. Yeah, at the party. Of course. Well," she ran a hand through Sean's hair, "good-bye, Sean. Have a nice time. Wish I was coming with you." Then she looked up at Venneker. "Well, ta-ta, Rupe. Come back, like I told you. We might give it a go."

Venneker was too quiet. He shook Mrs. Firth's hand, said he'd enjoyed himself and he'd think about what she'd said, then stepped up into the wagonette. Sean clambered up after him, whistled to make sure the kelpie was with them, then they were heading down the main street out of town.

They drove in silence for a mile or so. The road stretched away into the cold grey morning: in the far distance it became the colour of the winter sky and was lost before it had reached the flat bare horizon. A wedge of ducks went overhead, slim black arrowheads against the high grey clouds, heading for some unseen billabong. A troop of kangaroos moved diagonally across one of the wide paddocks: they came to a fence and went over it in a soaring concerted leap: in flight they were as graceful as the winging ducks above them.

"They can jump," Venneker said.

"Eh?"

"The 'roos. I said, they can jump."

"Yeah."

Silence again, but for the creaking of the cart and the steady plodding of the horses. They passed a side road; the red mud distracted the eye in the grey day. They crossed a bridge; the river flowed thickly and smoothly beneath them like a flood of yellow oil. Far to the west it was raining; the sky trailed a tattered veil.

"Looks like more rain," Venneker said.

"Eh?"

"Rain. I said, looks like more of it."

"Yeah."

Silence for another hundred yards, then Venneker said, "Well, for Christ's sake, say something! Sitting there in your bloody aloofness. What's on your mind?"

Sean looked up, surprised and frightened; Venneker was really angry. "Nothing. I thought something was worrying you. You don't look like you wanted to say nothing——"

Venneker stared at him for a moment, his lips clamped between his teeth and his nose coming down like a great blade, then his face relaxed and he turned and looked ahead at the bobbing head of the horse. The stiffness went out of his back and he sat there in a huge slumped heap.

"Something has been on my mind. I have been weak, son. Succumbed to the pleasures of the flesh, like some sixteen-year-old let loose at the prostitutes' picnic. Not that there is anything wrong with the flesh. The Devil protect me from the day when I'm too old to enjoy it. But I fell for a woman who bored me every time she opened her rarely unopened mouth. I spun lies and rash promises into her clam-like ear, and she believed them all. I cursed myself that first night for not saying good-night to her when we came to my door. Did you wonder where I had got to?"

"Sorta. I reckoned you must of gone down to sleep in Mrs. Firth's room."

"Lightning should strike me dead, render me impotent. I am trying to mould you into the shape of myself, and I set you such an example. Lured to bed, not once, but twice, God damn it, by a full bosom and a baying laugh. She laughed all night! Every time I woke, there she was, baying at the moon like a delirious hound. There was but one way to keep her quiet. Am I boring you?"

"No," said Sean. "I dunno what you're talking about half the time."

"Well, I am not going to explain the parts you don't understand. I don't believe there is such a thing as sin, but your mother obviously does and I don't intend undoing what she has taught you. No, I don't despise myself for my sin, as it would be called, but for my weakness. My weakness in allowing myself to be led to the bed by such a blatant siren, but above all, for my weakness in panting the incoherent things one does pant in the moments when all a man's thinking is below his belt. Son, I promised the woman I would come back and marry her."

Sean looked at him, dismayed. "Oh crikey, no! You couldn't, Mr. Venneker!"

"I know that. How well I know it. But the poor deluded creature believes it. That was what we were discussing when you and your mother came out of the hotel. I am a black-guard, Sean, a cad and a bounder, as I would be described in the circles where I originated. God knows, the woman is not my first. But none of the others ever believed what I told them. What makes it worse is that, for all her shortcomings, the woman is as kind-hearted as your own mother."

"What you gunna do?"

"I don't know. Battle with my conscience until a solution presents itself." He turned a mournful face towards Sean. " At this early stage in your career, son, let me offer a word of advice. When with a woman, no matter how hot your blood, always keep a cool mind."

"I'll remember that," said Sean, and knew he wouldn't stand a hope: his mind had stopped working altogether when he'd been with that Bateman sheila.

"You will remember it," Venneker said lugubriously, " only when it is too damned late."

In the middle of the afternoon the rest of the team began to move out of town. Several men had motor-cycles and they went off on their own bat, puttering and slipping in the mud like a covey of mechanical ducks. The remainder of the team, including those men with bicycles, got aboard Quinlan's truck.

Ida rode up front in the cabin with Quinlan. She felt com-fortable and content: the cushioned seat beneath her, the warmth of the engine against her legs, the prospect of good money ahead of her. As they drove out of town she nodded and smiled complacently at everyone they passed: royalty had never been more gracious towards its anonymous citizens.

"I think you've got a pretty good team, Mr. Quinlan," she said.

"Well, we'll see." Quinlan was driving fast down the gravelled road; now that he had at last signed a team, after so much trouble, he was eager to get at the first job. "I hope your old man's as good as he says he is."

"You haven't got to worry," Ida said smugly; she smiled absent-mindedly at a horse in a paddock. "My Paddy'll take some beating."

Her Paddy had already taken a beating. Resigned now to five months' hard work unless he broke a leg or sheared his hand off, he sat disconsolately in the back of the truck with the nine other men.

"Well, it's on again," Turk Tuthill said. "Another five months' hard yakka. It takes me the rest of the year to get over it. But you know, as July comes around again I'm looking forward to it."

"You're running out of money, that's why," Bluey Brown said. "You're probably putting water in your beer to make it go further."

"Not me," Turk said soberly. "I done some pretty crook things in me time, but I never done that."

Ocker Shand was sitting opposite Paddy. "Look, mate, I wasn't picking on your missus personally. I tell you, I was just pointing out that a woman is no good around a shearing shed——"

"You said that, Ocker," said Bluey. "You been saying it now for twenty-four hours. Why don't you think up something else to grizzle about?" He looked at Paddy. "Don't worry, Paddy. We're all on your wife's side. You're pretty lucky to have her, let me tell you. She's a happy piece, isn't she?"

"Yeah," said Paddy, himself as happy as a bird with mud on its wings. "Never stops laughing."

The truck suddenly came to a stop, skidding in the mud on the side of the road. The men were sent sprawling; the truck seemed to backfire with loud curses. Paddy extricated his head from between a man's legs, stood up and looked round the end of the canopy. Another truck was just up in front of them, turned sideways and completely blocking the road. Paddy jumped down, followed by the rest of the men, and walked up to join Quinlan who was just getting out of the driving cabin.

"Did you see that?" Quinlan's hair had gone even stiffer with anger. "The whole of New South bloody Wales for him to drive in and he's gotta try and run smack into us!"

Men were dropping from the other truck; the two groups met in the middle of the road, half-way between the two trucks. The main road stretched away to nothingness to the north and south. A side road, rutted red mud that looked like twisted entrails, went away between the fences of two paddocks and disappeared in the distance. The paddocks were flat and vast; on every side they ran away to the bowl of the grey winter sky. The two trucks and the two groups of men were just a dark spot in the wide landscape.

"Where the bloody hell did you think you was going?" The driver of the other truck was just as angry as Quinlan; his wrinkled walnut of a face looked ready to split apart. "Didn't you hear me blow me horn?"

"I heard you blow your horn," Quinlan bellowed. "What's that gotta do with it? Who taught you to drive—an abo? Don't you know anything about giving way to a truck on a main road? *This* is a main road," swinging his arm in an angry pendulum. "I was on this, going along at a steady rate, minding my own business, and you come barging up out of nowhere and try to push me off into a paddock."

"You was dreaming, that was your trouble," said the walnut-faced man. "I was half-way on to the road when you come down, scooting along like you owned the whole bloody countryside."

The argument went on; the two groups of men stood behind their spokesmen. There seemed no hard feeling between the two groups; they recognised each other for a shearing team, and grinned and winked at each other at the battle of words warming up the cold afternoon.

"Where you heading?" Bluey said to one of the men.

"We start at Mulgrue's shed to-morrow. What's your place?"

"Halstead's, a few miles down the road from here," Bluey said.

"Yeah, I know it. We ain't far from you. Might run into you again."

Bluey looked at the two trucks and grinned. "Yeah. We'll be looking out for you next time."

Quinlan and the walnut-faced man were still abusing each other, breath hanging like smoke from their mouths in the cold air. Then Ocker Shand took a hand.

"Righto, it's too cold to stand around here listening to you." He was talking directly to the walnut-faced man. "You were in the wrong and that's all there is to it. Now get your truck out of the way and let's get moving. Come on, shake a leg."

The walnut-faced man stopped with his mouth open in mid-sentence. There was suddenly a heavy silence; in the distance somewhere a cow bellowed. There was a shuffling of feet and a turning of heads: everyone had become interested in the argument.

A tall red-nosed man leaned forward and growled at Ocker. "You wanna pull your thick head in, sport. Nobody asked you to put your spoke in. I dunno if Herb here wasn't in the right after all."

This brought a roar of amazement from both Quinlan and Ocker. The two groups, at some unspoken signal, rearranged themselves; they lined up opposite each other, every man giving himself plenty of room.

"I dunno if anyone asked you your opinion," Ocker said. "You just keep your ugly snout out of this. All——"

Whatever else he was going to say was forced back down his throat by the tall man's fist. The walnut-faced man sprang at Quinlan, who leaned back to ride the blow, then delivered a swift chop that sent the small man sprawling into the mud beside the road.

Paddy cast a quick eye over the opposition, picked out a young bloke about his own weight, took out his gold tooth and put it in his pocket, then moved in swiftly. Bluey Brown picked himself up from the roadway and flung himself at the man who had put him there. Turk Tuthill was making a fool of a man a good four inches taller than himself: his fists went in and out with professional skill, and the man floundered helplessly.

Then suddenly there was the loud blast of a horn. The men looked up and saw Quinlan's truck slowly moving down on them. They swung away to the side of the road and Ida brought the truck to a halt right at the scene of the battle. She leaned out, her face flushed with anger and contempt.

"Why don't you grow up, you lot of mugs? Supposed to be grown men, and you're fighting over something that kids wouldn't argue about. You, Sawn-off," she almost spat at the walnut-faced man: the skin had been cracked by one of Quinlan's punches, "get that truck out of the way or I'll drive this one right through it. And you, Mr. Quinlan," she was no less venomous with him, "get back in here and get us on our way. Come on, don't stand there!"

"You take it easy!" Quinlan said. "I'm the boss of this team and don't you forget it."

"Well, try and act like a boss," Ida said. "Show some sense and climb back in here." She looked at Paddy, but spared his feelings: she spoke to the men as a crowd: "Righto, all aboard! The war's over."

The men stood their ground for a moment, then they grinned sheepishly and clambered back into the truck. They sat down, some of them mopping cuts on their faces, one or two scraping mud from their clothes. Bluey Brown looked across at Ocker Shand.

"If you hadn't opened your big trap, we wouldn't have been in that donnybrook. Fight your own fights from now on, Ocker. If Paddy's missus hadn't brought that truck up when she did, I'd have had my arse pushed in by the bloke I'd copped. He was too big and too good for me. I thought he was Jack Dempsey out here on holiday."

A short thin man in the corner of the truck, all slim bone and sinew, who had been introduced to Paddy as Clint Evans, dabbed at a graze on his long thin nose. "I dunno who I picked. I was just gunna ask him if he'd like to take a bet on who'd win the argument, and next thing he'd donged me."

"Yeah, I saw you," Bluey said. "You were like me, going

up and down like a lavatory seat. Every time I stood up, this big bastard knocked me down again."

Turk Tuthill grinned. "I was sorry it finished so fast, m'self. I was having the time of me life with my bloke. I felt like it was ten or fifteen years ago."

"You done some pro fighting?" Paddy had enjoyed his two minutes with the man he'd picked: the young bloke hadn't known much about blocking a punch. "I caught a look at you once there, and you looked pretty good."

"I fought for the middleweight title, back in 1911," Turk said. "Got put on me back in the ninth."

"I remember you now," Clint Evans said. "I never seen you fight, though."

"I was all right," Turk said. "I just wasn't good enough to be champ, that was all."

Nobody asked what had made him finish up out here in the West: the answer was in his pink eyes and red nose even while they thought of the question.

"That missus of yours, Paddy, knows how to throw her weight around when it's needed," Clint said. "She soon told Quinlan where to get off when he started telling her who was boss. But one thing I'll say for her. She didn't try to make you look small in front of us by picking on you."

"She wouldn't be game." Paddy blew on a skinned knuckle: he could handle anyone. "She knows me too well."

"You don't belt her, do you?" Chilla Peters said in his dry voice; one shrewd eye had begun to close slightly under a darkening bruise, but he seemed completely unperturbed by the fight. "I belted a woman once, and got six months for it. While I was doing time, she sued me for maintenance."

"How'd you get on?" Bluey said.

"When I got out, I belted her again. Then I went back in and did another six months."

"I don't belt my missus." Paddy returned his tooth to its proper place. "But I just let her know who's boss."

"My wife knows who's boss in our family," Bluey grinned. "She is."

"Well, I'm glad *she's* not with us," Ocker said; both eyes

were slightly swollen, but he was trying not to be aware of them. "Two women with us would just about finish everything."

"Listen to him," Bluey said. "The warmonger. You start any more stoushes before the season is out, and I'm drumming you, it'll be the finish of you. I gave up battling when I got out of the army."

Quinlan yelled from up front, "Hold on!" and the truck slowed, then dropped suddenly. The back wheels slapped in the mud, then they were moving slowly over a track that meandered almost aimlessly through thin scrub. The truck lurched and skidded and the track wound out of the back of it like red silk.

Bluey was sitting by the tailboard of the truck. He looked back at the shining mud and shook his head. "Wouldn't be surprised if they've got wet sheep." He turned to the men. "If they are wet, I, for one, don't want to shear 'em. I'm not taking any chances. Not this season, anyway."

"Well, if they are wet, we'll know who the jonah is, I tell you," Ocker said, then looked at Paddy. "No offence, of course."

3

But the sheep weren't wet. They were dry, and carrying fair wool despite the drought. There were perhaps four or five thousand of them in the woolshed paddock; they moved like a restless grey sea under the wind coming across the plain. There were more to come, another twenty thousand of them, but they were still out in the outer paddocks where the musterers had brought them these last few days. In the small pens at the rear of the shed there were already sheep waiting for the shearers to begin. The station was alive with activity; these next few weeks were the pivot of the whole year.

Wattle Run was not the biggest station in the district, but it was well established and had a reputation for the quality of its wool. The homestead stood on a slight rise, a squat rambling house with a wide veranda: it stood there with a sort of matriarchal dignity, the veranda coming round in front of it like two arms folded across a self-satisfied bosom. Close behind it was a steel-frame windmill, its blades spinning a silver circle in the shining morning air. A row of mulga wattles ran down the hill behind the house; at the bottom end of the line of wattles were the huts for the shearers and stockmen. A hundred yards farther down, like a huge ark anchored on the edge of the sea of sheep, was the shearing shed.

Paddy was testing the cutter of his shears. Now that he was back in a shed, caught in the hectic feeling of shearing time, glad of a chance to show off his skill, there was an eagerness for the bell to go and to have the first sheep between his knees. Pride was no sin with Paddy, but rather a defence: he had to show off his skills to prove he wasn't a complete failure: his father had been no good at anything.

Sean and Venneker came into the shed, Sean carrying his pots of sheep-dip. After the thin flat brightness of the winter sunlight, the shed was just a long darkness; it stretched like a tunnel to the doorway of light at the other end. This shed was an old one and the shearing seasons had left their mark on it. The interior smelled of wool grease: it hung in the air like an incense, as if the shed were some sort of temple. The grease had stained the floor and walls; light gleamed hesitantly on the smooth brown surfaces. Sean and Venneker walked down the middle of the shed together; the ridiculous disparity in their heights gave for a moment the illusion that the floor was on a slant.

Paddy looked up. "How's your mum doing?"

"Good-o," Sean said. "She's having the time of her life up in the kitchen."

"The men seem well satisfied with her cooking so far." Venneker was wearing an old football jersey; it stretched across his massive frame like a striped skin. "I must say last night's meal was better than I've ever had in a shearing shed before. I repeat, Carmody: you are an extremely fortunate man."

"Yeah," said Paddy suspiciously. He was unused to other

men being so frank in their praise of Ida. Venneker so far
hadn't stepped out of line, but he hadn't been backward
messing around with Mrs. Firth. Still, if he tried anything,
Ida would soon put him in his place: she wouldn't stand any
fooling around. With a smile he remembered the time she
had donged the bloke at Narooma: he looked up at Venneker
and felt better. "I just hope she don't try to work her guts
out, that's all."

Halstead, the owner of Wattle Run, came into the shed and
stood by the door. The men were all by their machines now;
Quinlan, who did his own wool classing, was at his table
under the big fanlight; the piece-pickers, roustabouts and
boys hitched up their pants and waited for the bell.

Everyone looked towards Quinlan as he raised his voice.
"Righto, men. Mr. Halstead wants good shearing, more than
fast stuff. Some of the sheep are still picking up after the
drought. Don't knock 'em around too much." The shearers
took no notice of this. Ocker Shand exaggeratedly cleaned his
ear with his little finger as if he hadn't heard right. They
knew how to handle sheep and didn't need to be told.
"Everybody ready?"

Then the bell went. Shearing was on again at Wattle Run.
Paddy dived into the pen, his body in the crouch in which
it would stay most of the day. He grabbed a sheep under the
forelegs, sat it up and dragged it out into the shed, on to the
"board." With the sheep's forefeet tucked under his left
armpit, his left hand pulled his machine into gear as his right
hand whipped up the handpiece. He worked with the automatic smoothness of one who knew his job and liked it now
that he was doing it; he was no relation at all of the man who
two days before had tried to dodge being signed up. He
wore a sleeveless flannel singlet; his lean brown arms moved
like thick striking snakes in the dust-flecked light.

The belly wool was thrown clear, then the wool on the
left flank, then the neck. The sheep was moved between his
knees like a sack: only an occasional bleat let you know
it was alive. From the neck to the forearm the cutter
ploughed, then the sheep was on its side and Paddy was
beginning the longest cut, the "long blow," from the flank

to the top of the head. Then he propped the sheep against his leg and attacked the other side. Stab, punch, a long sweep, heave, every movement part of a beautifully co-ordinated whole, then the sheep was finished and was stumbling, Paddy's knee aiding it with a push, down the chute into the counting pen. Paddy had gained five seconds on the other shearers with his first sheep; by the end of the day he wanted to be the "ringer" shearer.

Up in the cookhouse Ida heard the bell. She and the aborigine, Charlie, whom Quinlan had signed on as her helper, had just finished washing up the breakfast dishes. Ida dried her hands on her apron and walked to the door and looked down the hill towards the shed.

"There it goes, Charlie. They're at it now, going like scalded cats, I'll bet."

Light winked on the dark face as he smiled. "Too much hard yakka. Me wouldn't wanna be shearer."

"You sound like my old man," Ida said. "Well, we've got some yakka to do up here too. You get on with those spuds I've put there in the basin. I'm going to surprise them at dinner-time and give them mashed potatoes. They've probably never seen a potato without its jacket, not at shearing time, anyway."

She was about to turn back into the cookhouse when she saw a woman come out of the front door of the homestead and begin to walk down towards her. She was a young woman who walked with careful steps, as if she were used to pavements rather than the worn track down which she was now coming.

"My husband said you were cooking for the men." She smiled a little shyly; home was just behind her on the hill, but she looked lost. "I'm Mrs. Halstead."

"Hullo." There was no shyness about Ida's smile, nor any deference; without appearing rude, she could have been the owner of Wattle Run welcoming a stranger. "I'm the cook, till one of the men decides he wants a change. These shearers are pretty hard to please. I think they just like to grumble about the cooking, whether it's good, bad or indifferent. But men are like that, aren't they?"

"They must keep you busy." Her soft pale hair was shot
with sun; her large blue eyes were narrowed slightly against
the very faint glare from the ground. Ida couldn't remember
seeing a more beautiful girl and one who was more out of
place in this vast harsh land. "My husband tells me you even
have to bake to-morrow's bread each night after you've given
them their evening meal."

"I don't mind it," Ida said. "I like cooking, especially in
a kitchen. Well, I'd better get a move on, otherwise I won't
have dinner ready for them. We don't want a riot on the
first day."

"May I come in, or will I get in your way?"

Ida looked at her curiously, but kept the question in her
mind to herself. "Why certainly. Hey, Charlie, take the
spuds and carrots outside and do them. The missus and I've
got something to talk about."

Mrs. Halstead watched silently as Charlie picked up his
basin and the box of potatoes and carrots and carried them
outside. She looked at Ida. "You needn't have done that. I
didn't mind his being here."

"Oh, it's not that. He'd rather be outside. You'd make
him so nervous he'd finish up peeling his fingers instead of
the spuds."

Mrs. Halstead fidgeted nervously. "Look, perhaps I had
better go——"

"Don't be silly. Sit down and we'll have a talk. I think you
and I could do with each other's company."

Mrs. Halstead sank on to a chair. In the plain, almost bare
room, among the pots and pans and backed by the blackened
fuel stove, she looked like a rose growing out of a wood heap.
She sat half turned on the chair, with one arm over the back
of the chair and her hands linked. The pose was unaffected
but elegant: it gave Ida a thought.

"Excuse me asking, do you come from Sydney? Or anyway, from some city?"

"From Sydney," Mrs. Halstead said; her voice dragged a
little as if it had caught on a memory. "I lived at Vaucluse."

"I might've guessed it. Have you ever had your picture in

the society pages?" Ida had begun to chop up meat; the
chopper rose and fell rhythmically.

Mrs. Halstead looked up. " I don't know if I should answer
that. You make me feel a little ashamed."

" There's nothing to be ashamed about. I envy you.
Crikey, I've often dreamed of that sort of life. I'm not one of
your bolshies, Mrs. Halstead. You can't blame people if
they're luckier than others." The chopper beat a steady
tattoo. " You like it here?"

A pale hand picked at the blue wool of a sweatered arm.
" I try to."

" Meaning you don't?" Ida said. " Well, it's certainly different to Sydney. I was never there, don't suppose I ever will
be, but I've seen lots of pictures of it in the papers. The
Sydney Mail and things like that." She stopped chopping and
stared out through the window: in the high sky an eagle-
hawk hung, stiff-winged and lonely: as she watched, it
dropped like a sad note and went away in smooth flight.
" We can't all make ourselves at home anywhere."

" You could, couldn't you?"

" I dunno. Maybe." She had made her home anywhere for
the last sixteen years; the only thing they had never changed
was their economic position. " Some people are adaptable
because they've got to be."

" Why did you ask if I'd had my picture in the society
pages?"

" You have that look." She was an authority on class: her
text-books had been newspapers and magazines thrown from
passing trains. " It was just the way you sat there in the
chair."

" Yes, I used to have my picture in the papers. Never doing
anything worth while, just being at the races or parties or
going to theatres. I was proud of it, then. I used to keep a
scrap-book. Now I'm ashamed of it." She looked up at Ida
and said as if she were just opening the conversation: " You're
the first woman I've talked to in four months."

" What about the women in Cawndilla? And aren't there
any women on the other properties around here?"

" Yes. Oh, I've seen them. But I mean *really* talked to. I

couldn't have told them what I've just told you." She smiled
and picked at the wool of her sweater again. " I don't know
why I've told you this, unless it's because you don't live here.
You don't, do you?"

" Does the boss—does your husband know you don't like it
here?"

" I think he guesses it. I've never told him. I wouldn't do
that for worlds. He really loves this place. And I'm——"
The blush was the first colour her face had shown. " Well,
I'm like that about him. That's why I try to like it. For his
sake."

" Well, I don't have to ask what's wrong with it." She was
moving about the cookhouse; she might have spent all her
life in a kitchen, so at ease did she look. " This is good
country for sheep and not bad for men. But it's hard on us
women. We never get anything out of it. The men come
here because of the sheep and we come here because of the
men. And most of us women finish up looking like the
sheep. Wrinkled faces, knotty hair, not even much of a mind
of our own." She turned and smiled across the width of the
room. " Don't ever let it get you like that, Mrs. Halstead.
Don't ever finish up looking like one of the sheep in your
own paddocks."

Mrs. Halstead smiled; the two women were suddenly
friends, each sharply aware of it. " I'll try not to. I'd never
thought of that sort of future."

Down in the shearing shed her husband was standing
beside Quinlan. The men had got into the swing of shearing
now, were working off the rustiness of movement that is
always there at the start of a season, and it was becoming
evident that some of the shearers were a good deal better than
others.

" That little bloke at the end of the shed." Halstead was a
tall, angular man in his late thirties; he had a bony pleasant
face, reddish-brown hair and a big-toothed smile. " What's
his name—Carmody? He knows his job."

" I always try to get the best men I can in my team,"
Quinlan said. " This is the first time he's worked for me, but

I remembered seeing him shear down at—at Burrambang. I had to battle two other contractors to sign him up."

"Whom did you have to battle for the big bloke?" Halstead nodded down towards Venneker. "Wirth's Circus?"

Venneker was working at one of the tables, skirting the wool fleeces as they were flung on to the grating in front of him. At times he would turn his head and wink at Sean as the latter ran past in answer to a yell from one of the shearers. Sean, bright-eyed with the excitement of working in the shed, feeling the importance of having a job to do, was having the time of his life. Farther down the shed Bluey, Turk, Ocker and Clint were wrestling the sheep between their knees, working with the ease of long familiarity. They peeled the sheep as a waiter peels an orange: the fleece fell away like a discarded skin, was scooped up by the pickers-up and flung with a skilful throw on to the tables. Already the shed was working as a team.

"I always go out of my way to get the best men I can," Quinlan said; he believed the lie more than Halstead, who wasn't listening. "We'll be through on time, just like I said."

4

The day was over. Down the hill the shed was quiet: only in the ears of the men who had been there all day did it still hum. Beyond the shed the paddock was grey and moving in the last light; the musterers had brought in another mob of sheep in the afternoon. The men were tired: the first day was always the worst. Weariness was an atmosphere about the homestead.

"Gawd, I'm done in." Turk Tuthill lay on his bunk in the shearers' hut; at Wattle Run one big hut had been built for the men as sleeping quarters. "I must be getting old or something."

"Too much grog in your joints," Bluey said. "You want to be a clean-living sort like me."

Sean was sitting at the table in the middle of the room writing to McKechnie. This was the beginning of a new letter: Dear Mr. McKechnie, and the breathless words would fly across the page, describing the whole day, all the small, odd details that clung to a boy's mind like burrs to a sheep's wool; two hundred and fifty miles away McKechnie would learn more of the day here than the day on his own farm.

"Who you writing to, Sean?" Bluey said. "Your girl?"

Sean looked up and blushed. "Nah. Just a man I know. He's a mate of Mr. Venneker's."

Bluey looked at Venneker. "What's the matter, Lofty? Employing a secretary? How much does he pay you to write his letters, Sean?"

"It is his own personal correspondence. It has nothing to do with me." Venneker lay on his bunk with his feet sticking out over the end, most shearers were of medium height or less, and the bunks hadn't been built for men as tall as he. "And I'd deem it a favour if you would refrain from calling me Lofty."

"Well, what's your name?" Bluey said. "Lofty fits you."

"Rupert," said Venneker.

There was stunned silence for a moment in the hut, then Bluey began to laugh, rolling in his bunk. The other men joined him: the hut rocked with merriment. Sean sat in the midst of it, blushing for Venneker, but the latter was completely unconcerned. When the laughter at last subsided, he calmly said, "You may shorten it to Rupe."

Bluey wiped tears from his eyes. "Stone the crows, how's your form? A hulking great bastard like you, and your mother called you Rupert!"

"I didn't happen to be a hulking great bastard when I was christened," Venneker said. "Nor any other sort of bastard."

"I've only met one other Rupert," Bluey said. "That was when I was in the Salvos."

"Was you in the Salvation Army?" Clint said.

Bluey grinned; he looked no older than Sean. "Not for long. I went along for four or five meetings, but then I gave it away."

"What happened?" Turk said.

"They picked me as the poor bunny who had to hump the

big drum. I gave it up and became a Presbyterian. No drums there."

The conversation flapped around the hut like a tired bird. No topic lasted longer than half a minute: the men were too weary to sustain it, to argue on any points. Ocker Shand had already gone to sleep, snoring quietly and almost pleasantly. Clint Evans was sitting on the edge of his cot, soaking his feet in a basin of hot water; sleep hung on his face like a veil. After ten minutes or so, conversation died away. Sean's pen scratched away like a mouse at the silence.

Bluey stiffly sat up on his bed. "Well, I better write to the trouble and strife. I could hear her from here, yelling bloody blue murder, if I didn't drop her a line at least twice a week." He stood up and walked stiffly across to the table and sat down. "She's expecting a baby."

Nobody answered. Sean looked up from his letter, saw everyone had gone to sleep, and stared across the table at Bluey. "You talking to me, Bluey?"

"I think I must've been." Bluey looked round the hut. "I couldn't have been wasting my time talking to these logs. Yeah, I said the missus and I are going to have a baby. You probably don't care a damn, but I thought I'd let you know anyway." He grinned and winked. "It's our first. You wait till you're going to be a dadda. You'll want to tell someone, too."

"Well, I got a fair way to go yet," Sean said. "But I hope it's a nice baby and your wife's all right. What d'you want? I mean, a boy or a girl?"

"A boy." Bluey had an old black-covered exercise book in front of him; he worked the fingers of the cramped hand that had held the cutters all day, then took a pencil from his pocket. "You know, I'm glad it's you I had to tell. You'll understand better than these other blokes would."

Sean blushed and tried to look mature and understanding: he dug in the shallow depths of his experience for a few grains of wisdom. "Well, I dunno about that. Like I said, I got a fair way to go yet."

"That's why you'll understand. Because you're still a kid.

These other mugs have forgotten all the things you dream about at your age." Bluey looked about the hut at the men who had forgotten how to dream; Turk Tuthill rolled violently in the beginnings of a nightmare. " I want a boy, so he can someday play cricket for Australia against England. Do yor understand that?"

" Sorta," said Sean, and tried to look as if he did.

" When I was a kid like you, before the war, I used to dream of some day playing for Australia. I had a couple of games with the A.I.F. team in England, but I didn't get any further. But when I'm in Sydney and the Tests are on, I go to see 'em play and wish to hell I could be walking out there on to the field with that green cap on. But I'm not good enough, so all it can ever be is a dream. But if we have a boy——" He looked along the table at Sean: in the heavy yellow light of the lantern, throwing its black shadows, they were the same age. " You see what I'm getting at, Sean?"

" I hope he's good enough," Sean said, and wondered if his mother had had any plans for him before he was born: he knew that his father would have had no ambitions.

" He'll be good enough, I'll see to that," Bluey said. " All he's got to do is to be born a boy."

Paddy and Ida were in bed in their tent. When Quinlan had signed on Ida, he had mentioned that it might not always be possible to get separate accommodation for her. She had tartly replied that she had her own separate accommodation: she carried it with her, like a snail carrying its shell. When the shearing team had arrived at Wattle Run, Halstead hadn't been pleased to find the cook was a woman, and he, too, had asked where she was going to sleep. He hadn't offered to find her a room in the main house; knowing the independence of shearers, he had known that she, being a shearer's wife, would have refused. So two of the aboriginal roustabouts had put up the tent behind the cookhouse, and Paddy and Ida had become a separate establishment, as far as sleeping was concerned.

" Gawd, I'm tired," Paddy said. " Me back feels like some-one's shoved a poker up me behind." He tried to assuage the aching stiffness with a rubbing of pride: "But I done two hundred and twelve sheep. That ain't bad for the first day. It made me the ringer."

"Keep patting yourself on the back, you'll soon get rid of that poker that's worrying you. What d'you think I've been doing all day? Reading the paper?" Ida had only just become aware of how tired she was: it had been a long time since she had enjoyed herself so much.

"When we come up for dinner I thought you'd been spending all the morning talking to the boss's missus. I saw her come outa the cookhouse and scoot up the path. Then I saw her again at tea-time when we knocked off. She been giving you a hand peeling the spuds?"

"She's a pretty lonely girl," Ida said. "I feel sorry for her."

"What's the matter? Don't she get on with the boss? I wouldn't be surprised if he knocked her around a bit. He's got a bit of a cold look in his eyes, like he'd have his own way. I didn't see much of her. She looked a bit thin and scrawny. Maybe he'd like her better if she had a bit more meat on her. Maybe he's like me——"

"If he is, he talks too much." Ida moved uncomfortably on the mattress, trying to ease the heavy ache at the base of her spine. "No, I think they get on well together. But she's just out of place here, that's all. I might feel the same way if we went to live in the city."

"Gawd forbid," Paddy said reverently.

"But she's a nice little piece. I like her. She was telling me all about life down in Sydney. She used to live out with the toffs at Vaucluse. I wouldn't mind that sort of life, the way she told it. They certainly have enough to amuse them."

"They gotta have some compensations for living down there," Paddy said. "But think of all the drawbacks."

"I've been thinking of them." Ida lay silently for a while, only moving as the pain in her rump got worse: the seat of the wagonette had never made her ache as much as this. She had been on her feet fifteen hours, cooking meals, serving them, washing up, baking bread, and now the pleasure of the day had faded as the pain of fatigue lay like a weight on the end of her spine. "Darl, if Sean says he would like to be a

chemist or a tram-driver or something like that, would you like
to go and live in Sydney?"

Paddy moaned and flopped over, dragging the blankets
with him. Ida pulled the blankets back on herself, shivering
a little with the cold, and lay staring up at the darkness of the
tent. She didn't press the point with Paddy : she was too tired
to resume an argument that had been going on for years.

To-night she felt almost as tired in spirit as in her body.
Over the years she had built up defences that had kept out
disappointment, but the talk with Mrs. Halstead to-day had
worn a weak spot through which had leaked some of the frustration she had so long denied. Fundamentally she was not
interested in a rich woman's life. Long before she had met
Paddy she had decided that money alone had nothing to offer.
Had she had money, she would have been neither a spend-
thrift nor a miser : she would more probably have been a
philanthropist. But to-day Mrs. Halstead had shown her
glimpses of a life that, if no better, was at least no worse and
was certainly a great deal different.

In the first year of being married to Paddy she had liked
the life they had lived. To a girl who had spent all her life
in the limited confines of a small town, the mere thought of
travelling round the countryside, seeing new places, greeting
new faces, had been almost like release from years in an
attic. In that first year she had been happier than at any
time before or since; even the birth of Sean had not made
her as happy, because with the joy of bearing him had come
the first faint gnawing worry of what the future held for him.
In that first year there had been no future; they had roamed
from town to town, from job to job, and to-morrow had
always been still lost in the dark distances of the night.

Then as Sean had grown older had come the need for the
defences. They had been built up, like a thickening layer
across the eyes, until there had been a blindness protecting her
from the vision of what might have been had Paddy been a
different man.

To-day the blindness had been for odd moments swept
away. She had made no effort to protect herself : she had
̇ ̇ ̇ ̇ ̇ ̇ ̇ way to ask questions : she had been like an

emigrant seeking information on a new land. At first she had not thought much about the questions as she had asked them; they had really only been a means of drawing Mrs. Halstead out of herself. Mrs. Halstead had obviously missed Sydney; it had made her happier to have someone to whom she could talk about it. But then, quite without Ida's realising it, the purpose of the questioning had changed. Faint hopes of a new life, born perhaps in the thought that for the first time in years Paddy had signed to a job that would bring him good money, as good as he would ever earn, had begun to disturb her.

Suddenly now, her mind moving aimlessly in the darkness, she thought of home and her mother and father and sister. Her mother and father were dead. Her mother had died when she was two years old, when her sister Stella had been born. Her father had died three years after she had run away with Paddy: they had been in Queensland then and it had been too far and too expensive to go home for the funeral. Her memories of him were faint now and of course there were no memories at all of her mother. When she had left home the only thing she had taken with her, besides her own belongings, had been the wedding picture of her father and mother: she still had it, the glass long since broken, the picture faded and stained, the only tangible record she possessed of the life she had left. Her sister Stella had married after her father's death and had moved to Perth. They had never been really close, Ida gay and friendly, Stella quiet and clever: more than the width of a continent had separated them, and for ten years now no word had passed between them.

The tears were on her cheeks before she was aware of them. For the first time she realised the extent of their poverty: she did not have even a memory of home.

She turned in to Paddy, clinging to him with almost desperate hunger. He turned towards her, showing no surprise at her tears, and held her in his arms. " What's the matter, darl?"

She couldn't answer: she had no words for the sudden despair that had overwhelmed her: for the first time in her life she was lost, frightened by something that had the awful shifting insecurity of a quicksand.

5

The weather stayed cold but dry. Each morning the sky appeared out of the darkness like a lake of blue ice. In the paddocks there were white shadows of frost beneath the grey lonely trees. The mud of the past fortnight had turned into a hard crust around the homestead; down in the paddocks the sheep had reduced it to dust again. In the late afternoon the westerlies came moaning across the plains like a ghost army: the musterers, riding hunched in their saddles, turned their backs and faced east as if looking for to-morrow's sun.

The shearers had settled down to the rhythm of their work. The first stiffness had worn off; the cutters peeled the wool off at a steady rate. Paddy had established himself as the ringer of the shed: each day he shore ten or twelve sheep more than anyone else. No one resented his superiority; all the men admired him, and Clint Evans was talking of getting in touch with some of the other sheds to see if they had some-one to put up against Paddy.

"We might be able to get in a few side bets," Clint said. It was Sunday and the men were lying around the hut, glad of a day off. "I wouldn't mind plonking twenty quid on Paddy."

"I'd have a quid or two," Turk Tuthill said. "I ain't got your sorta money to throw around, but I wouldn't mind having a bet."

"You got as much as I got," Clint said. "You just ain't game to risk it, that's all. I always reckon, nothing venture, nothing win. You gotta lay out money to win money."

"Famous last words," Bluey Brown said.

"That's what you think, Blue. One of these days I'm gunna win a packet, and from then on I'll be set." Clint sat on his bunk and stared dreamily out through the hut window: all he needed was the fastest horse, the right cards, the correct call of coins, to own the world. "I knew a bloke once. He copped a double down in Melbourne. Four thousand quid for five. Eight hundred to bloody one. You wouldn't read about it, would you?"

"What would you do if you won four thousand quid?"
Turk said. "Would you give up work?"

"My oath, I would! Gawd, can you see someone sweating
his guts out with that much money in the bank? No, I'd get
some nice little system, something where I wouldn't lay out
too much and do the lot, and I'd just live off the bookies for
the rest of me life. Christ knows, they've lived off me long
enough."

"Well, I'd have a quid or two on Paddy if you can set him
up against someone," Turk said. "What about it, Paddy?
You feel like shaping up to somebody else?"

A team of draught horses couldn't have held Paddy back:
if the shed wanted someone to represent them, he'd help 'em
out. "Well, if you wanna risk your money on me," he said,
his head spinning with his efforts to be modest, "I'll give it
a burl. But don't go shoving your neck out too far. I ain't
any bloody world champion." He was dizzy with self-efface-
ment. "I'll just do me best."

"We'd better see Quinlan and the boss about it," Bluey
said. He had been elected the shed's union representative and,
while not officious, he was conscientious about both sides of
the contract with the station owner. "Halstead mightn't like
the idea of us having a race on his sheep."

"Well, we'll see 'em some time this week," Clint said.
"Then I'll go into town Saturday and see can I bump into
anyone from the neighbouring sheds."

"I wouldn't mind winning a few quid m'self," Bluey said.
"It ud come in handy. I might win enough to give the
trouble and strife a private room at the hospital. Let my kid
be born in style."

"You think he's going to notice where he's born?" Ocker
Shand was sitting on his bunk trimming his corns. "I tell
you, it doesn't matter where you start. It's where you finish
that counts."

"Keep going, Ocker," Bluey said. "We didn't know you
were a philosopher."

"I tell you, that's dinkum," Ocker said. "You see if it isn't.
I'd rather die in silk sheets than be born in 'em."

"I think you'll die the way you were born, Ocker," Bluey said. "Arguing with the doctor."

Ocker grunted and sliced at a corn. Bluey stood up. "Well, I'm going across to the dunny. Can I do anything for anyone?"

"Yeah, fall in," said Ocker, and almost cut his toe off as he fell back laughing.

Bluey grinned and went out of the hut and across the yard towards the small latrine that stood like a dilapidated telephone booth in the corner of the nearest paddock. He waved to Venneker and Sean sitting beneath a tree, then disappeared.

"There is a truly happy man," Venneker said. "He doesn't appear to want anything in the world but what he already has."

"Yes, he does." Sean sat with his hands wrapped round his knees. The wind coming across the paddocks and up the slope was cold, but the tree protected them from it and the winter sun was warm. "He wants his baby, when it grows up, to play cricket for Australia."

"Well, I suppose it is a laudable ambition. It is the only way to gain real fame in this backward country. Be a cricketer or be a jockey. Just don't annoy the populace by making any claim to brains."

"Fair go," Sean said. "Us Aussies ain't——"

"We Aussies aren't." Venneker had been working constantly on Sean's speech, but progress had been slow; Ida, realising she couldn't compete against the example set by Paddy, had long ago given up and let Sean go his own way. But Venneker had a more sensitive ear and consequently more determination in his self-allotted task: "Must I keep hammering at you as at a backward native?"

"We Aussies aren't," said Sean patiently: so far he hadn't seen the point of good speech: out here, all you wanted was a bloke to understand you, and there were some expressions here that were much more to the point than anything in the King's English, "as bad as all that."

"Yes, you are. Oh, this isn't the only country where sportsmen are idolised. In England Hobbs ranks next to the King, and in America there is this oddly-named character, Babe

Ruth, who seems to command more money than the President. And in France there is Carpentier. But in those countries they also respect brains. In this country they only *sus*pect them."

"Well, I dunno about that. We only put blokes with brains in Parliament."

"Do you? There *are* some intelligent men, of course, running the country, but there are a good many morons also gracing, or should I say *dis*gracing, the benches. This country seems to be lacking in men of vision. In fact it seems to be a national malady. A general inbred myopia when it comes to making plans for the future."

"You're picking an easy bloke to argue with," Sean said. "How can a bloke my age answer all the things you're saying? Here's Bluey. Try him."

Bluey was coming towards them now from the corner of the paddock, doing up his belt. His round plump face always reminded Sean of a freckled sun; it beamed like the bright beginning of a new day above the plump hill of his body. He came up, patting his stomach.

"Better out than in. How are you, cocks? What you sitting out here for? You'll get your manhood frozen off."

"It's all right in the sun," Sean said.

"I've just been over to the thunder-can, and the wind's coming through there like the breeze off the ice-works. But you're right, it's good-o in the sun. Mind if I park the rear end beside you for a while?" He sat down and leaned back against the tree beside Venneker. "Look at those plains, will you? Miles and miles of bugger-all. I wouldn't live way out here, not if you gave me the winning ticket in Tatts'."

"Where do you come from, Bluey?" Venneker asked.

"Coogee, in Sydney. Best damned place in Australia. When I'm home, I get up in the mornings, put on my togs and in three minutes I'm down in the surf. That's what I like. The beach and the surf. Out here I might have to go three days before I could paddle my feet in a water-hole. Give me the coast, and I'll give the rest of Australia back to the blackfellers."

"If the blackfellers had all this land, there wouldn't be any sheep and you'd be out of a job then," Sean said.

"No, not me, Sean. I'm not going to be a shearer all my life. I've got it all mapped out. I've told you before, I'm a bloody genius. I'm going to stick at this game for another three years. Then I'll have saved enough to set m'self up in business. I'm going into this wireless game, sell 'em and repair 'em, maybe even make 'em. I'm looking ahead. Wireless is going to be a bloody big thing one of these days, and I'm studying to get the good guts on it. Ten years from now I'll be known as the red-headed Marconi."

Sean looked at Venneker. "*He* must reckon there's a place for brains in this country."

"Of course there is," Venneker said. "God knows it could do with some brains. All I said was, one is treated with suspicion if one has brains. A pair of hands is worth more here than a set of brains. And a union card is worth more than either."

"What's this all about?" Bluey said with a grin. "Rupe sounds like a spruiker from the Domain. That how you spend your Sunday arvos, Rupe? Belly-aching against the way the country's run?"

"He reckons Australia don't want people with brains," Sean said. "And he said something about us not having any vision, whatever he means by that."

"Can't see beyond the end of your nose," Venneker said. "Or to put it more correctly, a total inability to see beyond Friday's pay packet. Everyone concerned with seeing how much money he can get for the minimum number of hours."

"You don't like Australians, Rupe?" Bluey said. "I don't like to say this, but if we give you a pain in the tit, why don't you go back where you came from?"

"A typical Australian parrot-cry, if you don't mind my saying so," Venneker said. "As indigenously Australian as the kookaburra's laugh or the cry of a two-up caller. It is an automatic utterance as soon as anyone makes a criticism of the country. As it happens, I like Australians. If I didn't, I should not have stayed here for the period I have. I am not without the wherewithal to pay my passage out of this mismanaged Paradise. But liking Australians does not make me blind to their faults. God knows, they have too many."

"Yeah?" Bluey had moved away from the tree to sit facing Venneker. The colour of his hair seemed to have drained down into his face; it was the first time Sean had seen him anywhere near to anger, and he was beginning to feel sorry he had brought Bluey into the argument. "Such as?"

Venneker had the faults of Australians on the end of his tongue; he rolled them off like stones into the rising pool of Bluey's resentment. "Laziness, ingratitude, the talent for taking too much for granted, stinginess, tardiness, xenophobia, bad manners——"

"That's enough!" Bluey snapped. "Now look, Rupe. I didn't think I'd ever want to get into a stoush with you, but you keep on that way and I'll hang something on the end of your nose. Christ, with what you've just strung off there, you haven't got a good word for us. Ingratitude, stinginess, tardiness. What do you mean by that last one? We weren't too bloody tardy getting into the war."

"That seems to be about the only thing you are quick to do. Jump into a fight or an argument. Witness the present case." Venneker was still leaning back against the tree; his temper was as cool as the wind stirring the branches above them. "But you are tardy when it comes to doing anything that might improve the country. Australians are too garrulous——"

Bluey looked at Sean and jerked a thumb at Venneker. "Get a load of who's talking?"

"——and expend most of their energy in words. The garrulity may be just a disguise, a camouflage for their laziness. They always seem to be able to find many reasons for *not* beginning a thing, and very few for beginning it."

Turk Tuthill had come across from the men's hut. As he came towards them he dropped into a crouch and bounced around, shadow-sparring and grinning at them. Then he straightened up and took a deep breath. "Makes you feel like a round or two. Fresh air, no grog, no women. I'll have to watch out. A bloke's likely to start getting healthy."

"Hang around," Bluey said. "I might need some support. Rupe's just telling us what's wrong with us Aussies."

"You're not letting that worry you, are you?" Turk

dropped into a crouch again and shot out his left. "The Chooms have been telling us what's wrong with us ever since they came out here with the First Fleet."

"Yes, but he's getting bloody insulting this time," Bluey said. "Reckons we're stingy, ungrateful, talk too much. You should hear him."

"Get up on your feet, Rupe." Turk danced back and forth, his fists punching holes in the air. "I'll knock your block off."

"Which further illustrates my point," said Venneker, not moving. "That an Australian's answer to everything is to knock the other bloke's block off."

Turk disposed of the ghost of Venneker with a vicious uppercut, then squatted down beside him. In the last couple of weeks the pink had gone from his eyes; but in the cold afternoon air his nose still had a purplish tinge. He patted the head of the kelpie lying by Sean's feet and looked at Venneker.

"What's the matter, Rupe? Don't you reckon we'll ever make anything of this land? You reckon we're a lotta worthless bastards who don't deserve it?"

"No, I wouldn't go as far as to say that. I think some day you will deserve it. But it will be a long, long time before you can make claim to being a nation. You'll never be a nation, not a real, hard-working, responsible nation, in my lifetime. Nor, I venture, in the lifetime of young Sean here."

"It beats me you haven't done something about organising us, since you seem to know everything that's wrong with us." Bluey's temper had cooled down; he had begun to suspect that perhaps Venneker was pulling their legs. "Why don't you try running for union secretary? That would be a start. You can be Prime Minister later on."

"That is another of the troubles here," Venneker said. "Too many unionists and not enough statesmen."

Turk looked at Bluey. "I wonder how long he'd live if he got up at the Trades Hall and said that?"

"They probably wouldn't touch him. They'd just think the long-legged bastard was off his rocker and ring up Callan Park."

Sean decided it was time the conversation was changed. He hadn't agreed with anything Venneker had said, but he knew it would be a long time before he had any argument to the criticisms. He moved his toes in the dust banked against a root of the tree. He scratched his name in the dust of the land: he suddenly felt proud, of what he did not know, and when he turned and looked over the wide plains, the miles and miles of bugger-all, to the tall cold sky, he could have wept with the joy of belonging.

He turned back to Bluey. "How's the baby coming along? Have you heard from your wife this week?"

"No, but I expect to hear something to-morrow when the postman comes out from town. The baby should be putting in an appearance any day now. He's dragging his heels a bit. He was due this week, we thought, but when Liz wrote she said the doc thought he mightn't turn up for another fortnight."

"It'll probably be a girl," Turk said. "They're always late."

"If it is, I don't care if it never turns up," Bluey said. "But I'm sure the old ball and chain wouldn't let me down like that. She wants a cricketer just as much as I do. Only thing is, she wants him to play for England. She's a Choom, like you, Rupe. I married her when I was over in the Old Dart during the war."

"Does *she* like Australians?" Sean said.

Bluey grinned. "She reckons there wasn't a bloke in England to come up to me."

6

The next day Liz Brown, Bluey's ball and chain, came to Wattle Run. The postman came across the paddock in his ramshackle truck and deposited Liz with a couple of dozen letters and three parcels on the doorstep of the homestead. Mrs. Halstead was there to meet her, and it was she, a little upset and bewildered, who brought her down to the cookhouse.

"Mrs. Carmody, we have a visitor."

Ida came to the door, her arms white to the elbows with

flour, and in an instant took in Mrs. Brown's advanced condition. "Gawd bless the blackfellers!" Then she squinted and leaned forward, sucking her lip pensively. "I'm making a wild guess, but you wouldn't be Mrs. Bluey Brown, would you?"

"I'm Liz Brown." Her voice was soft and clipped: the sound of Oxford mingled with the smell from the cookhouse. "Bluey doesn't know I'm coming." She put a hand nervously into the pocket of the coat that hung round her like a bathing tent. "He's going to be frightfully annoyed. But I just had to come." She bit her lip and looked anxiously from one to the other.

"Of course you did, Liz," Ida said. "Come on in and have a cuppa. You too, Mrs. Halstead. We'll fix her up, won't we?"

"Why, we'll do all we can," Mrs. Halstead said. "Of course we shall." She seemed to have regained her composure: all she had wanted was an example from Ida. "We'll put your husband in his place if he starts playing up."

Liz Brown sat down on a chair, shifting heavily as she tried to ease the tiredness of her body. "I thought I'd never get here. I've never been this far west before. I didn't realise distances in Australia could be so great, even though I've been out here five years now. But I'm here, and that's all I wanted." She took the cup of tea Ida handed her.

"God, I was lonely. Bluey has been away before, but this time——" She smiled weakly. "I'm a coward, I suppose. I just wanted him near me while I had the baby."

Ida sipped her tea. "Well, we're a long way from a doctor, so give us fair warning when you reckon your time's arrived. There's a doc in Cawndilla, isn't there, Mrs. Halstead?"

"I really don't know." Mrs. Halstead looked bewildered again. "Goodness, I hope so!"

"Well, if the worst comes to the worst, I'll deliver it," Ida said; she went back to kneading dough for a pie-crust. "It won't be the first one I've brought into the world. But we'll try and get the doctor for you, Liz?"

"You took a risk, didn't you?" Mrs. Halstead said. "Coming all that way in the train. You might have had it before you got here."

Liz Brown shook her head: she was too tired and relieved at being here to think what might have happened. She was a small girl, swollen now in her pregnancy, with a quick nervous manner and what looked like a determined effort to overcome an innate shyness. She was not pretty, but her large brown eyes, dull with tiredness now but hinting they could sparkle with humour, made her face more attractive than many with more symmetrical features. Her black hair was cut in a neat shingle and there was a slight stain of nicotine on her fingers; if she hadn't been pregnant she would have been wearing her skirt above her knees. But you knew the modern air would have seemed a little out of place on her: it was just another part of the effort to overcome her shyness. " Well, what we've got to think about now," Ida said, " is where we're going to put you."

Liz looked up. " I shouldn't have come. I just didn't think about what it would be like here. I'm a terrible bother——" She twisted her hands together; her knuckles cracked and she jumped. " But I had to be near Bluey."

" It's all right," Mrs. Halstead said. " Don't go worrying yourself over it. We've got plenty of room up in the house." She saw Ida looking at her. " It's all right, Mrs. Carmody. The boss isn't going to have any say in this. This is something for a woman to decide. Mrs. Brown can come up there and we'll see she's made very comfortable. One of our spare rooms has a double bed in it, and her husband can move in with her." She stood up; she seemed to have a new air about her, one of interest and decision. " You know, Mrs. Brown, I'm really glad you came."

Liz Brown went up to the homestead with Mrs. Halstead, and when the men came up for the mid-day dinner, Ida gave Bluey the news of his wife's arrival.

" Holy slithering Nellie! What the hell——?" Bluey dropped his plate on the table; gravy and peas shot out over the oil-cloth. " Where is she? Is she all right?"

" Hold on to yourself," Ida said. " She's quite all right and being well looked after. She's up at the house."

" Up at——!" Bluey simmered down: he doused his shock with a grin. " Trust old Liz. The old man can sleep and eat down here with the working-class, but she cops the first-class accommodation. What does the boss think about her being here?"

"He doesn't know about it yet," Ida said. "Mrs. Halstead was the one who invited her up. You'd better go up and see your wife."

"You bet your life!" Bluey was already on his way out of the hut. "But stone the bloody crows! Coming all the way out here——?"

He was gone, his voice trailing away as he hurried up the path. The men had just begun to comment on the news when Quinlan came stamping in the door.

"Where's Bluey? Gawd, what am I running? A flaming maternity home?" He looked about the long table, then came stalking down to Ida. "What's the strength of this? The boss tells me she came in this morning with the postie, that she's just about ready to have a baby, and that she's moved in with him and the missus. Did Bluey cook this up? Gawd, if he did, I'll fire him like a gun. What the hell does he think this is? Where are we going to put a pregnant woman? What happens if the baby turns up before we can move her back to town or wherever she comes from?"

"Shut up for a while and listen!" Ida said.

"Look, I told you before about talking to me like that!" Quinlan beat a fist into his open palm. "I'm the boss around here——"

Paddy stood up from the table. "I'm handing in me time. Nobody's gunna talk to me missus like that and get away with it. We ain't working for you any more, Quinlan. Come on, Ide. Take your apron off and chuck it in his face."

"You shut up and listen, too!" Ida said. "Now get this, Mr. Quinlan. Bluey had nothing to do with his wife coming up here. She came off her own bat and under her own steam, and I think she's a damn' brave girl to come all this way, especially when she's so close to having the baby. Mrs. Halstead asked her to stay up in the house, and she acted off her own bat, too. You men stay out of this and us women will look after it. Now that's all I've got to say and excuse my back while I get the rest of the dinner."

"Sit down, Paddy," Chilla Peters said. "Your resignation's been rejected."

Quinlan was on his way out of the hut, talking to himself. "I dunno. Talk to a man and you know where you are. I might just as well be talking to a brick wall as to her. She runs this team. It's just like being home with the wife——"

"Why don't you bring her up, too?" Turk Tuthill said; his broken nose spread across his face as he laughed. "We could start a sewing circle."

But the arrival of Liz Brown did not upset the scheme of things as much as Quinlan had expected. She was too far advanced in her condition to be of much help to Ida, but she proved to be no trouble. Mrs. Halstead came down to tell Ida that her husband had objected, mainly because he had wondered how the shearers would feel with two of the men having their wives with them when the others weren't allowed to bring theirs. But, she said with her new air of decision, she had politely told him that he and the men could go and jump in the billabong, and that Mrs. Brown was her responsibility.

"And how did he take that?" Ida said.

"It rather rocked him at first," Mrs. Halstead said. "Then I think he was rather pleased. He began to see it my way, that at last I have something around here to interest me." She smiled, her eyes shining. "You know almost overnight I've developed a proprietary interest in the Brown baby."

"Good for you," Ida said. "Have you ever thought of having one yourself? Or shouldn't I ask that?"

Mrs. Halstead picked at the sleeve of her jumper; the new air of strength suddenly left her. "I've thought about it a lot. But I had to make sure where I was going to live first. I think I must have felt a good deal like Liz Brown, when I first came out here. I came out in the train with Bob and after a while, just like Liz, I started to wonder if we would ever get here. I'd never been farther west than Katoomba before, and when we started coming across the plains, everything so dry and flat——" She walked to the window of the cookhouse and looked out. In the cold blue light of the afternoon her face reflected her thoughts: doubt and fright

were a complexion. "I wanted to go back. I didn't even
want to get out of the train when we got to Cawndilla. I
wanted to stay in it and go right back to Sydney and never
come west of the Blue Mountains again. But I didn't. Bob
asked me what I thought of it all and I told him it was perfectly marvellous." She turned her head, smiling self-consciously. "Everything down in Sydney is *perfectly marvellous*.
It just seems a foolish schoolgirl's exaggeration out here. But
anyhow, that was what I told him and I didn't want him to
think otherwise. But that very first night I decided I wouldn't
have a baby until I'd won out over this place." She looked
back at the window. "Or it had won out over me."

"And who's winning so far?" Ida said.

"I don't know." Mrs. Halstead turned away from the
window, turned her back on what she was fighting. "But I'm
still here and Bob still doesn't know. That's the main thing."

At the door Liz Brown said, "May I come in?"

The tired frightened look had gone from her face: it was
as if the ordeal was already behind her, as if she had borne
the child and found it healthy and sound: with Bluey beside
her in bed each night, the worst was now over. Ida looked at
the happiness in the thin dark-eyed face and said a prayer—
for the girl whose face was just a shadow against the light of
the window.

7

On the Saturday night Paddy came up to the cookhouse
after tea, his rebellious curls slicked down with soap and a
piece of cigarette paper stuck to his chin where he had cut
himself while shaving, and slapped Ida on the rump as she
stood at the table kneading dough for to-morrow's bread.

"How's it, darl?" He flashed the golden-toothed smile.

"What're you all dolled up for?" Ida said. "Expecting
visitors?"

Paddy rolled a cigarette very deliberately and casually.
"No-o. Just thought I'd put a clean shirt on for a change,
that's all. It's Saturday night, you know."

"How would I know? You men never stop eating, like you stop working. If you didn't eat on Sundays, I might know it was Saturday night."

"Well, you didn't have to take this job. Gawd, I tried hard enough to stop you. I didn't force you into it——"

"Nobody said you did. Keep your shirt on. Especially if it's a clean one." She stopped and looked at him. "My, you _ e a handsome beggar, aren't you? I'll bet if you were a single man now, you'd be gallivanting off into town to give the young pieces a bit of a thrill. You robbed the girls of a lot, didn't you, when you married me and decided to settle down?"

Paddy lit his cigarette and blew a smoke ring. "I told you before. I ain't interested in other women, young 'uns or old 'uns. I'm happy enough with you. And with Sean. Just having a quiet time, doing nothing in particular. Maybe having a drink with the boys now and again. But as for women——" He blew another smoke ring, then smacked it away with his hand. "Nah. You'll do me, Ide."

"So you got all dolled up for me?" Ida smiled and raised a pair of dough-encrusted hands. Paddy backed hastily away. "Well, wait'll I finish this, darl, and I'll go and have a wash and put on a clean dress. I dunno where we'll go once we're all dolled up, but we can come back here where there's plenty of light and sit and admire each other."

Sean came in the door. "Hey, Dad, are you going into town with the other blokes? They're waiting down near the truck. They said was you gunna be long?"

Paddy flung his cigarette to the floor and stamped on it. "Why don't you get lost in a wool bale some day? Why don't you get tonsilitis or laryngitis or even get something stuck in your neck? Anything, just so long's you keep outa conversations that don't concern you? You're always busting into something with your mouth wide open, yapping away——"

"Why, what've I said now?" Sean's hair was slicked down and his face shone as if it had been scrubbed with a floor brush. "Mum knows you're going. I heard you tell the blokes that you'd told her before tea that you'd be coming into town.

Clint Evans was just saying you're damn' lucky to have someone like Mum, that you can just say what you're gunna do and there's never any argument."

Ida was stretching the dough into long thin strips, running it through her fingers as if it were a rope, tying it in knots, twisting it into the shape of a hangman's noose. She appeared oblivious of the conversation going on between Paddy and Sean: she looked up as if surprised when Paddy turned to her.

"Look, darl, I didn't say nothing of the sort. I said you wouldn't mind me going in to have a coupla beers. I was just going to mention it to you, when Gabby-Guts here come busting in——"

"I thought we were going to sit here and look at each other?" Ida said. "I thought you said you'd got all dolled up for me——"

"I didn't say that! You said it. I ain't had a chance to say a flaming thing since I come in the door. Just when I look like getting a word in edgeways——"

"In comes Sean and puts your pot away," Ida said. "Well, I don't mind you going into town, but why couldn't you ask me to come along, too?" She looked at Sean. "And where are you going with your hair plastered down? You look like Rudolph Valentino's young brother. Don't tell me you're chasing after girls, too! I'm going to have a job on my hands, watching the two of you——"

Venneker filled the doorway. "Just for your information, Carmody, the truck is waiting and Quinlan is chafing at the steering wheel. Are you coming or are you staying to help your good wife bake bread?"

Ida stared at him. "Another blooming gigolo!" Venneker's mane lay on his head like a silver cap; he ran a self-satisfied hand over it. "What is this, a conspiracy or something? How long have you been cooking this up between you? I'd like to know what goes on down there in that wool shed amongst you men all day long."

Bluey Brown edged into the doorway beside Venneker; the light shone on the polished bronze of his hair. "Hey, Ida, Liz was wondering if she could come down here and sit with you.

She says you're going to be on your own, too, so you might as well keep each other company."

Paddy flung his arms wide in a gesture of despair and looked at the ceiling. "What chance has a man got? Try to have a word alone with his missus, and everyone keeps putting their spoke in, mucking up the whole works."

"What's the matter?" Bluey said. "You said just before tea——"

"I didn't say a bloody thing!" Paddy screamed; he beat his arms like a bird trying to battle its way out of a cage. "I ain't had a chance to open me trap——"

"Keep it closed then," Ida said. "You can go into town, but just remember when you've had enough. Stop drinking when you forget to pick up your change. And, Bluey, you tell Liz to come down here as soon as she likes." Then she looked at Sean again. "But that still doesn't tell me where you're going, all laired up like a sore toe."

"I was going to the flicks," Sean said. "Tom Mix is on and I ain't seen a picture in a long time and I thought you wouldn't mind and Dad said he'd pay for me——" He stopped and took a breath. "Can I go, Mum?"

Out in the yard Quinlan began to toot on the horn of the truck. There came impatient yells from the men already in the truck and, disturbed by the noise, the kelpie and several of the station dogs joined in the chorus. A minute later the truck was going down the track that led to the main road two miles away, and Ida was standing in the doorway of the cookhouse waving a dough-streaked hand and smiling broadly.

"I suppose it's safe to let them out on their own?" Liz Brown had come down the path and was standing beside her.

Ida turned. "I think so. But I don't know that I'd have let Paddy go if I'd been like you are. If I'd been you I'd have kept Bluey on the chain to-night. After all, you need your man around you at this time."

Liz followed her into the kitchen. "He didn't ask if he could go. I suggested it. I don't ever want him tied to my apron strings. I would rather he went in and celebrated in advance than wait until the baby is born. I think I should rather have him home then."

" Well, maybe you're right. I wouldn't have minded going in to see the pictures m'self to-night, only I'm too tired. And they wouldn't have wanted one woman in a truckful of men. Not if most of 'em are going to be on their ear when they're coming home." She began to pour the dough into baking tins. " But if Paddy comes home drunk he'll hear about it to-morrow."

In the truck Paddy was telling Bluey, " Now look, I ain't getting shickered to-night. I'm just coming in for a quiet booze and as soon as I look like I've had one too many I want you to tell me. Sometimes from where I stand it's a bit hard to tell."

" Well, I dunno how good I am," Bluey said. " I'm as weak as gin's water when it comes to calling a halt to the grog. I wouldn't mind having someone to look after *me*."

" I'll keep rein on the two of you," Venneker said. " As a man who has learned to hold his liquor, I can attend to my own drinking and watch those of you who don't know the difference between being happy and being helpless."

" You might be able to hold your grog," Bluey said, " but there's something else you can't hold. We'll probably have to come knocking on Mrs. Firth's door to let you know when we're coming home."

Venneker put a hand over his eyes and let out an immense moan. " Must we drink at her pub? Is there no other tavern in the town? I should not have come to-night. I should have stayed away from the town, put the woman and her temptation behind me. But no, my conscience brings me back——"

" You sure it was your conscience?" Turk Tuthill said. " That's the first time I've ever heard it called that."

" I tell you," Ocker Shand said from the darkness, " no woman ever brought any man any good."

" I'll bet that's what your father said when your mother gave birth to you," Bluey said, and laughter came out in a roar from the back of the truck.

" Hang on!" Quinlan yelled from the driving cabin, then the truck had bounced over a deep rut and in a moment was bowling along the main road towards Cawndilla.

8

"I tell you," Ocker Shand was saying, "Tibby Cotter is the fastest bowler that's ever played cricket. Jack Gregory is fast, but he's just not in Tibby's class."

"Look, I bet our Paddy Carmody is a faster shearer, and a better one, than any you got in your shed," Clint Evans was saying. "I got twenty quid that says he could towel the pants off anyone you wanna put up against him."

"My wife's gunna have a baby," Bluey Brown was saying. "He's gunna play cricket for Australia, too. I dunno whether he's gunna be a batsman or a bowler, but anyhow, he's gunna play for Australia."

"Yeah, I can sing a bit," Paddy was saying. "You ever heard *Little Town in the Old County Down?*"

"The other day when we had that fight," Turk Tuthill was saying, "you kept leading with your right all the time. That way you leave yourself wide open. Now you should always lead *this* way."

"Madam, the memory of your bell-like laughter," Venneker was saying, "kept calling me back, back here to this fine Scotch and the warm hills of your bosom."

The bar was thick with smoke: the lights glowed yellowly on the flushed faces of the men. The tangy smell of beer was as strong as the smoke: glasses sparkled like vessels of gold and patterns of froth on the counter winked like a scattering of gems. The talk was hard and loud: there was no filth, but no man had mistaken the bar for a drawing-room. In the harsh masculine atmosphere, Mrs. Firth and the one barmaid seemed out of place. Then you heard Mrs. Firth's full-bodied laugh and saw the girl's impudent eyes and you knew they were more at home here than they would have been at a ladies' tea.

Business was exceptionally brisk to-night. Beer flowed in a continuous amber stream from the taps; glasses slid along the counter as if on a production belt; the cash register tinkled like a pianola. The night was cold, a good night for drinking and arguing. All the town regulars were here to-night, and when Quinlan's team had arrived they had found the team from the neighbouring shed, the men with whom they had had the fracas on the road a fortnight before, lined up at the bar with two or three drinks already under their belts.

The fight had been forgotten: the cause of it had been too trivial to result in any lasting rancour. But that had not stopped further arguments from developing: what was the good of having a yarn with a bloke if you agreed with everything he said? Now here was one mug reckoning Charlie Macartney was a better batsman than Victor Trumper. Good Gawd——

"Anyone knows Trumper was on his own as a batsman," Ocker Shand said. "You ever see him play? Well, how would you know? Hey, Bluey, this bloke here reckons Macartney's better'n Trumper was. You seen 'em both. What d'you reckon?"

"My kid's gunna be better'n any of 'em." A grin slipped to one side on Bluey's flushed face; a hiccup chased his stumbling words. "Take note of the name, mate, for future ref'rence. Christopher. Me missus picked that: you know what women're like. Victor. I picked that: tells you what I think of Trumper as a batsman. Brown. That's me last name: Gawd knows who picked that. Christopher Victor Brown. He'll be playing for Aussie in—lemme see. Nineteen forty-four. Yeah, nineteen forty-four. He's gunna be young, but that don't matter. He'll be good enough to play when he's fourteen, but I don't wanna rush him. I'll hold him back a few years. I'm gunna see he ain't burned out too early." He took a drink and stood staring off into smoke-obscured space: he blinked and his head rolled a little unsteadily. "Gawd, it's gunna be a bloody marvellous day, the day he walks outa that members' stand at the Cricket Ground to open the innings. I'm gunna buy every bastard in the members' stand a drink. Dammit, I'll buy you one now! What'll you have?"

"I'll have a beer." The walnut-faced man had been arguing with Ocker with the same vehemence that he had argued with Quinlan on the first occasion of their meeting: the wrinkles in his face looked like a grimace of pain. "But if you reckon Macartney ain't as good as Trumper, then you dunno nothing about cricket."

"He dunno nothing 'bout cricket?" Ocker was hoarse with indignation. "Don't you know who he is? He's Bluey Brown!"

"Never heard of him," said the walnut-faced man, and took the beer Bluey pushed along towards him.

"Why, he bloody near played for Australia himself, didn't you, Bluey?" Bluey grinned modestly, but was saved from admitting how far he had been from being an international by Ocker himself. "There y'are, you see! It's only his bloody modesty, just because he ain't a skite like some people I know, that keeps him from telling you how good he is."

"Well, if he's so good," said the walnut-faced man, "why ain't he playing cricket, instead of being out here shearing sheep?"

"He's gotta live, ain't he? You ever heard of a cricketer who made as much money as a shearer? I tell you, mate, if you seen him play you'd know how good he is."

"Well, I'd like to see him play, that's all I say. I don't believe nothing I ain't seen."

"You didn't see Victor Trumper and you reckon he ain't much good!"

"That's different," said the walnut-faced man with a near-drunk's logic. "I'd just like to see this bloke play, that's all I say."

Ocker banged his fist on the counter, making the glasses jump.

"Righto, hold your horses!" the barmaid said. "I'll get to you in a minute."

Ocker looked at her blankly, then turned back to the walnut-faced man and banged the counter again. "Gawd Almighty, you *will* see him play! I tell you, we'll get a team from our shed and we'll come over and play your mob and if Bluey here don't get a century, I'll give you five quid!"

"Taken," said the walnut-faced man.

Farther down the bar Clint Evans was well on the way towards making another bet. "Righto, so you think this bloke of yours is pretty good, eh? Well, our Paddy Carmody's been doing better'n two hundred sheep a day ever since we started. I got twenty quid says he can beat this Herb Cooper of yours. We'll arrange it any way you like. Paddy'll come to your shed, your bloke can come over to ours, or we'll have a referee at each shed. I don't care how it's organised. I just wanna show you, you're talking through your neck. This bloke Carmody's the best man I seen with the clippers in a long, long time. I ain't interested so much in winning the money——"

Paddy was saying, " Well, I'll sing if you want me to. I don't like to push me voice on to anyone. It ain't everyone who likes a good song, sung the way it should be. What would you like? How 'bout *Little Town in the Old County Down*? You don't hear that much these days. Everybody's singing all them jazz pieces. I like a good ballad, meself. Well, here goes."

Venneker, bent almost double as he leaned down on the bar to talk into Mrs. Firth's ear, straightened up as the first sob-torn notes of *Little Town in the Old County Down* rose like a covey of wounded quail above the general hubbub. Then abruptly he leaned down towards Mrs. Firth again. " Let us away, Bugle Voice. There are things I must say that can't be said in this atmosphere."

" I wish I could, Rupe," Mrs. Firth said wistfully. " But I can't leave the till. Who'd ring up the money?"

" What is money beside love?" Venneker said. " Is a cash register my rival for your affections? Come upstairs and press me and hear the music I shall play."

Mrs. Firth quivered with laughter. " Crikey, you're a one, Rupe! But I can't buzz off just yet. Wait a while. Have a drink of water and cool yourself off."

" You talk as if the fire of my passion were just a schoolboy's flush. It is not to be cooled off. It is to be stoked up. Give me another Scotch."

" Well, hullo, Gert! Here I am back again and did you miss me while I was gone?" The portly man elbowed his way up to the bar beside Venneker; he reached across and patted Mrs. Firth's arm with a hand that looked like a bunch of sausages. " Gawd Almighty, I missed you, Gert! Been every bloody where, never thought I was going to get back home, kept saying to myself wonder what's Gert up to to-night? Course I knew you wouldn't be up to anything, knew you'd be missing your old Jack. How you been, love? How's the cold on the chest? How's the chest? Gawd Almighty, I missed you, Gert! Well, I'm back again. You miss me while I was gone?"

"No," said Venneker. "Nor would we miss you if you had cause to be gone again."

The newcomer turned and looked up at Venneker, his plump owl's face with its horn-rimmed spectacles blown out with surprise. "Who the hell was talking to you? Who's this, Gert? Where'd he spring from? Gawd Almighty, away from town a coupla months and the place is over-run with strangers!"

Mrs. Firth rang up the cash register, handed the barmaid some change, then turned back to the counter. "Hullo, Jack." There was no enthusiasm in her voice: she could have been greeting a creditor. "How was the trip?"

"I just told you! " The portly man seemed to talk in con-tinual exclamations. "Gawd Almighty, I missed you, Gert! Who's this?"

"This is Rupe Venneker, Jack," said Mrs. Firth. "Rupe, this is Jack Patchogue, the district magistrate."

"That all I am to you, Gert, just the district magistrate? How are you, Venneker, pleased to meet you! Gertcher, Gert, you're only pulling the man's leg! Tell him who I really am!"

"Jack is a friend, Rupe," Mrs. Firth said. "Sorta."

Venneker leaned down on the bar. "Madam, I came in from the back-blocks to-night to see you. First, I've had to compete with a cash register for your attention and affec-tions——"

Mrs. Firth laughed and winked at Patchogue. "Rupe's a real card, Jack. You're gunna die laughing at him."

"—and now this long-winded law clerk, this sort of friend of yours, comes busting in, wasting my valuable time——"

"Gawd Almighty!" Patchogue took off his spectacles; his face was suddenly as blank as a billiard ball. "Hark at

him! What's been going on while my back's been turned?
You been having me on?"

"Now hold your horses, Jack Patchogue!" Mrs. Firth
turned away, rang up the cash register, then turned back
again. "Nobody ever said anything about us tracking square
with one another! I'm free and over twenty-one and how I
spend me time is me own business! That's the worst of you
men. Give you an inch and you wanna move in and own
the whole caboose. Now you listen to me——"

"I'll wait for you upstairs, my bar-room-tulip," said Venneker, and tossed off the last of his Scotch. "Don't keep me
waiting too long. Good-night, Patchogue. It has been almost
a pleasure meeting you."

Down the street in the School of Arts hall, Sean was
perched on the edge of a canvas chair engrossed in the
adventures of Tom Mix. The cross-bar of the chair had cut
a deep welt in his behind, but if he sat back in the deep-
seated chair he could not see above the head of the massive
stately woman in front of him. And the picture was too
good to miss. Of course he didn't believe any of it, he knew
just as well as anyone that it was all made up, but it got you
in, all right. But this bloke Mix seemed to go looking for
trouble, and he was getting a bit tired of seeing him tearing
up and down hills on his horse Tony. It would have been
all right if Mix had been something of a rider, but he wasn't
in the same class as Sean's old man. And that saddle he had!
Cripes, even an old lady couldn't fall out of that. Still, he
was pretty good with a gun, or he looked to be pretty good.
Maybe they just slowed the picture up while he drew it from
his holster. That way he'd look pretty fast on the draw.

Mix and Tony came sliding down the screen from one
corner to another, and were lost momentarily behind the
woman in front. Sean swung to the right side of his chair
and picked them up again.

"Righto, son. Keep still," said a voice from the back.
"Tom Mix don't need your help."

Mix was now galloping across the screen. Down at the
front of the hall a woman was galloping up and down the
piano. At the back of the hall the town larrikins began

galloping in their seats. The picture cut to a scene of the heroine, wide-eyed and dishevelled, bound in a chair in a deserted hut. Suddenly she turned her head and looked off-screen.

"She's heard us!" a voice yelled from the back of the hall. "Stick to it, love! We're on our way!"

Then the woman in front of Sean stood up, shaking her head and clicking her tongue in disgust. The screen was gone from view as completely as if the back wall of the hall had fallen out. Sean wove from side to side, trying desperately to see, but the people on either side of him hemmed him in.

"Siddown in front!" a voice shouted. "Who paid to look at you, Mrs. Murphy?"

Mrs. Murphy paid no heed. Deliberately, still blocking the screen for those people in line with her as far back as six rows, she searched for her hat and gloves. Sean was bouncing on his seat in an agony of curiosity. The pianist was no longer galloping, but seemed to be doing her best to smash the keyboard to pieces. At the back of the hall now there were yells and grunts and whistles.

"Do him, Tom! You'll do me, you beaut!"

Then Mrs. Murphy had found her gloves. Slowly she began .o work her way out of the row of chairs as the pianist, exhausted, came to a thundering climax. For a moment there was silence, then there came the slow romantic music that Sean knew meant the end of the picture. He didn't even look at the screen; in disgust he got up and followed Mrs. Murphy down the aisle, wishing he had the nerve to kick her in her big swaying behind. Wasn't it enough to nark a bloke? Nearly four months since he had seen a picture and then he had to m s the most exciting part, all because of a big fat tart who didn't like people enjoying themselves.

He came out into the cold clear night and was almost knocked off his feet by Halstead, the boss of Wattle Run, as the latter came hurrying down the street.

"Sean!" Halstead grabbed him by the shoulder. "Where's your dad and the rest of them? What pub are they in?"

"They're over at Mrs. Firth's place." Sean wanted to

struggle away from Halstead's fierce grip, but he was afraid to; Halstead was as excited as if the homestead were on fire. "What's the matter, Mr. Halstead?"

"Bluey's wife is having her baby." Halstead was already crossing the road towards the Firth hotel. He looked down, surprised that he was still clutching Sean by the shoulder, and let go. "Sorry. I've been tearing round ever since she first got her pains. I can't get the doctor. He's out of town and he can't get back. The Cawndilla is in flood, washed away the bridge at Baker's Crossing, and he's stuck out at Mooney's Run."

"What's she gunna do?"

"Your mother and my wife look like being the midwives. I just hope your mother knows something about it."

Then they had pushed open the door of the bar and were looking in on the noisy, arguing crowd of men. Halstead looked around, then yelled, "Is Bluey Brown here?"

Silence dropped like a lid on the room. Everyone turned towards the door, then from the back of the bar Bluey said in a thick wobbly voice, "Who wants Bluey Brown?"

It was Sean who gave him the news. He couldn't contain himself: it burst from him like the announcement of a world-shattering event. "Your wife's having the baby!"

For a moment the silence was so heavy the room strained with it, then Bluey let out a full-throated shout that wouldn't have been out of place at a corroboree.

"It's come at last! Victor Trumper, you've had your day!"

9

Ida paused at the door for a moment as she came back into the bedroom. Earlier she had turned down the lamp that stood like an immense stylised mushroom on the chest of drawers, and in the shadowed room firelight taunted the dark corners. There was a low sharp moan from the bed and an arm came up in a convulsive movement: the fire suddenly blazed in the grate and for a moment the star-fingered hand was red, as if with pain. Then the fire just as suddenly subsided, the hand folded into itself, and the arm sank back into the shadows of the bed. Ida came into the room and put the towels she was carrying on a chair.

She wasn't comfortable in this room. She had noticed the feeling, without really putting her finger on what had troubled her, as soon as she had come up here from the cookhouse almost an hour ago. She didn't feel uncomfortable only in this room: in the rest of the house through which she had passed the feeling had persisted.

There was another moan from the bed and she turned, concern clouding her face. "How is it, Liz? Is he making a start?"

"Not yet. I don't think so." Liz Brown spoke with her lips almost closed: the clipped accent was blurred with pain. "How long will Bluey be?"

"Not long. He should be here soon."

"Why doesn't he come?" A fist beat fretfully on the bed. "Why doesn't he come home?"

Ida, hanging a couple of towels over the end of the bed where they would be easier to reach, stopped and looked around the room again. That was the trouble: the place had no feel of home. Bluey could come back from Cawndilla to this room where his wife was struggling in labour, but he wouldn't be coming home: Ida felt it was no more of a home to him than it was to the people who owned it. Throughout the whole house there was nothing that suggested the identifiable living of particular people: it had the barren personality of a room meant only for passers-by, people who hadn't come to stay. The tall dark wardrobe with the full-length mirror in which the fire glowed coldly; the chest of drawers with the white china knobs that somehow reminded her of giant staring eyes; the wide double bed with its brass glinting without warmth and its spring muttering metallically with every movement of Liz's body; the plain green polished linoleum and the darker green mats, like strips of preserved turf, beside the bed; it all had the impersonal stiffness of a shop window. You looked for price labels, then realised the window was already a home: the owner had just forgotten to move in.

A long shuddering moan burst from Liz; she seemed to chew on the sound as it came out of her. She flung an arm behind her head and it smacked against the brass bars of the bed: the room shivered with the sound.

Ida moved to the head of the bed. "There's nothing I can do to help you, Liz. It's a terrible thing, isn't it? This is the part you always have to do on your own. Pills don't help at a time like this." Her smile was as weak as the joke. "All you can do is pray. Though this is one time you wonder if there *is* a God. *I* believe there's one, but a woman can't be blamed for anything she thinks at a time like this."

Liz rolled her head on the pillow. Her eyes were closed and her lips were clamped tightly between her teeth; shadows lay in her face, making her old. Her legs moved convulsively, like animals trapped beneath the suffocating blankets. She opened her mouth and for a moment the breath hissed from the back of her throat before she spoke.

"God, I never knew it was going to be like this." She turned her head and looked up at Ida: pain was a scum on her eyes. "How long does it go on?"

Ida wiped the sweat from Liz's face with one of the towels. "I don't know, Liz. It's different with every woman. I had a hard time with Sean, but then I know some women who were all through in less than an hour."

Liz went to speak, waited, then shut her eyes and lay stiffly with both hands behind her head clutching the bars of the bed. The mound of her body beneath the blankets suddenly quivered: a cry was strangled at the back of her throat and came out through her lips as a thin pitiful moan. After a while she opened her eyes and looked up at Ida again.

"How long were you with Sean? How long?"

"Now look, Liz, it doesn't matter how long I took. It's different with every woman——"

"*How long?*" Liz was screaming; the bed rattled in a wild clangour as she shook it. "*How long?*"

There was the swift clatter of heels down the hall outside and Mrs. Halstead came running into the room. "What's the matter? Is it now? Goodness, I didn't expect it——"

Liz stared wide-eyed at both women, then her head rolled over and she began to weep. "Why doesn't the doctor come? Why doesn't he come?"

From outside in the yard there came the sound of an arriving car. A dog barked, a voice called to it, then the engine of the car was cut dead. Mrs. Halstead looked at Ida, nodded, then turned and went quickly out of the room and down the hall.

"It's all right now, Liz," Ida said. "It's the doctor. Mr. Halstead has just brought him out from town."

"Is Bluey with him?" Liz seemed ashamed of her tears; she kept her face turned away from Ida. "Can I see him for just a moment?"

The dog began to bark again and was joined by one or two others. Then there was the painful sound of a truck labouring up the rise from the paddocks, and behind it another sound that slowly emerged as the raucous singing of men who had stood too close to a bar for too long. The truck growled its way over the crest of the rise into the yard and the sound of its engine died away in the singing.

A caricature of a smile flickered on Liz's face. "Some-one's happy."

"Someone should tell them to pull their heads in," Ida said. "Do they think you're just sitting in here with your hands folded on your tummy, not feeling a damn' thing, but just waiting for something to happen? Men are so blasted thoughtless——" She picked up a slab of wood and poked it into the fire: sparks were reflected in her eyes. "Ah, what's the use? My Sean will probably grow up to be the same way. See you produce a girl, Liz."

"I don't care what it is," Liz said. "Just so long as it hurries up."

The singing stopped on a high note that rent the night like a knife running through tight silk; for a moment there was silence, then a shout rang out. "Good old Bluey! Good old Liz! You'll do me, you beauts!"

The dogs continued to bark and someone whistled loudly between his teeth. A grim look came over Ida's face and she started towards the door, only to stop as Mrs. Halstead came back into the room. Outside in the yard someone yelled, *Shut up, you lotta mugs!* but Ida didn't hear him. She stared at Mrs. Halstead, saw her shake her head, the beautiful face blank with dismay, then she turned back to Liz and said, " I won't be a minute, Liz. I'll go and get Bluey for you."

Outside in the hall Mrs. Halstead whispered that her husband hadn't been able to get the doctor. " What are we going to do?"

It had taken Ida only a moment to regain her composure. " We'll have to deliver it ourselves, that's all. But she'd like to see Bluey. Where's he?"

" Outside with my husband."

" Would you ask him to come in? She'll feel a little better if she can see him for a minute."

" He's drunk." Mrs. Halstead looked at the point of surrender : the situation was too much for her. " Bob has got him out in the yard, with two of the men holding him up. She shouldn't see him as he is now."

" Men!" Ida swung a fist against an open palm : the smack was like a whipcrack in the narrow hall. " God, if we could only do without them! How drunk is he? Can we sober him up?"

" Not before morning, I think." Mrs. Halstead looked towards the door of the bedroom; tears made her eyes shine. " That poor girl."

" Watch her for a moment," Ida said. " Don't tell her yet about the doctor. Or Bluey, either."

She went down the hall, walking quickly and determinedly, and out on to the veranda. She pulled her cardigan closer across her breast and did up the top button. She was still flushed with the warmth of the bedroom and her disgust with men and Bluey in particular : the night air pressed against her face with the coldness of bleached stone. She walked along the veranda and stopped opposite the laughing wavering men clustered by the back of the truck.

" G'day, darl." Paddy came out of the group on rubbery legs; Ida leaned away from his beery breath. " They tell me Liz's had a baby. Ain't that just like a woman? Always picks

the night-time. Why couldn't she had it in the day-time?
In the boss' time." He spun round towards the men. "Hey,
youse blokes! We oughta report Liz to the union. She's
labouring in her own time!"

Ida stepped down from the veranda and swung her open
hand against Paddy's ear. He let out a howl and twirled
round to face her, but she silenced him before he could say a
word. "I'll talk to you later! Sean?"

"Yeah, Mum?" Sean appeared out of the group of men.

"Take your father down to the cookhouse and give him
two or three cups of sweet tea. Keep giving it to him till
he's sick." Paddy went to say something, struggling for lost
authority, but she took him by the shoulder and pushed him
on his way, and he went down the slope followed by Sean.
Then Ida turned to the men. "Where's Bluey?"

The group of men parted and revealed Bluey propped up
against the back of the truck, a man on each side of him
supporting him by the elbows. One of the men nudged him
and he raised his head from his chest and gazed owlishly
about him. Then he focused on Ida.

"Well, stone the bloody crows, if it ain't old Ida! How's
the missus, Ida? She want any help?"

Ida looked ready to spit. "You ought to be ashamed of
yourself."

"Oh, I am, Ida. I am." Bluey bowed his head and struck
himself violently on the chest; he collapsed and the men had
to struggle to keep him on his feet. "Weak with remorse,
Ida. Not fit to be a daddy."

Ida looked about her. "Where's Rupe Venneker?"

"Well, how's the bastard's form!" someone said incredulously; in the moonlight Ida recognised the slightly unsteady
figure of Turk Tuthill. "He ain't with us! He must of
stayed in town with Cushion-Bosom."

"I tell you," said the lugubrious voice of Ocker Shand, "a
man ain't safe when there's a woman around."

"I wish I had a gun right now," Ida snapped. "I'd prove
you were right!"

Halstead came along the veranda. "Is that you, Mrs.
Carmody? Did my wife tell you I couldn't get the doctor?"

"What's that?" Bluey tried to struggle away from the two men supporting him; they had to grab him to keep him on his feet. "Where's the quack? Why ain't he here? Is the bastard drunk somewhere?"

"Mrs. Carmody!" Mrs. Halstead was standing in the doorway. "Come quickly!"

Ida turned and ran along the veranda, past Mrs. Halstead as the latter held the door open and down the hall. Even before she came into the room she could hear Liz moving in agony on the bed; the squeak of the springs almost drowned out her moans. As Ida came into the room, Liz cried out loud.

"Oh, Christ, it's coming!"

As Ida turned up the lamp, Mrs. Halstead came in with a big jug of hot water. She poured it into a basin on the dressing-table. Ida scrubbed her hands, then turned towards the bed. Liz lay with staring eyes and bitten lips; her face shone with yellow sweat in the bright light of the lamp.

"Where's the doctor?" she whispered.

"He couldn't come." Ida busied herself, getting things close to hand. "But don't you worry. You just get on with having the baby."

Suddenly Liz had another spasm. Her body quivered and her legs shot out as if she were trying to kick them off. Her hands went back over her head and grasped the rails of the bed. She pulled herself taut, moaning with agony, then an obscenity burst like a bubble from her white lips. The spasm lasted for what seemed a long time, while Ida and Mrs. Halstead stood silently and helplessly at the side of the bed, then at last it had gone. Liz slumped in her bed, her whole body seeming to collapse about the mound of her stomach.

She lay for a moment, her eyes closed and her mouth moving in and out as she panted. Then she opened pain-darkened eyes and looked up at them: "I'm trying to be brave. But I can't."

"It's all right, Liz," Mrs. Halstead said: in her own face there seemed to be a reflection of the pain in Liz's face. "Don't worry about anything but getting it over."

"Where's Bluey?" Liz said. "Can't I see him?"

"He's out in the kitchen helping Mr. Halstead keep the stove going," Ida said. "This is no place for him now, Liz. We'll bring him in as soon as the baby arrives."

Outside in the yard there was suddenly a shout, then a loud swearing. Voices were raised in argument and the dogs joined in the chorus. Then the voices died away, going down the hill towards the men's quarters, and as they did, Liz abruptly and shrilly screamed. Her body seemed to leap from the bed, and again the bed clanged as she flung her arms behind her to grasp the rails. Ida whipped the blankets back.

"Strain for all you're worth, Liz! It's coming at last!" Ida grabbed some towels and shoved them under Liz. "Some more towels, Mrs. Halstead! Quick!"

But Mrs. Halstead was standing quite still by the side of the bed, her face stiff with frightened revulsion and one hand tearing like a claw at the breast of her sweater. Ida stood up for just a moment, then she leant across the bed and slapped Mrs. Halstead hard across the shoulder. Mrs. Halstead jumped and caught her breath, then turned her head quickly and looked at Ida.

Ida wasn't looking at her. "Quickly, get me some more towels! It'll be here in a minute or two. Hold on, Liz. Hold on to me. Yell your head off if you like. But keep straining. It's coming."

She heard Mrs. Halstead move across the room behind her, then felt towels being pushed into her hands. She turned her attention to the lower part of Liz's body, and again felt, rather than saw, Mrs. Halstead move in behind her to comfort Liz. The room reeked of smoke from the fire, Liz's sweat and the blood of the birth. The fire had died down; the only sound in the room was the moaning of Liz, sometimes obscene, and the soothing murmur of Mrs. Halstead. Ida said nothing; she worked quietly and gently as the baby came into the world through pain and suffering of which it would never know, for it was a boy.

"The knife!" Ida said, and felt it pushed into her hand almost as soon as she spoke. Then she was aware of Mrs.

Halstead leaning over beside her; for a moment she thought
Mrs. Halstead was about to faint, then she saw that she was
blocking off the view of the knife from Liz. Quickly she
turned and nodded appreciatively at Mrs. Halstead, then she
had cut the cord and the baby was on its own, smeared with
the blood of its mother and blind to the battle ahead.

Ida lifted it by its heels and slapped it. For a moment
there was only silence in the room, the vast and ultimate
silence of the moment between living and not living, then
the baby whimpered and suddenly broke into full-throated
howling.

Ida turned towards the bed. "It's a boy, Liz! As healthy
and big as they make 'em!"

Liz smiled weakly, joy breaking through the cobwebs of
pain on her face, then weakness and suffering finally overcame her and her head rolled loosely on the pillow.

"She's fainted!" Mrs. Halstead exclaimed, and she looked
ready to collapse herself.

"Let her be," Ida said. "She'll be all right when she
comes out of it. Let's get the baby fixed up."

Mrs. Halstead visibly took control of herself again; she
straightened up and came towards Ida with her arms held
out. "Let me look after him. Please."

"This is as good a time as any to start learning," Ida said,
and gave her the baby. "Don't let what you've seen to-night
turn you off having a baby of your own. It's a lot of pain
and trouble, but it's worth every minute of it. I know."

Some time later, when Ida had bathed her and put her in
a clean nightgown and Mrs. Halstead had laid the baby in
the crook of her arm, Liz asked again for Bluey. Ida, after
hesitating for a moment, went out of the room and in a
little while returned with Bluey.

He came into the bedroom almost as if he were walking
into a court-room. He was white-faced and red-eyed; there
even seemed to be hollows in his plump cheeks. Gone was
all his brash cheerfulness; he was as quiet and hesitant as a
man about to be sentenced to be hanged.

Liz smiled at him from the bed. "My, what on earth has
happened to you? You look like a nervous wreck."

" It's played havoc with his system," Ida said. " He's been out there in the kitchen, giving you moral support. Look what it did to him."

" He looks worse than I must look," Liz said. She raised a hand and Bluey took it. " Darling, I didn't think you would take it as badly as this. You look like the new fathers in *Punch*. But it was worth it, Bluey." She turned her head to look at the baby beside her. " We got what we wanted, darling. Look at him. Christopher Victor Brown."

Bluey spoke at last; his voice came out of a throat round which the rope might already have been tightening. " He's a red-faced little bastard, isn't he?"

Outside in the hall Mrs. Halstead was saying, " But how on earth did they sober him up?"

" I don't know," Ida said, closing the bedroom door behind her. " When I got to the front door, they were coming up from the cookhouse with him. Turk Tuthill just said, ' There's enough to show his missus. The rest of him is down the hill.' So I grabbed him and brought him in. But unless he wants to tell her, she need never know he was drunk to-night."

" She looked happy, didn't she?"

" She couldn't have looked any other way. It was what they both wanted." Ida took off her apron: delivering the baby had been just another chore in the day's work. " Well, I'd better go down and see if my lesser half has sobered up. Gawd help him if he hasn't."

10

" Hey, Paddy," Clint Evans said, " I forgot to tell you in the excitement of the baby. I fixed it up for you to race this bloke over at Mulgrue's shed."

The men were sitting and lolling about the hut. Outside, a cold wind stampeded up the slope; trees bent vainly, holding desperately to fleeing leaves. Through the window the sky was streaked with thin cloud: against the pane it looked like sleet. Four of the men were playing cards; the rest lay about in odd restless attitudes. Most of Sunday was behind them: there was nothing to do but wait for to-morrow and work. Now that they were well into the routine of the shed, most of them would have preferred to sacrifice the Sunday lay-off for the chance of earning extra money. A day off, with nothing to fill in your time, wasn't much use to a man. Especially a day like to-day, with a wind cold enough to freeze the brass monkeys and everyone with a bit of a hangover from last night.

"You hear what I said, Paddy?" Clint was mending a rent in a pair of trousers; he handled the bag needle and the twine with careful, delicate skill. "When you gunna race this bloke over at Mulgrue's?"

"I'm dropping out." Paddy was sitting on Bluey Brown's bed glancing through an old *Bulletin*. "Better get someone else."

Clint looked up, and drove the end of the needle into his hand. "Holy Jesus!" He dropped the trousers and sucked on his hand; still with his hand in his mouth he said, "Wuddia mee you dupping out?"

"I ain't in the mood," Paddy said. "I don't want you risking your money on me."

Clint took his hand from his mouth. "What's the matter, Paddy? Cripes, you ain't dingoing it, are you? You can't toss in the towel now. I already bet one bloke twenty quid. I ain't got that sorta money to toss away on *any* shearer. There ain't anyone else in this shed I'd let carry that much cash for me. Waddia mean you ain't in the mood? Christ, who are you? Nellie Melba?"

Sean, lying on his stomach on his bed reading *Kidnapped*, lent to him by Mrs. Halstead, looked up at his father. He had been aware of something wrong all day. His father had come here to the hut right after breakfast and had only left it to go over to the cookhouse for dinner. When Sean had gone over to the cookhouse during the morning he had noticed that his mother, too, was quiet and had something on her mind. The old feeling of being lost had come back again. Neither of them had had a word for him.

He watched his father covertly, trying to read something

into the lean stony face staring blank-eyed down at the pink-covered *Bulletin*. All of a sudden it struck him that he was looking at the face of a stranger. He looked about him, scared : the hut was full of strangers. Then the unfamiliar face broke into the familiar smile.

" I ain't being temperamental, Clint," Paddy said. " But I just don't feel like straining a gut to see if I can shear more sheep than some other bloke. At least, I don't feel like that to-day."

" Well, I don't want you to shear against him to-day." Clint sucked at his hand again and bent to pick up the trousers from the floor. " I thought we might make it Wednesday. Or how about Saturday? That ud give you Sunday to get over it, in case you gotta work flat out to beat him."

" Can't make it Saturday," Ocker Shand said from the table; he had just drawn a hand that would give him *nap* in another minute or so, but he looked no happier. " We're playing cricket against Mulgrue's shed on Sunday. We all gotta be fresh for the game."

" Who's playing cricket?" Clint said. " When did you drum this up?"

" Last night at the pub," Ocker said. " I bet a bloke Bluey ud score a century. I bet him a fiver."

Sean had gone back to his book, but Alan Breck had lost all interest for him and soon he could no longer see the pages. He closed the book and rolled over on his back, closing his eyes as if he were dozing off. He was far from sleepy; what he had just seen had made him acutely and painfully wide awake. It had never occurred to him before that there might come a time when he could look with the eye of a stranger on his mother and father. They had all lived the one small life for so long : they were just a trinity and he had never imagined it would ever be any other way. But just a minute ago he had looked at his father and had not recognised or understood anything he had seen in the lean dark-eyed face. And now that he thought back on it, his mother had had the same grave isolated look about her,

A look of deep inner worry, as if each of them had a problem into which he didn't enter at all.

His first feeling was one of resentment, a repetition of the feeling he had had the night of the party at the hotel in Cawndilla. They had excluded him from something; he retreated into himself, hurt and bitter. Then the old sense of shame came back and he tried to brush away the fog of bitterness. His mother had always taught him to be fair-minded: the lesson came to her own defence. It occurred to him suddenly that this break-up of the old close feeling hadn't come without warning: it had begun the moment they had joined the shearing team. He opened his eyes and looked about the hut; these were the men who were coming between him and his mother and father. But he couldn't hate them. For the first time, without knowing what they were, but scared of the insidious way they worked, he was aware of the influences in one's life.

This wasn't the first time the family had worked in a shed. But in the past he had been too young to have a real job and his mother had never signed on for a full-time job as cook. They had been together, perhaps helping in the pens while Paddy worked inside the shed, and the influence of the other shearers hadn't touched them. Paddy hadn't usually been able to stomach more than a week or a fortnight's work and they had soon been on their way again, together as much as before.

But this was different. They had been at Wattle Run a month now, and they hadn't really been together once in all that time. Every time they ate there were so many others at the table; at night he slept here in the hut while his mother and father slept in the tent behind the cookhouse: somehow it had always been too far to go and say good-night; during the day he worked so hard there was no time to talk at all. In the past month he had had nothing to tell his mother and father and nothing to ask them. All at once he realised the only people he had talked to in the last few weeks had been Venneker and Bluey Brown.

"Hey, get a load of this." Chilla Peters was standing at

the window : his arid voice wasn't capable of showing surprise, but the men knew something was up. "Here comes Rupe in style."

The men moved quickly : anything to relieve the boredom of the day. Clint flung open the door and leaned out against the wind. He shivered and tried to come back into the hut for his jacket, but the push of men behind him sent him out into the yard. They stood in a tight group outside the door, oblivious of the wind and the cold, staring in admiration at Venneker.

He had got out of the driver's seat of the brand-new Hupmobile and had walked round to help Mrs. Firth out. He had regained something of his magnificent air : there was a mixture of baron and butler in the way he had got out of the car and walked round to fling open the door. He held Mrs. Firth's hand and bowed slightly; she stepped down from the running-board with her head held high and her bosom trembling with a suppressed giggle.

Venneker slammed the door of the car and turned to the men in front of the hut. " Can't a man bring his friend visiting without being subjected to the gawping stares of an asylum of village idiots?"

" Don't take any notice of him," Mrs. Firth said. " I know you ain't looking at me. You're looking at me new car. Ain't it a beaut? I only got it on Wednesday. All the way up from Sydney. I feel like Lady Muck, a real blooming toff."

" It's a bit of all right," Clint said, and began to walk round the car : his face was suddenly screwed up with shrewdness. " I've always liked the Hup."

" You'd like anything with four wheels," Turk Tuthill said. " Never even owned a push-bike, and he always liked the Hupmobile."

Ocker Shand was following Clint around the car. "I dunno, a car is better than walking, I suppose. But sometimes it's more trouble than it's worth. What happens when you have a puncture?"

" You turn it in and get a new 'un," Turk said.

" Mrs. Firth has come out to see the new baby," Venneker said. " I suppose it put in an appearance and last night's excitement wasn't a false alarm?"

" Yeah, it was a boy," one of the men said. " Here comes Bluey and the boss now."

Halstead and Bluey came down the path from the homestead. Halstead had lost the harassed, irritable air he had worn last night; he said something to Bluey and grinned, then came on down smiling outright.

" Well, who owns the hearse?" he said. " This yours, Rupe?"

Venneker looked as if he were about to spit a sarcastic retort, but thought better of it and instead turned and bowed towards Mrs. Firth. " It belongs to the good woman here. And I must say it complements her admirably."

Mrs. Firth waved a deprecating hand at him, then smiled at Halstead. " Hullo, Mr. Halstead. Just thought I'd come out and see how the new baby was getting along, seeing as how I had to drive Rupe home. He missed the bus last night."

" Like hell he did," Paddy whispered to Chilla Peters beside him. " I'll bet they didn't sit up all night talking."

" He does all right for himself," Chilla croaked back. " None of the sheilas I ever slept with drove me home next day."

" Would you like to go up to the house?" Halstead said. " Mrs. Brown is up there. My wife and Mrs. Carmody are with her. Just knock at the front door."

" I'll do that," Mrs. Firth said. " I just love kids. Always wanted a dozen of me own, but never got round to it somehow. Crikey, we oughta have a party, you know. A christening party. I'll talk to the women about it. Oh, congratulations, Bluey. Bet you was pleased it was a boy. Well, I'll see you later, Rupe. Don't sell the car while I'm gone."

She went up the path, one hand holding her hat to her head, still talking, her words whirled away into the distance by the wind that caught at her short-skirted coat and exposed her plump silk-clad legs to the men standing looking after her. At the top of the path she turned and waved to them, then she was gone into the house.

One of the men sighed deeply. "And here's me looking with lustful eyes on a sheep. How do you manage it, Rupe?"

"Finesse," said Venneker, "and experience. But don't let's sully the good woman's name by discussing her. Let's be gentlemen."

"You'll do me, Rupe," Halstead said, and laughed: he hadn't been as friendly as this with the men since their arrival. "But where's Quinlan?"

"He's gone down to the paddocks," Clint said. "He wanted to check on the sheep coming in to-morrow. Boss, there was something we wanted to ask you. How do you feel about Paddy Carmody here racing against a bloke from over at Mulgrue's shed? I mean having a race with the clippers?"

Halstead looked at Bluey. "I'm not keen on the idea. You're the union man, Bluey. Did you know anything about this?"

Bluey shook his head. "Clint mentioned it once before, but nothing had been done about it." He turned to Clint. "You haven't been to see the team at Mulgrue's, have you?"

"I saw 'em last night," Clint said. "I already put twenty quid of me own cash on. They reckon they can dig up a hundred quid for us to cover."

"Well, I wish you'd held off a while," Bluey said. "Until we'd seen Mr. Halstead. Paddy's a good fast shearer, but for all we know, this other bloke might be just a mangler."

"You always stand a chance of the sheep being knocked about when there's a race on," Halstead said. "Even if the man is a good shearer."

Clint was disappointed, but he hadn't given up hope. "Oh, we'd make sure this other bloke knew his job. And we can rely on Paddy."

"I told you," Paddy said. "I'd sooner you got someone else. I don't wanna work me guts out just to say I'm faster than some other coot."

"Ah, you're just saying that now." Clint tried to brush off Paddy's objection with a casual wave of the hand. But he was beginning to show signs of panic: here he was with a sure win on his hands, and everyone seemed to be against him. "You'll be raring to go, Wednesday."

"Don't you want to be in it, Paddy?" Bluey said.

"Course he does," Clint said quickly. "We all wanna be in it. I was just talking to the blokes. They all got some money they wanna lay on Paddy. He's just being modest. Come on, boss. Tell you what. If they cut any sheep, knock it around at all, we'll chuck in to replace it. You couldn't get any fairer than that."

Halstead said nothing. This wasn't going to be a good season and he had got that way over the last couple of months of the drought that he had been counting almost every sheep. The sheep were still feeling the effects of the drought, although they had picked up fairly well since the rain, and a careless shearer, intent only on speed, could quite easily knock them around. But these were a good team of men and he didn't want to antagonise them. They were just as independent as he, probably more so: they could walk off the job, but he couldn't walk off Wattle Run.

"Quit thinking about it, boss," Paddy said. "I ain't racing anyone, so that's all there is to it."

Sean looked quickly at his father: there was a note of temper in Paddy's voice. Everyone recognised it; a stiff silence settled on the group. Sean felt a flush of embarrassment; he looked from his father to Venneker and back again. Suddenly he wanted to help his father, but Paddy wasn't looking for help; he turned and walked across the yard and disappeared into the tent behind the cookhouse.

"Well, that settles that," said Halstead, and turned and went back up towards the house.

Clint was staring across at the tent, billowing as the wind slapped at it. "The dingoing bastard! Christ Almighty, did you see that? Here'm I, up for twenty —— quid, and he backs out like a yellow-livered quean! I oughta go and knock his —— head off."

"Take it easy," Bluey said. "Maybe he's got his reasons."

"Got his reasons?" Clint's thin face was livid beneath his tan: it had been money in his pocket, and now Paddy had welshed on him. "Christ, didn't the lousy bastard say he'd race the bloke from Mulgrue's? Why didn't he have his reasons before I put me money up? How'm I gunna look, going over there to tell 'em the bet's off, our bloke's gone temperamental on us?"

Sean walked away from the group. He had gone almost half-way towards the tent before he hesitated, then turned and began to walk slowly down the hill. The cold wind was sharp against his face; tears stung the corners of his eyes.

"Do you feel like company or would you rather walk alone?" Venneker had come after him.

"Oh, hullo, Rupe." He looked up, then back at the ground; he shoved his hands deep into his trousers pockets and kept walking. "We were wondering where you'd got to."

"You all knew damn' well where I'd got to," Venneker said. "You were wondering what I was doing, that was all."

"How are you doing with Mrs. Firth?" He really didn't care: anything to talk about while he tried to sort out the jumble in his mind. "I thought you weren't gunna see her again?"

"That was the intention," Venneker said. "But temptation is often stronger than determination."

"Is that why you went back last night?"

"Partly." Venneker raised his head and looked at the distant horizon; the wind caught at strands of his white hair under the seaman's cap and blew them across his face. "But mostly because it won't be very many years before I'll be too old to care about temptation."

Something in his voice made Sean look up; it was the first hint Venneker had given that he thought about his age. Nothing had happened in the past months to dispel Sean's first impression of him; he was a man to whom age didn't apply. He caught Sean's eye and smiled.

"I'm not immune to the decay of years, Sean. I don't consider myself old, not yet a while, but one can't deny the warnings one gets. Believe me, I was glad to come home this afternoon. Ten years ago, you wouldn't have seen me until to-morrow morning."

Sean looked down at the ground again to hide his blush. Although he had soon become accustomed to the hard male talk around the hut and shed, and had tried out a few of the words experimentally when alone, he still could not get used to Venneker's occasional comments on sex. He knew that Venneker wasn't being dirty-minded, only frank, but sex was too much of a mystery to him to be casual about it. He knew the theory and had seen it practised by animals; it had only made him more curious of the relationship between people.

"What's the matter with his nibs?" Venneker said.

"Dad? I dunno. Something's been wrong with him all day. I don't think he's dingoing the race, like Clint said. Dad ain't——"

"Isn't."

"Isn't like that." He walked a few more steps, then came out with the grave confidence: "I think he and Mum have had a row."

"Hum." Venneker walked in silence until they had come down on to the flat and were halted by a fence. In the paddock beyond, sheep stood close together in a great grey mass: the wind seemed to ripple across the mob as across a body of water. Venneker turned his back to the wind and leaned on the fence. "It is a terrible moment in one's young life when one's parents indulge in disagreements. I had parents who were always at it. They were very well-bred types, the very best of Victorian aristocracy, so nothing was ever thrown and no one was ever—er—belted. We had a large house and they would retire to opposite wings, and sometimes that ridiculous state of affairs would last for weeks on end. Meanwhile, we children would occupy the main part of the house, somewhat in the manner of comfortably established orphans. But I can remember that when I first became aware of these breakings-off of domestic relations, my small soul underwent agony. Later on, like my elder brothers and sister, I looked upon them as an opportunity to play merry hell with our nurse and governess."

Sean was leaning on the fence, his chin resting on his elbows, his eyes slitted against the wind. "I don't feel like playing merry hell with anyone. I just feel crook, that's all. What can a bloke do about it, Rupe?"

"What has caused the argument?"

"I dunno. I dunno if there's even been a row. I just *think* there has. They've both got something on their minds. And it ain't—isn't like Dad to do what he did just now. He doesn't run out on people."

"That's true," Venneker said: the feud between himself and Paddy had been almost dissipated in the company of the other men. "Why don't you go up and talk to him?"

"I'd like to, but I dunno that I can." He shut his eyes against a vicious gust of wind and made his confession: "Rupe, I don't feel he's my dad as much as he used to be."

Venneker inclined his head sharply, his eyes severe and concerned under the furrowed brows. "That's a serious statement, Sean. What do you mean by it?"

"I can't even tell you that. Oh, I'm all mixed up! But I was thinking this afternoon. Since we came here, I've hardly spoken to Mum and Dad. Not the way I used to." He turned his head and looked up. "I talk to you more than I do to them."

"Don't ever accept me as a substitute for your mother and father, Sean," Venneker said slowly, and Sean suddenly recognised the look he had seen on Venneker's face down by the creek on the day they had met: the years were apparent on the long angular face as he looked back through the past: "I had substitutes for parents all my life until I left home. Nurses, governesses, tutors. There was no love in our house, Sean. There is none still. My brother lives there, a dried-up bachelor who spends his life writing to *The Times,* a man who never married because he has never learned what love is. It would have been different if we could have learned something from the couple who spawned us. But they taught us nothing. But your mother and father are different. They know what love is. Don't ever let yourself think that I might take their place."

Sean said nothing for a while, intrigued by the sudden confidence of Venneker, but realising also that what had been said about his mother and father was true. He knew they were happy together and he could remember how unhappy and worried each had been when the other had been ill. There had been rows before, of course, but the days

immediately afterwards had always seemed twice as full of
happiness and laughter. But on those occasions he had
always had some idea of what the row was about, because
he had been too close to them to miss it. To-day's row was
a complete mystery.

"I think I'll go up and talk to Dad," he said.

"Do that," said Venneker. "But don't mention you've
been talking to me. Outsiders have no place in this *contre-
temps.*"

"What's that?"

"It is what you are about to walk into. Good luck."

11

Ida poised the milk-jug over the cups. "Who likes their
tea black or white?"

"I like mine white, not too strong," Mrs. Firth said.
"White for you, too, Liz? Mrs. Halstead? Just the thing to
pick you up, a good cuppa. I been living in a pub for fifteen
years now, and I still prefer a good cuppa tea to a bottla
beer. But I gotta get drunk now and again, just to set an
example to the customers. When is it tea-time for the baby,
Liz? You feeding him yourself? Good on you. I can't see
anything in this new-fangled business of shoving 'em on a
bottle right away. A woman might just as well be without
what she's got under her shimmy. Though that's the fashion
down in the city, ain't it, Mrs. Halstead? No bust, no
behind and practically all your hair cut off. It's a wonder the
men look at 'em nowadays."

"Oh, they still do." Mrs. Halstead was still a little nonplussed by Mrs. Firth; she had met her casually once or
twice before in Cawndilla, but this was her first experience of
Mrs. Firth full blast. "I've put on some weight since I've
come out here and I've let my hair grow, but I was a flapper
when I nabbed my husband."

"Well, I bet he likes you better now," Mrs. Firth said.
"I've never known a man yet who didn't like a woman to
look like a woman. Me and Ida ud be outa fashion down in

Sydney, but I bet we wouldn't have to spend our Saturday nights going to the pictures on our own. What you reckon, Ida?"

Ida sipped her tea and smiled without speaking. She was fighting the almost overwhelming desire to get up from her chair and go outside and look for Paddy. She couldn't remember who had started the argument last night; all she wanted was it to be finished. It had probably begun when she had slapped Paddy's ear in front of the men and had sent him down to the cookhouse with Sean. Her instructions to dose him with sweet tea had been carried out faithfully by Sean; when she had come down to the cookhouse Paddy had been white, sick and sober.

Paddy hadn't spoken to her then. He had got up from the table, walking a little unsteadily, and had gone across to the tent. In the next half-hour, until she had gone across to go to bed, he must have lain there brooding. She was no sooner in bed than he had told her he was handing in his time the following Friday and moving on. She had said nothing for a while, because it had been so unexpected, then her own brooding mood had set in. Finally she had told him he could please himself; she and Sean were staying on. She knew that had set him back; she had sensed his shock immediately. But the argument had gone on: he had been born with stubbornness and she, living with him so long, had acquired a good deal of it. She had argued in favour of the home they might some day be able to have with the money they were saving; he had argued against being tied down in the one place, working to a bell, living in a crowd where you got no privacy. The argument had been long and heated, but the wind that had sprung up had kept their raised voices within the tent. This time, not even Sean knew about the row. That was why she wanted it finished, even if she were the one to yield, before Paddy brought it out into the open by giving notice to Quinlan. But something held her back; she knew that, as much as anything, it was the ninety-two pounds stowed away in the jam-jar in the tent. They had never had so much before towards buying a place of their own.

"I had a great deal of trouble nabbing Bluey," Liz Brown

was saying; she was propped up among pillows, colour in her cheeks that seemed to have become plump overnight and not even a memory of pain left in her sparkling eyes. " I thought our Englishmen were bad enough, but an Australian practically has to be driven into marriage. Sometimes I used to wonder if Bluey was worth all the trouble he was putting me to."

" They're not very good lovers," Mrs. Halstead said, " but they take a lot of beating as husbands. Don't you think so, Mrs. Carmody?"

" They could learn quite a bit even there," Ida said with feeling.

" Oh, I dunno. My Alec wasn't bad, when he was sober." Mrs. Firth got up and moved to the tea-tray on the chest of drawers. " Mind if I help m'self to another cuppa? But I had the fun of cork last night. Are you broad-minded, Mrs. Halstead?"

" Why, yes." Mrs. Halstead almost spilled her tea in surprise. " I think so."

" What about you, Liz?" Mrs. Firth looked at her.

" Well, I swear and smoke and tell an occasional dirty story." Liz was smiling: Mrs. Firth somehow reminded her of the London charwomen who used to clean out the office where she had worked during the war. " Is this a dirty story?"

" Oh, no. Nothing like that." She came back to her chair, stirring her tea. She put her cup down on the table beside the bed. " Just a minute, these new corsets are killing me. There, that's better. A woman can breathe now. Course if I was built like the fashion, I wouldn't need these. There'd be nothing to hold in. Yeah, well, about last night. I've been having a bit of a fling with Rupe Venneker. I'll bet he's not like the Englishmen you complained about, Liz. He don't need no encouragement. Well, last night he come in, hinting he was gunna stay the night, and, bowl me over, who should come back to town but Jack Patchogue!"

" Who's he?" Mrs. Halstead said. " Seems I've heard the name."

" The district magistrate. I've been a bit friendly with

him, off and on, for a coupla years. He's no matinee idol,
but you can't be too fussy out here. I never could go to bed
and read a book." She sipped her tea. "Crikey, this is good.
When I get too old to run the pub, I think I'll start a tea-
shop. How do you reckon a tea-shop ud go in Cawndilla?"

"Not very well, I imagine," Mrs. Halstead said, trying not
to sound impatient. "But what about Mr. Patchogue?"

"Yes, come on," Ida said. "You're beating about the bush
like an old hen."

Mrs. Firth threw back her head and laughed; her bosom
shook and tea jumped from her cup into her saucer. "Got
you on tenterhooks, have I? Well, Jack comes back to town,
tell you the truth I'd almost forgotten him, and he's got the
idea everything's gunna be laid on just like before. You
know, the bed aired, the sheets rolled back, me just panting
for him to come home. What you smiling at, Liz?"

"I'm just using my imagination," Liz said.

"So am I," said Mrs. Halstead; it was impossible to be
shocked by Mrs. Firth, but she was picturing her at a Sunday
afternoon tea party in Vaucluse.

"Well, Jack didn't use his imagination. He was a bit slow
to catch on. Rupe had gone upstairs to," she took another
sip of tea, "warm the bed, and when I go up, crikey, who
should follow me but Jack! If I live to be a hundred, and I
hope I don't, I'll never forget the look on his face when I
opened the door and he looked in over me shoulder. There
was Rupe sitting up in bed as large as life, drinking a Scotch
and looking like he owned the place. I thought Jack was
gunna bust a blood vessel. He come storming into the room,
yelling he was gunna do this and he was gunna do that, and
for a minute I thought I was gunna have a murder on me
hands. That's all I'd need, the way the other women talk
about me already. Not that I care. Then, calm as you like,
Rupe gets outa bed, stark naked except for that damn' silly
cap which he's got on, grabs Jack by the scruff of the neck,
runs him outa the room, down the passage, and at the top
of the stairs gives him a boot in the behind with his bare
foot, and sends him on his way." She began to shake again
with laughter, rolling her head from side to side as if the

memory were too much for her. "I felt sorry for Jack, but he shouldn't of taken so much for granted. But, honestly, I thought I'd die laughing."

"Well, you certainly have plenty of excitement in your love life," Liz said.

Ida had enjoyed the story, but she was practical-minded. "How are you going to sort it out?"

Mrs. Firth shrugged. "I don't worry about those sorta things. If I was like that, I'd never married Alec. I made up me mind in a week, and I've never regretted it, not one single day. Alec drank, but crikey, we were happy. I'd of missed all that wonderful time if I'd tried to sort it out when he asked me to marry him. I know I ain't got many brains, so I don't over-work 'em. I just let me guardian angel look after me. He's done all right so far."

Mrs. Halstead was sitting in her chair, her hand to her eyes, weeping as she laughed. She looked past her hand at Ida, shook her head helplessly, then made an effort to control her near-hysteria. She realised with a pang that she was not so much sick from laughing so hard as from being unaccustomed to it: she was happily married, yet in the five months of her marriage she had found little at which to laugh.

"Mrs. Firth," she said, "why don't you come out here more often?"

"If that's an invite, I will," said Mrs. Firth. "Crikey, I've had a real good time this afternoon, listening to you women. In town, all I get to talk to is men. Not that there's anything wrong with men, but they weren't meant for talking to, were they? More tea, Liz? How about you, Ida?"

"No, thanks," Ida said, standing up. "I have to go and see Paddy. Excuse me. I won't be long," and went out of the room, knowing that once again she was going to surrender: she knew that in her own way she was every bit as weak as Paddy.

12

Paddy lay on the mattress with his hands under his head. Only his eyes moved, and the muscle at the side of his mouth; his body was stiff as the ridge-pole of the tent above him. He hadn't moved since Sean had come into the tent five minutes before; he had spoken only once and then in a voice that had the ring of the end of the world in it.

"But why are you blaming Mum for all this?" Sean sat on a box, twisting his hands together between his separated knees. "It's not her fault if you don't like the job."

The muscle moved at the side of Paddy's mouth, like something trying to escape from beneath the skin. He moved his lips as if he were about to spit, then changed his mind. He lay staring at the ceiling, then at last he said, "You're too young. You wouldn't understand."

Sean stood up, shoving his hands savagely into his pockets and turning away. "Oh, Christ!"

Paddy raised his head off his hands. "What you say? Don't let me catch you saying that again or I'll cut your bloody tail off. You know how your mother feels about Him."

"I didn't mean it that way. I wasn't swearing. Oh, I dunno, maybe I was. But gosh, it's enough to make anyone swear. *I'm not old enough to understand*. When the heck am I gunna be old enough? You say you're leaving here next Friday, and me and Mum are staying. Gee, Dad, I'm old enough to understand *that*! We been together all the time, all my life, and now you're walking out on us. I just told Rupe you weren't like that, you didn't walk out on people——"

"Who told you to talk about me with that interfering old ram?" Paddy's body went even stiffer with indignation. "What have our family affairs gotta do with him?"

"Nothing. He dunno nothing about this." The lie was firm in Sean's mouth: he suddenly felt old enough to argue with his father. "We were talking about you not wanting to race the bloke over at Mulgrue's. I was sticking up for you. So was he. He said you weren't a dingo, like Clint said you were."

"I'll fix that bastard later," Paddy said emphatically; the stiffness had gone out of his body now and he had begun to writhe a little. "Soon's your back's turned, everybody's ready to start talking about you. He wouldn't be game to say that to me face."

Sean didn't know where he found the courage: "I think you're a dingo for running out on me and Mum." He stood trembling in the awful silence of the tent: the wind died behind his back as his father came up off the mattress in one swift terrible movement, his fist raised and his eyes blind with anger.

"Don't hit me, Dad," he said softly, and it was neither a plea nor a threat: it was the plain statement of a boy who had made his first step into manhood, "or you can leave and I'll see that Mum and me never come after you."

Paddy stood with his arm upraised, his whole body shaking with anger and his mouth half open for the curse that wouldn't come. They stood there for a long frozen moment, the tent billowing about them as the wind rushed past outside, and each of them was afraid of the consequences of the next move. Then slowly Paddy's arm began to fall; the blindness went out of his eyes and he saw his son and the awful thing that he might have done to him. Suddenly pain scarred his face and he turned away and dropped down to sit on the mattress, his head resting on his hunched-up knees and anger going out of him in a long sigh.

"Don't ever talk to me like that again, Sean," he said: all at once he had recognised something from the past, a reflection caught in Sean's eyes, and within himself he had felt the ghost of his father: "I might of killed you."

Sean stood awkwardly, weak with relief but aware of an as-yet-unrecognised strength: it would be a long time before he was fully familiar with the climate of adulthood. He had crossed into another state without remarking the boundaries: there was no Customs at the border to tell him childhood was behind him for ever. He looked down at his father, then as Paddy raised his head to look at him he smiled tentatively.

"You're not going, are you, Dad? Please."

Paddy stood up slowly and put a hand on Sean's shoulder as Venneker's voice bellowed from outside, "Hey, Carmody, are you there?"

Paddy swung back the flap of the tent and he and Sean stepped out into the wind. Venneker was there, backed by Bluey, Clint, Turk and Chilla Peters.

"What's on?" Paddy said, and looked at Clint. "I hear you think I'm a dingo."

"Well, I don't think much of any mug who leaves me holding the bag like you done," Clint said.

"Retract your horns," Venneker said to Clint, "and let me look after this. I know how to handle our friend here."

Paddy turned on his heel and prepared to go back into the tent. Sean grabbed him by the arm. "Hold on, Dad. Let's hear what Rupe's got to say."

"I don't wanna hear nothing he's gotta say," Paddy said. "He can handle me! Why, I'd have the bastard on his back before he could lay a finger on me."

"Slow down, Paddy," Bluey said. "We just want to get things straight before Clint goes over to Mulgrue's to call off the race. You really don't want to have a go against this bloke?"

"No," said Paddy.

Sean looked at his father and recognised the lack of adamancy in his voice. With a sudden flash of intuition he knew that his father now wanted to show off his shearing skill, but couldn't think of a way of changing his mind without appearing to give in to Clint.

"Well, that puts the kybosh on it," Turk said. "Maybe it's just as well. A bloke might of lost his money."

"Yeah," Clint said. "He might of wanted to give up half-way through, after we'd placed our bets."

"The boss didn't seem too keen on the idea, anyway," Chilla said. "At least he'll be pleased."

"I dunno, I think he might've let us have the race," Bluey said. "I don't think he's that much of a nark."

"Have you all had your say?" Venneker said with grand patience: he looked about him as at a group of pupils.

"Now we shall place the matter back in the hands of the one man competent to negotiate it, shall we?"

"Meaning you," said Bluey.

"Meaning me," said Venneker, and turned to Paddy. "Carmody, I have refrained from expressing, or even entertaining any opinion on your decision not to represent this shed in the projected race. I am sure that you must have adequate reasons for refusing."

Paddy looked at him suspiciously. "Quit beating about the bush."

"Refrain from interrupting," Venneker said. "Now before you went into retreat, Clint here perhaps didn't give you the full facts of this suggested contest. Certainly we wish to show the opposition that we have a man of whom we are proud—"

"Cut it out," Paddy said: modesty choked him.

"—but the main object was to raise money for a worthy cause."

It was Clint's turn to look suspicions. "Go on, Lofty."

"We would rather have kept this from Bluey's notice until a later date, but circumstances have forced upon us the announcement of the purpose of the race. In short, the money won upon the superiority of your skill was to have been presented as a christening gift to Bluey's son and heir."

Paddy turned to Bluey. "Well, crikey, that changes the whole thing. I didn't know it was anything like that. Gawd, I'll be only too glad to have a go. I just hope I can win, for the nipper's sake."

Bluey looked about the men, then at Paddy. "This has sort of bowled me arse over Charlie. I—well, thanks. I'd better go and let Liz in on this." He turned and went up the hill, walking quickly as if he had nothing more to say and didn't want to be embarrassed by his silence. He went hurrying by Ida without seeing her. She came on down to the group of men.

"What's got into Bluey?" she said.

"He is a little stunned, I think," said Venneker, "by the magnificent gesture of your husband in consenting to attempt to win a substantial gift of money for the newly-arrived infant."

Ida looked blankly at Sean. "What's he talking about?"

"Dad's gunna race a shearer from Mulgrue's shed." Sean wanted to put his arm about his father, only a bloke just didn't do that sort of thing; but crikey, right now he loved the old man. "And when he wins, all the betting money goes to Bluey's baby."

"It was his idea." Paddy jerked a thumb at Venneker. "I ain't taking credit for it. I just hope I can win the cash."

"You will," Venneker boomed: the old Olympian air was back with a vengeance. "You won't let the other fellow win, if you have to brain him with your clippers. Well, all is settled then. Clint has his bet on, the Brown infant is assured of something in the bank before he has a brain in his head, and you will have a further opportunity of showing you are better than us ordinary mortals when it comes to peeling the hide off a sheep. Everyone would appear to be happy."

He turned and stalked back towards the men's hut. Ida looked after him and in her mind's eye saw the grey wig replacing the seaman's cap and the black robes billowing in the wind: no counsel had ever made a more triumphant exit from a court. He's a wonder, she thought and felt a rush of gratitude and affection for him. She didn't know the words he had used, but he had been instrumental in preventing Paddy from giving notice. She had come down here and might have spent the rest of the afternoon pleading with Paddy to stay, or even yielding completely and promising that she and Sean would leave here with him at the end of the week. But Rupe, with his gift of the gab, had saved her all that. There would be no way of thanking him, because he hadn't known what he had really done, but some day she would make it up to him.

Paddy was looking at her, but she could say nothing to him now with Sean standing beside him. Casually she began to walk towards the cookhouse. "How about a cuppa?"

"Too right," said Paddy, and quickly fell in beside her. "How you feeling, darl?"

"Pretty good," Ida said, and winked a glistening eye.
"You coming, Sean?"

Sean couldn't trust himself to speak for a moment: without pride but only thankfulness, he knew he had just won the first major battle of his life. Somewhere in his mind a prayer struggled for expression: his mother had taught him that everything worthwhile was due to God: defeat and failure were your own accomplishments. But the prayer couldn't break through the knowledge of the fact: he looked ahead at his mother and father walking side by side, and God was forgotten.

"I'm coming," he said. "I'll get my cup. It's in the hut."

In the hut Clint was walking up and down like a man with boils on his behind. "Christ Almighty, what a turn-up! Here I am, fixing meself to win a few quid, and you go and donate the whole bloody lot to charity."

"I doubt if Bluey would appreciate his child being referred to as a charity," Venneker said. "Do you begrudge the babe the gift?"

"Now don't go trying to put me up a tree," Clint warned: he shook an angry finger. "I don't begrudge the kid nothing. But I can do with the money just as much as him. I ain't got no father working for *me*. Any other time I'd been glad to throw in for the nipper, but this time—— Ah, what's the use? You all think I'm a tight-arsed bastard, just because I want the money meself, instead of giving it to the kid." Anger had gone now and his voice was almost weeping with disappointment. "But Christ, this was the only time in me whole life when I had a sure winner!"

"You wouldn't have had even a starter if it hadn't been for Bluey's infant," Venneker said. "As it is, you can still bet on a winner. The only thing is, you will pass your winnings on to me. I have elected myself fund secretary and treasurer."

"I might of bloody well known it," Clint said. "But if Paddy loses——"

"He won't lose," said Venneker. "Apart from being driven by his own conceit, I shall be standing over him with a whip. I take no chances with things that I organise."

13

Early on Wednesday morning Herb Cooper, the shearer from Mulgrue's shed, came over to Wattle Run.

"Holy cripes," Ocker Shand said. "I tell you, if I'd known you were Herb Cooper, I'd have called the bet off. How much money are you trying to take us for, anyway?"

"I ain't trying to skin you on this one," said the walnut-faced man. "I didn't know this job was on till they told me I'd been nominated. I'm just interested in that bet on the cricket match on Sunday."

"Now don't go talking like that, Herb." One of the men from Mulgrue's shed had come with Cooper as his second; two men from Wattle Run had gone over to replace them for the day in the other shed. "You gotta be a trier all the way in this. You beat this bloke for us and we'll beat their mob for you at cricket."

Herb Cooper's face wrinkled into a grin: his features were lost in a maze of lines and you had the impression of looking at him through a screen. "They're gunna be as poor as church mice by the time we're finished with 'em. Well, where's this bloke of theirs?"

"Here he comes," Ocker said.

Paddy was coming down the shed in state: he had a retinue of seconds that Jack Dempsey might have envied. Sean was walking in front, carrying a bucket of water and a towel, a sporting acolyte. On Paddy's right was Venneker, a spare grey singlet draped over his arm and a spare pair of clippers in his hand. On Paddy's left Turk Tuthill carried an extra pair of sandshoes, a brown-paper bag of sandwiches, and Paddy's jacket. At the rear Clint Evans and Bluey were relatively unburdened: Clint had only a sheet of paper on which he had listed the bets and Bluey was carrying another towel. The group came to a halt beside Cooper and his second.

"Are you the challenger?" Venneker said.

"Well, I dunno——" Cooper began: he wasn't sure that

he hadn't come all the way over here just to have his leg pulled.

"No, he ain't the bloody challenger," interrupted Wilson, the second. "It was your bloke here who done all the talking. I just took him up on the bet to shut him up."

"Stone the crows!" Clint said. "You were doing all the skiting——"

"Would you kindly leave all the talking to me?" Venneker spoke over his shoulder to Clint, then looked down at the two men from Mulgrue's. "Well, it really doesn't matter. After this contest there won't be any doubt as to who is champion and who is challenger. We shall, of course, expect to be paid all winnings before you leave here to-night."

No Derby thoroughbred had ever received better pre-post preparation than Paddy got in the next five minutes. Cooper and Wilson stood by with ill-concealed sneers on their faces as Paddy, stone-faced and silent, was slapped and massaged by Turk, had the laces of his shoes untied and retied more carefully by Bluey, was given a shadow run-through on an imaginary sheep by Clint and was finally approved by Venneker.

"You'll do," he said. "Now you understand your instructions. A steady pace for the first hundred sheep, speed it up for the next hundred, rest off for the next fifty, then a spurt at the end for the last fifty. Three hundred sheep should be good enough to win."

"Well, I seen some bull in me time," Wilson said, "but this takes some beating. Who you trying to kid?"

Venneker turned a slow head. "Were you speaking to me?"

"I wasn't talking to the dummy you been mucking around with for the last five minutes——"

"Who's a dummy?" Paddy jumped back into character: the stone cracked on his face and he stepped forward, jaw out-thrust and fists bunched. "I got a tongue in me head——"

"How well we know it," Venneker said, and put a large hand against Paddy's chest and pushed him back. "Please hold it, and save your breath for the contest. Now it is almost time for us to begin. I see the boss and Quinlan have arrived."

Halstead and Quinlan came down to the group. All the men in the shed were down by Paddy's stand. Outside the shed the aboriginal yard-boys were the only Wattle Run personnel not interested in the race: even the stockmen out in the paddocks had sent in their bets. Halstead pushed through the crowd and held out a note.

"Here's a tenner," he said. "Who's taking the bets?"

"I am," said Wilson, and took out a crinkled sheet of paper and a pencil. "Who's putting this on?"

"The missus and I," Halstead said. "What are the odds? Even money?"

"You oughta be giving me odds," Wilson said, "judging by all the bull that's been handed out about your starter. No, it's even money and all bets are paid to-night before we go home."

"We'll be glad to accept them," Halstead grinned, and turned to Paddy. "Good luck, Paddy. Mrs. Halstead sends hers, too. And there was a last-minute message from your wife. She said if you don't win, you needn't come back to the tent to-night."

The men roared, and Halstead joined in their laughter. He felt a closer bond with these men than with any team that had come to the shed: their presence, or anyway the companionship of their wives, seemed to have made a difference to Jean too. He wondered how things would be when the team moved on: Wattle Run would be lonely again, and Jean might lapse back into her mood of the last few months. In the meantime, it was good to have these men around: with the drought and the worry over Jean, he had almost forgotten how to laugh.

"Well, how about we get started?" Quinlan said. "We've still got to get this job finished, race or no race."

Quinlan was accustomed to the independent outlook of shearers, but this team was beginning to get his goat: this race had been arranged without a word to him, and the first he had known of it had been this morning when Halstead had asked him if he were going to have a bet on the result.

They were a good mob of workers, as good as he'd ever had, but Gawd, now and again a man liked to know he was boss.

Paddy took the gold tooth from his mouth and handed it to Sean. "Look after it for me."

Cooper opened his mouth and took out all his teeth. He handed them to Wilson with elaborate care. "Keep an eye on these."

Wilson, straight-faced, took the teeth. "You gunna un-screw your wooden leg?"

With his teeth out, Cooper's wrinkled face had almost collapsed inwards. "Nah. Don't wanna embarrass the champ here."

The Wattle Run team looked towards Venneker for a retort, but at that moment Quinlan blew a blast on the whistle that he carried on a cord round his neck. The group broke up, the shearers going to their places along the board, the piece-pickers to their tables, and the roustabouts spread-ing themselves along the shed where they could conveniently handle the wool shorn by two or more shearers.

"Good luck, Dad." Since Sunday Sean had felt a closer bond than ever with his father: they were men together now, and he expressed his confidence in adult terms: "I put five bob on you' m'self."

In the engine-room at the end of the shed the power had been turned on. The long steel shaft running the length of the shed began to spin slowly, gleaming blue in the dull light. The machines above each position at the board began to hum; the men picked up their clippers and were ready.

The bell went, a little louder this morning. Paddy and Cooper, working side by side, went into the pen together. They came out together, each dragging a sheep, and the clippers went down into the wool at the same moment. The other shearers stood watching them for a moment, then they went into the pens after their own sheep. It was going to be a good race; there didn't appear to be much between Paddy and Cooper.

Paddy had been lucky. He had grabbed an old ewe, a "rosella," with most of the wool along her belly worn off, and he had just that much start on Cooper. He moved the

heavy sheep roughly but deftly between his knees; its dark
eyes stared with stupid panic at him as he leant over it. He
pulled the head back, cleared the wrinkled neck, went on
down the flank, wrestled the sheep round, and finished on the
other flank. He stepped away, dragging the sheep with him,
leaving the fleece lying like a soft, disarrayed mat on the floor
behind him. He heard the picker-up step in and scoop up the
fleece, but he heard him only on the fringe of his mind:
with a shock he realised that, for all his start with the old
ewe, Cooper had kept pace with him. They pushed their
shorn sheep down the chutes together and, still together, like
a dance team performing some interpretative routine, went
into the pen for their second sheep.

Paddy counted the first twelve sheep, listening for the
clatter of hooves going down Cooper's chute, then time and
the sheep began to merge into a fog in his mind and he
worked like an automaton. He had never had to work as fast
as this, Cooper was no mug and it wasn't going to be a
walk-over. Sweat sprang out of him, soaking and blinding
him; the brown striking arm, buried wrist-deep in the wool,
was streaked with shining gold. His ears lost all sound but
the humming of the machine; when he breathed, his lungs
seemed full of wool. At the end of the first hour he was no
longer straightening up when he dived into the pen for a
sheep. He was just a stooped hunch-backed caricature of a
man, bent half-way to the floor, a simian-like creature that
had been trained to do only one job and that with all the
speed it could muster.

When the bell rang at the end of two hours for the rest
period, he leaned against the fence of the pen. Sean came
down to him with a mug of tea, followed by Venneker.

Paddy gulped the tea and handed the mug back to Sean.
He took the towel Venneker handed him, wiped his face and
arms, then tucked in his singlet and straightened up.

" Fit as a bloody fiddle," he said, and looked towards
Cooper, who leaned against the fence, drinking tea in slow
deliberate mouthfuls. Cooper looked at him, folded his face
inwards in a grin, lost one eye in a wrinkled wink, and

jerked a thumb at him. Paddy grinned back, then turned and strolled nonchalantly towards the door of the shed.

Once outside he turned to Sean and Venneker, who had now been joined by Bluey and Clint, and said, "Christ, I never been so glad to see a smoke-o turn up. I was just about done in when that bell went. This bloke Cooper's good."

"You'll beat him, Dad," Sean said. "He's just as done in as you are."

"How's the score?" Paddy said.

"You're even Stephen so far," Clint said. "But you're dead right. He *is* good. You'll have to keep your finger out the rest of the day."

"What you think I'm doing now?" Paddy snapped. "Picking me flaming nose?"

"I've been watching you, when I got the chance," Bluey said. "You've been flat out like a lizard drinking, but this cove is right with you all the time. The worst of it is, he didn't look half so knocked up as you."

"Maybe the bastard ain't human," Paddy said; his pride was as sore as his frame. "He don't look it."

Clint was worried: it looked as if twenty quid might be going down the drain: well, his luck was running true to form. "Pity we couldn't of laid some of the money off somewhere. We might of covered ourselves, just in case you don't win."

Venneker had been standing silently aloof from the discussion; suddenly he exploded in a thunder of wrath. "Holy God Almighty, what a bunch of defeatists! The day is only one-quarter of the way through, we're running a dead-heat with the opposition, and already you're talking as if we have had the pants licked off us. Where's your backbone?"

"I might do better without one," Paddy said, and twisted his arm round to massage his back. "This one feels like it's got a permanent kink in it."

"Then he must feel the same," said Venneker. "You notice he hasn't come outside? Have you thought that perhaps he's too worn out to walk as far as the door?"

The thought of the possible defeat of Paddy had communicated itself to the other shearers; when they moved back into the shed, several of them stopped by Paddy, wished him luck in pessimistic tones, and went on to their stands as if they were already wondering how long it would be before they could make up the money they had lost.

One of the aboriginal stockmen had taken the progress scores up to Ida at the cookhouse. She was in the middle of baking a cake; she had intended that to-night's meal should be a sort of party to celebrate Paddy's win.

" I'll have to have a word in his earhole when he comes up for dinner," she said to Mrs. Halstead. " I'm not going to spend my time baking this cake, just to celebrate him taking a hiding."

Mrs. Halstead was at a bench outside the cookhouse, washing napkins in a tub. She looked in at Ida and smiled through wisps of blonde hair that hung down in front of her face. " Could we keep it for Christopher's christening?"

" No, I'm putting on a special one for that occasion. I dug up a recipe out of those Sydney papers you gave me. It's some American recipe, got everything in it but a cupful of prickly pear. No, this one's just a sponge cake. If Paddy doesn't win, I won't let on about it and us women can have a blow-out to-morrow afternoon." She slid the cake into the oven, then walked to the cookhouse door, wiping her hands on her apron. " If Paddy loses, I don't expect he'll be able to keep a thing in his stomach. He was only telling me in bed last night how he wasn't going to make too much of a show of this man from Mulgrue's. Said he was just going to shear fast enough to win." She smiled, looking out over the plains, grey-green under the clear winter sunlight, and seeing nothing but the intimate darkness in the tent last night. " I'm married to a real wind-bag, Jean, but I wouldn't swap him for ten modest men."

Down at the shearing shed the wind-bag was almost completely deflated. He was silently and breathlessly cursing for having allowed himself to be talked into this race. Here he was, busting a gut, racing in and out of the pen like a cut cat, working harder than he'd ever worked in his life before, ad all because he'd been soft-hearted about winning a present for Bluey's kid. Would the kid ever grow up to thank him? Not on your bloody life! Twenty years from now the kid would be somewhere down in the city, living in the flaming lap of luxury. And where would *he* be? Up here in the bush nursing a hernia, the poor brainless bastard who'd worked himself bloody near to death just to start the kid on his way to being rich.

At the mid-day break the two men were still even. Paddy, in a shining skin of sweat, walked slowly up the hill surrounded by his principal backers, who took one look at his exhausted face and asked no foolish questions.

"Go and lie down in the tent, Dad," Sean said. "I'll bring your dinner over to you."

"You'll do nothing of the sort," said Venneker. "Appearance is everything at this stage. It would give Cooper an immense psychological advantage if it were known your father was flat on his back, ready to expire."   -

"That's right," Clint said; the shock of the possibility of losing his money on what had seemed a sure thing had made him almost as exhausted as Paddy. "We gotta keep up appearances."

"Give us a grin, Paddy," Turk said. "It ud be better if you could laugh out loud."

Paddy couldn't have raised a smile if his supporters had tickled him. He walked flat-footed across to the bench outside the men's hut, slowly stripped off his singlet, and began to wash his upper torso. He was standing there, white with soap and pale with fatigue, when Cooper and Wilson came up the hill from the shed.

"You notice he isn't hurrying?" Venneker said. "Obviously he is just as done in as you are."

"I dunno about that," Ocker said. "I tell you, right now I wish I had money on *him*."

"You happy bastard," Bluey said.

Paddy found a towel on a nail beside the hut door and carefully dried himself. He picked up the clean singlet Sean had laid on the bench, pulled it over his head and tucked it into his trousers. He took the comb hanging on a string from the nail where the towel had hung and deliberately parted and slicked back his hair. With the towel he wiped away the sweat that had already begun to shine on his face again; then he painfully straightened his back, squared his shoulders and was ready to keep up appearances.

At that moment Cooper, half-way across the yard now, let out a roar of laughter, hearty and strong as a Queensland cyclone, and swung his arm in a mighty slap against Wilson's shoulder. Then he abruptly picked up pace and with a hop, skip and a jump, bursting with energy, went up the steps of the cookhouse and disappeared from view.

There was silence for a moment among the group outside the hut. Then Paddy spoke for the first time since they had left the shearing shed.

"I'm going over to the tent," he said. "He can shove his psychological advantage."

14

Cooper won the race. At the end of the day he was seven sheep up on Paddy and looked as if he could have gone on shearing until the mobs had run out. He popped his teeth back in, partly filling out his face again, went round the shed shaking everyone's hand while Wilson collected their money, and finished up in front of Ocker Shand.

"Well, see you Sunday, eh? We'll be waiting for you. I seen the town clerk of Cawndilla and he says we can have a lend of the oval. Don't forget to bring your money. Well, hooray. I've enjoyed meself. Thanks for asking us." And he hurried out of the shed, followed by Wilson, and was gone in a cloud of dust in the truck in which they had come.

"I tell you," Ocker spoke to the shed at large, "he didn't even have a drop of sweat on him."

"If he plays cricket like he shears," Bluey said, "we'd better send a telegram to Sydney and see if Jack Gregory's available."

Paddy was an old man, ready for the boneyard, but he remembered to make a gesture. "Sorry I didn't win for your nipper, Bluey," he said hollowly.

"Don't worry about it," Bluey said: he was both disappointed and relieved that he wouldn't have to accept the money on behalf of his offspring. Since Sunday night he and Liz had several times debated how they would invest the money for young Chris, but always in the back of his mind had been the thought that he would be sure to feel some embarrassment when the moment came for the money to be presented. "You did your best."

"Yeah, that's right," Paddy said matter-of-factly, and cursed again for having allowed himself to be talked into working himself into the grave for a kid that right now was probably hanging on its mother's tit, not caring a hoot about how the rest of the world was going. That was the way it was: the ones who come after you never appreciate what you done for them. The world was taken for granted: history was only someone else's boasting. Then, fair-minded, he tried to think of someone who might have done something for him when he'd been at his mother's breast: the milk turned sour in his mouth, and he went up the hill to the tent, berating himself for a mug who was always on the wrong end of the stick.

Although everyone had lost his money, disappointment didn't stop them discussing the race that night. The men sat about the hut and expressed their opinion of Cooper's remarkable stamina and skill. Nobody complained that Paddy had lost; he was just forgotten, as the men began to compare Cooper to the great shearers they had met or heard about in the past. Venneker, no longer interested in a race in which his charge had run second, had gone to sleep almost as soon as he climbed into bed. Sean, the only one in the hut still interested in the loser of the race, sat at the table and scratched away at another letter to McKechnie.

This was the third letter and it already ran to nine pages. It was beginning to show the effects of Venneker's persistent, if haphazard efforts, to improve Sean's education: written from week to week, the grammar and expression improved as the pages increased. There were still mistakes, but a good many of them had been crossed out and corrections written in above them. Education hadn't quickened

Sean's letter-writing; rather, it had slowed it up. Each time he sat down with the pen in his hand he began a mental steeplechase in which the hazards were punctuation, grammar and correct spelling. Two hundred and fifty miles away McKechnie, a blind man with no more education than Sean, would appreciate none of it.

Sean was now beginning to find the letters to McKechnie a chore rather than something he enjoyed. The first letter had been almost an adventure: it had been the first he had ever written. There had also been the good pleasant feeling of writing to a lonely ma   he had inherited much of his mother's warm sympathy for the world and its unfortunates. But now, harassed by an educated conscience, the memory of McKechnie as a personality already a little dim in his mind, he was continuing with the letters only because he couldn't bring himself to think of McKechnie's disappointment if they didn't arrive. There had been only one acknowledgment that they *were* arriving: a fortnight ago he had received a short one-page note, written for McKechnie by his daughter, asking after everyone's health, telling them the drought had broken, and laconically advising them not to get caught in any more bush fires.

With no more response to his letters than that short note, McKechnie had become more of a symbol to Sean than anything else. As he laboriously moved the pen across the paper in a small neat script, putting down almost a diary of what was happening at Wattle Run, he was hardly ever aware of addressing McKechnie as a person. The letters were going to *someone,* but always when he wrote the address the picture in his mind was of the letter being delivered to a place, and not to a person. Sometimes he would stop in the middle of a sentence and stare with unseeing eyes across the hut towards the shadowed corners: clear in his memory was a sunlit road and a neat newly painted farmhouse beneath the upsurge of steep green hill. He would sit sometimes like that for almost five minutes, if no one disturbed him, and when he would finally go back to the letter there would be a feeling bordering almost on despair. The world would never stand still: so much could happen to the farm, it could be sold, burned, fall to pieces, before *his* time came round. The world moved so quickly, but why did you always take so long to grow up?

There was no doubt in his mind that some day they would go back to Bulinga. Whether they would settle there or pass on through, as they had passed through so many towns, was something he preferred not to contemplate. But the farm, still really unknown to him in detail, had become a part of his life: it crystallised all the vague dreams and yearnings that had stirred him for so long. Home had become an ambition.

With his mother's honesty, he now told McKechnie about his father's defeat in the shearing race. He ignored the drama of what had happened; in his disappointment he searched for excuses for his father's defeat, but could find none, and in the end he told the story flatly and objectively. His father, had he known, would have set a match to the paper on which he wrote.

He finished the letter at last, twelve pages, and signed his name. This was the last one that would be written from Wattle Run: the shearing would be cut out within the next fortnight and the team would be moving on. He got up from the table and walked to the door of the hut and stepped out.

The night was cool but not cold and the westerlies were only a soft song in the wattles climbing in a patient line up the hill. At the top of the hill, beside the squat bulk of the house, the windmill turned slowly, spinning the bright moonlight into a silver web. Under the high moon the paddocks, stretching away to the blue darkness of the sky, were almost white. Distantly there came the bark of a dog: sharp and nervous, it was a lonely sound.

Sean stepped farther out into the yard and looked about for the kelpie. He whistled and called softly, then the kelpie came silently towards him, a shadow out of the shadows, and slid under his hand.

"Not so stuck up, eh, Nigger? A bit down in the mouth like me, eh?" Sean turned his head and saw the silhouette of his mother cross the window of the cookhouse. "Hullo. Mum's still working. Let's go and blow down her ear, mate."

Ida was just finishing tidying up the cookhouse when Sean came in the door. The kelpie stayed at the door: he had already learned that Ida believed the cookhouse was no place for animals. He sat down on the top step and turned his back: he hadn't wanted to come in, anyway.

"I thought you'd be in bed long ago," Ida said. "I'll be glad to get there myself."

"I been writing to Mr. McKechnie." Sean sat down at the kitchen table and rested his head on one hand. "I been thinking about that place of his, Mum. You think we'll ever have a place of our own?"

Ida was hanging dishes on nails above the sink; they clattered slightly as they were dropped against the wall. The kitchen hadn't been so well organised since it had been built: everything was in its place and easily at hand; there were even newspapers, cut with scalloped edges, lining the shelves of the cupboards. Ida had established an atmosphere of permanency about her: this was a place of her own, and next season's cook would never own it as she did now. She turned round, aware of the sadness in her son.

"That's up to us," she said, and sat down at the table opposite him. "You and me, I mean. If we leave it to your dad, we'll never own anything but what we stand up in."

"It's gunna take a fair bit of money to get a down payment on a farm. How long do you reckon we can keep Dad working?"

"I dunno," Ida said, and leaned her head wearily on her hand. "He almost moved out last Sunday."

"I know," Sean said.

Ida looked at him, her eyes moving quickly but her head staying stiffly within her hand. "How did you know?"

"I had a row with him." Sean was tired, too tired to care about embarrassment; at another time he would have found difficulty in speaking so frankly to his mother. "He got pretty stirred up."

"Why?" Ida hadn't even suspected this battle within her own family: afraid, she looked for wounds and bitterness. "He didn't say anything to me."

"I reckon he didn't want to." Sean looked across the table at her. "I'm sorry I opened my trap now."

"You've opened it too far to shut it now. Why did you have the row?"

"He told me he was gunna leave here this week. Said he was gunna leave you and me to look after ourselves." He looked up, a little afraid of his mother's reaction: "I called him a dingo."

Ida sat unmoving and completely wordless. She stared across the table at her son and had difficulty in recognising him. Suddenly her family had grown up.

"We nearly had a fight," Sean said. "It got that close."

Ida put both hands to her head, as if weariness had overcome her. She closed her eyes and tried to shut out the scene in her mind. Fights between herself and Paddy were nothing, one or the other would sooner or later surrender; but a fight between her husband and her son had the anguish of tragedy about it. She took the easy way out.

"Don't tell me any more of it," she said. "It's past, and that's how I want it to stay."

"It wasn't my fault," Sean said.

"I don't care whose fault it was!" Her voice was sharp with her fear. "This family is too small for me to be taking sides. For any of us to be taking sides. Your father's pig-headed, and I make mistakes too, and you aren't going to go through life without treading on our toes. But I want no more rows than we can help, and if there have to be rows, I don't want any bitterness afterwards. We can't afford it, or in no time at all we'd be breaking up. God knows, I wanted a big family. A big family can afford fights. But all I got was you, and I'm not going to have you following in your father's footsteps, running away because he couldn't get on with his father!"

"I wasn't thinking of running away. Dad was the one who was going."

"That was on Sunday. Next time, if there was going to be a next time and I'll damn' well see there isn't, it might be you who'd want to be on your way." She put her hand tentatively across the table towards him: suddenly older, he might rebel against a too-affectionate gesture. "Sean, you and I have got to make allowances for your dad. That pigheaded pride of his could take him away from us, if we didn't turn a blind eye towards him now and again. I know things are all right between you and him right now. Sunday's all forgotten. But in future, when an argument looks like cropping up, a serious one, hold back a bit. If Dad wins for the moment, it won't matter. In the end, in this family we do what *I* want to do. And in time, if you handle him right, he'll finish up doing what *you* want to do."

Sean realised his mother, by not wishing to know everything about Sunday, had completely misunderstood the argument. He had got into the argument only because he had taken her side; and now she didn't want to hear about it. He felt a sense of injustice, but he was too tired to care. He knew suddenly, with clarity and the first hint of an adult's cynicism, that Sunday's victory was something he could never share.

He stood up. "Well, when the time comes, I hope I can get him to buy a farm. That's all *I* want."

"I want the same," Ida said, following him to the door and switching out the light. "And we'll get it."

She said good-night to Sean and watched him walk through the moonlight with the slightly rolling gait, so much like his father's, that he had developed in the last couple of months. She bit her lip, as sad now at finding her son no longer a child as she had been when she had found him no longer a baby, then she turned and went into the tent to seek the comfort of Paddy's arms and perhaps console him on his licking.

She turned up the lantern and looked down on that useless object, a worn-out, snoring mate, and disgustedly she almost spat as she blew out the light. In a rare mood of defeat, she climbed into bed beside Paddy. He stirred restlessly and rolled away from her, as if even in sleep the shame of his own defeat was too much for him. She pulled the blankets savagely towards her, exposing him to the cool night air, and turned away, hoping sleep would come before tears.

15

Sunday was a cold grey day. Far off the sky was supported by thin columns of sunlight in the very early morning, but they faded before breakfast and the sky became just a grey canvas that sagged and bulged as if it were heavy with water. A cold wind came across the paddocks and the trees sang sadly with bowed heads. It was no day for cricket.

"Maybe we should of played 'em football," said Clint.

"Don't start complaining." Ocker said, casting a doleful eye at the miserable sky. "We've got to beat these bastards. We'll never be able to hold our heads up if we don't."

Both teams had arrived at the Cawndilla oval some fifteen minutes before. Two trucks, one from Wattle Run and the other from Mulgrue's, were parked side by side on the edge of the field and the men stood close together in groups like sheep huddling together for warmth.

"When are we gunna start, Ocker?" Sean said.

"If we don't start soon," said Bluey, "we'll get a wet arse and no runs."

"We'll be starting in a minute," Ocker said. "Everybody's here, except Rupe. Where's he got to?"

"He didn't come home last night," Sean said. "He got a lift into town with the boss. He probably kept Mrs. Firth company."

Venneker had a talent for appearing on cue. There was the sudden insistent blowing of a horn, then out of the scrub surrounding the field there charged the only new Hup-mobile in the district. Venneker was sitting up straight behind the wheel, like the master of a China boat running before a typhoon, while Mrs. Firth crouched beside him, one hand holding her hat and the other clutching for dear life to the side of the car. Crows rose in a black raucous explosion from the scrub, then Venneker had swung the car round in a wide circle of dust and rolled it with airy casualness in beside the Wattle Run truck.

He and Mrs. Firth alighted simultaneously, he with his usual grand dignity and she with some haste, as if she were glad to get out of the car before it bolted off again.

"Crikey," she said to the world at large, " he's a demon driver, if ever I seen one."

"I believe in punctuality," Venneker said. " It took me longer than I had expected to get dressed this morning."

"Get a load of the get-up," Turk Tuthill said.

"He's got his trousers at half-mast," Bluey said. " Someone must've died."

"Probably the bloke who owned the pants before him," Chilla Peters said.

Venneker seemed to have come prepared for either football or cricket. The black seaman's cap was perched at the usual jaunty angle on the white mane; the red-and-green striped football jersey curved its way tightly round the angles of his upper frame; a pair of black labourer's boots, topped by green socks, anchored him firmly to the ground. Between the tops of the socks and the bottom of the football jersey, his legs and middle were encased in a pair of very tight, startlingly white trousers.

"How's he look?" Mrs. Firth had walked over to join Ida, Liz Brown and Jean Halstead, who had just arrived in the Halsteads' car. " That's a pair of my Alec's duds he's wearing. We had to get him into 'em with a shoe-horn. Gawd help him if he bends. He'll give away all his secrets."

"I wouldn't want to miss that," Liz said. Her baby was asleep in the back of the car, and she herself looked remarkably fit. Her face had filled out, seeming to glow with colour; her figure, once athletic, had now become soft and curved with womanliness. Beside her, Jean Halstead, more beautiful, appeared pale and lustreless.

"You look real good, Liz," Mrs. Firth said, nodding appreciatively, as if Liz's pregnancy had been her own suggestion. "There's nothing like having a baby for improving a woman. I wonder if I got time for improvement?"

"Keep working on Rupe," Ida said. "You've got him half-way hooked."

"It ain't for want of trying," Mrs. Firth said.

"We're all on your side," Jean Halstead said, then saw her husband among the group of men and smiled at him with love: she hadn't felt so happy for months.

Then Venneker let out a roar. "What are we standing about for? Who's the opposing captain?"

Herb Cooper, dressed in a faded grey flannel singlet, patched navy blue trousers held up with an old tie, sand-shoes and a greasy felt hat, as if shearing matches and cricket matches were all the same to him, came forward from the group clustered about the truck from Mulgrue's. "I'm the captain of our mob. You wanna toss?"

"That's one way of getting started." Venneker took a penny from his pocket. "You call."

"Hey, wait a minute!" Ocker Shand stepped up beside Venneker and glared up at him. "Who said you were captain?"

"No one," said Venneker blandly. "I never for a moment assumed that it would be otherwise."

"That's where you came a gutser then," Ocker said vehemently. "I organised this match and I'm going to be the flaming captain!"

His brow was almost as dark as the sky above him. The wind had increased: leaves whirled in the air like startled birds, and the dust had its last fling before it turned to mud. The edge of the plains was lost in a dark grey curtain and the moving air was already wet. But Ocker had forgotten the elements in the shadow of something far worse.

"Stone the bloody crows, you had nothing to do with this match! Everything was left to me and now you want to step in and take over!"

Clint Evans looked doubtfully at Ocker. "I dunno whether you'd be any good. Why don't we pick Bluey as captain? He's supposed to be our best cricketer."

"I don't want the job," Bluey said with a grin, and turned his back to the first thin drops of rain. "I know you mugs. If we lose the game, you'll blame me. I nominate Turk."

"What's he know about cricket?" demanded Ocker. "I tell you, I oughta be captain. You wouldn't have had a cricket match if it hadn't been for me!"

"That's right," a man said. "If it hadn't been for Clint, we wouldn't of had a shearing match either."

"And we'd of still had our money," Turk said.

"We better hang on to what we got," Chilla Peters said, and began to walk away. "You play 'em on your own, Ocker. I'm getting in outa the rain."

Ocker's answer was lost in the first swishing gust of rain, then as everyone began to rush for the shelter of the trucks the whole countryside was blotted out by a grey swirling curtain. For a while the rain lashed viciously at the ground, driven by the bustling, businesslike wind, then the wind had gone on, dragging clouds with it, and the rain settled down to a steady steep fall that pocked the earth with puddles. The hills and the scrub became the colour of the sky. The birds had disappeared and the animals, the occasional kangaroo or wallaby that came this close to town, seemed to have gone underground. The only sign of life was in the trucks and the Halsteads' car.

Mrs. Firth had scrambled into the car with the other women. "Why don't we go back to my place? I ain't supposed to open the pub on Sundays, but you could all reckon you were travellers in need of food and drink. I can get round the law that way. Let's have a party, eh?"

"Both truckfuls?" Ida said. "There'll be quite a mob."

The invitation was shouted across to the men in the trucks and didn't need repeating. Almost before Mrs. Firth had closed her mouth, the drivers of the trucks had let in the gears and started off, flinging a fine spray of mud behind them. Jean Halstead drove the car with the women in it back to town, and Venneker and Bob Halstead made the trip in Mrs. Firth's Hupmobile. The rain had set in as a steady downpour, washing out the whole landscape, reducing the world to small isolated groups. It was a hopeless day for cricket, but it looked like being an ideal day for a beer and an ear-bash.

The trucks had pulled into the rear yard of the hotel and

the men were already waiting politely, but impatiently, in the
bar when Mrs. Firth and the other women arrived. Mrs.
Firth laid down the law immediately.

"Now I don't want you to make a welter of it," she said as
she walked in behind the bar, tying on an apron. "Anyone
who gets noisy drunk or tries to start a fight gets locked up
until he sobers up. I ain't supposed to be serving you on
Sundays, but the way it is to-day I don't think anyone will be
snooping around. Nobody comes in behind the bar but us
women. I want some of you fellers to help me put a brand-
new nine-gallon keg on the taps, and when that runs out
we'll put another on. When the party's finished, we'll add
up how much it cost and you can pay me what I paid for it.
Righto, who's gunna help me put the keg on the taps?"

There was a rush of volunteers and the party was under
way. Jean Halstead helped Mrs. Firth in the bar while Ida
and Liz Brown went out to the kitchen.

"You take it easy," Ida said. Liz had gone upstairs to put
the baby in one of the bedrooms, and now came into the
kitchen as if looking for work. "You don't want to go
knocking yourself out just to make it a good day for that
mob out there."

"If someone doesn't help you, *you'll* be the one who'll be
done in," Liz said. "What are we going to feed them with?"

A sheep had been delivered to the hotel the day before,
and in the larder Ida found a bag of potatoes and a bag of
beans. She walked through to the bar and called for volunteers to work on the potatoes and beans. The rush was not
quite as enthusiastic as that for setting up the beer keg, but
finally four men went out, carrying their glasses with them,
and began to peel the potatoes. Ida cut up the sheep, got it
ready for roasting, then set about preparing a treacle pudding.

Cawndilla had become a sodden ghost town, pale and
phantom-like behind the heavy screen of rain. The streets,
rivers of yellow mud, were deserted but for an occasional
dog, hump-backed in dejection, creeping from doorway to
doorway like a derelict human. The rain drummed monotonously on the town's tin roofs, containing each house in its
own world of sound, and there was little chance of the party

in the hotel being heard elsewhere. Which was just as well:
two dozen men, lubricated by cost-price beer and stimulated
by a diversity of opinions on a diversity of subjects, were a
long way from mute.

It was Clint Evans who found the large storeroom built
on as an extra wing at the rear of the hotel. He had been out
to the men's lavatory, affected by two quick beers and the
cold day, and coming back had glanced in and seen the open
space among the paraphernalia for which the storeroom had
been built. The sight of the sawdust sprinkled on the floor
and the memory of last Wednesday's lost bet met in his
brain with a shock that almost paralysed him. He stood for
a moment, blinking his eyes and trying to recover from his
amazement at his own genius, then he had bolted inside to
the bar as fast as he could work his bandy legs.

"Who's for a game of two-up? Got just the place out the
back. Even got sawdust on the floor, so's the pennies won't
roll. Waddia reckon? Who wants to give it a fly?"

Everybody wanted to risk their money, it seemed. Clint
headed for the storeroom, his thin face flushed with anticipa-
tion and his eyes shining like two-bob pieces, and the men
streamed out after him. They formed a ring, bets were made,
a piece of wood was found that made an excellent kip, two
bright brand-new pennies were miraculously produced and
placed side by side on the kip, and Clint stood ready to toss
them into the air.

"Righto, we want a coupla bob to see him go!"

"I'll bet two bob he heads 'em!"

"Dollar he tails 'em! Who'll cover a dollar he tails 'em?"

"All bets set? Righto. Come in spinner!"

And Clint had sent the pennies spinning into the air.
They spun high, drawing the men's faces upwards, and the
room for a moment seemed to glow with the reflected light
from the upturned faces, then the pennies had begun to fall
and the faces went down, dimming the room again. The
pennies landed, rolled, then fell flat: two heads. The men
were set for the rest of the day, or until their money ran out.

In the bar Mrs. Firth and Jean Halstead were drying
glasses. Jean did it slowly and conscientiously, as if she had

never had to dry glasses before; Mrs. Firth breathed on the glasses and used the towel as a polishing cloth, a barmaid who took pride in her work.

"I'd get twelve months' gaol and lose me licence if I was found out," Mrs. Firth said. "Serving beer on Sundays, running a gambling joint."

"You could tell them not to play two-up," Jean said. "You asked them not to make a welter of it."

"Ah, let 'em go." Mrs. Firth polished a glass, then looked at it critically. She breathed on it and went on polishing. "Let 'em have their fun. I've never been able to be a spoil-sport, Jean. Not since I come out here, anyway. Men, the men I meet here in this pub, ain't got much but what they can pick up from day to day. I believe in letting 'em have all the fun they can get while they can get it. They battle all their lives, working like slaves just to stay ahead of nature and what it can do to you, never having a holiday, keeping this part of the country alive, and when they're dead they're forgotten. Nobody thanks 'em for what they done. All they get is abuse and called a lotta silly bastards for wasting their lives out here. You've heard what they call 'em down in the city. Bushwhackers. The mugs from the mulga."

"I know," Jean said. "I've called them that, myself."

"You've changed your mind?" Mrs. Firth looked at her sharply, then smiled when Jean nodded her head. "You've only gotta be out here a while and you soon realise who's the mugs. I know. I was the same as every other city smart aleck when I arrived here, but I soon changed me mind. Now nothing's too good for 'em, as far as I'm concerned." She breathed angrily on a glass and polished vigorously. "Getting drunk on Sundays and gambling may be against the law, but the law was made by city wowsers. They dunno nothing of what it takes to keep a man alive out here."

Jean Halstead slowly went on drying glasses. She was in complete agreement with everything Mrs. Firth had said: it was a lesson she had been learning painfully these last six months. The soft easy life she had led in the city now seemed a long way off, more a dream than a memory. She knew that Bob was really not one of the men Mrs. Firth had been talking about: Wattle Run with its fifty thousand acres and its twenty-five thousand sheep, was not a cocky's farm. No, she had meant the cockies with their couple of hundred acres, the men who did all the work themselves, the lambing, the shearing, the milking, the ploughing, the sowing, the harvesting, every year just a calendar of work until their sons grew up and the burden was lightened, but a man still died tired. The small-selection farmers, the drovers, the shearers, the stockmen—these were the men Mrs. Firth meant and they were men Jean Halstead had come to know in the last six months. Like everyone else in Sydney she had used and believed the glib phrase "Australia lives off the sheep's back"; but now she knew that, of course, Australia lived off the backs of men. Men such as those outside in the store-room; and the farmers standing behind their windows looking out on the rain, thankful for it but remembering the floods of five winters before; the stockman squatted beneath his horse somewhere out in the scrub; and the drover, riding his horse and leading two others, who was now a mile out of town and heading, unwittingly, for the two-up game and the turn of Paddy Carmody's luck.

Paddy had been having a tough trot in the storeroom. As soon as Clint had suggested the two-up game he had felt the old pull: cards and two-up were like a magnet to the money in his pocket. He had bet on the first spin of the pennies and after half an hour still hadn't succeeded in calling them correctly. He was having worse luck than a blind man in a brothel this last week: not a flaming thing was going right. He had allowed Sean to have a couple of small bets, just for the fun of it, and to add insult to injury Sean had called tails correctly both times.

For the first hour all the men had had some interest in the game. Then when a few of them had begun to notice the run of their luck, they had wandered back into the bar. Venneker had had only one win in five bets and was now back in the bar, lending his personality to the enhancement of the women's day. Bluey, still a little distracted that he was the father of a future Test cricketer, his distraction helped by four or five beers, had gone upstairs to see if the baby had

the makings of a good bowling arm. Clint, almost running a
fever with excitement, was glad he had suggested the game:
he had been winning continuously almost from the first spin
of the coins.

Paddy continued to chase his luck down a dark alley, and
by the time Ida came out to the storeroom to call the men to
mid-day dinner he had exhausted all his assets. Ida noticed
it at once.

" Where's your tooth? " she said.

Paddy smiled at her weakly, the gap in his mouth seeming
to make him more shamefaced. " I think they're playing with
double-headed pennies, darl. The way me luck's been this
morning, I couldn't win an argument."

" You've never won yet," Ida said. " Who's got your
tooth? "

" I have," said Herb Cooper, halting beside them as he
headed for the dining-room. He flicked a stubby forefinger
at the gold tooth pinned by its wire brace to his shirt. " I'm
thinking of knocking out one of me uppers and putting this
one in its place. Might give me more chance with the girls,
you reckon? "

" How much do you want for it? " Ida said.

" Well, I dunno," Cooper said. " I'd have to have it valued.
I bet a quid against it, but it might be worth more than that.
I wouldn't wanna rob meself."

" You'd be the only bastard you wouldn't rob," Paddy said,
then turned back to Ida. " We ain't gunna buy it back. If
I'm gunna get it back, I'll win it back."

" What with? " Ida said. " Are they allowing credit in this
game? I'll buy it back, even if Mr. Cooper here charges me
two quid for it. You think I want you hanging around me,
grinning like a toothless old hag——"

" If that's all you're worried about, you can buy it back
and wear it yourself! " Paddy shouted; he could have cut his
own throat when Cooper, of all people, had been the one to
reduce him to an absolutely penniless state. " All you think
about is a man's looks. Here I been trying to win us some
extra money, something to add to our jam-jar, and all the
luck's been against me, and all you think about is how I look

without Mickey!" He stalked in towards the dining-room shouting over his shoulder to Cooper, "Don't sell it to her! Keep raising her price!"

Cooper looked at Ida and winked. "I hear you're a good cook, missus. You can have the tooth for a second helping of whatever's on for dinner."

"There should be enough for second helpings all round," Ida said. "But you'd better keep his tooth for a while. If he hasn't won it back from you by to-night, I'll come and get it from you. Though Lord knows where he's going to get the money to get back into the game. Most of the men won't want to stake him after seeing the way his luck's been running."

But Paddy didn't need to approach the men for a loan. He sat next to Sean at dinner, commenting on the latter's luck, smiling widely every two or three minutes, throwing in an odd remark here and there on how even a terrible run of luck had to change sooner or later. At the end of the meal, having eaten two helpings of everything, because Sean had done so, and having tasted none of it, he walked back to the storeroom with Sean, wondering why he had reared such a thick-headed bastard who couldn't take a hint. He stood watching the coins go into the air for the first spin, debating whether to ask Sean for a loan or clip him under the ear for being so dense, then Sean had turned to him and was holding out a note.

"Want a lend of ten bob, Dad? You can pay me back next pay-day."

Paddy took the note and winked at his son: no doubt about it, the boy was a chip off the old block, knew that a bit of gambling never hurt a man and wasn't afraid to stake him when the luck was going the wrong way. He looked about him, saw Bluey and Ocker had seen Sean hand him the money, and nodded knowingly: if Bluey's kid grew up to have Sean's gumption, Bluey would have someone to be proud of.

His first bet was a cautious one, just two shillings. He won, and with his next bet doubled his stake. Within half an hour he was once more flashing the golden-toothed smile

and had run his luck back into the bright light of everyone's
envy. Clint Evans, who was a superstitious gambler and had
had a reverse of fortunes since dinner-time, came and stood
beside him in the hope of being brushed by some of his luck.
Then the stranger arrived.

There was a banging on the door of the storeroom and the
two-up game suddenly ceased. The pennies and the kip disappeared and the men did their difficult best to look inno-
cent. They stood there, waiting for the door to burst open
and the town's wowsers, supported by the one policeman,
to come rushing in, but the banging just continued.

"If they're going to raid us," Ocker Shand said, "why
don't they get it over with?"

Then the hammering stopped. For a moment nothing
happened, then the door slowly opened and a head came
round the edge of it.

"Hullo," a cracked voice said, "a two-up game in progress?"

"Depends who's asking," Chilla Peters said. "We might
be holding Sunday school."

The door opened a little farther and the stranger came
round the edge of it into the storeroom. He didn't appear
to walk into the room; it was almost as if he had climbed
round the door, as you might round the corner of a cliff. He
was thin and tall almost beyond the point of caricature; no
artist would have drawn a character so thin, for fear it would
have been spoiled in reproduction. His face was almost twice
the length of an ordinary face, and half as broad: the
features seemed to have been put on askew, so that all might
fit and none would be left hanging like some weird growth.
Lank black hair hung from the top of a high narrow dome,
and one was left with the final impression of a badly-treated
mop that had been dressed to end its days as a scarecrow. His
clothes were faded and nondescript, wet through as far up as
his knees, and he carried a stained worn raincoat and a hat
that could only be classed as a relic.

"Do I look like a copper?" the stranger said, then
laughed: it was a sound that split in the middle, then was
shattered completely, so that the room was full of this flying

sound, like birds darting to and fro, up and down, in a mad effort to escape the enclosing walls. The men stared at the newcomer, then looked at each other as if wondering what to do with this lunatic. The stranger slowly stopped laughing: he gathered together all the flying pieces of sound, made the laugh whole again, then swallowed it. The lopsided mouth dropped a little farther in a smile. " You haven't got to worry, friends. I heard the clink of the coins and I looked in, hoping for a game."

" Where you from?" Clint said. " Do you belong around here?"

" I belong nowhere, friend. But I have just come from Becker's Lagoon, where I delivered a thousand head of sheep. I am heading north now, chasing the sun "—he shook water from his hat and the laughter struggled in his throat—" and all I'm seeking is a pot of beer, some tucker and a chance to try my luck. Am I in?"

" You're in," Turk Tuthill said. " We'll get you a beer and something to eat. Sean here'll show you where to put your horses outa the rain. How many you got?"

" Three," said the stranger. " And four dogs."

" I'll look after them," Sean said, and went out, leaving the stranger at the mercy of the spinning pennies. In the backyard of the hotel three horses stood with heads bent against the rain. In the open doorway of a wood-shed four bedraggled dogs stared out with unhappy eyes at Sean as he ran through the rain and led the horses to some stalls at the bottom of the yard. One of the dogs barked and came skidding out into the mud as he took hold of the reins of the horses, but he whistled at it and it sidled up to him wagging its tail. The other three dogs followed it, and Sean went across the yard surrounded by animals.

He took the saddle and packs off the horses and stood for a moment watching them as they dipped their muzzles into the bins of chaff. Two were just ordinary stockmen's horses, solid in the leg and chest and with the suggestion of endurance and intelligence that a man looks for in a horse he works every day. But the third horse wasn't built for plodding all day after sheep, or drafting a bullock out of the scrub: he wasn't the sort of horse usually to be found in a stockman's or drover's string.

Sean walked round the back of the two stock horses and took a closer look at the black stallion. Standing quietly, shining like black porcelain, the horse had a look of sleekness and speed that reminded Sean of a hawk in the moment before it folded its wings and dived. He put out a hand and stroked the wet coat and the horse raised its head from the bin and rolled a nervous eye.

"You're a real beaut," Sean said, then turned and ran back through the rain to the storeroom, wondering why such a beautiful animal should be led about the country at the end of a drover's lead rope.

At the moment the stranger had entered the storeroom another visitor had entered the side door of the hotel, without knocking and using his own key. Jack Patchogue, the district magistrate, had been sitting at home watching the rain stream down the windows and thinking to himself that there was nothing worse than being a widower on a rainy day.

When he could no longer stand the thought of his sitting alone at home and Gert twiddling her thumbs up at the pub, he had put on his hat and raincoat, struggled into a pair of gumboots and had come up the street through the cold teeming rain to the hotel. With stiff wet fingers he had searched for the key Gert had given him eighteen months ago, put it in the side door and had gone in to find that Gert was a long way from twiddling her thumbs.

"Gawd Almighty, what's going on? I come up to keep you company and I find you entertaining behind my back! What's got into you, Gert? Is that the way to treat a bloke?"

The bar was deserted but for Mrs. Firth and Venneker. She had been leaning on the bar counter listening to his suggestions as to what they might do if they went upstairs and had just allowed herself to be talked into his invitation when Patchogue walked in. She straightened up and restrained herself from telling Patchogue not to take his hat off, but to go straight back home.

"Hullo, Jack. Did you want something? I didn't expect to see you out on a day like this."

"Looks like you didn't!" Indignation and the running up the street through the rain had left Patchogue almost without breath. "Gawd Almighty, Gert, I didn't think you'd act like this!"

Venneker had remained leaning across the counter until now, when he stood up and squinted down at Patchogue with an irritated eye. "My man, can't you take a hint, or do you want the good woman to take out a restraining order to stop you from bothering her? That would be a trifle embarrassing for you, wouldn't it? Signing a restraining order against yourself."

Until now, blinded by wounded pride and rain on his glasses, Patchogue had only been aware of his opposition as someone tall in trousers. Now he took off his glasses, disturbed by a faintly familiar voice, and peered up at Venneker. "Gawd Almighty, you!"

"A case of mistaken identity," Venneker said. "I am not the God Almighty."

Patchogue hadn't heard him. He turned to Mrs. Firth and threw out his arms imploringly. "Him, of all people! Gert, what's going on here?"

Turk Tuthill came into the bar . "Can I have two more beers, missus? One for me, and the other's for a bloke outside who's just got in from Becker's Lagoon."

Mrs. Firth drew two glasses, while Venneker turned to Turk. "How is the game going? The fall of the coins favouring you?"

"Off and on," Turk said. "I'm about square now."

"What's going on out the back?" Patchogue said.

Turk had accepted the fat, owl-faced man as a friend of Mrs. Firth. "A two-up game. You wanna come out and try your luck? Thanks," he said to Mrs. Firth and took the two glasses from her. "See you later."

Patchogue swung round towards the bar again. "You know what you're doing, Gert? Serving beer on Sundays, letting them run a gambling game on your premises!"

"What are you getting so worked up about?" Mrs. Firth

said. "You often come up here for a drink on Sundays. And we used to play cards every Sunday night, once. Penny poker. Ain't that gambling?"

"No! We were friends! You were entertaining me!" Patchogue was almost beside himself with rage and frustration now. The only woman in his life he had ever been able to dominate had died five years before, worn out by his demands, and ever since he had been seeking someone else who could satisfy him without having any hold on him. Cawndilla was too small a town to have girls who could be bought, and though there were not enough men for a girl to be too hard to please, none of the younger girls had given him the slightest encouragement. Mrs. Firth was the only older woman who was unattached and for the last two years, mistaking the nature of her affection, he had been building up in his mind the thought that it was only a matter of time before there would be another Mrs. Patchogue. Now jealousy had brought him to the brink of apoplexy. "You're just running an open house now! In more ways than one, too!"

Venneker didn't actually punch him. He just straightened to his full height, raised his fist on high, then brought it crashing down against Patchogue's cheek. The tight fat flesh burst like a ripe fruit and blood began to run immediately. Patchogue staggered back, put a hand to his face and stared at it with amazement when it came away streaked with blood, then he had turned and stumbled out of the bar, half-moaning, half-muttering, and in a moment there was the loud slam of the side door being closed.

"I apologise for my conduct," Venneker said, breathing a little heavily. "I am not in the habit of fighting before women."

"Good Gawd!" Mrs. Firth was almost overcome. "Don't apologise. That's the first time in all me life I've had a man stick up for me. When I been insulted before, I've had to dong 'em meself!"

Venneker picked up Patchogue's spectacles from the bar where he had left them. "Will he be able to see his way home without these?"

"It ain't the first time he's left here without 'em," Mrs.

Firth said. "Coupla times I've kicked him out for taking too much for granted, and he's gone off without his specs. Once he left here without his shoes and socks."

Ida, Liz and Jean Halstead had been washing up the dinner dishes in the kitchen. They came in the bar now, looking a little washed up themselves, and Jean Halstead walked in behind the bar counter.

"What'll it be, ladies?"

"Could I be expensive," Ida said, "and try a whisky and soda?"

"I'll just have a lemonade," Liz said. "I have to go up and feed Christopher in a moment."

"How is the infant progressing?" Venneker said.

"He's very well," Liz said. "I'll be taking him back to Sydney in another week or so, when the shearing finishes here at Wattle Run."

"Is it only another week?" Mrs. Firth looked startled.

"That's all," Jean Halstead said, setting drinks on the counter. "I was talking to Bob last night about it. I'm sorry it's finishing."

"So am I," said Mrs. Firth, and looked at Venneker. "Where do you go next, Rupe?"

"I haven't the faintest idea," Venneker said, and Ida looked sideways at him: is he beating about the bush? she wondered, and felt like kicking him in the shins: he had no right to treat Mrs. Firth this way. "I make a point of never looking ahead."

"It's often better than looking back," Ida said.

"Agreed, madam," Venneker said. "That's why I live only in the present."

"Stumps you every time." Mrs. Firth shrugged her shoulders. "Always gets the last word in.. What would you be like if you couldn't talk, Rupe?"

"Still better than average," Venneker said, and excused himself to walk out of the bar and back to the storeroom.

"D'you think I should break his leg?" Mrs. Firth said to the other women. "That ud keep him tied here a bit longer."

As Venneker walked into the storeroom a shout went up from the men and for a moment he thought they were greeting him. Then he noticed that those closest to him had their backs to him; those farther away were facing him, but were oblivious of him. They were gathered in a loose ring about Turk Tuthill, holding the kip from which he had just spun the two pennies, Paddy Carmody and a tall thin stranger who seemed to be suffering from some sort of fever that caused him alternately to clap his hand to his chin and to break into a laugh that was a mixture of wild merriment and something approaching hysteria.

"What is going on?" Venneker said to Bluey Brown.

Bluey turned a happy, flushed face; his breath smelled of beer, but that didn't appear to be the only cause for his slight drunkenness. "Paddy's having a run of tinny luck. He hasn't lost a toss in half an hour."

"Who is the lost cadaver standing opposite him?" Venneker said.

"The lost——?" Then Bluey grinned; he knew that Paddy had been downcast about the result of Wednesday's race and he was happily excited that Paddy was having such a run of luck. "Oh, him. Dunno his name. He came in a little while ago, and now he's the only bloke betting against Paddy. He's in the hole for over fifty quid already, I reckon. He's worse than Clint for wanting to try his luck. Look at him. You'd think he was ready to go off his nut."

The stranger was leaning forward, bent in the middle as if he were ill, his eyes shining and a queer smile widening his lop-sided mouth. He looked across at Paddy and croaked, "Eight quid he tails them. All I have, friend. Eight pounds that our colleague here throws tails!"

Paddy hesitated for a moment. His own eyes were bright with the excitement of his run of luck, but he had recognised the look in the other man's eyes: a gambler knows a gambler. The stranger had become almost desperate now: he had forgotten the value of money and all he wanted now was to win, to snap his losing streak and thumb his nose at the fates that had ridden the pennies to the floor wrong side up. Paddy held back: the other men had dropped out of the game, and he was reluctant to clean out this sporting stranger;

but even as he hesitated he knew the stranger was too far gone in the fever to take *no* for an answer.

"Taken!" Paddy said. "Eight quid he heads 'em!"

Turk placed the pennies on the kip, held them steady, then flipped them quickly into the air. They went up, whittling the air into curls of bright bronze light, then they fell, hitting the floor with two sharp sounds that were loud in the quiet room. They rolled a short distance, teetered on their edges, then fell.

The stranger remained bent forward, staring down at the coins, then, without moving his head, he raised his eyes and looked across at Paddy.

"I have a horse outside," he said. "A thoroughbred, one that could run like a mountain wind if I had the time to train him."

"What you getting at?" Paddy said.

The stranger slowly stood upright. "The horse against everything you've won to-day. I bet the horse that the spinner tails 'em!"

"No, mate," Paddy said. "It's gone far enough. I don't wanna take your horse off you."

"Yes!" The stranger flung out a long arm, a gesture that could have meant anything: a plea, a threat, a gesture of despair. "Don't back out on me now, friend! I bet the horse!"

Paddy looked about him at the other men, then at Sean standing beside him. "What you reckon, Sean?"

Later Sean would be ashamed of himself, but the words escaped him now: "It's a good horse, Dad! I saw it a while ago. It's a beaut!"

"You'd like it?" Paddy said. "You'd like to own it yourself?"

"Crikey, Dad! You mean it? For me?" He had never owned a single thing in his life, and the thought was too much for him: "Toss him, Dad! For Gawd's sake, take the bet!"

Paddy looked back across the ring. "Taken. Everything I won this afternoon against this horse of yours. You bet he tails 'em."

Again Turk placed the pennies on the kip. He took his time, deliberate over the small action, held the kip for a long breathless moment, then jerked his wrist and the pennies were in the air. They climbed towards the bare electric globe, drawing the whole room together into one small flashing, whirling spot, then they fell straight, almost without spinning, and hit the floor with a flat and heartless sound.

The stranger straightened as if he had been hit in the small of the back, threw back his head and laughed. It was a full-chested laugh, like the one he had uttered when he had first come into the storeroom: it roared and whipped about the room, splintering against the walls, and there was no hysteria in it, only a great feeling of relief, as if the man had sighed and it had come out as laughter.

The laugh was at last recaptured and swallowed again. He put out a long thin hand and took Paddy's shaking it with enormous gusto. "Congratulations, friend! You took a risk on that last one, stayed with your luck when it might have been at the end of its tether, and you won! The sort of gambler I like to meet."

"I feel like a bastard taking your horse off you," Paddy said.

Sean was suddenly aware of what had happened to the stranger; shame overcame him and he stammered confusedly, "Take him back, mister. I'm sorry I asked Dad to take you up on the bet."

"I won him in a game of cards," the stranger said. "Why shouldn't I lose him at two-up? He's yours, friend. Make more of him than I did. He'll be a champion if you bring him along the right way."

"Well, we'll go and have a look at him," Paddy said. "I might of won us another Poitrel."

The stranger put on his hat and opened the door. Patchogue and a burly unhappy-looking man stood just outside, Patchogue with his fist raised to knock on the door that had been opened away from him. He opened his fist and pointed.

"There they are! Playing two-up! Arrest the lot of them!"

The unhappy-looking man looked a little unhappier.

"Why don't you sleep on this, Jack? They aren't doing any harm. Your liver might feel better t'morrow, and they'll be outa here, back working in the sheds."

"This has nothing to do with my liver!" Patchogue's face was now decorated with a cross of sticking-plaster; without his spectacles, he blinked his eyes continually, like an owl caught in a bright light. "To-morrow we'll have nothing on them! Lock 'em up and I'll hear the case first thing in the morning!"

"You the town policeman?" the stranger said to the unhappy man.

"Yeah," said that character. "Wish to Christ I wasn't right now. What sorta bastard are they gunna think I am, working on Sundays to run in a few two-up players?"

"You're the man I've been looking for," the stranger said. "I have a message for you. I'll get my horses and follow you down to the police station." He turned back to the men in the storeroom. "I hope all this works out satisfactorily for you, friends. I warned you of the wages of sin, but you heeded me not." He winked at them, then turned back to Patchogue and the policeman. "I'll get my horses and dogs, then later we'll talk about a hall for my reform meeting."

He went out across the yard: laughter was lost in the hiss and drum of the rain. Patchogue stared after him for a moment, then spun back and flung an arm that almost knocked off the constable's hat.

"Go on, arrest the lot of them! Lock 'em up for the night! And make sure you get the big bloke, Venneker or whatever his name is!"

16

"Hey, Bluey," Paddy whispered. "You asleep?"

"Not a bloody chance," Bluey said. "I've got Turk, Chilla and Ocker all using me as a bolster. It's my own fault for being built for comfort. What's on your mind?"

Paddy sat up. The light in the hall outside threw the pattern of the cell bars across his face: both eyes were hidden behind bars of shadow. He wriggled on to one hip, reached into his pocket, then withdrew his hand and leaned across towards Bluey.

"Here." The word didn't come at first as he tried to whisper and he had to clear his throat. "For your kid."

"What is it?" Bluey took the object Paddy had given him and held it up to a strip of light. "Ah, cut it out, Paddy! Stone the crows, you don't want to go handing out money like this! It's yours. Here take it." He held out the roll of notes tied with string.

"No, it's the nipper's," Paddy said. "I should of won it for him last Wednesday. Then yesterday washed out the chance of winning it for him at cricket. It's his. Put it in the bank for him."

Bluey lay stiffly on the floor of the cell, trying not to disturb the three men whose heads were pillowed on various parts of his body. He had been disappointed when Paddy hadn't won on Wednesday, he had admitted to himself that night, but since then he had forgotten what a win might have meant for the new baby and hadn't given a thought to what might have resulted from yesterday's cricket match, if they had been able to play it. Yesterday had been such a wonderful day, including being thrown into the lock-up last night, that the future of Christopher Victor had never crossed his mind. Now here was Paddy offering him well over a hundred pounds, an amount that would look good in the baby's bank book, but would look equally good in Paddy's bank book, if he had one.

"No, mate." He tossed the roll of notes back to Paddy. "Thanks all the same. It's bloody nice of you, but we couldn't take it."

Paddy picked up the money from his lap and threw it back to Bluey. It hit Ocker Shand in the face and he sat up quickly, looking around dazedly.

"Was that a rat? Did it bite me?"

"You were dreaming," Bluey said. "Put your head back on my gut and go to sleep."

"Balls, I was dreaming! Something bit me, I tell you." Ocker began moving his hands about him, feeling for rats.

One hand brushed against the string tied round the notes and he hurriedly jerked it away. Cautiously he felt again for the rat's tail, seized it and held it high. "There's the bastard!"

"What's the matter with you?" Chilla Peters said, and squinted up at the dark object dangling an inch or two above his nose. "What the hell's that?"

"I thought it was a rat," Ocker said, and Chilla rolled his head quickly to one side. "But it looks like something else."

"It's a roll of notes, if you must know." Bluey reached up and took the money from Ocker. "Paddy dropped it."

"What's he doing with money at this time of night?" Chilla said. "He ain't counting it, is he?"

"Mind your flaming business," Paddy said. "Me and Bluey were having a quiet chat, and every bastard in the cell's gotta put their oar in."

"Shut up and go to sleep," someone said from the far side of the cell.

"You know what you can do," Paddy said, then turned back to Bluey. "You keep the dough, Blue. I did all right yesterday. I won a horse, and he looks to me as if he's gunna be as good as the bloke claimed. If Sean wants to race him, we'll make money outa him."

Bluey was silent for a while, then he said, "All right. Paddy. And thanks a lot. For me, Liz and young Chris."

"I wish someone ud tell me what's going on," Ocker said. "Or can I have a guess?"

"Just pull your head in and go back to sleep," Chilla said, and rolled over. He looked over the hill of Bluey's body to Paddy, lying back now in shadow. "Good on you, Paddy. But you didn't have to do it."

"It's a load off me mind," Paddy said. "See you in the morning."

In the morning Constable Thomas opened the door of the cell and looked in with a sad face. "Look, you coves, I got some bad news for you. The wife says she isn't gunna cook for you. Says the lock-up was only built to handle overnight drunks, no more than one or two at a time, and she didn't marry me to cook for two shearing teams for a week."

The cell was exceptionally big for a country police station, having at one time been the storeroom of a grain and feed merchant who had since gone out of business. It was built of galvanised iron on an iron frame, with a concrete floor, and would have held no self-respecting criminal longer than five minutes if he had had a mind to escape. But the twenty-four shearers had filed in here yesterday in the very best of humour, after Patchogue had given them seven days, with no option, for gambling. They had spent Sunday night here also, when the constable had first locked them up, and that night, still feeling the effects of the beer they had drunk, still in a party mood and holding no real grudge against Patchogue, had stayed awake almost till dawn, singing dirty songs in which Patchogue's name figured in almost every chorus. When Monday had come, a fine day but with the sheep still wet from Sunday's rain and therefore bad for shearing, with a slack day on their hands anyway, they had treated the court proceedings with great hilarity and had almost drawn extra sentences for contempt of court. Halstead had come in from Wattle Run to plead leniency for the men as first offenders, pointing out that they were needed out at the shearing sheds, but Patchogue, smarting under the contempt in which the prisoners so obviously held him, aware now that his victory was as hollow as a back tooth and twice as nagging, had been stubbornly adamant.

The court hearing had been held in the School of Arts, under the dusty, withered decorations remaining from last month's Masons' dance, and Patchogue had wasted no time handing out sentences. Because he still believed the affair with Venneker was only a passing one and because he didn't want to ruin his chances completely, he had ignored the fact that Mrs. Firth should have been charged for allowing gambling at the hotel. Venneker was the man he wanted; he didn't even mind that the stranger who had had a message for Constable Thomas had walked out into the rain from the storeroom and had disappeared. That twenty-three other men had to be sentenced with Venneker was just bad luck for them.

Venneker and the other prisoners were now standing in a group around Constable Thomas, the door wide open behind him and nobody giving it a second look.

"You mean you're going to allow us to starve?" Venneker said. "We are now charges of the State, I would remind you. For the next six days it is your duty to clothe, feed and house us, no matter what inconvenience it may be to you and your wife. You may remember that it was you who delivered us to this outpost of Dartmoor. It has caused *us* a certain amount of inconvenience."

"Ah, Christ, don't lay it on," said Constable Thomas; his dark heavy face drooped like a bloodhound's. "I didn't wanna bring you in. You heard me ask him to think it over. Nobody'll talk to me around town since yesterday. Calling me all the bastards they can lay their tongue to. Me, who's lived here all my life, who wouldn't have been a copper if they could've got someone else to come out this far. Struth, don't make it hard for a cove. Let's think this over and find a way out. You got any suggestions?" He looked around hopefully.

"I tell you, it's bloody poor management," said Ocker Shand. "Bringing us in here, then not being able to feed us."

"It's going to make criminals of us," Bluey said. "I'm already getting the urge to break gaol. Dunno what my kid's going to think of me. An escaped convict for an old man."

"I ain't gunna escape," Chilla Peters said. "This is one of the most comfortable gaols I ever been in."

"I could of done with a coupla more blankets last night," Paddy said. "How's it for more blankets to-night, warder?"

"Don't call me the flaming warder!" Constable Thomas waved a protesting hand and looked ready to end his life and his misery. "You coves are just making a joke of it. But it isn't funny. You wait till about tea-time to-night, when you've got empty bellies and nothing coming along. You dunno my missus like I do. When she says she isn't gunna cook, she isn't gunna cook. Many's the time I've gone hungry myself."

"Can't you cook?" Venneker said.

" Struth," said Constable Thomas, " if I cooked for you, I'd be burying the lotta you by t'morrow morning. No, come on, quit acting the goat. What're we gunna do about this?"

" You could let us go home," Bluey said.

" Yeah, and lose my job," Constable Thomas said. " Think of something else."

" No, listen to me," Bluey said; he had suddenly remembered that he was the union representative and that there were still sheep to be shorn out at Wattle Run and Mulgrue's. " Look, we've got almost another week's shearing ahead of us, the shed is supposed to cut out on Friday or Saturday, and we're due down at Long Billabong on Monday to start shearing there. I dunno my law, but I think you're the boss of your own lock-up."

" That's correct," Venneker said. " You are entitled to use your discretion in running it according to circumstances. Our friend Patchogue is supposed to inspect the gaol once a week. If at the end of the week we are starving we can lay a complaint against you for ill-treatment and neglect of duty."

" Yeah, I think you're right," Constable Thomas said. " I think I remember reading that somewhere in some of the books they sent up from Sydney. It was all in legal pidgin and I couldn't make head or tail of most of it. But I seem to remember something along those lines. Anyhow, what're you getting at?"

" This," said Bluey. " Let us go out to the sheds each day, we'll feed out there and we'll come back here each night to sleep. How's that?"

Constable Thomas thought about it for several minutes. There was no change in his unhappy face but for a deepening of the lines in his brow as he concentrated on the various aspects of the proposal. " How'm I gunna know you coves'll come home every night?"

" You'll know where to find us if we don't," Bluey said.

" I'm not going out tearing around the country for you," Constable Thomas said. " Not these winter nights, anyway. If I let you go, I'll expect to see you back here every night at eight o'clock. And you'll have to supply your own transport. All I got here is a pushbike and a horse and sulky."

" We'll get our trucks in," Bluey said, and looked at Herb Cooper. "That all right with you blokes?"

" It's righto with us." Cooper had forgotten to put his teeth back in after his night's sleep, and his voice hissed through his gums. "Just so long as we can get a full day's shearing, we don't mind spending the night in gaol."

" What about the money you earn?" Constable Thomas was still considering every point of the pact. "You coves will be earning more than prisoners make down in the city gaols."

" We'll donate it to charity," Venneker said. "The local branch of the Prisoners' Aid Society, of which I happen to be treasurer."

17

So the shearing, about which Halstead and Quinlan had begun to despair, got under way again. A phone call was put through to Wattle Run and Mulgrue's, and Quinlan came into town in the truck at a speed that could have had him gaoled for reckless driving. He came to a stop in front of the police station, the truck bucking fiercely at the suddenness with which he applied the brakes, leaned out and yelled. The Wattle Run men, hungry now, came out of the police station like a crowd coming out of a hotel at closing time: Constable Thomas came out after them, completing the illusion. He stood on the steps of the police station and shouted a final warning for them to be back before curfew. The men scrambled aboard the truck, then Quinlan had roared it away down the main street. As it headed out of town, it was passed by the truck from Mulgrue's coming in to collect the shearers still in gaol.

" Convict labour, that's all we are," Bluey Brown said. "I'm back where my great-grand-dad started."

Ida, with less than an hour's warning, had prepared a magnificent welcome-home breakfast. Jean Halstead and Liz Brown had come down from the homestead to help her, and when the men trooped into the cookhouse, they were met

with steaming porridge, thick steaks and fried eggs, hot bread
and butter, strawberry jam that Ida had been saving for the
farewell meal, strong tea, and a kerosene tin full of apples.
The men sat down to enjoy it, but they had reckoned without
Quinlan. Worried by the upset schedule, aware of the six
thousand sheep still out in the paddocks, he rode herd on the
men while they ate, and within half an hour, belching loudly,
some still with their breakfasts in their hands, they were on
their way down to the shed.

And so it went for the rest of the week. Five minutes
after the shearers had left on the first morning, Patchogue
heard about what was happening and came to the police
station. He stood in the centre of the empty cell and
threatened Constable Thomas with suspension, dismissal,
imprisonment and every other punishment short of hanging.
He stamped and swore and beat the air furiously with his
pudgy hands, reading a liberal interpretation of the Riot Act
to the sad-faced Constable Thomas and his stern-faced wife,
putting on a show to convince himself as much as anyone
else, then he abruptly shut up and went back home, determined to lie low until Venneker and the rest of the shearers
had moved on. He stood in front of the mirror in his bedroom and stared at the blank owl-like face that hid the
frustrated mind: his wife smiled at him from a faded photograph, a plain timid woman having the last laugh after all.
He swept the photograph from the dressing-table with an
angry motion, then sat down to wait out the week.

At Wattle Run Ida was also looking towards the end of the
week, but not with the same expectation. These last few
days she had found herself sometimes standing motionless
and staring about the kitchen with a warmth of feeling that
surprised her. She would put out a hand and touch the table,
a dish, the pots on the stove; a breeze would disturb the
curtains she had put up at the window, and she would smile
with pleasure at the distraction. About her she had almost
enough to take the place of home: she was a prodigal who
was satisfied not to continue the journey all the way.

But of course the journey had to be completed. This
kitchen, the pleasure of what she did here, this atmosphere

of temporary permanency, didn't mean anything to Sean.
Home was a state of mind he had yet to acquire, and the
process would be a long one: he hadn't even begun to
think of Wattle Run as home. She took down the jam-jar
from a shelf and counted the money in it: home, at present,
was a roll of crumpled notes, some silver, a few pennies.
Another year maybe, she thought, and looked out of the
window at Sean waving good night to the men as they
clambered into the truck for the trip back to the lock-up.

"Where's Clint?" she heard a voice shout. "Always late.
Does he want us to be locked out?"

Other voices began to shout for Clint Evans, and she saw
him come hurrying through the dusk, doing up his belt. He
was dragged aboard the truck, and it went down the hill
with the motor roaring and the dust rising greyly into the
dusk behind it. Sean stood watching it for a while, with the
lost air of someone on the outside of things, then he began
to walk slowly down to the yard built in one corner of the
home paddock.

Ida put the money back in the jam-jar and returned the
jar to the shelf. She called to Charlie, the aboriginal helper,
saw him coming across the yard, dark as the night behind
him in the sky, then turned to the sink and began to clear the
plates and dishes for washing up. She would have a talk to
Sean later: they had enough money in the jar now to begin
to think of a farm as something they might really own
within a year or two. Or at least they would have made the
down payment on it: she and Paddy might be dead before
it was ever theirs outright. Suddenly frightened, she blessed
herself: you could ask the Lord for too much. . . .

Walking down to the home paddock Sean was wishing he
were old enough to be in gaol. When the policeman had
herded the men out of the storeroom on Sunday, he had
pushed Sean aside, calling him Sonny and telling him to
buzz off, and he would never know how close he had come
to being the victim of assault and battery. Sean had gritted
his teeth and drawn his fist back, possessed for the moment
of his father's temper and pride, and had only been halted
by Venneker's restraining hand.

" We may need you on the outside," Venneker had whispered hoarsely. " See if there is a solicitor in town. Failing that, see if you can procure two or three rough files."

But there had been no solicitor and no need for one, the men all having decided to plead guilty, and there had been no need for the files. And Sean was still annoyed that he had been so summarily dismissed from the raid. The men must be having a wonderful time in gaol; the hut was lonely without them. There were still a few men left on the station, a couple of stockmen and one or two of the shed hands who had not turned up at the cricket match before the rain started and consequently had not gone on into Cawndilla and the two-up game; they were men who had always kept to themselves and Sean found no pleasure in their company. No, he should have gone to gaol, where all the blokes were. He leaned on the fence rail and looked with admiring eyes at the black stallion in the yard.

" He's a beaut, isn't he, Nigger?" he said to the kelpie at his feet, but the dog, neither jealous nor interested, didn't even look up at him. It stared across the yard at the horse, raised a leg and wet on a fence-post, then turned and trotted back up the hill: it had better things to do than stand around looking at horses.

Sean spat after the dog, then turned back to look at the horse. Even in this lustreless light, the black coat, moving over smooth sliding muscles, seemed alive with a blue sheen. When he called to it, softly as if this were a secret tryst, the horse raised its head, its ears pointed and its eyes bright with intelligence, and Sean caught his breath: the beauty of it, head raised, neck quivering, the deep chest tensed with power, the legs planted firmly, the tail moving gently in the breeze, all was a sudden pain inside him.

Then the horse had whirled, arching its neck, and was galloping round the yard, leaning forward and inward, hampered by the small space. At last it slowed and came towards him, snorting a little, not frightened but a little reserved, and Sean vaulted the fence. It shied away as he landed, its head going high and the eyes rolling white, then it came on and in a moment boy and horse were together, its nose buried in the crook of his arm and he stroking the muscles bunched in the trembling shoulder.

"I got a horse," he murmured, "a real horse," and at the moment owned the world.

The shearers-by-day-prisoners-by-night carried out their contract with scrupulous honesty. Every man increased his usual daily quota of shorn sheep and by Thursday night Quinlan knew the Wattle Run shearing would finish on schedule. Each night, when the evening meal was over, every man reported to the truck and was driven back to the lock-up, where Constable Thomas, now hailed by the towns-folks as the only copper they had ever met with initiative, welcomed them with an unhappy grin and locked them up for the night. On Friday night he told them they were being locked up for the last time: Halstead had been in to see Patchogue, and the latter, still in retreat, had sent a note to the police station that he was reducing the men's sentence because of their good behaviour. Saturday morning they would leave the lock-up as free men.

"I dunno how I'm going to react to all this freedom," Bluey said. "Out with decent honest citizens again, I'll probably need rehabilitating. What's the chances for an old lag in the outside world?" he asked Constable Thomas.

"I dunno," said Constable Thomas, and almost succeeded in looking happy: if he were the laughing sort, these coves would have given him a lot of laughs in this past week. He heard his wife's voice somewhere in the private living quarters of the police station, and wished there was some way he could get a remission of his own sentence. "Just don't land back in here, that's all. I got enough troubles already."

The Wattle Run shed cut out at four o'clock on Saturday afternoon. The last sheep went clattering down the chute, the last shearer straightened, the bell rang and the man in the engine-room cut off the power. The long shaft slowed gradually, still moving after the hum of the engine had died away, the driving-belt flapping loosely, having stretched with the constant usage of the last few weeks, then the shed was suddenly still, as if all noise and movement had followed the last sheep down the chute into the long races that led to the dipping-trough and finally to the wide silent paddocks beyond. The shearers stood empty-handed, ankle-deep in the foam of fleece, looking at each other as if lost. Quinlan, his table empty for a moment, looked up blank-eyed, seeing nothing but the fleece he had been classing all day. The whole shed was still, the men looking slightly embarrassed as if posing for a photograph, then the moment was broken as a picker-up moved down to collect the last fleece for the tables. Shearing at Wattle Run was finished for another season.

After the evening meal some of the men went into Cawndilla again for a last binge: they knew that the next shed was sixty miles from the nearest pub. Venneker went with them, hair slicked down and boots shining like glass, a Saturday night Lothario who had already said his good-byes to the Halsteads and Liz Brown and had made arrangements to be picked up on Sunday morning at a rendezvous on the main road. Bluey and Liz Brown, whose last night together this would be until the shearing season was over, came down to the kitchen where Ida was just taking off her apron, her work finished until Monday, when she would start all over again.

"Where's Paddy and Sean?" Bluey said.

"Down by the home paddock. They're down there looking at next year's Melbourne Cup winner. Seems we're going to be rich."

"I don't believe Paddy will ever be rich." Liz sat close to Bluey at the kitchen table and held her hand on his; the after-smell of cooking, the strong taint of disinfectant in the sink, hung about their love for each other. "Not unless he has a tremendous windfall."

Ida smiled across at them. "You've noticed, too, that he doesn't like to work?"

"That wasn't what Liz meant," Bluey said. "Did he tell you what he'd done with the money he won at two-up last Sunday?"

"No," Ida said. "I heard he'd won some, but I thought it had been confiscated by the police."

"The copper wasn't interested in us or our money," Bluey

said. "No, Paddy had a hundred and twelve quid on him when he went into gaol."

"He did?" Ida couldn't help the quick glance at the jam-jar on the shelf: she was suddenly sitting in the kitchen of their own farm: the world had changed suddenly, swiftly as the spin of a coin: then she looked back at Bluey and the dream was gone: "Has he still got it?"

"Only two quid of it, what he started with on Sunday morning." Bluey's hand turned over under Liz's. "He gave the rest to us, Ida. For young Chris. We want you to take it back."

"What did he say when he gave it to you?" Ida said.

"Just that it was a load off his mind. He blamed himself for losing to that bloke Cooper in the shearing race." Bluey took the roll of notes from his pocket and pushed it across the table. "It would be a load on *our* minds, Ida, if we kept it. Just don't let him know we gave it back to you. We wouldn't want to hurt his feelings."

"And a man who did what your Paddy did must have wonderful feelings," Liz said. "I cried when Bluey told me about the money."

Ida picked up the roll of notes and stuffed it into the pocket of her dress as Paddy and Sean came into the kitchen. She looked up at Paddy, her eyes glistening, and couldn't find a word to welcome him. He sat down beside her, putting a hand on her thigh and squeezing, looking happier than she had seen him in a long time, the old Paddy eager to be on the move again. "Well, darl, all ready to go?"

She smiled at him, ducking her head to hide the shine in her eyes, then she turned back to Bluey and Liz. "Can't wait to be out of here."

"It's not that," Paddy said: the gold tooth gleamed and a curl bobbed animatedly on his forehead. "It's just I'm always interested in seeing new places. Ain't you, Bluey?"

"Sometimes," Bluey said, and turned his hand over under Liz's to entwine their fingers. "But when I've got enough money to set m'self up in that wireless shop, I'll be happy to settle down. We're going to raise our own cricket eleven. They can all grow up and play for Australia, then come into the business with me. Bluey Brown and Sons, all eleven of 'em. When you finally settle down, come to us for your wireless set. We'll give you a discount."

"Yeah, we'll do that," Paddy said, and changed the subject. "They tell me you ain't coming with us, Liz?"

"No," said Liz, and for a moment envied Ida. "I'm staying here for a few weeks with Jean Halstead. Then I'm going back to Sydney."

"You get on well with the boss's wife, eh?" Paddy had the common suspicion of any boss and anyone connected with that boss: Halstead was a good bloke, better than most bosses; but the homestead was an enemy camp and no worker worth his salt ever stepped across the boundary.

"We all get on well with her," Ida said, then looked at Sean sitting on the end of the table and gave the conversational wheel another twirl: "How's the world-beater?"

Sean's face lit up. "He's looking better every day. We been curry-combing him to-night. When we get to the next place, we're gunna start working him, getting him ready to race. Dad and me both had gallops on him to-night. Dad reckons he's never been on a horse with so much speed in him."

"That's right." Paddy nodded sagely: no one could tell *him* about horses. "I think he's even good enough to win at Randwick or one of them other big courses."

"Then we may see you down in Sydney some day?" Liz said.

"Well, I dunno." Paddy wasn't going to commit himself: there were limits to how far a bloke would go, even for a good horse.

"How're you going to move him on from here?" Bluey said. "You've got a dray and three other horses, haven't you? It's forty miles from here to Long Billabong."

"I'm taking 'em down," Sean said. "I'm leaving here at five in the morning. We'll make it all right, even with the dray. Once we get there, all they gotta do is loaf around in the paddocks." He looked along the table at his mother. "I think the new horse might win us a lotta money, Mum."

"It'll be welcome," Ida said, and put her hand into her

pocket. "All we have to do is to persuade your father to always ride to win."

"I never pulled a horse in me life." Paddy glowed with righteousness. "I'll ride him to win, you see."

Ida smiled at Bluey and Liz. "You must come and visit us when we have our farm." Her hand held tightly to the roll of notes: "It shouldn't be long now."

In the morning Sean was on the road with the wagonette and horses before anyone else was out of bed. The kelpie rode on the back of the wagonette, staring sullenly back at the three horses as they plodded along at the end of their lead ropes. It was a cold clear morning with the sun still on its way in from the faraway sea. Sean's breath hung in front of him, and he drove with his hands, clutching the reins, tucked in his pockets. Ice crackled on the road as the horses walked through pools that had escaped yesterday's sun, and frost lay like dried salt on the edges of the sea of paddocks. A flight of ducks climbed from the silver blaze of a billabong, their wings brushing stiffly in the sharp still air, and drew a long black line across the sky as they headed south. A crow rose from a crippled monument of a tree, cawing harshly at the sun now coming over the distant hills, and the cry lingered in the ear. A few kangaroo-grey clouds turned pink as they rode into the path of the sun, then they had moved on, clear and white against the morning blue.

Sean felt the first touch of the sun and sat up straight. He took his hands from his pockets and slapped the reins against the rump of the grey gelding ambling with bent head between the shafts of the wagonette. The morning was lonely, but Sean began to sing, the words meaning nothing but the music coming out of him like a cry of joy: the road stretched ahead to better days than this. Last night his mother, unable completely to contain a secret, had told him of the extra hundred and ten pounds the jam-jar now held.

The rest of the shearers left Wattle Run after breakfast. Turk Tuthill helped Paddy strike the tent and it was loaded on to the truck with the team's belongings. Those men with motor-cycles kicked over their starters, startling the dogs and upsetting the broody hens, then they had gone sliding and bucking down the hill and were soon out of sight in the scrub bordering the main road. The rest of the men boarded the truck, some looking for comfortable spots where they could stretch out and pamper last night's hangover, and Quinlan blew the horn for those who were still saying farewell.

Ida, wearing the dress she had bought in Cawndilla and a straw hat Jean Halstead had given her, feeling a regular ball of style but wishing she didn't have to freeze to be fashionable, took a last look round the kitchen, then walked out to the truck.

"It's just like leaving home," she said.

"I'm glad you think so," Jean Halstead said: she stood with her arm linked in her husband's, her eyes watering perhaps from the cold, and put out a hand to Ida. "We want you to come back whenever you can."

"Any time at all." Bob Halstead knew the last six weeks had somehow allowed him to keep both his wife and Wattle Run: he had known that, if things had gone on as they had been going, he would have had to choose. He shook hands with Ida, and wondered that he could owe so much to a woman who was still almost a stranger to him. "Don't worry about the season. Just come back, that's all."

"We'll do that," Ida said. "Won't we, Paddy?"

"Yeah," said Paddy, leaning over the back of the truck: he'd have to have a yarn with Ida about getting so matey with the boss and his missus: if this was kept up, by the time they'd finished the shearing season they'd be on visiting terms with half the upper crust of the State. He sniffed, to show his independence, and indulged himself in some brilliant wit: "You'll have to come and visit us, too."

"Just what I was going to say." Ida laughed up at him, enjoying her secret, then turned back to the Halsteads. "It won't be too long before we've got our own place."

Bluey and Liz had been saying good-bye to each other up at the homestead. They came down the path now, Bluey carrying the baby and Liz struggling under the weight of Bluey's two suitcases. Bluey took in the group with a plump, satisfied smile.

" Take a good dekko at him," he said, and held up the baby for all to see. " Another twenty years, when he's walking out on the Cricket Ground to towel the pants off the Chooms, you'll be able to say you knew him when you couldn't tell which end was which." He looked down at the baby and grinned. " Isn't he a handsome little bastard?"

" Just like his dad," Ocker Shand said. " Which end is which?" and he fell back into the truck, laughing as if the demons he'd drunk last night were tickling him to death.

Then it was time to go. Ida, suddenly overcome, quickly kissed Jean and Liz and clambered up into the cabin of the truck beside Quinlan. Bluey clung to Liz and the baby for a moment, the smile gone from his face, then the men were pulling him into the back of the truck as it went rolling down the hill. The yard seemed suddenly empty.

" The best season we've ever had," Bob Halstead said, and knew that the women, who knew nothing of the value of a season's clip, understood him.

Then the baby began to cry, and they turned and went up the slope to the homestead. In the kitchen Charlie, the aborigine, was beginning to wash the breakfast pans and dishes. He did them carelessly: from now on he wouldn't have the cook missus to jump on him if the bottoms of the pots didn't look like mirrors: the sandsoap would dry like a rock on the shelf where he had hidden it last night. Later he would sweep out the cookhouse, disturbing the dirt but not disposing of it. He'd liked the cook missus, but she'd worked too hard. He looked at the curtains hanging limply in the window and wondered how soon he'd be able to pinch them for his Mary. From the window he could see the truck disappearing into the scrub: the moan of its engine came faintly, then slowly it died and there was just stillness.

Venneker and Mrs. Firth were waiting for the truck on the main road. They got out of the Hupmobile as the truck swung in beside it, and neither appeared to care that they were more than a little dishevelled. Venneker went to the back of the truck and laboriously climbed in: he had spent all night saying farewell and there was nothing further to say: a good-bye kiss would be only anti-climactic. Mrs. Firth,

tired but still bubbling, still happy from last night but afraid
of to-morrow, looked up at Ida.

" Couldn't pin him down." The sun was reflected from
her face : the smile, the glasses, the whole face seemed suddenly blank with light. " But I ain't giving up hope."

" I'll work on him," Ida said. " He'll weaken eventually."

" He'd better," Mrs. Firth said, and laughed out loud :
her bosom shook, and she took off her glasses and wiped her
eyes. " He dunno how determined I can be."

Then Quinlan had moved the truck forward, gathering
speed as he took it out into the middle of the road. Ida
looked back at the figure of Mrs. Firth standing beside the
Hupmobile, one arm waving vigorously and the other clutching the car for support. Behind her in the distance, the
Wattle Run homestead was a dark quiet shape on the hill,
the windmill flashing in the thin sunlight above it.

Ida drew back into the cabin of the truck. She struggled
into her cardigan, took off her hat and relaxed : the farewell
was over. " I hope the next place is half as good."

" You never know," Quinlan said, and took the truck round
a curve. Wattle Run was lost behind a hill, gone as a shell
of a house, a windmill blinking a meaningless message, and
pitifully naked sheep waiting in the paddocks for next
season's wool.

Chapter Four

1

THE WEEKS had vanished, chased by steely winds into the
past, and the team moved from shed to shed, out of winter
into spring, their bodies getting leaner and their bank-rolls
fatter, and the end of the season came in sight, like a
horizon finally reached. Spring grew ripe and the winds
turned soft, caressing the cheeks where recently they had
cut, and the nights were quiet enough for wide-awake dreaming. They moved into country where the land was shared

between sheep and wheat, saw the dust of the mustered mobs drift like a thin fog over the green-gold sea of young wheat, and began to count the days to the last pay-day. They swung east, climbing the slopes from the plains, and the season was over.

Mountains stood against the eastern sky, glittering with the last of the winter snow, grey in parts like tarnished helmets, flying plumes of tattered cloud. Snow gums posed in frozen corroboree along the ridges and far below them the boiling streams, dark with melting snow, raced down through the gorges to the plains and away to the sea. The sun rode high, coming back from the north with a soft warmth that loosened a man's muscles, stirred the sap in him, and darkened his shadow on the earth that quickened like a living thing. Flowers blazed on the hills, white like morning frost, yellow as the noon sun, blue as the evening sky, and birds rose and fell like their own song on the shining air. And Sean said good-bye to the men who had helped him cross a border.

"You may not know it," Bluey said, "but you've grown up since I first met you."

"You think so?" Sean said, and hoped it was true.

"You have a way to go." Bluey was talking carefully, searching for the right words: some day he would have to repeat them to his own son. "You probably don't feel different, but you are. But you'll be different again, before you can look back and say: when I was a kid. I dunno what you've learned, Sean, but among these blokes you couldn't have learned much that will do you harm. You've a way to go yet, but when you're a man you have only one thing to remember: *be* a man." Then the plump freckled face was grinning, was shining like the rising sun warm on Sean's back. "So long, mate. Look after yourself, and don't go spending your money on loose women."

Sean choked the blush somewhere at the base of his throat; he shook hands with Bluey, man to man. "No sheila's gunna get me in. I can take 'em or leave 'em."

"Don't ever leave 'em," Bluey said. "That's a waste of God's material."

The other men also said good-bye to him as a mate, hoping they'd maybe see him again next season. None of the others had any advice for him; some of them felt they were in no position to offer it. Turk Tuthill looked at the mountains with eyes that were slightly pink again from a binge that had celebrated the last night of the season.

"Those mountains," he grinned. "Are they moving up and down?"

"Not to me they ain't." Paddy was helping Sean load the wagonette; work at last was behind him and he felt like a lifer who had just been pardoned. "You oughta lay off the grog, Turk."

"That's right." Turk was amiable enough: they had begun lecturing him on the evils of drink years ago. "If water had the same effect, I'd drink that. I'm not keen on grog just for its own sake."

"Where you heading now, Turk?" Sean began to tie ropes to keep the load from slipping. "Back to Cawndilla?"

Turk shook his head, then closed his eyes in pain. "Shouldn't of done that." He sighed, then blew out heavily: the spring air took on the tang of a brewery. "No, I don't reckon I'll go back there. I've worn out me welcome, I think. I'll try somewhere new."

"Where d'you come from originally?" Sean said. "Where's your home?"

"Maybe that's his business," Paddy said, a little too sharply for a question that had been an idle one.

Turk hadn't noticed Paddy's tone; he blinked his pink eyes and grinned absently. "Woolloomooloo, in Sydney. Down in Plunkett Street, not far from the wharves. It ain't the best place in the world, but I'd give anything to go back."

"Why don't you?" Sean said.

"Just like his flaming mother," Paddy said. "Wants to know the ins and outs of everything."

"There ain't any point," Turk said. "Me old man died before I gave up the ring. Died the night I fought for the title. And the old lady's died since. I'd go back now, and there'd be nothing there. Strangers in our house. The blokes I grew up with, married and moved away. I liked the 'Loo, a real friendly place, but I dunno that it's the place for me now." He looked away towards the mountains, clear-sighted and long-sighted as a man could ever be. "Out here, the grog I drink is good grog. I'll die drunk, but I'll die decently drunk. Down there, I'd finish up in the gutter, a plonk fiend, maybe even drinking metho, someone that people ud spit upon and the kids ud laugh at. I seen it meself when I was a kid, and it ain't gunna happen to me." He began to walk away and his voice came back, faintly as if it were lost in his throat and he were talking to himself: "I take after me old man, but I got something he never had." The last word was just a whisper to his two listeners: "Pride."

The two Carmodys stared after him, then Paddy looked up at Sean kneeling on the load in the wagonette. "Don't ever stick your nose into people's business like that, again. Not while I'm around, anyway."

"How was I to know?" Sean said.

"You did your best to find out." The alum of memory twisted his mouth: "Some people got things they like to forget."

But none of the other men seemed to be worried by memories of the past. Clint Evans was going back to Sydney, to chase the bookmakers whom he'd been chasing for years: some day the right horse would come home at the right price. This was Chilla Peters' last season: the hand had begun to slow, the back to stiffen, and it was time to go home for good to the ham-and-beef shop he had bought in Maitland. Quinlan was taking the truck back to the ice-carting business he ran in Bondi during the summer: as he confided to Bluey over the bar on the last night, you couldn't afford to relax, you never knew when the bottom was going to fall out of the boom. And Ocker Shand, suddenly remarkably happy, was going back to marry the girl he'd been engaged to for eight years.

"I've been thinking it over," he said, "and I think it's about time I settled down. A bloke needs someone to look after him when he gets to a certain age, and I'm not getting any younger, I tell you. She's a good cook and doesn't mind work. I think we'll make a go of it."

Then Paddy and Ida were sitting side by side on the seat of the wagonette, Sean and Venneker were on their horses, and the team was no longer a team, just a number of people going their various ways.

" Good luck! " the men shouted, and the cry came back like an echo: the toss of a coin, the fast horse, the right fork in the road decided your future; and the wagonette and the horsemen went down the slope, disappearing behind shoulders, coming into view again at a bend in the road, getting smaller and smaller, losing identity, becoming nothing but a dark moving speck that was eventually nothing. The men turned and went in to prepare for their own departure.

" A good mob," they said, and there was no higher praise.

2

The racecourse, like so many bush courses, had no barrier, just a starter with a flag and a strong voice, and the hardest part of any race was the first hundred yards. Everything was taken for granted but actual mayhem, and old-timers could remember when even that had been attempted. Whips were flailed like lolly-sticks, not always at the horse under the jockey holding the whip, and the bony projections that were elbows and knees were used as weapons that could have been classified as felonious. Language was also a weapon, blunt and crude as a stone axe, and failing all else there was nothing in the rules that said a horse couldn't be used to thrust another horse out of the way.

Paddy, who had ridden in these races before and who had too much respect for the horse under him to risk him in a free-for-all, had got away with the leaders but was wide out. He continued riding wide for the first hundred yards, confident of the speed and stamina beneath him, then he swung in as the field went into the first bend.

There were twelve horses in the race and now, the weak having been separated from the strong, they were in two bunches, with Paddy tailing the leading four horses. They passed the mile-post, with a grey horse leading a length, two bays and a chestnut running together, and the black striding freely in fifth place. They passed the half-mile, still holding the same positions, and the second bunch was already out of the race. They came round the bend, leaning in as they swung a little wide, legs flying and tails streaming, the jockeys' silks a blur of colour, racing away from the spinning dust that was always at their heels, and Paddy knew it was time to start riding.

For the last month now he had been working the black, galloping him in paddocks, on smooth stretches of back road, on a deserted bush course they had passed, and he knew he was riding a good enough horse to win this race with ease. He flicked the reins, urged the black forward with his knees, and went down towards the winning-post, a winner all the way over the last furlong.

" Holy God Almighty," Venneker roared, and the yelling of the crowd seemed for a moment to fade to a whisper, " we own a phantom! See him run!"

He, Sean and Ida were standing at the rough rail fence that separated the stand enclosure from the track. Behind them the small stand bulged with the excitement of its occupants; at the rear of the enclosure other spectators jumped up and down on the backs of trucks, on wool wagons and on the seats of sulkies. The judge's box, mounted on shaky legs of silky oak, leaned forward towards the track, as if peering for a closer view of the finish. The four book-makers, standing on their upturned butter-boxes, shouted themselves hoarse like prospectors who had struck it rich: there had been practically no money bet on the horse that had just gone past the post, the easiest winner the track had seen in years.

Paddy brought the black back to the enclosure, swung down, took off the saddle and weighed in. Sean, feeling twice as large as life, and Venneker, swollen to giant size, took the horse down to the stalls, while the crowd trotted along behind them, still breathless from what they had seen, eager to see at close quarters this horse that would one day be a champion among the best.

Venneker kept the crowd at a safe distance while Sean

dried the horse down and gave him a light feed. Paddy, his dark eyes shining like opals, the curls almost ringing merrily as they danced on his forehead, came down to the stall with Ida.

"Wasn't he wonderful?" Ida's straw hat was slightly askew and there was a smudge on the front of the best dress where she had jumped up and down against the fence rail in her excitement. "I've just collected five pounds off the bookmakers. I wish we'd bet more, now."

The crowd stood about, passing comment on the black and how he had won, remembering other champions that had begun on bush tracks and finished at the top on the city courses. The other horses in the race were now back at the stalls, but no one was interested in them. There was only one horse at this meeting, the black stallion munching quietly in the rough bark stall.

"Our Place," someone said. "How'd you pick that name?"

"It's a long story." Ida smiled at the crowd: they were all her friends. "But that's what he means to us. Our Place."

There had been a long argument when the time had come to name the stallion and register him for racing. Paddy, who hadn't expected that anyone else would want a hand in selecting a name, hadn't been able to make up his mind between something Gaelic and something aboriginal. He had been surprised when Ida had said she liked Swift Wind as a name. Then Venneker had chimed in with the suggestion that a horse with such classical lines needed a classical name: something from the Greeks, preferably. Paddy had replied that the Greeks weren't going to have anything to do with naming his horse, then Ida had reminded him it wasn't *his* horse, but Sean's. That was so, Paddy had replied, but what did Sean know about naming horses? The argument had gone on for an hour, with much muttering and scribbling on scraps of paper, and finally it was Sean who had solved the problem. He had been swimming in the river near which they were camped, and had said, *let's call him Our Place,* and that had been that. The money the stallion had won to-day was already marked for the jam-jar.

That night Sean wrote to McKechnie, the first letter in weeks, the words running away from him as he described the race and what they were planning to do with the horse that looked as if it could make hacks of anything else on legs. He borrowed phrases he had heard Venneker utter, and on the pages the horse emerged as a cross between Carbine, a phantom and a peregrine falcon. The Melbourne Cup was already as good as won, the cup shining on the mantelpiece in the living-room of the farm which the Melbourne Cup prize-money would have bought, and they were afraid that eventually he would be limited only to weight-for-age races, otherwise he would be weighted into the ground in handicap races. When his racing days were over, and they wouldn t race him once he was turned seven, he would be retired to the stud and there would found what Venneker called a dynasty. The last page of the ten-page letter dealt briefly with the health of the humans, then the formal signature was affixed, elaborate as the lettering in an illuminated address, the envelope was addressed, and McKechnie had been brought up to date on the people whose voices he had almost forgotten. The one person whose voice he did remember, and so well, had written nothing since the three-line postscript to Sean's first letter.

But then it seemed Venneker wrote to no one. There had been three letters for him from Cawndilla, presumably from Mrs. Firth, but he had written none in reply and finally Ida, unable to mind her own business any longer, tackled him about it.

She and Venneker were riding in the wagonette, she on the seat and he lolling comfortably on the folded tent in the back, and Paddy and Sean were a quarter of a mile ahead, riding their horses close together as they talked of where they would next race Our Place. It was a warm blue day, with the far sky seeming to drain down into the hills that bordered the broad valley through which they were travelling. The scent of the eucalypts was heavy on the air, sharpened occasionally as they passed close to a clump of peppercorns. Cattle stood motionless in the paddocks, small patterns of colour against the green that was already beginning to fade, and on the far side of the valley wheatfields rippled like liquid gold. Rabbits were crouched quietly in the ruins of haystacks and the line of telegraph poles, crucifixes stretching to the horizon, held their rows of sleepy birds. A lazy day, no day for problems such as Venneker's.

"What are you going to do about Mrs. Firth?" Ida said.

Venneker stared up at her, his eyes peering out from the overhang of his brows. "At the present moment I intend doing nothing. I am doing my best to enjoy what, up till now, has been an almost perfect day. Don't let us drag clouds across the sky."

"I ought to drag you by the hair of your head back to Cawndilla."

Venneker said nothing, but his eyes retreated beneath the shaggy brows. He lay without moving except to roll slightly as the wagonette bounced over a rut; dark lines of shadow were traced on his forehead like corroboree markings. Ida was aware that he had forgotten her; she looked down at the leather-brown face, carved in the heroic style, and suddenly felt as much sympathy as she had felt contempt a few moments before. He was independent, but she knew all at once that he had become as much part of her family as Paddy and Sean.

He was like all of them: rootless as locusts, afraid to commit himself, in danger of losing that which he needed because he had become so accustomed to insecurity. His independence teetered precariously on sand: he was like a man who foolishly defies the sea while behind him the land waits for the backward step that will mean safety. He lay there, judging himself, unaware that Ida was also judging him, then he moved his head back and looked straight up at her.

"I'll need time, Ida," he said, "and in any case I shan't go back to Cawndilla."

"What'll you do?"

"I don't know. But if I went back there I'd be only moving in to take the place of her late-lamented Alec." The old fire flamed again for a moment: "I'll take the place of no man, in bed or anywhere else."

" They're going to have trouble with you in the next world," Ida said. " Anyhow, how about dropping Mrs. Firth a note? You owe it to her to keep her happy till you make up your mind."

Venneker thought about it with large concentration, although he had already made up his mind five minutes before. " I think I shall. Just a few well-chosen phrases to remind her of my ardour. Also to take her mind off that caricature of a magistrate, Patchogue, in case he has managed to ingratiate himself back into her favours again."

" He hasn't, I'll bet," Ida said. " And you should be ashamed of yourself for thinking so."

Venneker looked back at Our Place, walking quietly on a lead rope behind the wagonette. " I never knew what a conscience was until I joined this family. The day is not far distant when I expect to find myself with a full set of morals."

They continued to move north, beneath a sun that every day was becoming warmer, that had almost completed its southward journey and now hung in a sky that looked as if it had never known clouds. They followed the route of the smaller towns, racing Our Place at two picnic meetings and winning easily, all of them now dreaming of next spring when they would try him in the big country races, the town cups, and would win with the same ridiculous ease. The roll of notes in the jam-jar had increased steadily; Ida still maintained from Paddy the secret of the extra one hundred and ten pounds. Life had become like the season all around them, getting better every day.

Then they got the letter from McKechnie, addressed to them at a town Sean had mentioned they would be passing through. It wasn't long, written in a scrawl on one page, as if McKechnie's daughter had been in a hurry and had had other things on her mind, and it asked them to come to Bulinga early next month and enter Our Place in the Bulinga Cup. The prize-money was a hundred pounds, and even if they didn't win it, he would be glad to see them.

" What d'you reckon?" Paddy said.

" I'd like to go, Dad," Sean said, and wondered how the farm looked now.

"So would I," said Ida. "I'd like to see the Batemans again, just to see how they've got on."

"Well, we'll go then," Paddy said, then looked at Venneker. "You coming, too?"

"I'm glad I was asked," Venneker said; he and Paddy still occasionally clashed, but it had now developed into a matter of temperaments rather than opinions. "For a moment I thought I was to be carted along, just like so much baggage, without even a voice in the decision."

"You mean you ain't coming?" said Paddy.

"I mean no such thing," Venneker said. "When do we start?"

3

Sean was surprised at just how memory had lasted: the farm was as familiar as a calendar picture which had hung before him all year long. The paint had faded a little, a burnt skeleton had taken the place of one of last year's trees; with a small shock he saw that part of the fence needed mending. But it was the farm as he remembered it; the scars were the fault of time, not of his memory.

An invisible magpie was carolling liquidly, a mongrel dog was barking at the aloof kelpie, and McKechnie was standing beside the wagonette, his sightless face cracking happily like a mask. "Gawd, it's good to see you! How you all been? You all here? Rupe, Mrs. Carmody, Mr. Carmody, Sean? How are you? Get down, get down. Gawd, Gawd!"

He was pathetic in his gladness; the excited feet stumbled on familiar ground and he put up his hands as if defenceless. Venneker swung down from the big chestnut and slapped an arm about the suddenly nervous shoulders.

"You old bastard!" The magpie and the dog shut up; there was another, mightier voice in the land. "Holy Jesus, I didn't realise I'd missed your ugly countenance so much. Where's the rest of the household? Are you batching?"

"No, Rose and Ted are in town getting some things. They were as happy as me to know you were coming back."

He sought Venneker's hand and pumped it; he turned his head, searching for the others, who had remained apart until the two old friends had finished their reunion. "Mr. Carmody——"

"I ain't ever met you before," Paddy said, jumping down from the wagonette, "but call me Paddy. How are you, mate?"

"Good-o. Right as rain. Where's your missus and Sean?" The face moved questioningly; without the expression of the eyes, it seemed that the excitement was almost too much of a strain on the rest of his features.

"We're here," Ida said, and tried not to sound as her heart felt: this was more than just the end of a journey. "And I'd like nothing better than a good cuppa."

While the adults drank their third cup of tea and answered questions with questions, the conversation of re-union, Sean went out to look at the farm. Behind the house a small orchard marched in regular ranks up the slope of the steep hill, marched and got nowhere; decorations of peaches and apricots hung on the breasts of the militant trees. The sheds, their white paint now almost a grey flake, housed the milking stands, a two-wheeled dray, two oil-darkened ploughs, warm-smelling harness hanging like shrubs and vines on the walls; and Sean wandered quietly through the sheds with the feeling of one who had entered a shrine. The analogy wasn't clear to him, but he was aware that this was more than an idle tour of inspection. The feeling turned to tremors as he stepped out of the gloom of the sheds into the brightness of the afternoon: the farm stretched away before him, shining paddocks and green-flaming trees, satin cattle and the waving inquisitive heads of corn down by the creek, the brown carpet of a fallow field and the pattern of fences that somehow made the whole scene permanent; and he turned away and went into the house trembling with tears he couldn't understand.

An hour later McKechnie's daughter and her husband came home. She was a plain girl with beautiful eyes: she had the habit of staring downwards, as if trying to keep from her father the joke that had been played on him. Ted, her husband, was a man of big bones and no flesh; it looked as if it hurt him to sit down. He stood in front of the empty fireplace, his bony arms crossed easily behind his back, and spoke in a flat, squeezed-out voice that was as expressionless as a written word.

" I suppose Dad told you what we're trying to do with the farm?"

McKechnie ducked his head from side to side as if he had been trapped and was seeking a way out. "No, I ain't told 'em yet. Plenty of time. Let 'em get acclimatised first. Gawd, they only just got here!"

"What's happening? Don't keep us in suspense." Venneker lolled in a faded red plush rocking-chair; it creaked beneath him, as if welcoming back an old friend.

Ted Anderson looked at his wife, then at his father-in-law; both seemed to be staring at the floor. He shrugged, his skull almost disappearing into the cradle of his shoulders. " Well, I dunno. I thought Dad would've told you——"

" Well, I didn't!" It was the first time any of the Carmodys had heard McKechnie speak sharply : the quiet voice was suddenly shrill, then fell away apologetically to a whisper : " I'm sorry. I didn't mean to get off me bike like that. No, I didn't tell 'em, Ted. I was gunna leave it till later. But we might as well tell 'em now." His voice was still a whisper : " We're gunna sell the farm."

The Carmodys said nothing, although Sean had to bite his tongue to keep quiet. Venneker rocked back and forth in his chair for a few moments, then he asked the question that had been straining at the room.

" What's gone wrong?"

" Nothing's gone wrong," Ted Anderson said, and looked down at his wife. " We just want to go back to Sydney, that's all. Isn't it, Rose?"

" That's all," she said in her father's soft voice, but her very tone implied that that wasn't all; she was a girl who would spend all her life trying to be neutral. " Nothing's wrong with the farm."

" What are you going to do in the city?" Venneker had assumed the role of magistrate; Ida, watching him, had the sudden realisation that he was very attached to this farm, had settled back in here as if he had never been away. The chair creaked comfortably beneath him in an old rhythm; his tea cup, brought in from the kitchen without its saucer, rested in an old stain-ring on the faded red of the table-cloth. " Are all three of you going down there?"

Rose Anderson looked nervously about the room, then she stood up and was already moving towards the door when she said, " About time I started getting tea."

Her husband stood irresolutely for a moment, as if he had just been abandoned, then he too was on his way out of the room. " I've got to bring the cows in for milking."

" Can I come with you?" Sean said, and was on his feet ready to go, so that it would have been hard for Anderson to have refused him. But Anderson was glad to have Sean come with him : he felt the atmosphere of the room had become too tense in the last few minutes, and he did not want the visitors to think they were unwelcome. They would have realised they were most welcome if they only had known what was going on in his mind.

Ida, left with the three men in the living-room, felt she should have gone to the kitchen with McKechnie's daughter, but curiosity and some sixth sense that told her she was needed kept her here, waiting for McKechnie to explain something that was obviously a touchy subject around the farm.

" Well," said Venneker, " are you going down to Sydney with them?"

McKechnie ran his hand through his hair and leaned back in the deep leather-covered armchair : dressed in brown shirt and brown trousers, thongs of veins showing beneath his weather-tanned skin, he looked a part of the chair.

" I don't wanna," he said. " I just got the feeling I couldn't stand up to life in the city. It ud kill me."

" Yeah." Paddy had just discovered a friend : he was on McKechn ͻ side, no matter what the argument was about or with whom. " I'd feel the same way. Some people just ain't built for city living. I remember once I met a bloke——"

" Very interesting," said Venneker, and chopped Paddy off
as if he had decapitated him; he looked back at McKechnie.
" What do you intend doing?"

McKechnie's hand was still exploring his head. " Christ, I
dunno, Rupe. I just dunno. You see, I don't own all the
farm. Oh, I know you think I do, but I don't. When Ted
come up here with Rose late in nineteen-nineteen, just after
he got outa the army, I gave 'em half the farm as a wedding
present. It was the least I could do. Me brother Don, who'd
lived here with me and the missus, had worked the place,
with me helping him the best I could. First the missus died,
then a coupla months later he went, and I was left on me pat
malone. I got a coupla hands to come in and work, but they
were no bloody good, and in the end I wrote and asked Ted
and Rose to come up here. You can't pay your relatives
wages: it don't work out. Ted was a good willing worker, so
I give him half the farm and what we made we split fifty-
fifty. You can see what a job he made of the place. He
worked like a flaming nigger. When you come along, of
course, he was able to slacken up a bit."

" You mean I lived here for three years and didn't know
of this arrangement?" Venneker said.

" It was about the only thing you didn't know," McKechnie grinned. " But I kept it to meself for Ted's sake. He
don't say much and when he didn't tell you himself, I
reckoned he wanted it kept quiet. He ain't ever said anything, but I've never known how he took it when I offered
him a share in the farm. He didn't have a razoo when he
married, not a penny to bless himself with, although I don't
hold that against him, but he could of taken what I done as
charity and resented it. I dunno. Anyhow, as far as people
have been concerned, it's always been *my* farm up till now."

" And that's where the trouble lies now?" Venneker said.

" Yeah." McKechnie put both hands to his head; his
lean face was stretched tight on the rack of its bones. " He
wants to sell. He wants his share of the money to start a
bakery down in Sydney. He used to work in one before the
war. He knows the game and I'm sure he'll make a go of it."
He was silent for a moment, then Ida knew what had held her

back here in this room: "Once your boy said to let him know if ever I was gunna sell the farm. I thought you might have enough money to buy Ted's half."

"We ain't got enough," Paddy said quickly: suddenly he was closer to being trapped than he had ever been in his life before. He had been watching the way McKechnie's conversation had been going, aware that it wasn't just idle talk, and his answer had been ready on the tip of his tongue. He had begun to realise over the last couple of months that he couldn't go on for ever denying Ida and Sean the chance to settle down, but he hadn't reckoned on things happening so soon. Christ, here they were with a horse that might be a champion, with the opportunity to keep moving about the bush and yet living in style in pubs and boarding-houses instead of in the tent, with money to spend and new clothes to wear, with everything in their hands to make a bloody wonderful life; and now here was this old codger trying to spoil the whole works by asking them to settle down here and run this farm for him. Paddy almost spat into the aspidistra beside him, and went on: "You'd want at least fifteen hundred quid for a half-share in a place like this——"

"Twelve hundred," McKechnie said. "We're letting it go as cheap as we can, because Ted wants a quick sale."

"Twelve hundred, fifteen hundred, it's all the same to us." Paddy began to feel safe again: McKechnie evidently thought they were made of money. "It'll be a coupla years before we can raise that much. You'll be down in the city by then, probably breathing your last."

"That's the stuff," McKechnie said. "Make me real cheerful. I ain't got enough to worry me right now."

"Sorry, mate, but I'm only trying to be realistical about it." Paddy sat back, safe as he had ever been.

Then out of the blue Ida said, "What's the bank like about mortgages? Are they easy to get in this district?"

"Easy?" McKechnie's voice quickened. "Cripes, they practically beg you to take one."

"I can vouch for that," Venneker said. "I can remember——"

"You stay outa this!" Paddy cut Venneker off sharply,

evening the score. "Or are you gunna get commission outa the sale?"

"Interrupt me again like that," said Venneker, "and I shall take five per cent off you."

Paddy was on his feet instantly: it was a good opportunity to change the subject. "Like to step outside and try your luck?"

"Sit down!" Ida said.

"He ain't gunna talk to me like that——"

"Sit down!" Ida glared and Paddy subsided; then she looked back at McKechnie. "We've got just over five hundred pounds, Mr. McKechnie. Do you think the bank would back us for the other seven hundred?"

"It's a dead cert they would!" McKechnie's face came alive: even the sightless eyes seemed to sparkle. "Gawd, you'd have no trouble at all. We could go in t'morrow if you liked and fix it all up——"

"Hold on a minute!" Paddy had been left temporarily speechless by Ida's brazen lie about the amount of money they possessed. He had done some quick calculating and he knew damn' well that at the most they couldn't have more than four hundred quid. And here she was upping the amount by a cool hundred. No doubt about it, when a woman wanted something she became downright dishonest, just so long as she got it. "We ain't got any five hundred quid. The missus is just pulling your leg."

"That's what you think!" Ida was on her way out of the room, determined to have her way now while the going was good. "I'll be back in a jiffy."

"I think we have under-estimated her," Venneker said to Paddy. "I was inclined to agree with you that your bank roll couldn't exceed four hundred pounds."

"How would you know?" Paddy said. "Christ, I never met a bastard with such a long nose for other people's business."

"Just common-sense reasoning," said Venneker, unruffled. "I know what the three of you drew in wages while we were shearing. Living with you as I have been, I have a fair idea of what your expenses have been. Subtracting one from the other and allowing for the fact that you had nothing when I met you——"

"Insulting cow, ain't he?" McKechnie said; then Ida came bustling back into the room.

She walked to the table in the centre of the room and placed the two jam-jars side by side on it. The notes in the jars looked like some vegetable growth; green leaves, pink leaves, blue leaves were pressed tightly against the glass, as if the plant had grown and was now straining to be released.

"Hullo, where did we get the second jar?" Paddy now began to understand the extra hundred quid: she had found some poor bastard's savings, had picked it up on the road somewhere and, just like a woman, hadn't said a word about it.

"It's ours," Ida said, as if she had read his mind. "There's the money I saved while we were at Wattle Run. There's the money we won on Our Place, stake money and betting money. And," she took a breath, reluctant to give away her secret, having held it so long she had become proud of it, "there's the hundred and ten pounds you gave to Bluey Brown for his baby."

"Bluey?" Paddy sat up. "Did you ask him for that? How did you know I'd give it to him?"

"He told me himself, when he and Liz gave me back the money." Ida's voice softened: "They didn't want me to tell you, darl, because they didn't want to hurt your feelings. But they reckoned we needed the money more than young Chris. It was a kind thing you did, darl, but I agreed with them. We got someone of our own who's just as important as their boy."

Paddy looked up at Ida standing with the money now sprouting from her hands. He was angry at Ida for not having told him about the return of the money and yet glad that she knew what he had done. He had given Bluey the money out of true kindness of heart, knowing that Bluey must have been disappointed after the upset in the shearing race, but later he had begun to regret that his good act hadn't been a little more public. Bluey obviously hadn't said anything to the rest of the shearers, and the only other man who had guessed what had happened, Chilla Peters, had been too close-mouthed to go talking about it. Now and again a bloke likes the world to have a good opinion of him.

But Ida was right: they did owe something to Sean. "Righto. So you got all that money. Now what you gunna do with it?"

"Five hundred and seventeen pounds," Ida said, and dropped the money on the table. "If we can get a mortgage for the rest, we'll buy half the farm."

4

Early next morning Paddy and Sean took the stallion out to the racecourse. They drove through Bulinga, only just beginning to stir awake, smoke climbing weakly from one or two chimneys, a baby crying fretfully in a house, roosters asserting themselves in a world of sleepy surrender, then they were out on the other side of town and approaching the course. They were not the first to arrive.

Sulkies and carts were drawn up on the outside of the track; five cars were in an aloof rank to one side. In the stalls behind the grandstand half a dozen horses were being dried down and fed. In the enclosure in front of the stand men stood in groups and watched the dozen or so horses that were being worked out on the track. Paddy and Sean sat in the sulky they had borrowed from McKechnie and looked at the competition they would meet on the coming Saturday and Monday.

The horses came galloping past, sometimes singly, sometimes in pairs, their hoofs drumming on the firm earth, a tattoo that beat its way right into you, so that it and your heart had the same rhythm, the sound coming clearly as the horses came towards you, drumming into you so that for one moment your whole body seemed to pulse with the sound, then the horses had gone past, the sound lingering then swiftly flying after them, dying away in the sound of another horse already coming at you, and you knew that a racetrack in the early morning, without the cheering heartless crowd, the brass-voiced bookmakers and the sound and smell of money, with just the beauty of horses galloping and a cool sun smiling on a distant ridge, was the best place in the world at the best time of day. Sean drew a deep breath and his vision blurred with the ecstasy of it all.

"What's the matter?" Paddy said.

"Cripes, Dad, why can't it always be like this?" Sean opened both arms and embraced the horses, the valley, the whole morning; then he looked at his father and dropped his arms, grinning foolishly. "I got carried away."

"I don't blame you." Somewhere in Paddy there was a touch of poet: an ancestor had strummed a harp and told tales compounded of magic and music and blarney, and the old blood still ran with the new in Paddy. "I was thinking something the same, meself. Makes you pity people who never get outa bed to see it. Makes you sorta feel this is one of the true things in life. Ain't that right?"

"Ye-ah," said Sean, who hadn't got around to being intellectual about the matter. "Yeah, I suppose you're right."

"Course I'm right," Paddy said. "I'm only wrong when I'm arguing with your mother."

They watched the other horses for a while longer, sizing them up and remaining convinced that Our Place would have no more competition here than he had had at his three previous starts, then Paddy saddled the black and took him out on the track. He was aware of the quick interest of the men in the enclosure, but he saw to it that they learned little that would help them in laying their bets for Saturday. He took Our Place round the track twice, working him at only half-pace, riding with a loose rein so that it wouldn't look as if he were holding the stallion in, knowing that he was not the sort of horse that tried to jump out of his skin as soon as he walked on to a track, and the second time past the enclosure he noticed some of the men were already turning to go, convinced that this black newcomer had nothing that would trouble the fancied horses on Saturday. At the far side of the course, where he was too far away to be timed, Paddy let the black stretch out over three furlongs, then brought him back to the stalls where Sean was waiting to dry him down.

As Paddy swung down, a fat ball of a man came rolling slowly towards them from the corner of the stand. The course was almost deserted now, a vast silence hanging in the morning air and the stand and the stalls lonely and small in the wide flatness of the valley at this point, and the fat man came towards them with a furtiveness that sent a chill up Sean's back.

"You got a nice horse there." His fat wasn't soft and flabby; he was three hundred pounds of solid meat spread over a frame that was too short. His head was a round ball on which his features seemed to have been painted, hardly breaking the smooth contour, and his neck was lost somewhere in the fat of his shoulders. His body sloped away gradually, four ways, to its widest circumference round his middle, then reversed the slope back to the ridiculously inadequate base of his small feet. He carried his hat in one of the hams he used as hands, and brilliantine shone on his neatly parted dark hair. His eyes were dark and dull, like berries, and his voice suited his appearance, fat-sounding and heavy. "You running him at the meeting? By the way, my name's Martin. Lew Martin. I'm one of the stewards for the meeting. Run the butcher shop in town the rest of the year."

"I'm Paddy Carmody and this is me boy Sean."

"Pleased to meet you." Martin took Paddy's hand, but didn't look at Sean; the latter felt he had been dropped into space, thrown away with the rest of the kids for whom Martin had no time.

"Yeah, we'll be running at the meeting," Paddy said: he had noticed how Sean had been ignored and his voice had an edge of anger to it. "I believe old Sam McKechnie filed our entry. Our Place is the name of the horse."

"Oh, sure, I remember now." Martin smiled, but his teeth didn't appear and his eyes were lost above the rising bulbs of his cheeks. "How d'you fancy your chances?"

"You never know at these sorta meetings." Paddy had become as cautious as a tortoise; this bloke didn't look the sort who'd waste his time on greeting strangers. "There may be some good 'uns around here."

"We got one or two," Martin said. "But I had the glasses on you when you let your horse go, over there on the other side of the track. He didn't look like he was standing still."

"He's got some toe, but he can't hold it." Paddy's face was as bland as an archbishop's; Sean turned away so his own face wouldn't give away the lie. "If he could run a mile like that, we'd be in clover."

"We all wish we had another Carbine, don't we?" The smile again creased Martin's face. "Well, best of luck, anyway. You'll find it a pretty good meeting. Biggest we've ever had, we hope. You might pick up a few quid."

He walked away, rolling from side to side, treading delicately on his small feet as if trying to keep his weight off them, heightening the effect of furtiveness that had been Sean's first impression of him, and disappeared round the corner of the stand.

"He knows more than he let on," Paddy said. "I wonder if he's seen us race at those other places?"

"It don't matter, does it, Dad?"

"Well, we don't want the price backed down to odds-on," Paddy said. "We wanna make a few quid if we can. Now your mum's decided to be a landowner, we can do with all the money in the kitty we can get."

Sean had been told last night of the opportunity that had been offered them of buying a half-share in the farm and he had lain awake into the early hours of the morning, his mind somersaulting with visions of the future, mapping plans and then discarding them, till finally he had fallen asleep from sheer exhaustion. The excitement was still a lively thing within him, but the late hour of getting to sleep and the early hour of rising to come out here to the course kept it in check, and on the drive back to the farm there was little conversation between the two Carmodys.

For which Paddy was glad. He had had a bad night with Ida last night when they were alone, and when she had at last turned her back on him and gone to sleep he had been only half-way through his argument against taking out the mortgage. It was all very well for Ida to say that thousands of people took out mortgages and managed to survive them; there always had to be one unlucky bastard, and you could bet his name would be Paddy Carmody. Bad luck didn't worry you when you were on the track: you had nothing to lose and you could always drive on and let to-day's bad luck slip back into yesterday. He had pleaded with Ida to wait another year, till they had enough money saved to do without the aid of the bank, but she had snapped something about chances like this waiting for nobody and then had turned her back on him. So help him Christ, for a moment he had felt like booting her in the behind, but he knew that wouldn't have helped his argument, and in the end he had turned over to go to sleep, dragging the bedclothes towards him as a final gesture of defiance.

Paddy spent the morning in a one-sided conversation with McKechnie, offering moody grunts as his contribution, while Ida, Sean and Venneker toured the farm with Ted Anderson, taking an inventory and learning some of the idiosyncrasies that would need to be watched. Venneker knew most of them, but it seemed that some had developed in his absence: there were two new milkers that were inclined to be skittish if not handled rightly, one of the plough horses had taken to letting the other horse do all the pulling, the dam across the creek would need strengthening before next year's rains; but the farm could have been falling apart at the seams and carried nothing but unbroken horses and dry cows, and Sean would still have had the same feeling of walking on invisible clouds.

To-day was Friday and because it was expected that it would be a busy day at the bank, with the long week-end coming up and plenty of visitors in town, they had agreed to wait until Tuesday to see about the mortgage. Late in the morning Ida and Venneker drove into town in the sulky, Ida to buy herself a new pair of shoes to wear to the races and Venneker to draw on the cheques that had been held for him at the bank while he had been away and to send off a lengthy telegram that he had composed last night in bed. When they returned the mid-day meal was on the table and everyone was eating heartily. Everyone, that is, but Paddy. His stomach had become a shrivelled gourd lined with acid; there was no power in his jaws to chew his food; and his tongue was just a withered strip of leather that got in the way of everything he put in his mouth. He knew he'd never again eat well while he had a mortgage hanging over his head.

In the afternoon, again borrowing the sulky, the Carmodys drove out to see the Batemans, something Ida had mentioned they must do as soon as they had arrived in the valley last night. They climbed the winding road into a breeze that blew gently through the trees on the tops of the ridges, and stopped and looked back at the valley.

" It's going to be a wonderful place to live," Ida said.

" All the places we been," Sean said, " and I still ain't seen anything as good as this valley."

Paddy said nothing, and after a moment they drove on along the road between the razorback ridges. They drove out of the green sweet-smelling timber into the forest of dark stumps and gaunt crazy-armed trunks that marked the wide path of the fire that had roared through here months before. Grass now hid the scorched earth, but the ridges were marked for a lifetime by the charred trees that stood unmoved by the breeze, their only sound that of the crows nesting invisibly in their black trunks. The sulky bowled down the road, dragging a thin trail of dust after it, hurrying through the desolate scene, then they had come round the shoulder of the hill and Mrs. Bateman was standing at the mailbox by the side of the road, a bundle of papers in her arms and some letters in her hand.

She stood waiting for the sulky to come down to her, smiling at them but not recognising them, then they had pulled up beside her and at once her face almost fell apart with amazement. She dropped the bundle of papers and reached up to take Ida's hands as the latter got down from the sulky.

" Gawd bless me ! You said you'd come back some day, but I never dreamed——! " She leaned forward and kissed

Ida's cheek: it was much more than a polite gesture. "Come up to the house. Ern and the girls will be tickled pink to see you."

But for the background of blackened forest, there was little evidence that the fire had swept through here and destroyed all that the Batemans had owned. The house had been completely rebuilt: only the scorch-darkened chimney reminded you that this was the second house to stand here. As if to defy further disaster, Bateman had built the house larger than the original; two rooms had been added and the veranda lengthened. It was a house now, not a shack: the fire had improved the Batemans' social standing. Half a dozen head of new stock grazed in the great bottom paddocks, and the sun was bright on the yellow wood of new fence-posts. Behind the house Bateman and the two girls were working in an almost-completed new shed.

They looked up as Mrs. Bateman called to them, then the three of them came running, still carrying the tools they had been using, and the two families went into the house in a laughing, hand-clasping group.

"I got some beer I been saving for me birthday," Ern Bateman said, "but stone the crows, this is more important than birthdays! This don't happen every year."

"You done a good job of rebuilding," Paddy said: usually he had nothing but contempt for cow cockies, working their guts out from morning till night just to stay alive, but he couldn't help the admiration he felt for Bateman. "You must of started on it the very day we left here."

"The day after," Bateman grinned. "I had to get me breath back. But it's been pretty tough, I can tell you. We're up to our necks at the bank, but we'll get by, I reckon."

At the mention of the bank Paddy glanced towards Ida, but she was busy talking to Mrs. Bateman. Then he looked at Sean, but he was sitting in a corner listening to the two girls. Paddy reluctantly looked back at Bateman: nobody was ever bloody well listening when something important was being said.

Ida was telling Mrs. Bateman of their intention of buying

S.-L

a share in the McKechnie farm. "It's time we settled down and gave Sean a chance to get a good start. Now we'll be neighbours, I hope we'll see a lot of each other."

"I suppose your husband likes the idea of having a place of his own?" Mrs. Bateman said.

Ida had to restrain herself from putting her finger to her lips: she looked over her shoulder, but Paddy was telling Bateman about the horse they now owned, advising him to lay out a few bob if he managed to get down to see Saturday's races.

"He can't quite get used to it just yet," she said to Mrs. Bateman. "He's been on the move so long, he's got to get himself into another frame of mind. But he'll settle down," she said determinedly, and Mrs. Bateman smiled at her: she knew what some men were like: she was just lucky in having a worker like Ern.

Sean, sipping ginger beer, was wondering when he would get a word in edgeways with the two Bateman girls. He had managed to tell them that from now on he would be living in the valley and that he owned a horse that would be running at the Bulinga races, and from then on he hadn't been allowed to say a word. The elder girl, Mary, was going into Bulinga to-night to stay with a friend: she was going to do so many things over the week-end, Sean wondered if she would have time for eating and sleeping. Marge, a little older in manner and fuller in the body, was going to the races with her mum and dad on Saturday and Monday, but cripes, she had to come back home each night, instead of being allowed to stay in town.

"Pity you ain't already moved into the farm," she said. "I could of come and stayed with you."

"You want to wait till you're asked," her sister said. "You don't go pushing yourself on people."

"I won't get anywhere if I don't," said Marge: the time would come, you knew, when this farm wouldn't be able to hold her. "Any rate, it don't matter whether I ask meself or he asks me. I can't go, so that's all there is to it. But just wait till I'm sixteen." She looked at Sean and winked: the ginger beer went up the back of his nose and he spluttered all over the front of his shirt.

Sean's embarrassing moment broke up the small conversations and drew the group together again. Mary went out to the kitchen to put the kettle on for a cup of tea, and Marge was told to go down to the garden and pick a lettuce and some tomatoes for sandwiches. Sean volunteered to go with her.

"Been reading any more books?" he said as they walked across to the large square of garden at the edge of the timber.

"What sorta books?" Marge said.

"Oh, books," he said, wondering what had made him bring up the subject. "You were reading one when I was here last."

"Oh, *that* one. I've read a couple since then. I just finished *What Married People Should Know*."

Sean looked at her a trifle dismayed. "You're ahead of yourself, ain't you?"

"You can't know too much." She bent down to examine a lettuce. "Gee, Sean, I'd like to get married!"

Sean felt it was time to be careful. "Why? Because of what you read in the book?"

She looked up at him without straightening her body and he felt a thrill of weakness pass through him. "That ud be good-o. It reads pretty good. But that ain't the real reason. I just get lonely, that's all. And when you're married, if you pick the right man, you don't get lonely."

"What happens if you pick the wrong bloke?"

She straightened up, a lettuce in her hand. "You get a divorce and start all over. Just like Dad did here when the fire burnt us out."

Sean shook his head. "You're too fast for me. Crikey, I ain't even thought of having a girl yet, and here's you already thinking of getting divorced."

"Is your mum and dad happily married?"

"Of course!" Then he put out his chin and said: "When I get married, all I wanna be is as happy as them. If I am, then I won't need any divorce."

Marge smiled, an open smile that had no hint of coquetry in it. " I like you. I'm real glad you're gunna be living close to us from now on."

Sean grinned, at ease with her now. " You can lend me that book. I'll see if it's worth while getting married."

The Carmodys stayed on till late afternoon. Ern Bateman took Paddy over the farm, pointing out where the fire had struck worst and what he had done since then, and Paddy's admiration of him grew. As they came up the long paddock, Bateman driving the cows ahead of him towards the milking-shed, Ida came to the front door of the house with Mrs. Bateman.

" Time we were getting back, darl," she said. " We've got to have you in bed early to-night, conserve your strength for to-morrow's race."

" We'll be cheering for you," Mrs. Bateman said. " And I hope your horse is as good as you say he is. I'm gunna put five bob on him."

" I ain't one to tell people how much to bet," Paddy said, " but I reckon you could easily risk five quid, or even more. You'll get a good price. You could win enough to pay off some of that note at the bank."

" You shouldn't discuss other people's mortgages," Ida said delicately.

" Why not?" Paddy said. " We're gunna have one too, ain't we?"

Ida smiled at the Batemans, promising herself she would clip Paddy under the ear as soon as she got him alone. " A regular joker. When you get to know him properly, he'll keep you in stitches."

" We joke about our mortgage," Ern Bateman said, and laughed. " It's the only way we can bear to think about it."

Driving back to the McKechnie farm, Paddy was very quiet. He sat staring ahead at the flopping ears of the horse while Ida and Sean talked of the wonderful job the Batemans had done in rebuilding their place.

" That's what home comes to mean to you eventually," Ida said. " We'll feel like that about our place in a year or two. We'll hang on there, no matter what happens."

They had reached the top of the road leading down into the valley. Paddy brought the horse to a halt and sat looking out over the wide dip in the land, his face screwed into a knot of concentration and one hand tapping slowly on a knee.

" It ain't a bad-looking valley, is it?" he said, hardly opening his mouth.

Ida said nothing, but Sean agreed with his father. " I'd be satisfied to live here for good, Dad."

The valley was still and peaceful in the late afternoon. Shadows flowed lava-like down the western slopes; on the eastern slopes, the sun blazed in green and yellow reflection. The floor of the valley was veined with the blue macadamised main road and the brown dirt side roads. The river was a silver road on which no one travelled: it appeared from nowhere out of stacked rounded hills and disappeared in the shining distance, going nowhere. The trees in the lower part of the valley were dark against the paddocks; on the far slopes a breeze disturbed them, and the sun sparkled in them as in breeze-rippled pools of water. Fences marked the paddocks like long, widely spaced furrows, and farmhouses squatted determinedly in the paddocks, silent and seemingly unoccupied. The high air was still and shining, and below the Carmodys a crow went sluggishly down towards the river flats, its wings blue in the slanting sun. The bird's cry came up to them, empty, unmusical, bitter.

" What are you thinking about, darl?" Ida said softly.

" I was thinking about Ern Bateman. What he's done back there, and how much it means to him and his missus. His wife's as proud of that house as if he'd built her a mansion." He turned his head to look at her, his face still twisted as if he were in pain. " Darl, I still don't like the idea of us getting a mortgage. But could we risk some of the money we've saved to try and win the rest at the races?"

Ida said slowly, " How much?"

" No more than a coupla hundred quid. I dunno what price we'll get about Our Place, but I don't reckon it'll be less than five to one. If we give two hundred quid a fly at that price, we'll have our money to buy the share in the farm. And have a few hundred over besides."

Sean turned excitedly to his mother. "Go on, Mum! Our Place can't lose. Just think. We'll own our half of the farm by to-morrow night, instead of having to wait till we paid off the bank. Go on, Mum. Give Dad the two hundred quid."

Ida wasn't allowing herself to be rushed. She had become very attached to the money she had accumulated in the jam-jars and when it finally left her hands she wanted something concrete in return for it. She had faith in the stallion's ability to win races, but a betting ticket was nothing concrete till a race was over and then often it was nothing more than just a piece of cardboard, no more concrete than a broken promise. She had bet on Our Place at each of the three meetings where he had run, but there was a difference between risking two pounds and risking two hundred. The Bulinga meeting was bigger than any of the previous ones, and for all they knew there might be some exceptionally good horses entered. Our Place was a champion, but he hadn't yet had to prove himself.

"I'll tell you what," she said. "If Our Place wins to-morrow, I'll give you two hundred pounds to put on him in Monday's race."

"Hell, that won't be any good," Paddy said. "We'll win so easy to-morrow, we won't get any five to one on Monday."

"Take it or leave it," Ida said. "I'm not risking two hundred quid till I know what we're racing against."

5

There was an air of urgency, of high emotion, about Bulinga, as if over this week-end it had to cram in all the bright excitement of twelve months. The main street, startled out of its usual somnolence, gay and uncomfortable in its banners and placards, was alive with people, friendly bush people stiff and unhappy in their best catalogue clothes and loud-talking city visitors self-consciously casual in what was supposed to be the latest in country wear. The pubs were doing a roaring trade, with some customers already too blind to know whether it was Saturday or Monday, and the bar at the course was already running low in its stocks.

The racing committee had done a fine job at the course. The one-decker stand had been newly painted and its green decking and red roof were splashes of colour in the wide expanse of brown-topped grass. The committee had erected a flagpole and a foot from the top, because the pulley had stuck, a faded but clean Southern Cross made a brave attempt to be a standard in the breeze. The single white rail on the inside of the track showed thin and clear against the wooded hills on the far side of the course, and the track itself looked fast and firm enough to speed even the slowest plug. A band, brought from the nearest big town, their instruments a dazzle of sound and shine in the bright sun, played hits from musical comedy, while a dozen bookmakers shouted themselves hoarse above the music.

From the stalls behind the stand Sean heard the shout of the crowd as the horses went past the post in the second race. He stood in the shadow of the stall, Our Place moving nervously behind him, while two boys stared at him in plain envy.

"You ever ride him in a race?" The freckled-face boy looked uncomfortable in his tightly laced black boots and kept moving his feet as if they were hurting him.

"No, but my dad says I can next year." He raised a hand and caressed the nose of the stallion. "We'll be here for next year's races."

The second boy was eating a toffee-apple and now he said something, but the words couldn't get past his locked teeth.

"Pardon?" Sean said.

The boy chewed for a few moments, swallowed with some difficulty, ran his tongue round his mouth, then repeated his question. "How many races has he won?"

"We've only had him in three and he's won all of 'em. He'll win again this arvo, too."

Local pride flared; the freckles stood out on the first boy's face. "Yeah? You think you're pretty good, don't you? We got a champion horse around here named Murrumbidgee. Your old man won't even see him in the race."

"My dad don't look back over his shoulder when he's riding," Sean said.

Venneker and McKechnie, coming across from the stand, heard the last part of the conversation.

"A good rider never looks over his shoulder," Venneker said.

The two local boys looked up and gaped. "Cripes, it's old Venneker!"

Then they had turned and sprinted away, the boy in the tight boots running as if he had forgotten he was wearing them and the other boy holding his toffee-apple high like a torch-bearer tearing down the road from Olympus.

"Where's Mum and Dad?" Sean said.

"Talking to the Batemans," Venneker said. "I heard the younger girl inquiring as to your whereabouts."

"Ah, she'll find me if she wants me," Sean said, turning his blush towards the back of the stall.

McKechnie edged his way into the stall, walking close to the stallion with the confidence of a man who had more than the usual trust in animals. He placed an inquiring hand on the black flank and slowly felt his way along the whole length of the horse till both hands were moving gently over the neat head.

"This is about the fifth time I done this," he said, "and each time he seems to be a better-looking horse."

"He's a good-looker, all right," Sean said. "But I wish you could see him run."

Venneker's eyes glared under his painful frown; Sean made a quick gesture of disgust with himself. But McKechnie seemed oblivious of the awkward moment. He patted the horse on the nose, then came out of the stall as Paddy and Ida and the Batemans came pushing through the crowd towards them.

It was the first time the Batemans had seen Our Place and Mrs. Bateman was so impressed she went away and doubled her bet. Ern Bateman stood discussing the black's good points with the men, while Ida kept a watchful eye on the young girl who was so interested in Sean.

"Your mum's invited us out to your place for tea," Marge said.

"Oh?" said Sean; he wasn't sure, but she seemed to be giving him the glad-eye more than usual this afternoon. That fact didn't upset him so much, but he wished she would lay off a bit in front of his mother. He stole a glance at his mother and didn't feel any better when he saw her watching him with more attention than usual.

"We'll be staying for a while after tea," Marge said, " so you'll be able to show me over your farm."

"Yeah," said Sean.

"Your mum might let you and me take our tea out into the paddocks and have a picnic."

"Too many flies," said Sean.

"Well, we could go for a walk after tea," Marge said. "We don't wanna hang around listening to grown-ups talking."

"You can learn a lot by listening," said Sean, almost going cross-eyed trying to watch his mother's reaction to all this.

"Listening ain't the only way of learning things," Marge said, and Sean stepped close to Our Place, hoping the stallion would suddenly rear and kick him to death.

"That's a nice hat you're wearing, Marge," Ida said. "It makes you look at least seventeen."

"Anyone could tell I ain't seventeen," Marge said. "I ain't wearing lipstick."

"I don't always wear it," Ida said. "This is the first time in months I've had any on." She ran her tongue round her lips. "I keep licking it off, thinking my mouth is dirty."

"But you're married," Marge said. "You don't have to wear it. But if you were younger and didn't wear lipstick, the men wouldn't look at you."

"Well," Ida said, "all I can say is, I'm glad I'm married."

"I wish I were, too," said Marge, and at once Ida lost her suspicion of the girl. She put out a hand and squeezed Marge's plump arm.

"You will be one day," she said, "and you'll find that it isn't important whether men ever looked at you or not. Just so long as the man you're married to keeps looking at you."

"But if I don't get him to look at me in the first place," Marge said, "how will I get him to marry me?"

Ida was saved by the arrival of two newcomers. They came on unsteady legs, each leaning against the other for support, the man with the grey-and-yellow moustache half leading the grizzled man who peered about him with eyes chronically affected by myopia and alcohol.

"G'day, Rupe," said the man with the moustache. "When the hell did you get back? Hey, Joe, look who's here!"

"How the hell can I look who's here?" said Joe. "I ain't got me flaming specs. Where's the bar?"

"You two topers still at it?" Venneker said. "Have you been sober at all while I've been away?"

"Can't remember it," said the man with the moustache. "You been gone a fair while, too, ain't you? Last time we seen you, you were belting the daylights——" Then he noticed Paddy for the first time. "Struth, you were the bloke he was belting!"

"He's never laid a hand on me," said Paddy loudly: cripes, the way these rumours grew, a man's reputation was never safe.

"Hey, Mick." The grizzled man squinted about him, sniffing like a dog seeking a scent. "Where's the bar? Gawd, I'm dying of thirst!"

But Mick had just recognised Paddy's attire. "You a jockey, eh? This your nag? Think you gunna win?"

"He'll win," said Venneker. "You just watch the race."

"Well, I'd like to," Mick said. "But——"

"Hey, Mick." The grizzled man leaned away from Mick, then fell back against him: they stood rocking precariously on the quaking earth. "Where the hell's the flaming bar? If I had me specs, I'd find me own way. Standing around gabbing while all the beer's being drunk!"

"See what I mean?" said Mick, and suddenly the two of them had plunged forward; they staggered through the crowd, trailing their heavy breath, towards the bulging tent that housed the bar and the large number of other men who, like Joe, were dying of thirst.

Then the bell rang for jockeys to mount for the next race. Mrs. Bateman came back to the group outside the stall, clutching her betting tickets as if it were a passport, and exhorted Paddy to ride for all he was worth or she would never speak to him again.

"Good luck," everyone cried, then the horses were on their way out to the track.

Paddy, better dressed than he had ever been in his life before, in a new emerald green jacket and yellow cap, white breeches and shining yellow riding boots, took Our Place at a mincing gallop down the track and round to the starting-post. The Bulinga Stakes was a race of a mile and a half and the horses would pass the stand twice before the winner was known. The winner of the Stakes was expected to be the favourite for the Bulinga Cup on Monday.

There were fourteen runners in the race and Paddy had drawn number six marble. The local champion and favourite for the race, Murrumbidgee, a rangy chestnut with a good head and a suggestion of power in every line of him, was third from the rails. Paddy looked along the line of restless horses, wondering how far they would be behind him when the winning-post was reached, feeling as cocky as a rooster in a yard of chickens, then the starter had called them into line.

A hush fell over the course. The sun suddenly seemed to become hotter, beating down out of the clear raw sky, throwing deep nervous shadows beneath the moving horses, and Paddy, his nostrils thick with the smell of leather and sweating hides, squinted his eyes against the glare as he stared up the track. There was only the sound of excited hoofs in the dust and the curses of the jockeys, then from the timbered slope behind the starting-post there was suddenly the satirical laugh of kookaburras, and the starter had yelled *Go!* and they were off.

Paddy got Our Place away quickly, to escape being pocketed, and when they settled down to the running he was on the rails, tucked in behind Murrumbidgee and, two lengths out in front, a small grey, all three of them running easily and each of the jockeys watchful of the other two.

They stayed that way, with the rest of the field tailing off, past the stand the first time, with the crowd already beginning to yell, round the far side of the course, then they were coming round the bend into the straight for the run home and Paddy moved Our Place up. He caught Murrumbidgee in half a dozen strides and the two of them went up together on the leader. The grey made a race of it for a few yards, then she suddenly folded and the black and the chestnut went on together, Paddy riding hard on the outside and Murrumbidgee staying with him all the way as they went down through the roar of the crowd towards the winning-post. The white board rushed at them, Paddy heaved in the saddle and Our Place had gone away, the winner by a length.

Paddy slowed the black down, the other horses going past with their last effort coming too late, and all he could hear now was the roar of the crowd. He turned the stallion, now panting and trembling with the effort of those last few seconds, and cantered back to the saddling enclosure. He smiled widely at the crowd, pleased as a kangaroo with two pouches: he'd just shown the mob what a good horse and a good jockey could do to the local competition. One of these days he'd be as famous as Bobby Lewis or Steve Donoghue or Tod Sloan; he felt no older than an apprentice coming in from his first win.

He swung down, took off the saddle and stepped up on the grain merchant's scales just outside the stewards' tent. Lew Martin, sleek as a fat seal but so much more shrewd-looking, stood beside the scales.

"Nice ride, Carmody," he said. "Like I said, you got a good horse there."

"Thanks," said Paddy, and stepped down off the scales: weight was correct and the bookmakers could now begin to pay out on Our Place at six to one.

Paddy was surrounded the moment he turned away from the scales. Ida kissed him, Sean wrung his hand, Venneker, McKechnie and Ern Bateman thumped him on the back, and Mrs. Bateman and Marge stood on the outskirts and waved and smiled their congratulations.

"Oh, you beaut, Carmody!" Venneker was roaring. "To coin a phrase, you bloody bobby-dazzler!"

"Listen to Rupe," said McKechnie. "Talking Australian!"

"To-day I'm as Australian as any of you!" Venneker's voice was still thundering round the enclosure: people ducked instinctively, then turned their heads and laughed at him. "I'll take on any bastard who denies it!"

At last everyone's excitement had simmered down. While the others went away to collect their winnings, Paddy and Sean took Our Place round to the stalls.

"If your mum had bet that two hundred quid," Paddy said, "we'd of had the money to buy the farm."

"Yeah," said Sean. "Well, maybe we'll win enough on Monday."

"If we're lucky. We won't get no flaming six to one then. We'll be bloody lucky if we get two to one. I tried to tell your mum, but I might as well talk to a post."

"Yeah," said Sean, and took the stallion into the stall, while Paddy walked on to the jockeys' tent.

Sean had cooled down the black when Paddy, now out of his silks and back in the new blue shirt and grey trousers Ida had bought him specially for the meeting, came across to the stalls.

"You can take him home," he said. "I told Rupe and Mac and Ern I'd have a drink with 'em. Just one to celebrate."

"You oughta come and have one with me." Lew Martin stood behind them, balanced precariously on his tiny feet, looking from side to side as if waiting to be called away.

"Some other time, thanks," Paddy said. "I promised these blokes."

"I know how it is. Nothing like a drink with your cobbers. Specially after a win like to-day's. You gunna run on Monday, too?"

Paddy grinned, smug as a man with second sight. "Gunna win again, too."

Martin with difficulty inserted a fat hand in a pocket and pulled out a packet of Capstans. He held it towards Paddy, but the latter shook his head. Martin put a cigarette in his mouth, looked away for a moment, then struck a match and with his hands cupping his mouth, said, " Are you interested in not winning?"

Paddy had thrown an old rug over the horse and now he stopped with his hand flat and stiff on the faded check pattern and looked over his shoulder at Martin.

" What you mean?"

Martin took the cigarette from his mouth and the smoke was still round his lips as the words came out.

" I'll make it worth your while if you don't win."

Paddy's fingers bent and the rug screwed up into his palm. Over near the stand the band began to play *If You Were The Only Girl In The World,* and Paddy said, " You fat——" Then he looked at Sean and stopped. " Get to hell out of here, Martin."

His voice was soft, but Martin caught the disgust and anger in it. He opened his mouth to speak, then changed his mind and turned quickly and went back towards the stand, his fat shadow hurrying along behind him, and the crowd began to sing with the band.

Paddy looked after him, his hand still clenched on the rug, then he looked down at Sean. " That's one of the things I got against money. Some people think it can buy everything."

6

" I like this farm," Marge said. " It's much better looking than ours. And it's closer to town."

" Yours will look as good as this some day," Sean said.

" It still won't be as close to town."

" Maybe you'll have enough money by then to buy a car."

" Gee, that ud be a bit of all right, wouldn't it?" Marge sat with her arms holding her knees close to her chin; her eyes darkened with the dream of wealth. " Some day—ah, what's the use of day-dreaming like that? By the time Dad's got enough money to buy a car, I'll probably be married and

have a coupla kids. Unless I marry a man who's already
got a car." She looked at him. "You gunna have a car
some day?"

"I dunno," Sean said, as if it were just a matter of choice.
"I suppose so. Depends how we do here on the farm."

They were sitting in the long sweet grass on the shelving
bank of the creek. They and their mothers had come back
to the farm in the wagonette, while the four men had stayed
in town to have one drink to celebrate the win in the Bulinga
Stakes. The one drink had been multiplied: after waiting an
hour for the men to turn up, Ida had got tea for herself, Mrs.
Bateman, Marge and Sean. When they had eaten, the two
women had sat at a table, redecorating the house in talk,
poring over a catalogue Ida had found, spending money with
the gay abandon of people who had money. Ted and Rose
Anderson had gone visiting friends, already beginning their
farewells, knowing they would be gone from here within a
couple of weeks, and Marge and Sean had been left to find
their own amusement. It had been Marge who had suggested the walk and Sean, after a careful glance at his
mother, eye-deep in the catalogue, had agreed.

They sat now on the bank of the creek, two tall white
gums standing silently like chaperons behind them, and
below them the water whispered its way towards the river a
half-mile away. Frogs chanted hoarsely and somewhere in
the evening a mopoke called mournfully to the shadowed
hills.

"How long are you gunna stay here?" Marge said.

Sean, who had been thinking of what they might some
day be able to afford if they could develop the farm still
further, turned a surprised stare towards her. "How long?
For good, of course."

"You're a real country boy, ain't you?" Marge mused.

"I ain't ever wanted to be anything else," Sean said, and
lay back in the grass. He put a tentative hand on her back
and slowly traced the ridges in her spine. "Disappointed?"

"No-o." Marge was still gazing down towards the dark
stream, one side of it just catching the rising moon, so that a
yellow fire seemed to be eating its way slowly across the

water. She shivered a little as his fingers touched a nerve in her back. "You must have electricity in you."

"The cows ain't gunna like that," he said.

"Who cares about the cows?" She dropped back in the grass beside him, pinning his hand beneath her. "You dunno much, do you?"

He was too honest to deny it, but his answer was barbed. "I don't get the chance to read books, like some people."

"At least I know what's what."

"It ain't helped you much." The only defence was attack: "You still only got your books. You ain't got a boy."

She lay silently, her breathing lost in the whisper of the creek, her body stiff on his numb hand, and he knew he had hurt her. He stared at the sky lightening under the rising moon, wondering why he couldn't speak the language that led you on from here: he hadn't advanced far enough beyond the border to have thrown off the cruelty of childhood. He had hurt Marge, deliberately and sadistically, and now there was remorse but no words to express it.

All he could say was the inadequate, childish, "I'm sorry."

She turned her head and looked at him, her face turned away from the moon, dark and older than he would ever be: the moon, coming over her shoulder, made his innocence transparent. His whole arm was numb now, pins and needles driving into his flesh, but he couldn't move it: he was paralysed, lost at the cross-roads till this girl, older than he by all the time that breeds instinct, should show him the way. She rolled towards him, blocking out the moon, and he felt her soft lips on the stiff board that was his mouth. Weakness ran through him, removing the bones from his body, and something he couldn't name uncoiled within him like a snake coming awake in the summer sun.

He had never kissed a girl before, he had never kissed anyone but his mother, and never like this. He was clumsy and a little brutal: Marge jerked her head back, straining against the arms he had locked about her. Instantly he was afraid he had hurt her again; he raised a nervous hand and ran the fingers lightly down her soft jawline.

"I'm no good at this," he said: the words were thick in the back of his throat. "Am I doing what the book says?"

"No." She lay with her head on his chest, her face still lost in darkness. "I don't want you to."

Then he knew, with a sudden flash of intuition, that there was really little between them: being a woman she was farther along the road than he, but the books hadn't helped and the bold talk had been merely whistling in the dark: she turned her head, and innocence lay on both of them like the moonlight. He hadn't the words to express what he felt, but he knew that from now on he need not be frightened of her.

"I'm going to be your boy," he said, the dominant male: he saw himself like Venneker, striding through life with women panting at his heels; then he remembered his mother, and he rolled out from under Marge, letting her head fall with a thump in the grass, and stood up. "Come on, we better be getting back. Your mum'll be wondering where you are."

He hadn't fooled Marge: "So will yours. I bet she thinks we been up to no good."

They brushed the grass seeds off each other, went up across the faintly shining paddocks to the house and arrived there at the moment Ern Bateman drove into the yard in his sulky.

The kelpie had greeted the horse and sulky with several bored barks, not even troubling to rise from its bed under the wagonette. The back door of the house opened and yellow light was splashed across the sulky. Ern Bateman sat stiffly and primly in the very middle of the seat, as if afraid of falling out.

Ida and Mrs. Bateman came out into the yard. Bateman turned a stiffly held head and looked down at his wife. He blinked slowly and spoke through delicately pursed lips.

"I come to take you home."

"Full as a boot," Mrs. Bateman said to Ida. "If he's like this and managed to get home, I wonder what the others are like and where they are?"

"I don't suppose it's much use asking him." Ida looked up at Bateman, still blinking slowly in the light from the doorway. "Where's Paddy and the others?"

K

But Ern Bateman had only one answer: " I come to take you home."

Mrs. Bateman shrugged. " Well, we better go then. I hope yours turns up soon, and not too much under the weather. Come on, Marge. Hop in. You sit on one side of your dad and I'll sit on the other. We'll have to hold him in going round the bends. Good-night, Ida. I've had a real lovely day and I'm looking forward to seeing you again Monday. Fact, I'm looking forward to seeing you a lot from now on. Come on, Marge, say good-night to Sean and let's get home before your dad falls asleep. I don't wanna have to carry him into the house."

Marge, standing out of the path of light, pressed Sean's hand, then moved across and got into the sulky. Her father blinked at her, smiling without recognition, then Mrs. Bateman had climbed in on the other side of him and in a moment they were driving out of the yard and soon were lost in the shadows of the road leading out of the valley.

Ida looked at Sean. " Well, what have you been up to?"

" Cripes, nothing!"

" Righto, don't jump down my throat. But you sound as if your conscience is worrying you. You've been behaving yourself, haven't you?"

" Mum "—Sean was suddenly quiet and serious, defending the girl he loved—" Marge is a real nice girl. She ain't anything like she sounds."

Ida said nothing for a while, aware that her boy had taken another step away from her, was that much closer to being independent of her, then she smiled. " I'm glad to hear it, Sean. I hope you see a lot of her."

Sean felt the confidence had gone as far as it could without embarrassment: he would never be able to talk about girls with his mother. He turned to a subject that, through long familiarity, embarrassed neither of them. " Well, I suppose Dad's drunk again. You reckon we better go looking for him?"

" I should be wild with him," Ida said, " but I know I won't be. He deserves a celebration after the way Our Place won to-day."

"You gunna let him put on the two hundred quid on Monday?"

"Of course," Ida said: she looked about the moonlit yard, already feeling the pride of ownership. "We can't lose, after what we saw in to-day's race."

Sean put the grey gelding into the wagonette and they headed for town. The night was warm and very beautiful. The paddocks sloped away from the main road, silver-green and no more solid than the landscape of a dream, to the dark timbered hills that seemed suddenly closer in the moonlight. The moon was still climbing, paling the stars; the trees rose like gushers out of black wells of shadow. They crossed a bridge, the planks rattling like gunfire in the stillness, and below them fireflies were tracer bullets without targets. Farmhouses stared at them with yellow uncurious eyes; in one they heard the sound of a piano, and Ida hummed the song till they were out of earshot. A car came towards them and was gone and the hail of its occupants was flung at them like confetti. They drove on, taking their time, travelling a road that was already becoming habitual to them. They had fitted into this valley long before they had arrived here.

They were still more than half a mile from town when they heard singing ahead of them. It came out of a long tunnel of shadow where the road ran between an avenue of white gums; tuneless and with the words unintelligible, coming suddenly out of nowhere, it was like the wailing of aboriginal spirits.

Then two figures came out of the darkness on to the long stretch of moonlit road. For a moment they were two separate and distinct shapes, then abruptly they had moved together into one huge misshapen figure that came weav ng down the road, its mournful song rising and falling above it like a keening ghost.

Ida brought the wagonette to a halt. "Your dad isn't with them. He could stick to a tune better than that, no matter how full he was."

Venneker and McKechnie, arms wrapped about each other, McKechnie lost under the stooped figure of Venneker, came to a staggering stop by the head of the horse.

McKechnie, his head hidden in the shadow of Venneker, said, "Who's there?"

Venneker straightened, leaning one hand on McKechnie's shoulder to maintain his balance, and looked past the horse at Ida and Sean. In the moonlight he looked a wild and terrible figure. His cap was gone and the silver hair hung about his head like the trappings of a witch doctor. Beneath the sheif of his brows his eyes were just black holes of shadow: his nose stood out between them like a great blade of bone. His mouth was a wound that spread into the hollows of his cheeks and his jaw was as savage as an upraised club.

"There they are!" The words boomed out of him: the horse pulled its head back sharply. "The keeper of the conscience! Mother Grundy and her offspring!"

"Dunno either of 'em," said McKechnie, still faceless in Venneker's shadow.

"On their way to cut short our pleasure! Bound for town, their noses quivering to smell our breath, words of pious advice hanging on the tips of their tongues! But Jesus God Almighty!" He flung high an arm: somewhere a bugle blew and banners were unfurled. "We beat them! Without advice, without the goading of these temperance workers, of our own volition and intention, we defeated them! We left the pub before closing time!"

"Are you all finished?" Ida said.

"Temporarily, madam." Venneker stood leaning with one hand on McKechnie, like a speaker beside his rostrum: he was prepared for questions from the opposition. "You may utter a few words if you wish."

"If I get down off this cart," Ida said, "I'll lay you flat as a board."

"Willing to use force, you see?" said Venneker to McKechnie. "A sister of Carrie Nation."

"Dunno her, either," said McKechnie.

Ida wasn't annoyed by Venneker's insults: if she hadn't suddenly become worried about Paddy, she would have been laughing outright. She hadn't seen Venneker as drunk as this before: she knew he could carry his liquor, and this was as if he had squeezed every last ounce of effect out of every drop he had drunk. But how or why he was drunk was of no concern at present.

" Where's Paddy?" she said.

" Good Gawd, it's Mrs. Carmody!" McKechnie had leaned away from Venneker and with both ears free had at last recognised Ida's voice. " Time you was in bed, missus."

" That could go for other people I know," Ida said. " But that doesn't tell me where Paddy is."

" He ain't with us," McKechnie said, and waved an arm about himself as if to make sure.

" The woman can see that for herself," Venneker said, and Sean drew in his breath, waiting for the moment of remorse, but Venneker had gone trampling on: " For all her myopic outlook, she is not blind."

Ida suddenly blew up. " Shut your mouth, you drunken, overgrown brute! Get out of my way before I drive the horse right over you! Out of my way! Quick!"

She slapped the reins against the horse's rump and he jumped forward. Venneker and McKechnie separated, Venneker leaping away to one side with a curse that almost stopped the horse dead in its tracks, then the wagonette had swung past them and was creaking and swaying down through the darkness between the avenue of trees.

" I should've run him down!" Sean could hear his mother panting, her voice almost sobbing with anger. " Talking to that poor man like that! God, what got into him? Drink ——!"

She slapped the reins again, urging the horse on with an angry shout, and they went on into town with the wagonette swaying drunkenly, and Sean clinging to the seat and wondering what had happened to the peaceful bliss that had been with them when they had left the farm.

At the edge of town Ida dragged the horse to a stop, pulling him back so sharply that the wagonette tipped and for one sickening moment Sean thought they were going to be overturned and crushed beneath it.

" Righto, hop down!" Ida had already jumped to the

ground. "You take the pubs on the left side of the main street, I'll take the ones on the right. If you find Dad, bring him back here. Go on, get a move on!"

And she had gone storming up the street, angrier and more worked up than Sean had seen her in a long time, not since the morning when she had stood in the clearing back by the river and told Paddy that Venneker would be coming with them on the droving trip. But now her anger was directed at both men: Venneker's drunkenness seemed suddenly to have aroused her temper at the thought of Paddy's being drunk. Sean felt momentary sympathy for any drunk who might get in her way in the pubs she was about to visit.

There were three hotels on his side of the street, including the one where Paddy had first had a drink in Bulinga. He stood shyly inside the bar door, looking about the sweating, noisy smoke-hung room, looking for the dark familiar face that would be flushed and sleepy-eyed, listening for the shredded notes of *Little Town In The Old County Down*, bending down to see if there was a slumped figure passed out among the unsteady feet of the other men, but there was no sign of Paddy. It was the same at the other two hotels.

His mother was already back at the wagonette when he arrived there. "You couldn't find him?"

"No," he said. "I asked a coupla blokes, but they hadn't seen him for more than an hour. He's just disappeared."

"Where could he go?" Ida stood with her fists on her hips: she was breathing heavily, from anger and her whirlwind tour through the hotels. "There's a dance on at the School of Arts. I had a look in there. And he wouldn't go to the pictures. He couldn't sit still long enough, not even if he was drunk. I wonder——"

"Wonder what?"

"Nothing." Could Paddy at last have gone off with some woman? She forced the thought from her mind before it could hurt her too much. "We didn't pass him on the way into town."

"He'd of been in the sulky. I wonder where that is? I didn't see that anywhere, either."

"Well, we're going to wait for him, till to-morrow morning if necessary. He's got to pass this way to go home. And my God, when I get him——!"

They sat there in the wagonette by the side of the road while the town, like a drunk who hated to leave the party, slowly and reluctantly fell asleep. Sulkies, drays and cars passed them at intervals, some of them carrying silent figures already half asleep, others bulging with wide-awake revellers whose raucous singing came back long after they were out of sight. Lights went out, the houses suddenly blank and anonymous, and the town at last turned over to sleep.

Ida and Sean hardly spoke. They sat in the back of the wagonette, both of them now utterly weary, and stared with heavy-lidded eyes up the main street. The high moon blazed like a cold silver sun on the glistening macadam of the roadway: the shadows beneath the awnings of the shops were dark as eternity. A white dog, almost invisible, crept above his solid shadow across the street and disappeared round the corner of a building. A bat scraped its wings against the moon and somewhere a cat cried at the night. Sadness came down, cold as the moonlight, and the town huddled deeper in its bed.

They had no way of knowing the hour when Paddy finally came down the street. They saw his tiny figure at the far end of town, walking in the very middle of the road as if afraid of the shadows on either side, coming towards them with feet that dragged like those of a man who had seen the end of his days, his head bowed and his hands jammed deep into his pockets, and he was opposite them before Ida spoke.

"Paddy!" Her voice was sharp: she stood up, towering against the moon: Sean crouched in her shadow, and stared at the broken man who had his father's face. "Paddy!"

Paddy stopped, raising his head as if he weren't sure he had heard rightly. Then slowly he looked across at them, the moonlight full on his face, and Sean almost cried out at the pain and suffering he saw there.

"Leave me alone," Paddy croaked, and turned and began to stumble on: he tripped, his feet searching desperately for ground, then he had fallen face down into the blackness of his shadow. Sean went over the side of the wagonette in a single swift movement and in a moment was cradling the bruised head, wondering at the tears on the dusty, grazed face, his whole being torn with the anguish of the mumbled " Oh, Christ Jesus, what've I done? Jesus, Jesus, Jesus!"

7

Sean lay in bed, staring out of the window at the coming morning, hearing a cock crow on the edge of his mind, seeing the sun coming up, red and bright, to light a world that should have remained dark for ever. Beside him in bed Venneker lay on his back, snoring through his wide-open mouth; sometimes jerking nervously, making the bed rattle; and on the table beside the bed the clock ticked monotonously and with increasing irritation, like a bomb for whose explosion he had waited all night.

Lying close to Venneker he could smell the liquor on the latter's breath. The room seemed to reek with it: Venneker's every deep loud gasp added to the atmosphere. Sean turned over, burying his face in his pillow, trying to escape the smell, to get away from the evil that permeated the room. He had never seen anything wrong with drink. He had seen plenty of drunks, including his father, but living in the bush, always on the move, he had never seen any of the wrecks on whom the social workers worked so vainly. Drinking was just a man's pastime, something he'd grow up to, and there was no more harm in it than in, say, eating too many green apples. You had your fun and you paid for it and no one was ever really hurt.

But now he knew that was all wrong. Drink was a terrible evil and he would never, never touch a drop of it. It had withered the heart of his father and dried himself to a tearless husk who, at two o'clock this morning, had seen the end of the world.

" I was drunk, otherwise I wouldn't of got into the game. Those two blokes we saw at the course, Mick and Joe, asked me to go with 'em. They were full, too." Paddy had lain in the back of the wagonette, his head pillowed on Sean's lap, talking to the sardonic moon, while above them Ida's stiff and silent figure threw a shadow as black as her mood. " I thought I was doing us a good turn. I was gunna have the same luck as I had at that other two-up game at Cawndilla. There was all the money in the world at this game, and I was gunna win enough to buy the farm. I was gunna surprise you both."

" It's all right, Dad," Sean had said, " it ain't the end of the world."

But he had been wrong. Paddy had gone on, as if he hadn't heard Sean. " I started to lose right from the jump. I lost everything I had, every bloody penny, and I kept on losing, and then I got sober. Oh, Christ," he shut his eyes and rolled his head. " I should of stayed drunk. I got sober and I started to sign IOU's."

The wagonette had come to a sudden stop and Ida had turned swiftly on the seat. " What IOU's? What for?"

" Four hundred quid," Paddy said, and Sean felt the tears running down over the dry leather of the cheeks into his hands.

" Oh, no!" Ida was still turned in the seat, holding with both hands to the back of it, her body bent as if in pain. " No, no, no!"

" It was like I was at the top of a steep hill." Paddy's face had still been turned away: he spoke into his tears cupped in Sean's hand. " I couldn't stop. All the time I was going downhill, losing money hand over fist, and all the time I kept signing IOU's. In the end they told me to go home."

Home: the place they had almost owned, the farm now stretching away in the morning beyond the window. A sense of pain, of loss, burned behind Sean's closed lids; bitterness was a taste he was now old enough to recognise. During the night he had hated his father, but now there was nothing: he remembered the tears in his hands, the first he had ever seen his father shed, and he knew his wasn't the only pain.

Then there was a gentle tap on the door. " Sean. Get dressed. We're going to Mass."

When he came into the yard five minutes later his mother

S.—M

was waiting for him in the sulky. They had gone almost a mile into town, driving through the immaculate morning, before she spoke. "We're going to pray. There's nothing we can do about the money, but we need help in other ways. Or I do."

"Are you gunna pay the money? Have you gotta? Couldn't we say it was our money, that he was drunk and didn't know what he was doing?"

"I thought of that." She had been thinking all night, sitting stiffly in a chair by the window, refusing to go near Paddy, sprawled fully dressed and restless on the bed. He had spoken to her twice and each time she had answered him by staring out of the window. She had thought of everything: her brain had wept with anger, sorrow and an immense frustration, while her eyes had remained dry. Tears were a weakness: once she had begun to cry, she could not have held Paddy off. "But it's our debt as much as his."

"I don't see that it is. We didn't sign the IOU's. The money was mostly ours. Only some of it was his——"

"Stop it!" The church lay ahead of them: Ida urged the horse to a faster pace. "I got enough to pray for. Don't let me have to pray for you."

The sulky drew into the side of the road before the church and Sean slowly got down. "I don't see how praying's gunna help."

Ida looked down at him. "It's all we've got. That, and one hundred and seventeen pounds. I was talking to Mrs. Bateman last night." She stopped: last night was like some time spent in another country: she looked back at the memory of happiness. "She told me she hadn't missed one day, saying a prayer, since their place was burnt out. That was what helped them. Praying, and Mr. Bateman's guts."

Sean had no control of his tongue. "Dad ain't Mr. Bateman."

"He's your father," Ida said, and fought to hold back the tears: she suddenly felt alone, pierced from both sides. "Don't ever compare him to anyone."

But in the bare wooden church, kneeling uncomfortably on the hard floor, listening to the priest's Irish brogue making a mockery of the Latin, Sean found that praying didn't help at all: the sense of loss and pain, the bitterness on the tongue, remained like the after-effects of an operation, something physical for which prayer had never been meant. He looked sideways at his mother. She was bent forward, her face in her hands, and he wondered if she felt as hopeless as he did.

They drove back to the farm. Ida spoke only once to Paddy during the morning, telling him to let Ted Anderson know that they wouldn't be buying his share of the farm, then she busied herself about the house. She worked with almost feverish enthusiasm. Brusquely brushing aside Rose Anderson's protests, she scrubbed the floors of the hall, the living-room and the big kitchen; she cleaned windows, dusted furniture, polished door-knobs, left her imprint on the house like a former owner.

Paddy spent some time out near the milking-shed with Ted Anderson, then without saying anything to anyone saddled the grey gelding and rode towards town. Venneker and McKechnie, silent as two trees, leaned on the fence of the yard, only now and again showing they were alive when one or the other turned his head to spit over his shoulder. Sean, lost and empty-minded, went out of the house and over to stand at the fence beside them.

Nobody said a word for a while, then Sean said, " Did you know where Dad was last night?"

McKechnie's head came up, waiting for Venneker to answer. Venneker spat over his shoulder, then said, " Yes, we knew. We also knew he was losing. Losses such as he sustained are soon news on the bush telegraph. Everyone in the hotel where we were detained knew that your father was on his way to being the biggest loser the town has seen in years."

" Why didn't you tell us that last night, instead of abusing Mum?"

" Perhaps when you're as old as I am, you'll understand why," Venneker said quietly. " I am really only beginning to understand this morning why I acted as I did last night. Many things possessed me then. Drink, disappointment, grief for your mother. And for you, too. I only wish now that I had shown the control that Mac here did. Or it might have been better if we had told you the truth and gone back into town with you. But I had little courage last night. All I had was words. Too many of them and none of them well chosen."

McKechnie, standing between the two of them, his face old and slack and all the spryness of the last two days gone from his body, turned towards Sean. "What you gunna do now?"

"Christ knows." The world stretched before him as a bleak plain: he would never grow older, was old enough to be cynical and bitter and profane. "I ain't even thought about it."

"What's your mum said?" McKechnie said.

"Nothing. Nor Dad, either. Nobody's said anything, not a thing about where we'll go, not even when we gunna leave." He sighed. "But we'll be on our way again, you can bet."

"Well, maybe it ain't so bad," McKechnie said: his voice was as blind as his eyes: the words meant nothing to him.

Venneker said, "Don't talk bloody rot! Of course it's bad."

"Maybe it ain't." McKechnie's voice was now dogged: it was as if he were suddenly reaching out to help Sean in any way he could. "He's gunna be on the move again. He's gunna see things, new places, new people. If he stayed here for ever, maybe he'd finish up like me, never seeing anyone, blind in more ways than one. Christ, you dunno what it was like when you were away, Rupe. But Sean'll be travelling. Ain't that something?" He seemed to shrink, leaning back against the fence. "I always wanted to travel. I used to listen to you, Rupe, and I used to envy you. You been everywhere, all over the flaming world. You seen everything. There were places I wanted to go, things I wanted to see. I remember once hearing you say the name of a mountain I wanted to see. In Mexico I think it was. Poco—something or other."

" Popocatepetl," Venneker said.

" Yeah, that's it. I ain't gunna ask you how you spell it. I just liked the sound of it and I always wanted to go there. There were places I wanted to go to, here in Aussie. Places with lovely names, ones I liked the sound of. Deniliquin, for instance. Ain't that a good sound, just like a ripple of water? Sean's done a lotta travelling and he'll do a lot more. He'll finish up with a lotta memories, something he can really settle down with. Not bugger-all like I got."

" None of us is ever satisfied," Sean said. " I'd swap places with you any day, Mr. McKechnie."

Venneker said, " There is always someone with whom we'd swap places."

Envy lay about them like a corruption, a disease of every man : even the holy man envies the saint. Somewhere there was peace and truth, some far billabong where nothing was comparative and no man had to seek further, but the distance was immense and two of them were old and the other might never find the road. They could only hope, and hope was envy masquerading as a prayer.

Paddy arrived back from Bulinga just before tea-time. Ida was sitting on the front veranda talking with McKechnie, but as soon as she saw Paddy turn in off the main road and come riding up towards the house she abruptly got up and went inside, leaving McKechnie wondering what had happened.

Paddy hailed McKechnie but had ridden on past the house before McKechnie had time to recognise the voice. He took the grey on across the yard and swung down at the gate into the small paddock where Sean was exercising Our Place. He stood, holding the reins of the grey and with one hand leaning on the fence of the paddock, watching his son ride the stallion with the skill that comes only from inheritance, feeling a thrill of pride despite the worry in his mind, then at last he called Sean.

Sean jumped down from the stallion and led him over to the fence. " He's full of go, Dad. He'll win by a street to-morrow."

He hadn't spoken to his father at all this morning. There

had been nothing to say: all anger had drained away out of him during the long night. During the day he had several times felt a surge of bitterness, but it hadn't lasted: he was still young enough to feel disappointment more than anything else. All the adult emotions had come crowding in within the last twelve hours: he had been wounded almost before he had been aware of the battle: he had cried out and the echo had come out of childhood. There was nothing that abuse or recrimination could do about disappointment, and now he was prepared to accept his father on the old footing.

Then Paddy said, " He ain't gunna win to-morrow."

" What you mean? Ain't he gunna run?" Small panic crept into his voice. " Are we leaving here so soon?"

" No, he'll be running," Paddy said. " He just ain't gunna win, that's all."

Sean frowned. " I don't get you, Dad."

" Now look, Sean, you gotta keep this under your hat." Secrecy stole in on the yard: the house was quiet behind his lowered voice. " I been around town and the price for Our Place is odds-on. In one place he's three to one on. We'd have to put three hundred quid on to win one."

" We ain't got three hundred quid."

" You being sarcastic or something? You want a clip under the ear?"

" No, but like I said, we ain't got three hundred quid."

" Righto, so we bloody well ain't got three hundred quid! Christ Almighty, does it matter?" Paddy found his voice getting away from him, climbing above them; he brought it back to a whisper between them. " What I'm getting at is, if we had three hundred quid or even six hundred, we couldn't make enough to buy the farm. I told your mum the price ud be short on Monday, but she *knew*. She always bloody well knows."

" What you gunna do then? What's this about Our Place not winning?"

" Murrumbidgee, the local nag, is now six to one. He's the lowest price of all the other horses. That's what they think of Our Place. I'm gunna put the rest of the money on him and he's the one that's gunna win."

The frown had remained on Sean's face. He was still puzzled: this man on the other side of the fence from him was a stranger, the stranger with the familiar features whom he had seen months before in the shearers' hut at Wattle Run: you could trust no one. He bit his lip.

"You mean you're gunna pull Our Place? Crikey, Dad, ain't that what Lew Martin wanted you to do yesterday? Ain't that—ain't it dishonest?"

Paddy turned and began to take the saddle off the grey. "You want the bloody farm, don't you? This way we can get it."

"I dunno whether I want it *that* much." Conscience dragged at him like an anchor: across the yard, in the silent house, almost as if she were watching him from the window, he felt the presence of his mother.

"You're only half of it! What about your mother? If we go on from here, you think she's ever gunna let me forget what I done last night? I ain't gunna forget it m'self. I ain't proud of it. But Christ, I don't wanna spend the rest of me life being reminded of it!"

"How you reckon she's gunna take this idea of winning the money on another horse? You know what she's like. She don't go to church very often, but she acts like people who do. I mean the good ones."

"She ain't gunna know." Paddy hung the saddle on the fence, opened the gate and led the grey into the paddock. He slapped it and it went slowly across towards the un-walled shed where a feeding-box was built into the corner of the fence. "Not till it's over, anyway. She'll probably kick up a shindy then, but it'll be too late and there'll be nothing she can do about it."

"Where you gunna get the money to back Murrumbid-gee?"

"Out of the jam-jar, just before we leave to-morrow morning. There's over six hundred quid in there now, including the stake money we won yesterday. We gotta pay out the

money I lost at two-up, but we'll have enough left to make
a decent bet on Murrumbidgee. At six to one he'll win us
what we want to buy the farm."

"I still don't reckon Mum's gunna like the idea." He
turned and looked about the yard, at the house and down
over the paddocks: it was a pity honesty wasn't something
you could *see,* something you could compare with the beauty
of this farm. "I ain't happy about it, m'self."

Paddy had been standing beside Our Place, running a
hand up and down the black nose. He suddenly took his
hand away and spun round. For a moment Sean thought his
father was going to hit him and he tensed, ready to move
away. Then he saw that there was no strength in Paddy to
hit anything. He leaned against the fence, completely
beaten.

"For Christ's sake, Sean, you think I'm happy? You think
I *wanna* do a thing like this? What sorta bastard d'you
think you got for a father?"

8

Early on Monday morning Sean was wakened by Venneker getting out of bed. He had spent another restless
night and now at six o'clock cared little why Venneker should
be getting up and dressing. He turned over and went back
to sleep.

So that when he finally got up and went out to the kitchen
for breakfast Venneker was back from Bulinga with Mrs.
Firth. She had come in on the 6.55 train and was now just
finishing her third cup of tea, tired from the long journey
from Cawndilla but still the same old Mrs. Firth.

"Gawd, hasn't he grown! How are you, Sean? Didn't
expect to see *me* here, I'll bet. Didn't expect to see meself
here, tell you the truth." She smiled around the large
kitchen table at the others: Venneker, Paddy, Ida, McKechnie, Rose Anderson: she was already thoroughly at home.
"I got Rupe's telegram Saturday. Trust him to pick the
busiest day of the week. The bar was chock-a-block wher

they give me the telegram. I won't tell you what was in it, but it said something like: drop everything, come at once. Expected me to come running, just like that." She snapped her fingers and took a sip at her tea. " Well, I did."

Sean sat down to his breakfast wondering if Mrs. Firth knew what had happened since Venneker had sent the telegram. He guessed that Venneker must have told her of the crisis on the way out from town, but there was nothing in her manner to suggest that she knew she was in the middle of a very strained situation.

" Crikey, this is a lovely valley, ain't it? Driving out here this morning I kept saying to Rupe, when he'd let me get a word in edgeways——"

" A remarkable woman," Venneker said to McKechnie.

" She sounds it," McKechnie said. " Just the sort to keep you in place."

Mrs. Firth leaned across and slapped McKechnie on the shoulder. " Go on, you're only pulling me leg! But I'm gunna get on well with you, I can see that. Me and you is just what Rupe needs. We'll straighten him up proper."

" What did you do about the pub?" said Ida, practical-minded as usual.

" It'll be all right. I counted up the money that was in the till when I left and so long as there's no less when I get back, I'll be happy. Anyhow, the girls will look after it. And I told Bill Thomas, the policeman, to keep an eye on 'em now and again. It'll be all right, don't you worry, Ida."

Ted Anderson came into the kitchen, having finished his outside chores, and was introduced to Mrs. Firth.

" So you're the one who wants to sell part of the farm?" she said, and Sean looked up from his toast and jam.

Ted Anderson looked embarrassed for a moment, then he seemed to pull himself together. He sat down at the table and drew towards him the cup of tea his wife had poured for him. He leaned forward, his shoulders hunched up about his ears, and stirred his tea with a spoon that was lost in his great bony hands. Sean, looking at him, had the feeling the whole Carmody family was hated by Anderson.

" Yes, I'm selling," Anderson said. " Leastways, I'm *trying* to sell. You know anyone who's interested in buying half a farm? The quicker, the better."

Rose Anderson's hand came up towards her husband and she drew in her breath as she went to say something. Then the old habit of neutrality came back to her: she lowered her hand and picked up her cup to drown the words she was going to say. The whole room was quiet for a long moment, even Mrs. Firth aware of the sudden bitterness of Anderson, then Paddy scraped back his chair and stood up.

"Well, I gotta be getting into town. There's a few things I gotta do before the race this afternoon."

Mrs. Firth leaned back in her chair, turning away from Anderson, and looked up at Paddy. "Rupe was telling me you can't lose this afternoon. I'm gunna have some money on you. I ain't seen a race meeting in a long while, not since I went up to Cawndilla from Newcastle fifteen years ago, and I feel like having a bit of a fling. How much would I win if I put fifty quid on your horse?"

Sean swallowed the last of his toast with difficulty and looked up at his father. Paddy was looking at the ceiling, one eye shut and his lips moving soundlessly.

"Between sixteen and seventeen quid," he said. "He's three to one on. I'll give you a tip, Mrs. Firth. I wouldn't back him. It ain't worth it at that price."

"Three to one on!" McKechnie said: eyebrows rose foolishly above the blind eyes. "Gawd Almighty, I never thought his price ud get that short. Someone must of put a packet on him, to back him down to that price."

"Well, it wasn't us," Paddy said. "We ain't gunna make anything outa his win but the stake money. We should of had *our* bet on Saturday."

Ida stood up and began to gather up the breakfast dishes. "Saturday is past history. We're not going to get anywhere moaning about what should have been done on Saturday. When you've finished your tea, Gert, I'll show you where you can have a bath."

"Crikey, and can I do with one! I feel like I been rolling round a paddock for a week."

"With whom?" said Venneker.

Mrs. Firth almost flattened him with the swing of her arm. "Gawd, ain't he a beaut! I really missed you, Rupe. I ain't had a good laugh since you left!" And she lay back in her chair and had a good laugh that took all the tension out of the room and brought smiles to the faces of everyone. Sean, smiling across the table at her, loved her at that moment as he might have some favourite aunt: she was the best thing that could have happened to the farm that day.

A little later Paddy left for town, winking at Sean as he walked out of the house, saying he would meet them at the course in time for the first race, and Sean went out to give Our Place some walking exercise in the small paddock. McKechnie followed him.

"This Mrs. Firth," he said, walking beside Sean as the latter led the stallion up and down the paddock, "what's she like to look at?"

"All right, I suppose," Sean said. "She's a bit old for me."

"Yeah, I reckon she is," McKechnie said. "But if you were a bit older, would you think she was a bit of all right?"

"Well, she wears glasses," Sean said.

"Yeah, they don't improve anyone. Still, she can't be too bad. Rupe was always telling me about the raving beauties he used to know, and I don't think he's the type to finish up with a crow."

"What d'you wanna know for?" Sean said.

"Oh, just trying to get her pictured in me mind. I got an idea she's gunna be around for a long time. She sounds all right, got a bit of life in her, but I always like to know whether they're good or bad-lookers. Makes me feel better if they're good-looking. Me own missus was a good-looker."

"Well, if she had her glasses off, I think she'd be pretty good." Sean tried to alter his standards: he added twenty years to his age and tried to imagine himself lost with Mrs. Firth on a desert isle. "She's got a pretty decent sorta figure, plenty of padding, if you know what I mean, and she's got a nice smile, real friendly and sorta open, and her legs are good-o. All round, I'd say Rupe's done all right for himself."

"She may be a bit old for you, but you been keeping your

eyes open, ain't you? But she sounds all right. I think I'm gunna like her."

"Good," said Sean, and felt he had accomplished something.

After an early lunch everyone at the farm, including Ted and Rose Anderson, drove down into town to the races. The day was hot, the sun beating down out of a bright smooth sky, and the smell of eucalypts and peppercorn was heavy on the warm still air. Cattle stood listlessly in the yellow-topped paddocks and in the trees the birds were motionless and silent. When the wagonette turned off the main road the dust billowed away like red smoke behind it; beyond the course the sudden flash of sun on the river was like an explosion of silver flame. The heat of summer flooded the whole valley.

Nevertheless, everyone had spilled out of town to the races again. The men clamoured about the bar, downing a glass of beer in quick time while the previous glass had already started to ooze out of their pores, and swapped the yarns of last year and the year before. The women sat beneath their parasols and fanned themselves and talked about each other, the locals about the city visitors and the city visitors about the locals. The children, wiser than any of the grown-ups, had brought their swimming togs with them and would spend the afternoon between the river and a vantage point just opposite the bend into the straight. The bookmakers shouted and sweated, cursing the band and its music, and the bandsmen, cursing everybody, worked their way lethargically through their repertoire. Above all, still stuck a foot from the top of its mast, the Southern Cross hung like a limp and defeated standard.

Paddy, in his silks, carrying his saddle, walked across to the stalls.

"Did you cop any extra weight, Dad?" Sean stood beside the stallion in the stall, out of the glare and heat of the sun.

"Another ten pound. I'm carrying fourteen pound of lead now. But it don't seem to be holding back the money." He threw the saddle across Our Place. "They're laying it on

thick on him. Some of the bookies won't take any more
bets."

Sean's voice was quiet, hesitant: he would rather not have
known: "Did you get any money on Murrumbidgee?"

"Two hundred quid at six to one. What we should of got
if we'd backed Our Place on Saturday. I got Mick Hanna,
the bloke who took me out to the two-up, to put it on for
me."

"Didn't he ask any questions?"

"I told him the money belonged to Ted Anderson. He
knows enough not to ask too many questions."

There was a stiff silence, the music of the band and the
laughter of the crowd faint on the outer edges of it, and
Paddy turned round to tighten the saddle straps.

Then Lew Martin, his face livid and shiny as the sun,
came quickly, almost rolling like a ball, over the bright dusty
strip of ground between the stand and the stalls. He stopped,
standing in the sun and the dark round pool of his own
shadow, and said, "Carmody, I wanna see you."

Sean kept looking at the fat perspiring figure in the sun,
but he knew his father hadn't moved.

"Righto, I'm listening," Paddy said.

Martin stood for a moment, rebuffed, then he stepped into
the stall. Sean, staring at the bright light outside, hardly
aware of the passing parade of people, lost him in the dimness of the stall. Then the voice, deep and fat, came
clearly:

"Carmody, just forget all about what I said on Saturday.
You go ahead and ride your own race. And," his voice had
a cold quiet menace against the heat of the day; somewhere
a woman laughed hysterically at a joke, "if you lose this race
to-day, I'll rub you out for life. On this course and every
other course in the State."

Then he was gone, but Sean didn't see him go and he was
left with the feeling that Martin's shadow had remained
behind in the stall. He stood under the curve of the stallion's
neck and looked at his father.

"What you gunna do, Dad?"

"That bastard!" Paddy's voice had the venom of a man

balked at every turn. "He's the one who started the rush on Our Place. He's the —— who laid all the cash to back him down to —— odds on."

The hard words were like slaps against Sean's ears: he had never heard his father swear so obscenely. He put out a hand and rested it on Paddy's arm: he knew suddenly that his father was at the end of his tether.

"Take it easy, Dad. Let's scratch Our Place and we'll pack up and get out of here."

Paddy slowly turned his head as if he had just become aware of Sean. He said nothing for a moment, staring with puzzled worried eyes at his son, then at last he understood what Sean had said.

"That wouldn't do any good. They wouldn't let me scratch him this late. They'd rub me out anyway, if I tried it. I don't wanna be rubbed out, Sean. Christ, I'd never be able to hold me head up again. I ain't only thinking of meself. You and Mum would be in it, too." He was a roamer, but his world was small: to be disbarred would make him a public figure on the bush tracks. Honesty was something he could stretch to meet the circumstances, but shame was cut to size, something he could never alter nor throw off: he wore it like an inner garment, hidden from the world. His values were simple: it was what people thought of you that counted. "No, I gotta ride. There ain't anything else for it."

"What you gunna do then?"

Paddy's decision was quick: "Get down to the seven furlongs post as quick as you can. Wait there till I'm going down to the start and I'll chuck you some lead. Bury it in the bush, then come back here. Go on, quick."

Sean went out of the stall at a run, running away from the shout of Marge as she came round the end of the stand with her mother and father, catching a glimpse behind them of his mother and Mrs. Firth, running with the desperate urgency of someone who didn't want to stop to think. Till now his only part in the attempt to swindle the public had been to keep his father's secret; now he ran with the weight of sin about his neck. He dodged round the end of the

crowd, went down through the paddock where the cars and
sulkies and drays were parked, and was running into the
timber at the edge of the track before he noticed the kelpie
was loping along at his heels.

"Go back, Nigger," he panted, but the kelpie ignored him,
and he turned and ran on into the timber. Here, the trees
formed the outer edge of the track: if any horse, rounding
the bend, ran off the course it would finish up lost and
bewildered among the tall gums. Behind the trees a low
ridge climbed sharply and ran in a curve behind the far
side of the track: it was like another, natural grandstand
on which the trees stood like impassive spectators. Beyond
the ridge the valley stretched away as flat paddocks to the
slope of the distant hills.

Sean crouched down behind a tall red gum, leaning back
against it as he tried to regain his breath, and the kelpie lay
down at his feet.

"Where's it gunna get us?" Sean said, but the dog had
turned its head away, bored beyond words: Sean was alone
with his despair. "All our friends, even Mum, backing our
horse and he ain't gunna win. Doing everything that's wrong,
and is it gunna be worth it? Is it?" he said to the trees and
his voice went away among them, dying away as a hopeless
whisper, and he turned and saw the horses coming down
the track for the start of the Bulinga Cup.

The twelve horses came striding down, running singly,
with Our Place bringing up the rear. Sean saw his father
riding high in the stirrups, holding the stallion back, then
they were opposite him and he stood up and whistled.
Paddy's hand came up in a swift movement, there was a dark
flash in the air, then the bar of lead skidded into the dust
right at Sean's feet.

He quickly scooped a hole with a stick, the kelpie for the
first time showing some interest, buried the length of lead,
then stood up and ran back out of the timber towards the
stand and the excited murmuring crowd which thought its
money was safe on the black stallion that couldn't be beaten.

He would have had no trouble finding his mother and the
others, if he had been looking for them. He had no sooner

come through the maze of cars and sulkies into the general
enclosure when he heard Marge shouting his name at the top
of her voice. He looked about for escape, he suddenly
wanted to be alone, but she called him again and he was
trapped.

"Where you been?" she said as he joined the group at
the rail in front of the enclosure. "I saw you buzzing off a
while ago, like you'd been stung by a bee or something."

"Yes, where'd you go?" Ida said.

"Just down there." He nodded vaguely towards the end
of the valley.

"Yeah, but what for?" Marge said.

"I wanted a leak," he said, and blushed and ducked as his
mother swung her open hand at his head. "Gee, you can
ask some questions."

Marge wasn't embarrassed. "The way you were running,
it didn't look like you wanted to do that."

"Righto," Ern Bateman said, "don't let's argue about
whether he oughta run or walk to do it. Let's look at the
race. They're ready to go."

Even as he spoke the cry *They're Off!* went up to the hot
sky like some religious exclamation: the crowd crossed its
fingers and prayed for a winner. The group at the rail leaned
forward, their shouts held ready in their throats, and Sean
envied them their ignorance. He looked at his mother
pressed excitedly against the rail, at Venneker ready to split
the world apart with his roar of triumph, at Mrs. Firth,
Marge, her mother, her father, and at Bert McKechnie, the
blind eyes staring away to nowhere and the excited mouth
working soundlessly, and he felt his despair rise like a giddy
sickness within him. He knew all at once that the farm
wasn't worth it.

At the back of the course, having gone a furlong, Paddy
was holding Our Place in sixth place, running on the rails
in a pocket that so far was not worrying him. The thunder
of the hoofs came up off the ground at him; dust spun up
round him like a storming cloud; the flying mane of the
black whipped across his face; he felt the pressure of an-

other jockey's knee against his, and he moved Our Place forward.

They passed the stand the first time round, the crowd yelling its encouragement, a bay horse bowling along in front in a brief hour of glory, and the stallion, well within himself, galloping freely beneath Paddy with a smoothness of movement and power that brought a thrill to his horseman's heart. The mile post went past, then the seven furlongs, still with the bay out in front and Murrumbidgee tailing him, but Paddy and the man outside him had moved up to take third and fourth place and the rest of the field had begun to fall away.

The bay had clapped on the pace, his jockey hoping to steal a march on the others, but Murrumbidgee had gone after him and now Paddy moved Our Place up, running into third place and into the dust of the bay and the big chestnut. The half-mile and the three furlongs dropped behind and now they were swinging into the bend, urged on by the soprano screams of the kids who had come out of the river and stood in a dripping yelling crowd on a small mound just off the edge of the course, and the race had really begun. The three horses went round in a tight bunch, all three boring in as if afraid of losing the white rail spinning at them out of infinity, then the bay suddenly went wide, taking Murrumbidgee with him, and Paddy took the black up on the inside.

They came round the bend, the chestnut, the bay and the black, colours bobbing, legs flailing, tails streaming, the most beautiful sight in the world against the whirling background of their own dust, and went down towards the roar of the crowd and the thin white board that was the finish.

They flew down the straight, locked together, an entity of terrific strength and wild thrilling speed, the jockeys riding with goading hands and heels, one shouting at the top of his voice and using his whip savagely, and the long red nose of Murrumbidgee reached out as the post came with tremendous swiftness towards them.

Then Paddy leaned forward, rising as if lifting the stallion with him, feeling the surge of strength as this beautiful honest thing beneath him plunged forward with the awful suddenness of stepping off into space, and the post flashed by and the chestnut and bay were behind him.

Gradually he slowed Our Place to a canter, patting the black shining neck, heartsick for this courageous horse that had won a race that was already fixed against him, then he had turned the stallion round and was riding back to the saddling enclosure. The crowd was ecstatic, standing on its toes and yelling its head off, and in the betting ring the bookies wondered if they should shoot themselves or light out for the horizon before the punters came to collect their winnings. The small group by the rail in the main enclosure was hugging itself in an orgy of excitement: Venneker's roar could be heard even above that of the crowd. Sean surrendered himself to Marge's hug and kiss, then turned away and ran across to take the reins of Our Place while his father took off the saddle.

Paddy, carrying the saddle over his arm, stepped on to the scales. Lew Martin, his red face blooming above the tourniquet of his stiff white collar, stood beside the scales and grinned.

"Nice race, Carmody."

The weighing clerk fixed the bar and looked at it. He leaned closer, frowning slightly, then looked at Martin and raised his eyebrows. Sean saw Martin squint at the scales without moving from where he stood, then duck his head in an almost imperceptible nod.

"Righto," the weighing clerk said. "Correct weight."

Sean felt his heart jump and saw his father turn sharply, almost overbalancing on the small platform of the scales.

"Come on," the clerk said. "Move out and let the next bloke on."

Paddy stepped slowly down off the scales, moving as if he had all the time in the world and nothing at all mattered, and looked at Lew Martin. The latter stood with his hands in his pockets, teetering back on his heels so that he seemed to be hiding behind the mound of his stomach, his eyes lost completely in the grinning triumph of his fat face, and Sean, turning away to follow the slow dejected figure of his father, knew suddenly and clearly who had put so much money on Our Place over the week-end, who had backed the stallion down to odds-on before the course betting had even begun, who had prepared for every emergency by even bribing the weighing clerk.

They had almost reached the stalls, pushing through the congratulating crowd, when Mick Hanna, his moustache sparkling with beer foam, came lunging up beside him.

" Christ, Paddy, you won!" Only Sean and Paddy were aware of the indignation and shock in his voice: the crowd was too excited to be aware of anything but its own good fortune: *everybody* had backed Our Place. " Jesus, all that money! I put ten quid of me own money on, too! And you won! Did you see it, Joe?" He turned round and appealed to his cobber, who had just forced his way through the crowd and now stumbled along beside him.

" I seen it, all right." Joe looked shrewdly at the world through gold-rimmed spectacles. " Something's wrong some-where. There's something I don't understand——"

" Me neither." Mick shook his head; he ran his tongue along his moustache. " I gotta go and have a drink. Two hundred quid on the wrong nag, a tenner of mine up the spout——"

" Let's have a drink." Joe took off his spectacles and put them in his pocket. " The bloody world looks a bloody sight clearer when I can't see it."

They fell away into the crowd, then the crowd, too, had begun to fall away, and soon there were only Paddy and Sean and, suddenly as if she had appeared out of nowhere, Ida.

" Where's the others?" Paddy said.

" Gone to collect their money," Ida said. She hesitated for a moment, then she said quietly, " I heard those two drunks. I heard what they said about you winning and I heard them mention two hundred pounds. I had a look in the jam-jars before we came into town. What happened to the money?"

The band had begun to play: it wasn't gonna rain no more, no more. The crowd laughed and counted its winnings: even at odds-on they had gained something. The sun shone bright and hot: the shadows had a gaiety about them, rushing nimbly over the ground under the people who could see nothing wrong with anything. The Carmodys stood in the dimness of the stall, removed from the whole scene like aliens who had just been deported.

"Tell your mum all about it," Paddy said to Sean, and turned to walk out of the stall and over to the jockeys' tent. "Tell her everything. And try to tell her why I done it."

9

"So we're gunna get married," Mrs. Firth said. "I wish you could be here for the wedding."

"If it was in the next week, we'd stay," Ida said. "But you've got to go back to Cawndilla and fix up things there. It'll be nearly another month. We couldn't wait that long."

"I can hardly wait, meself," Mrs. Firth said, and bounced with laughter. "I feel just like a girl getting ready for the first time."

"Where are you going for your honeymoon?"

"Down to Sydney. We're gunna look up Bluey and Liz Brown, and drop in and see Jean Halstead—she's gone back to Sydney to have her baby: she wanted to have it at Wattle Run, but her hubby made her go down and let a specialist treat her—and go to all the places I ain't seen in so long. When I told Ted Anderson I'd buy his half of the farm, I said I'd do it only if he would stay on and work it till I'd had me honeymoon. I wouldn't miss that for all the tea in China. I never had a honeymoon with Alec. He couldn't get anyone to look after the pub. We just went to bed early every night for a month, instead." She leaned against the wheel of the wagonette and looked at Ida. "It's fifteen years, damn' near sixteen, since I was as happy as I am now. I laugh a lot and I have a good time, but that ain't everything. A woman *needs* someone, don't she, Ida?"

"She does," Ida said, and turned to help Paddy as he came

out of the house with two hessian-wrapped bundles under his arms. " Is that all, darl?"

" That's the lot," Paddy said, and swung the bundles up into the wagonette. He was still subdued: he smiled at the two women, but his face creaked with the effort. The shadow of all he had done in the last few days clouded his eyes: he knew he had a debt to pay. But it couldn't be paid *here*. He had to get out of this valley, over the hill to a new start, and then they could perhaps begin to look for a place to settle. Remorse and the knowledge of what he had done had filled him with an utter weariness. He looked about the farm, feeling a sudden regret, a sense of something lost, then quickly he looked back at Ida. " All set to go. Where's Sean?"

" Coming up the road," Ida said. " He's with Rupe and Mac."

Sean was walking between the two old men. The three of them had left the farm an hour or more before and had walked down the main road to the bridge that spanned the slow-moving river. They had leaned on the rail, two of them watching the olive water swirl past the piles and the other listening to it, all three of them looking old in their quietness and the unhappy curve of their backs, then at last they had begun to walk back to the farm.

It was only then that Venneker had begun to talk. " Don't hold what has happened against your father, Sean. I talked to him last night, and he is not really to blame for what he is and what he has done. His trouble began long before you were born."

" I know that," Sean said. " He ran away from home."

" He ran away from home to look for something, something that I don't believe he recognised he possessed until this last week. What he wants, just as much as you, is a home. He *has* a home, really. It is up there," he flung an arm across the paddocks towards the farmhouse, " in that wagonette. What you and your mother want is perhaps no more secure and permanent than what is in that wagonette when the three of you ride together on the seat."

"I still would like to settle down on a farm," Sean said.

"You will, some day, Sean." McKechnie spat into the dust of the road. "When you want a thing as much as you do, you get it in the end."

"Mac is right, there," said Venneker. "You've been on the road a long time, but I don't think you'll finish up like most sundowners. Most of them never reach the end of their road. But you will, Sean. Just keep plugging away. Never mind the disappointments you've had, don't be influenced by the Lew Martins you'll meet, just go your own way with your eye on what you want, and you'll get there."

"I hope so," Sean said.

Then they had come up the road from the main road and had reached the wagonette. For a moment there was an unreal silence: the group stood like strangers waiting to be introduced; then Paddy, the only one who had no ties with this farm, stepped across to Mrs. Firth and took her hand.

"Hooray," he said. "And I hope you and Rupe have a lotta happiness."

"We will," Mrs. Firth said. "And I hope you have the same."

Paddy turned to Venneker and put out his hand. "Hooray, you old bastard."

Venneker's voice was just a whisper; the real good-bye was in the clasp of his hand. "Good-bye, Paddy."

Ida could say nothing. She kissed Mrs. Firth and each of the men, then turned away and climbed up to the seat of the wagonette, blind and dumb with emotion. Paddy got up beside her, picked up the reins and waited for Sean to join them.

Sean shook hands with Mrs. Firth and McKechnie, not looking at their faces, trying not to see the tears, then he turned and took Venneker's outstretched hand.

"Good-bye, Rupe," he said, then the tears came and he leaned forward against the bony ribs, feeling the arms go round his shoulders, and prayed to God that he would some day see this old man again.

Then the wagonette had rolled down the road to the main road, the grey gelding straining between the shafts, glad to be on the move again, and the black stallion walking quietly behind at the end of a lead rope. The kelpie trotted in the shade beneath the wagonette, indifferent to the place they were leaving, already bored with where they might be going, and soon the farm was lost to sight round a bend in the main road.

They began to climb out of the valley, following the road that would take them past the Batemans, where there would be another farewell, and in the late afternoon they stopped at the spot where they had camped the first night on the droving trip to Cawndilla.

Paddy turned in the seat and looked down at the valley as it lay beneath them. The long shadows of the afternoon crept eastwards and a homing bird slid down a shaft of sunlight to a tree that glittered like a yellow fire. On the far side of the valley a mulberry cloud came up from behind the slumbering hills.

" We'll find another valley," Paddy said. " I promise you."

Ida put her hand on his knee. Disappointment still lingered in her, like a pain, but it would go. There had been so much of it in the past: this now was like an unexpected tide in a sea: it would subside. Her family was here about her, bound close to her again, and that was what counted in the end. " Some day there'll be a farm known as Carmody's Place. And we'll keep the door open for everyone. For people like Rupe and Mrs. Firth and Bluey Brown and all of them. And we'll keep it open for people like us. Because there must be others like us, and we might be able to help them. You think we might, darl?"

" I know we will," Paddy said; the last of the sun winked on the gold tooth and he took her hand in his.

The wagonette moved on and Sean lay on the hessian bundles and the folded tent in the back and saw the land disappear below the lip of the valley. He lay there listening to his mother and father talking above him and he knew that neither of them knew his secret. Eventually they would learn it, for none of us can hold a joyful secret completely within himself and in time he would want them to know anyway, but for now the knowledge was only his. Down

there at the farm, leaning against the hard body of Venneker.
he had cried the last remnants of childhood out of himself.
Ahead of him now lay nothing but the battles, the joys, the
griefs of a grown-up.

He stood up behind his mother and father and put an arm
about each of them. The wagonette went down the turning
road, with always a bend ahead of them, and behind the
valley was lost in the flood of its own shadows.

Long Island,
Sept. 1950—*Aug.* 1951.

THE END